ZADA 5

PATH OF THE ONE

R D MORENO

Publishing Services provided by Paper Raven Books LLC
Printed in the United States of America
First Printing, 2024

ISBN

CONTENTS

CHAPTER I

THE RESCUE

THE YEAR IS 3565. PLANET CASTIA IS EMBROILED IN A LONGSTANDING CIVIL WAR. THOUGH ITS PEOPLE THINK THEY ARE ALONE IN THE UNIVERSE, UNBEKNOWNST TO THEMSELVES, AN EXPANDING EMPIRE IS ON THE VERGE OF APPROACHING THEM. SIX MONTHS EARLIER, THE EMPEROR DECIDED TO BRING CASTIA INTO THE FOLD. YEARS OF WAR HAVE DEVASTATED THE PLANET, ONCE GREEN WITH MOUNTAIN RANGES, LAKES, RIVERS, AND ONE LARGE OCEAN.

IN THE SKY IS A SQUADRON OF FUTURISTIC-LOOKING crafts, dark grey, triangular ships with loud, roaring engines. Looking down towards the ground, the pilot in the craft sees nothing but burned-out buildings with small patches of green where the planet continues trying to heal itself with sections of the bombed-out mountainous area to their side, and an industrial complex ahead of them.

As the ships head towards their target, they dodge rockets launched at them. One rocket strikes a craft, which is deflected by its shield, but explodes right after, pushing the craft off course. It regroups with the other ships back to attack formation just in time to fire missiles at their designated target. As missiles hit their aim, a voice comes over their radio: the deflected missile took down their shield when it exploded. The voice over the radio is Adam, Duke Balcazar's oldest son. As they pull up, there is a massive explosion below.

They have just damaged their enemy's main weapons depot, but the craft with no shields is struck by debris and crashes to the ground. The pilot ejects, but the copilot is struck and killed. Adam hits the ground and drops his chute, with a gun in hand, and his sword drawn, then hides behind large rocks in a group of trees near the clearing. Far from where his ship crashed, he takes cover behind the remnants of an exploded building, giving him a better chance of avoiding capture. In the air, one craft comes back to find Adam on the ground. The pilot spots him as he runs to the rocks, who then notifies Eric, the acting general for this battle, but Adam is too far behind enemy lines with too many of the enemies' troops nearby to send a rescue team.

Adam realizes his communication device has fallen out of his pack. *Shit!* he says to himself as he rushes to piece it back together. *I can't reach the command center.* Being on an unfamiliar planet, the device does still give him location information, so he can find his way back if he can make it through enemy lines without getting spotted. Still, behind the rocks, Adam gets his bearings, puts his weapons away, then maps his way to get across the front line. Amidst the flames from the explosion, he slowly moves, staying out of sight of the enemy.

Near the front line, Eric reaches out to Connor, Adam's younger brother, letting him know Adam's ship went down behind enemy lines with no way to communicate. Connor pushes Eric to help get Adam back. Eric is adamant it cannot be done at this time with no communication and Adam as far behind enemy lines as he is. He then tells Connor, "Look, this is the first time you have been this involved in any type of battle or war. Yes, all your training has prepared you, but this is the real thing, not a simulation."

Connor thinks to himself that Adam could be badly hurt with no way to communicate. "I understand this is real, and that is my concern. We have no way of knowing if Adam will be able to find his way back."

Studying Connor, Eric realizes this young kid could get hurt himself doing something foolish. "I understand your concerns. They are the same as mine, but you need to trust me on this. Your brother knows how to take care of himself."

Without Eric's approval, Connor plots to go rescue Adam, not knowing Eric is working on a plan, even though he told Connor there was no way. Eric has been very close to the Balcazar family. He's been there since both Adam and Connor were born. Eric feels like they were his sons and could not bear anything happening to either of them. This was their reason for training the boys in the art of war. They felt this would help keep them safe, no matter where they were or what they were involved in. Even though Eric is concerned, he knows Adam could handle himself in danger till Eric can help get him back, as this is not the first time Adam had found himself in a situation like this.

Part of Eric's battle strategy has been secretly working with rebel forces behind enemy lines and having direct, secure communication with them. When the Balcazar boys were very small, their parents implanted trackers in them in case of trouble. Only their parents, Eric, and his brother John Aristo are aware of this. Eric has a special device allowing him to locate and track both boys. Eric reaches out to the rebels to let them know where Adam is. One of Eric's staff, hearing Connor is working on a plan to go after Adam, even though he was ordered against it, rushes in to inform his boss. Eric is forced to track Connor down to tell him what he has secretly been working before he was ready so Connor does not ruin the scheme.

Eric tells Connor about the trackers, then shows him the device used to follow them.

Connor appears surprised over this revelation. "You mean you and my parents have been able to locate me all this time and have known everywhere I have been?"

Eric laughs, "No it has not been like that. This was done just in case something happened to you two, like what is going on with Adam now."

Eric then sets up a plan for Connor to meet with one rebel near the front line to assist with Adam's rescue.

He is the only one aware of the rebels and their location; he also tells Connor he will need to go on his own with the rebels after Adam. Eric tells Connor he can get him near the front lines, but being so close carries risk. Since this is Connor's first time in a war, Eric is very concerned, but knows that Connor will go on his own to save his brother either way. He tells Connor to remember his training and not to take any risks he does not need to. This may be a good time to try stretching his abilities for protection. Eric says, "I know you have been trying to learn everything you can about your family's inherited physic abilities. Maybe this will be a good time to put them to use. They could help keep you out of trouble. I have a tracker for you as well, allowing me to know where you are all the time, the same way you will track your brother." Again, he says, "Do not take any risk you do not need to, and when the time is right, I will get you both out."

Connor asks, "What do you mean by that?"

"Just trust me. I have things going on that you are not aware of, and when the timing is right, I will act on them."

After working with the rebels and setting the meeting location, Eric takes Connor alone so no one else knows what they are doing. Eric gets him close to the frontline to meet with one of the rebels. Upon getting Connor there, he hands him the tracker to help find Adam. Connor quickly reaches the meeting point where a rebel called Bennet is waiting. After validating who they each are, Bennet takes Connor to the meeting point and the others already waiting. While on their way, Bennet asks Connor, "Aren't you a little young to be involved in this? It looks like you do not even shave yet."

Connor smiles. "I may look young, but I am very capable. Trust me."

Bennet, still looking him over, adds, "Trust has to be earned. It is not given lightly, especially with someone as young as you." They then travel to a secret tunnel, getting them behind the front lines, where they meet several other rebels. Bennet then asks Connor, "How far away is Adam?"

He replies, "Based on the tracker I have, he is about 200 miles from here."

"We will need some kind of transport to arrive there, or it will take a long time for us to reach him, assuming Adam is on foot trying to head this way. This will be tricky as we are in enemy territory. The team hijacked a vehicle that should help. There was a small craft available, but that would draw too much attention. Also, no safe place to land it. We should make it about halfway there with this vehicle. Let's get going. We only have a few hours of night left."

While Connor, with the rebels, winds their way toward his brother, Adam works his way to the front, not knowing help is on its way. As he tries to progress, a lot of troops move around, making it difficult to achieve good forward advancement. With morning coming soon, Adam looks for a good place to take cover. He suddenly comes upon a guard station with three men who spot him as they move toward him. Before they can warn anyone, Adam quickly takes them out with his sword, trying to keep things quiet. He then grabs one of their communicators and runs for cover before the dead guards are discovered. Shortly after getting away, he hears over the communicator the dead men have already been detected and they are scanning for whoever killed them. He continues searching for cover with daylight quickly approaching. Adam makes it about two miles. The troops will struggle to glance at who dispatched them and know what direction the killer took. Adam comes up to an abandoned warehouse. Once in the building, he finds a safe place to hide out, waiting for the troops in the area to move away.

On the way to Adam, Connor can see from the tracker: Adam is clearly on the move toward them. "Adam is a little erratic in his movement and may be looking for a place to hide, so we need to get there ASAP."

Bennet replies, "I understand that, but we are behind lines, and all of us are at risk, so we still need to be careful. The morning is almost here. We will need to ditch this transport, then head our way on foot, trying to stay out of sight. We're coming up to an area with cover shortly, so we could continue in the daylight." After hiding the transport, Connor and the rebels start their way through the forest, using the mountain path the rebels travel through to get in and out of the battle zone.

"This fight has been going on for too many years and killed more people than I can count, but with help from your emperor, his men, and the damage just done by them at the Ammo depot, this war should come to an end shortly, we are hoping," says one rebel.

Bennet says to Connor, "If your troops had not come into this fight when you did, we may have lost this war, but with you here, it has revitalized us and given us the hope we needed to finally win this fight. The General started this war years ago to take control. He wanted complete world domination and to be the absolute ruler and dictator. If all us rebels had not started fighting back against his army, we would have been under his control by now."

Connor demurs, "We have not come here to destroy, but to stop the fighting and unite the planet. By seizing some key locations, we should be able to stop this fighting as we have done on other worlds."

"That sounds good in theory, but our enemies want to rule or eliminate us."

"Eric understands this. That is why we took out their weapons depot, which will cripple them from being able to continue the fight much longer. This is the same plan we have used on other worlds, and Eric should be able to bring this to an end quickly."

While they are hiking through the forest toward Adam, Connor gets a flash in his head, a vision of Adam being captured, blindfolded, and taken for interrogation. Not sure he should tell the team of his abilities, he continues, thinking of a way to present this information to them. He also checks the tracker. Adam is still in the same area as earlier, so Connor decides to hold on to what he observed until something changes. Bennet, seeing that he checks Adam's tracker, asks if anything has changed, to which Connor replies, "No, he seems to have stopped moving and has been in the same place for a little while. Maybe he found a place to hide, but I will keep checking it as we go to make sure we keep moving in the right direction."

Adam, still hiding in the warehouse, hears movement in the building. He turns off their communicator, so they do not hear anything from his location. Noticing them coming closer to him, he slowly moves to another location in the warehouse, continuing to stay out of sight, but since it is still dark in there, he has some trouble seeing where he is going and misses the broken glass on the floor. As he steps on it, the soldiers that came in hear the noise and rush towards Adam. He gets behind them quickly, killing four and incapacitating two, to rapidly exit the warehouse, but runs into another squad of soldiers right outside. They capture him, but not before fighting a few of them. They tie him up. Then the captain says, "Blindfold him and take him to the general. He will have a lot of questions for this guy."

As this is going on, Connor looks at the tracker and sees Adam's movement. Connor says, "There must be something going on with Adam. I am seeing too much change, and it looks like he is now going the wrong way." Without revealing his vision, he says, "They may have captured him. If so, we will need to figure out what location they are taking him to."

Bennet says, "I am afraid they may bring him to their general. We know where that is, but it will be very difficult to get him out. Also, the path that way is much more difficult to get through. There are a lot more checkpoints. After we emerge from the cover of this forest and hills, we will need to find a place to rest. We have been going for almost two days with no sleep and will lose our edge, risking us all."

Still in a hurry to get to his brother, Connor requires some convincing, but finally agrees. Shortly after changing direction, they find a cave that will keep them out of sight near the top of a hill. The entrance is recessed so they can view out and not be seen. They also check to make sure they have an alternate path out, just in case it is needed. They then settle in to get some rest. While doing so, Bennet agrees to take the first watch, with Connor taking the second. This would also allow them to come out of the forest at dusk for better cover. Connor steps out to communicate with Eric, letting him know where they are and what the new plan is. Eric responds, "Ok, good. I have been tracking you the same way you are tracking Adam. I saw you change direction. Once you are close to Adam, let me know so I can prepare to get you out."

Connor says, "Ok, will do."

After a few hours, Bennet wakes up Connor to take his turn on watch. From where they are, Connor can see down in the valley. While on watch, he observes some movement down below. He monitors it, staying out of their sight. After the movement stops, he wakes the rest of the team so they can get started back after his brother. They maneuver their way down to the valley floor just as the sun sets. Heading down the road for a while, they run into a small scouting party. Getting in behind and surprising them, they overtake and kill them off, but since this is Connor's first actual battle with any kind of enemy, he finds it difficult to truly kill the person he is fighting. Bennet notices his hesitation and eliminates the enemy for him. Bennet asks, "You look a little green. Is this your first kill up close?"

Connor is a little embarrassed over his inaction. "Yes, I have been training my whole life, but this is the first time I have been this near to someone being eliminated."

"Sorry, but war is hell, and if we had let them live, they may have compromised where we are going. Also, if I had known how green you are to all of this, I would not have agreed to bring you along, but it is too late now. You are going to have to toughen up quickly. No telling what else we are going to run into before we get to your brother."

"Sorry, I will not hesitate or let you down next time."

"Ok, we'll see. We need to hide the bodies and get their communication equipment." Bennett spots their vehicle parked off the road. "This will speed things up a bit."

Enemy soldiers take Adam to the General; they lock him in a room while he is still bound and blindfolded, then tell the General about their capture and all the damage Adam caused. He sits in the room for several hours before someone unlocks the door and takes off his blindfold. The gruff older man peers at him and says, "If I untie your hands, are you going to give me any trouble?"

Adam replies, "No, I am not sure where I am."

The gruff man unties Adam. "Ok, you need to follow me." They leave the room and head down a dark hallway with two more guards behind him. They come to a large lit room with an older gray-haired man with wrinkles and scars. He has lived a lifetime on his face. The gruff soldier pulls Adam by the arm and pushes him into a chair in front of this old, gray-haired man. The gruff man barks, "This is our commander and general."

The general says, "So this is the guy that has been causing us the problems. I hear you have been a lot of trouble for us and taken out some of my men. Why are you here? I do not recognize your uniform. Are you part of the team taking out our ammunition depot? That has caused us so much harm, and if you are not part of the rebels, then again, why are you here? This is not your fight."

Adam answers with a stern look. "We were sent here to stop this war by our emperor."

"What emperor? I am the ultimate power here."

"On this planet, that may be true, but we are the masters of multiple planets."

"I do not understand. We have just started to travel into space."

"Yes, you are correct, and that is part of the reason we are here now. Your civilization is mature enough for us to approach."

"I think you have lost it; we do not have time for this right now. Your damage has caused us a lot of pain, and I need to come up with a plan to recover from it before we become compromised, even more so." The General looks at the gruff soldier. "Take him back and lock him up for now. Have someone keep an eye on him till we figure out what to do with him."

The gruff soldier grabs his arm. "Come with me." He says to Adam when they get back into the dark hallway with no one else around, "Is it true you came from another planet?"

"Yes," Adam says.

"This is crazy. How is that possible?"

"There is a lot more going on here than you know," says Adam. "If you will help me, I need to get a message out to my team about where I am."

"Sorry, there is no way. I need to escort you back to the room, but will see what I can do while you are in there."

AT ABOUT THE SAME TIME, CONNOR AND BENNET overtake the scouting party. After they clean up the bodies and take their equipment, Bennet says, "It may be a good idea to change uniforms with the soldiers we killed. This could help if we come across a roadblock or checkpoint." Once Connor changes, he also looks at the tracker for Adam, sees he is much further behind enemy lines now, and tells the team.

Bennet says, "Ok, that is what I thought. We believe that is where the General is." Then he repeats it again. "This will not be a simple task to get him out." They all pile into primitive transport with wheels touching the ground, not hover above the ground like Connor's transport back home, and head towards Adam, unsure of the obstacles they will encounter.

They venture down the road, then come upon a checkpoint and are waved through. Since it is dark, the guard there cannot clearly see who is on the transport, just that they are wearing the correct uniforms. While in primitive transport, Connor has another vision of his brother. This time, he sees Adam being tortured and feels intense pain like he is the one being harmed, as if he was in his brother's place. Connor says, "We need to hurry. They are going to torture my brother."

Bennet replies, "You do not know that."

Connor's now concerned about how he can explain it. "Yes, I do."

"How? Why do you think they are torturing your brother?"

"I have witnessed it. There is something I need to tell you. I can see things that are or will happen. This ability has been passed down through my family from time to time."

Bennet is not sure he can believe what Connor is telling him. "If this is the case, what else can you see that may help us get close to your brother?"

"Right now, I am still learning how to control it, so these visions just come to me."

"Ok, then if this is true, I am not sure I believe it. If you get any more visions, do not keep them to yourself while we are on the way to your brother. From what I can guess, we are still about two hours away at this pace if we do not run into any trouble."

ABOUT AN HOUR AFTER BEING PUT IN THE LOCKED room, the General demands to have Adam brought back to him. Another soldier transports Adam to the general and ties him down to the chair he was sitting in during their first meeting. The General demands, "If you are really from another planet, then you must have superior weapons. This would be a big help for us. Where are they?"

Adam stares icily. "They are well protected, and I would not think of telling you. We came here to stop this war, not escalate it."

The General booms in a loud voice, "When you blew up our ammunition depot, you damaged our chances. Now we need your weapons if we are going to win!"

"As I said, you will not get your hands on our weapons!"

"Take him to the table and strap him down. We need those weapons, and he is going to tell us where they are." The soldier drags Adam to another room with a steel table. Adam hits the soldier, trying to get away, but three other soldiers run in. Adam puts up a good fight for a bit, but they finally force him to the steel table and tie him down. One soldier clips electrodes to the end of the table, then takes off his shoes, clips electrodes to his hands and feet, and then pours water on the table. Just as the General walks in, he says, "You can make this easy or hard, your call."

Adam glares at him. "I guess it will be hard. I cannot, nor will I, tell you where our weapons are."

"Hit it. Let's see how he likes that." One soldier pulls the switch on the wall; the lights go dim. There's a loud hum, and Adam's body goes rigid after a minute. The General says, "Ok, that is enough." The soldier pushes the switch back, the hum stops, and Adam drops onto the table. "Now will you tell us where they are?"

Adam yells at him, "No way in hell! You can flip that switch all day long. I will never let you know anything."

"Hit him again longer this time." The soldier flips the switch. They hear the hum start once more. This time, they wait a few minutes longer.

Adam, with all his might, gives out a loud shout, "I will never tell you anything."

"Stop it. Get him off the table and take him back to the room. Double the guards on him. This is not working. We need a new plan here or we are done," says the General. The soldiers take Adam, who can barely move, back to the room, tossing him in on the floor, and lock the door.

CONNOR, FEELING EVERYTHING ADAM HAS BEEN, SAYS, "We need to hurry. What they are doing to Adam is very painful. I can also tell that the General is getting desperate and is trying to get answers from Adam, and he will not let anything slip."

Bennet answers, "We are about thirty minutes away, but we will have to ditch our transport, or we may not make it in. We will need to see how many soldiers are there and how the building is guarded. If you are truly having visions, try to see where Adam is in the building. This will help us in trying to get him out."

BACK WITH ADAM, THE GRUFF SOLDIER LOOKS AT THE other soldiers guarding him. "I need to check on the prisoner. The General wants to make sure he is ok." They unlock the door and let him in.

One soldier guards the door. "Knock on the door when you're ready to come out."

The gruff soldier picks up Adam from the floor and moves him to the bed. "You don't look so good," he says to Adam.

"I feel worse," says Adam. "But I will not let that maniac in the other room know that. What's your name?"

"Ray," the gruff soldier replies. "I think I have found a way to get a message out if you can tell me who and how to reach them, but I need to be careful. The General has lost it and will do anything to win this war that has been going on far too long. If you are truly from another world and can stop it, I will do whatever I can to help. No one seems to know why we are fighting anymore, and all the General is looking to do is to be the victor at all costs."

Adam smiles at Ray. "Ok, if you can get a call out, they are monitoring your radio channel 41. Ask to speak with Eric. Tell him you are asking for Adam and where we are. He will take care of it from there."

"Let me see what I can do. I will also get you some food and water. I am sure you have not eaten in a while. It will help you recover quicker."

"Thank you. I will make sure you are taken care of when this is all over."

"I was not looking for that. I just want this to be done. I cannot remember life before the war anymore. If you can help end the combat, it is worth any risk I have to take." As Ray heads to the door, he says, "If I am not back before too long, I did not get through and was caught."

"Understood. Thank you."

Ray knocks on the door, then leaves the room and tells the soldiers he will be back with some nourishment for the prisoner.

One soldier says, "Why would you do that for him? He killed some of our own men and has information that could help us."

Ray replies, "I am tired of all the killing, and I am just trying to do what is right, no matter what he is responsible for."

"I get what you are saying. I am not there, but I will not stop you if that is how you feel." Ray continues down the dark hallway. At the end, it splits right to the kitchen and left to the radio room. When he gets to the end, he heads left. The radio room appears to be dark inside. He then peers behind him to see if anyone is watching. There is no one around, so he goes down into the radio room. As he opens the door, a blast of heat hits him from all the active equipment. He then locks the door behind him. He chooses to leave the lights off, goes to the radio, dials channel 41, grabs the mic, and softly asks if anyone is there a few times.

Finally, someone responds, "Yes, who is this?"

"My name is Ray. I was told to ask for someone named Eric. Is he there?"

The voice on the other end says, "Hold on one minute."

THE PERSON ON THE OTHER END, ONE OF ERIC'S STAFF, drops the mic, then runs to the other room to get Eric. "Sir, someone on the radio channel 41 is asking for you."

Eric, with a surprised expression on his face, asks, "What? Who is it?"

"The man said his name is Ray and was told to ask for you."

Eric runs to the other room and grabs the mic. "This is Eric. I am here. Who's this and what do you want?"

"My name is Ray, and I was instructed to tell you I am calling for Adam. He requested me to reach out to you."

Eric excitedly asks, "Adam! Is he ok? Where are you?"

"They tortured him, but he is doing ok. He communicated why you are here, and I want to help. Will you be able to send men to assist him?"

"I already have a group on their way. Can you help free Adam?"

"No, I do not think that will work. He is too heavily guarded, but I should be able to help smuggle your men in. A door at the back of the building is not being watched. I can unlock it. The door has the number 26 on it."

"Thank you, Ray. The team is not too far away. I will let them know."

"Ok, I must go. I have been talking too long already."

"Understood. Let Adam know we are en route."

Eric reaches out to Connor, letting him know about the call with Ray and how to enter the building. He also tells Connor he has been tracking him the same way Connor was with Adam. Once he is with Adam, Eric will send in reinforcements to rescue them. Connor tells Bennet and the team someone on the inside is going to aid them and about the plan to break into the building.

Bennet responds, "Outstanding. I feel a little better about our chances of getting your brother out, but we will need to stay on our toes till this is over."

WHILE ERIC TALKS WITH CONNOR, RAY, NOW SWEATING from the heat in the room, unlocks the radio room door, but as he starts out, someone walks that way. Another soldier asks Ray, "What were you doing in there?"

He replies, "It is dark in this hall, and I thought the kitchen was this way."

"No, it is the other hall," says the soldier.

"Yes, I figured that out as soon as I walked in. I saw the glow from the radio, so I turned around."

The soldier, with a puzzled look on his face, says, "Ok, I guess that makes sense."

Ray heads down the hall and enters the kitchen while the guard watches. Once in the kitchen, Ray grabs some food and gets a cup of water. He then returns to the room where Adam is. Once at the door, the soldiers look over what Ray has in his hands, then unlock the door and let him in.

The soldier again says, "Knock on the door to be let out." Ray continues to walk in. They close and lock the door as he enters.

Adam asks in a soft voice, "You were not gone too long. Were you able to make contact?"

"Yes," said Ray. "I was told a group is already close by coming to get you out. Here is food and water. Get ready to leave. I need to open the back door so they can enter. Once you get out, your weapons and pack are in the next room. If I do not see you again, good luck to you."

Adam has a smile on his face. "Thank you for all your help. I will not forget what you have done for me here."

"In the sound of desperation, you're welcome. Please help us end this war." He then knocks. "Let me out," he says. The door opens, and he walks down the hallway in the opposite direction, maneuvering his way to the back door numbered 26. He glances around to see if anyone is there. With no one in the area, he unlocks it and quickly paces away into one of the other hallways. Ray again runs into the same soldier that saw him come out of the radio room.

The soldier gazes at him. "Why are you here? There shouldn't be anyone in this part of the building."

"I got lost looking for a place to sleep. All the hallways are dark."

The soldier says, "The sleeping quarters are in the next hallway. I repeat, you should not be here."

Ray answers in a stern voice, "I got it. I'm leaving the area now." Ray heads towards the sleeping quarters, and the soldier continues to the back of the building.

OUTSIDE, CONNOR AND BENNET APPROACH THE building where Adam is. After hiding the transport vehicle, they slowly get to the back of the building near the door marked 26. There is a small open area past the trees. While in the trees, they scan for any soldiers nearby. Not seeing any, they go to the door. Bennet opens it and goes through, just in time to see Ray knock out the soldier. Ray looks at Bennet and says, "I'm the one who unlocked the door and called Eric to let you know how to get in. Bring the rest of the team, and I will lead you to Adam." Ray slowly leads the team down the dark hallways to Adam. When they get close to the room, Ray sees the door open. "He's not there," Ray says.

Connor asks, "Where else would he be?"

"They may have taken him back to the General." Just then, they all feel a slight shake from the building and look at each other,

"Did you feel that?" asks Connor.

"Yes, what was it?" asks Bennet.

Ray puts in, "Probably an earthquake. We get them all that time around here."

Bennet answers, "Yes, that's true."

"The general is in the next room. We will have to be careful."

As they get to the door, the general says, "I know you are out there. Come in. Did you think we did not know what was going on?" As they all enter, they see the General with his arm around Adam and gun to his head. "Drop your guns and step away from them."

Adam sees Connor. "Connor, I am glad you made it." He then quickly steps back into the General, grabbing his arm and pushing it up as the General fires his gun towards the ceiling. Adam continues to twist his arm behind his back, knocking him to the floor. He then pulls the gun out of the General's hand and holds it to his head. "It is time for you to surrender."

The General barks, "My soldiers are outside the building, and you will not get away."

"I am not going anywhere," says Adam. Just then, soldiers in strange uniforms flood the room, and Eric walks in. Adam looks at Eric. "Glad to see you made it."

Connor gapes at both Adam and Eric. "What is going on here?!"

Eric smiles at Adam, then says, "Well, do you want to tell him, or should I?" Connor, Bennet, and the rest of the team wear a puzzled expression on their faces.

Adam steps forward. "I will. Connor, did you wonder why I was bringing up the back for the fighter squadron instead of leading like normal? It was the plan from the beginning. After the bombing of the depot, I would crash and be captured. Then you would be sent to rescue me. But when I lost my communication device, it messed up the arrangement. We had to capture the General, and this seemed the best way. Eric and I thought this was the optimal way to give you battle experience with a protection team around you, without your knowledge. Once we were together, Eric knew we were both with the General in the building. The boom you felt earlier was a sonic bomb to knock out all the troops in the area without having to fire a shot. Then Eric and his troops could fly in and take over."

Connor asks, "Wait, so none of this was real for me?"

"Not true. It was all real, even more so when we lost communication with Adam. I was just talking with Bennet about all you went through, and I am very proud of how you have handled yourself. We tried to make sure you had protection going after Adam. This was a great way to get you involved, and you did an excellent job!"

Eric and Adam then look at the General. "You are done. We needed to take you alive so we could prove that the head of the snake had been cut off, and get your army to surrender. If they question it, we have proof we are merciful. Now is the time for you to rebuild, not destroy."

The General says, "I will never surrender."

Adam replies, "That is our point. We do not need you to. Showing we have captured you without firing a shot is enough. No one in this world even knows what they are fighting for anymore. You have been so bent on winning you did not care about the cost, but it is all over now. The reason we came here in the first place is our emperor discovered the resources you have. We can show you how to mine them without destroying your planet. Once we teach you, you will be able to rebuild what was destroyed during your war. We have teams sent here to do this. Your planet is yours. We have not come here to take it over, merely purchase what resources you do not need at a fair price. This will help rebuild your economy, and we will get the minerals we need; everybody wins."

Eric adds, "Bennet and Ray, we want you to be the first to lead your people into a new life. Since you are each from opposite sides, you can show your world a new, peaceful, and hopeful life for all. It will require some time, but we can teach you how quickly things can be rebuilt with our technology. I will be excited to see what things look like here a year from now. We have already sent word the war is over, and teams arrive as soon as tomorrow. In the meantime, we will use our base as a staging area."

Adam says, "This is our way of saying thank you for your assistance in stopping this war. We have already spread the word over all your communication channels that everyone can lay down their arms, and we will help you rebuild. We will leave tomorrow when the other teams get here, but I agree with Eric. I will be enthusiastic to see how great your future will be. Good luck to all of you."

CHAPTER II
A HERO'S WELCOME

ERIC, ADAM, AND CONNOR RETURN TO THEIR HIDDEN base with Bennet and Ray. Adam shows them around, sets them up, and returns to meet Eric and Connor. Connor looks despondent, and Adam suspects he's upset about how Eric and he schemed together.

He walks over to Connor. "I am sorry, but since this was your first time in a war like this, we wanted to make sure you were ready to deal with it. Based on what I have seen and heard, you are more than prepared, other than not being able to kill someone, but that will come as the need arises, I have no doubt. Eric did not want to tell you we have used these same tactics on other planets in the past, and it has worked out well. Now that you have proven yourself, there will be no more secrets."

Connor sighs. "I get it. I'm not happy about it, but I understand."

Eric puts in, "Well, you have been training your entire life, but it has been merely training. This was the real deal."

"Understood. So where do we go from here?"

Adam answers, "We go home tomorrow, once we've had a good night's sleep."

Eric agrees. "Yes, after six months of building up for this final win, I am ready to go home."

"Me too," Adam and Connor say at the same time.

The next morning, Connor steps outside. Just as Adam said, ships begin to land. Adam tells Ray and Bennet the new arrivals know who they are and will work with them on the next phase, bringing their planet back to life without hostilities. Together with Eric and Adam, Connor wishes them both good luck before leaving. They then board a smaller ship and are gone.

On the ship Adam is piloting, he states, "I have put in the coordinates to our home planet, Hmar 4. We should be there in a few hours."

"I cannot wait. I am going to sleep for days." Connor smiles broadly.

Eric leans in. "Sorry, we are not done yet. We will have to build, then present our report to the emperor in two days. He always wants the readout immediately. You should be able to rest after that unless the emperor has other plans for us. When we get home, you can see your family, and I can tell your father how well you did. You and your brother are the legacies of the Balcazar family, protectors of the royal family, and heads of the royal military. He will be eager to know your progress."

Several hours later, they land at their home port. As the ship descends, Connor spots their father, Duke William, and mother, Duchess Sara, along with Eric's brother John. As they walk off the ship, the duke says, "My boys, I am so glad you are both back safe. Eric, as always, thank you for watching out for them. I take it the mission was successful."

Adam beams. "Yes, Father, very, and you will be pleased to hear how well Connor did."

"Great. I look forward to hearing all about it, but let's get to the Villa. The emperor is already there."

Eric splutters, "What? We are not ready to meet with him. Our report is not prepared."

"Do not worry. He wants to celebrate the completion of your mission. The information can come later. The emperor brought his daughters with him."

"Great. I look forward to seeing Christina." Adam perks up.

With a wink and a smile, Sara turns toward him. "I am sure you do." Adam blushes.

"I am not sure what you mean. It's simply that we have not seen her in a while."

Connor jeers. "Yeah, right." Grinning, he pats Adam on the shoulder.

THE GROUP DEPARTS FOR THE VILLA, A LONG JOURNEY to the country. As they approach, they glimpse guards protecting the emperor. With a quick security communications check, the shield opens, and their ship lands at the front door of the villa. There, they stand face to face with a grand entrance. An ornate staircase leads to the front door. As they all walk in, Emperor Esteban stands on the other side of the entrance with his arms out and hands raised high. "There are my heroes, world conquerors! I cannot tell you how pleased I am with what the three of you have done. Let's celebrate and honor you. Eric, William, and John have been updating me the whole way through as you have updated them, so I am up to speed with your success. My daughters, Christina and Emily, are in the other room. Let's go in there and get this celebration going. Then we can talk about how it went and what's next."

Connor proclaims, "Great, I am hungry. Let's eat," as everyone walks into a grand hall, at the center of which is a long table stacked with delicacies. Two blonde, nearly identical girls greet them. Before they can introduce themselves, one springs forward and yells, "Adam!" putting her arms around him in a warm embrace.

"Christina!" her father admonishes.

"Sorry, Father, it has been so long since we have seen each other. I was just excited to see him and Connor, too."

Connor responds, "Well then, where is my hug?" As Christina embraces him, they all laugh.

"Why don't we take a seat so we can eat?" William encourages. "Adam and Connor, you guys can sit next to me."

Esteban interjects, "No, I would like them by me. William, you have raised fine sons, and I want to hear what they accomplished during this last campaign." Looking at the boys, he adds, "Why don't you sit on either side so we can also discuss what's next? Sorry, Sara, I know you have missed your boys, but I will make sure you have time with them before I send them off again."

"Yes, sire, as you wish." Sara smiles.

Over the din of multiple conversations, Esteban stands. "I would like to raise a glass to the Balcazar and Aristo families. Your outstanding support to my descendants and efforts to expand our universe make things very profitable for us, not simply financially and with technology, but in changing people's lives for the better. If it were not for your guidance and direction, none of this would be possible. Now, with this last success, William, you should be very proud your legacy will continue with your sons. John and Eric, I also want to add that, if not for your training, they would not be who they are either. Thank you. When it is my time to go, I will be happy to know what we accomplished in my lifetime."

Williams stands. "Thank you, sire. I can speak for everyone when we say none of this would have been possible if not for your support and vision, along with the trust and freedom to do what needed to be done."

Connor jumps up. "Thank you, and I am not trying to be rude, but can we eat now? I am starving." Everyone laughs.

Esteban has a big smile on his face. "Sorry, yes, I forgot how young you still are and how important food is to you." Everyone laughs again, and with that, they eat.

"While I let Connor swallow, I hear this campaign was rough this time, and you were tortured before Eric could come to fetch you."

Adam nods. "Yes, but I focused on the fact that I would be rescued at some point. I was also surprised Connor got to me when he did. We wanted to offer Connor exposure, but the amount he got and what he accomplished was outstanding. I would be happy to have him cover for me the next time."

Connor adds, "Yes, it was very intense, but I thought my brother was in serious danger, and reaching him as soon as I could was the only thing on my mind."

Adam looks toward Connor. "Sorry if you thought I was not at risk. If you and your team had not got there, it could have been a lot worse for me."

"I did not think about that. Then I feel much better about what we did to reach you."

Esteban asks, "Connor, what do you mean?"

"Well, I really did not want to talk about it here, but we had to slaughter everyone in a patrol party." He glances at Adam. "This was the first time I have been that close to killing anyone."

"Really? I am impressed even more. Well done."

Christina and Emily, sitting near Adam and Connor, hear all this. Christina blurts out, "Oh my, Connor, I am so sorry."

Connor says, "No, it is okay. That is what I have been training for all my life."

"I appreciate that, but it was your first kill, and that had to be hard for you."

"Yes, it was. Thank you for understanding." Adam, who knows Bennett did the assassination, says nothing.

Connor offers, "Let's change the subject."

Esteban agrees. "Yes, let's take this back to a happier conversation. Boys, I have big plans for you. The two of you are the future, and I anticipate what is possible when you lead the charge. Your father, John, and Eric cannot survive forever, and with your success, you will continue our legacy."

William, John, and Eric laugh. Then William puts in, "We are not that old or ready to retire yet, and the boys have barely started, but we appreciate how you feel about them. We share your sentiment and will help them mature and succeed."

"Great, that is what I want."

Christina hears all of this. "Hey where do I fit in?"

Esteban laughs a little. "I am sorry, my dear. You will own everything when I am gone. But, in the meantime, now that you are older, I will include you in my plans for our empire and what Adam and Connor are doing to help us. This means you will spend more time with them as we make new projects."

"Great, thank you, Father. That is all I was looking for."

"Ok, I think we have talked enough about our business and the future. Let's continue eating and drinking while having a great evening."

Connor looks at Adam. "Can I talk with you privately for a minute?"

Adam says, "Sure." They step away from the table to a corner of the room.

"Thank you for not telling them I did not succeed. I was embarrassed, and I did not want the emperor to lose faith in me and my abilities."

Adam grabs his shoulder. "I have your back, as you have mine. Do not worry. When the time calls for it, you will do what you need to. Of this I have no doubt. There is no need to discuss this further." Then he rubs his head. As he does this, Christina and Emily stroll over.

"Hi, Emily, it has been a while. How are you?" Connor says to her.

Emily smiles. "Yes, I know too long. I am well. What were you guys talking about?"

As Adam cannot stop staring at Christina, he says, "Just an unfinished conversation, you know, brother stuff, nothing too important." Adam then reaches for Christina's hand and asks if she would like to take a hike with him outside so they can catch up.

"Yes, I would love to," she replies.

Esteban, noticing Adam and Christina walk off together, looks at William and Sara. "I think there is more than the friendship the two of them had growing up."

Sara wears a big smile on her face. "Oh yes, Adam has been smitten with Christina for a while now, maybe always. It's hard to tell, as he is very private with his thoughts."

Esteban speaks as a proud father. "If this grows into something more, that would make me very happy. I could not think of anyone better for my daughter. It will also bond our families together."

William and Sara concur. "We would be very pleased as well, but it is up to them, and we have to keep our hopes quiet, so they do not feel pressured into anything," Sara says.

"Yes, very wise," Esteban replies. All three, with big smiles on their faces, watch Adam and Christina leave. Connor and Emily come back to the table.

Connor inspects his parents. "What are you smiling about?" They laugh.

"Nothing, we are merely happy and proud of you boys," says Sara. "So, Emily, what have you girls been up to?"

Emily replies, "We have been away at school and go back in a few days. We will both graduate in a few months."

"You and Christina are attending the same school?"

Emily beams. "Yes, thanks to our father. If it were not for him, who knows what would have happened to me? When my parents were killed, he and Christina took me in and allowed me to attend all the same schools Christina attended. We have become like sisters, and I have learned a lot."

"Sounds like it has worked out well. The two of you look so much alike you could be blood sisters. I bet you hear constantly."

Emily wears a big grin. "Yes, we do, and do not always correct them, which makes it fun for us."

Sara laughs. "I bet it does. What are your plans once you graduate?"

"That is up to our father and the projects he has for Christina. Hopefully, I can support her, but we both have a science background from our studies."

William puts in, "If you girls are as close as you say, that should not be a problem. I would think Christina would want to keep you close to her."

While William and Sara talk to Emily, Adam and Christina walk out to the garden. She looks at Adam and always says what she feels. "Our life has been an exciting ride. Remember when we were last together, meeting our fathers on Lucas 2 after they stopped the civil war—or so they thought? Then we went for a hike after ditching my guard unit, not knowing we stepped in the middle of the enemy territory and had to fight our way out?"

Adam, normally a little reserved with his feelings, now thinking about it, laughs. "Yes, I thought you were going to kill those two before the three others I took care of, and we escaped. Fortunately, your guard unit found us shortly after not telling your father or mine, as they would have been in trouble for losing you."

"Maybe mine did. That's probably why he sent Emily and I away to school." She chuckles.

"Ha, that's about the same time my father had me stay with Eric. He trained me harder and brought me with him on his missions. Maybe if we did not get into that battle, we wouldn't be where we are now."

"If you and Connor hadn't trained me when I was younger, we might not have made it out either. Emily and I train at university, and she's pretty good at keeping me on my game."

"I want to see for myself."

"Oh yeah." Christina smiles back.

With that, Adam reaches for her hand again, pressing his lips to hers, and gives her a big kiss, almost taking her breath away. "How was that?"

"It was okay, but I was looking for something more physical." This time, he pulls her to him, puts his arms around her, and gives her another kiss. Her knees buckle.

Christina, lightheaded, can barely breathe. "That's better."

With a big grin, "Good," Adam says. Just then, Connor and Emily stroll down the path and interrupt them. Adams backs away from Christina a bit.

Connor says, "Sorry, don't let us stop you. We just came to see what you two were up to."

"No, that's ok. We were just talking."

Emily grins. "That did not look like talking to me."

Christina blushes a little. "Maybe we should get back to the party."

Adam agrees, "Yes, maybe so."

Christina begins to walk away with Emily. She grabs Emily's hand tight, looks at her with an excited smile, then says in a quiet voice, "He does like me." They giggle.

Connor sighs, "Sorry brother."

Adam says, "No, it's ok. I needed to know if she likes me the same way I like her, and she does, but with the whole family here, we could not take things further, anyway."

"Ok good, I am happy for you. Also, so you know, according to Emily, they return to school in a few days, so if you cannot move things along before they leave, you may have to wait a while longer."

"Good point. I will have to see what I can do then in the next day or so."

"But if we are all here at the villa, it may be a problem. Well, good luck."

Back in the great hall with the rest of the family, they sit down again. Adam's mom Sara asks, "Did you all have an enjoyable walk?"

Adam nods. "Yes, we did. We also discovered what occurred at Lucas 2 was not as quiet as we thought it was."

William and Esteban laugh, and Esteban says, "Whatever do you mean?"

Then William smiles. "Did you think we would not have found out what the two of you got involved in? We receive a guard report every night when they are watching you, no matter what happens, even when you lose them."

Esteban is still laughing. "I am surprised it took you both this long to figure it out."

Adam shrugs. "Since we have not seen or talked with each other till now, we had no way of knowing we both got sent away since nothing was ever said."

"We felt since you were both ok, your father and I agreed not to say anything. When I read the report, the one thing that made me feel good was that Christina was very capable of taking care of herself. We also knew maybe you were both ready for the next phase of your lives while separating at the same time to keep you out of trouble."

Connor puts in, "So that is why Adam left when I was younger and I did not see that much of him after he went with Eric?"

William nods. "Yes, I figure if Adam could get into that kind of trouble, it was time to up his training. That is also why John pushed you harder in your training, making you the capable young man you are now, and why we agreed to send you to fight with Eric and Adam. John and I felt you were ready, and Castia would be an excellent test for you. We have a legacy to protect. The Balcazar family has been guarding emperors and leading their military for generations. We had to make sure the two of you were going to continue this legacy as the next generation, like John, Eric, and I did when we took over from our fathers. You two are well on your way, and we could not be prouder."

A few more conversations go on. The entire time, Christina and Adam keep looking at each other and grinning. After a bit, Esteban says, "Well, this has been a great night. It could not have gone any better." As he winks at Christina, she blushes a little. "But we have to leave in the morning, and it is late."

Adam watches his plans to spend more time with Christina slipping away. "Tomorrow? I thought you guys were staying for a couple of days."

"As much as we would like that, I have business requiring me to be back tomorrow, and the girls need to get ready to go back to school." Esteban starts to walk out. "William and Sara, thank you very much for hosting this evening." He looks at William. "You have been a good friend and partner." As he shakes his hand with both of his, he turns and hugs Sara, then looks at Christina and Emily. "Are you coming?"

"Yes, Father, we will be right there," responds Christina. He strides out of the room, and Christina walks over to Adam, leans in, and whispers in his ear, "Meet me back in the garden in about an hour." Adam nods his head. Then Christina and Emily exit as well.

Sara beholds Adam with a big smile on her face. "What's going on?"

Adam grins at her. "I do not know what you are talking about."

Connor laughs, "I do."

Sara says, "If things are getting serious between you two, we could not be happier for you."

Adam cannot stop grinning. "Thank you, but we are not there yet. This is the first time I have seen her since you guys sent us away."

William demurs. "No, do not say we sent you away. We knew you needed to grow, and we gave you a better way, or else you and Christina may have gone down the wrong path if we kept you together. She needed to go to school, and you needed some direction to help our family as the next generation. We always knew we could not really keep you two apart."

Sara adds, "It has been a long day for all of us, and I am ready to retire to my room."

"Sounds good," the boys say. They all go upstairs to their chambers. Shortly after, Adam sneaks out of his room to the garden below. A few minutes later, Christina walks out. When she sees Adam sitting there, she smiles from ear to ear. Adam looks at her and starts smiling himself. "What are you smiling at?"

Christina gazes into his eyes. "I could not stop since our last kiss."

"I know, me either." Adam reaches for her hand. She sits down next to him.

"I wanted you to meet me out here because I need to make sure that kiss was as real for you as it was for me."

"I have thought of doing that since we were on Lucas 2, but then we were in that fight and the guards found us, then rushed us off. Tonight, I had to do it before I lost my nerve."

"I am glad you did, but where do we go from here?" says Christina.

Still holding her hand, he looks into her eyes and kisses her softer than earlier. "I am not sure. You are leaving in the morning."

Just then, a guard walks through. They jump apart on the bench.

"Oh, I am sorry, sir. I did not know anyone was out here. We are getting ready to lock everything down for the evening."

Adam says, "Ok, give us a few minutes."

"Yes, sir," the guard replies.

With a slight laugh, "SIR! You have grown," Christina says.

Adam chuckles. "We do not have much time, to go in, I mean. We have waited this long. Being apart from you now will kill me, but knowing you feel the same way, I am willing to find a way to make this work if you are."

Christina states, "Then you better give me a kiss that will hold me until we can be together again." Adam stands and pulls her up to him as he put his arms around her, this time leaning over her. He gives her another longer, harder kiss that takes her breath away, making her lightheaded. Adam feels her start to drop but holds on, then brings her back up.

Christina peers into his eyes. "I'll wait for you no matter how long it takes." She gives him a big hug, then grabs his hand and says again, "No matter how long." They then both walk in. The guard stands there waiting to lock the doors.

Adam looks at the guard. "Thank you for waiting. You can lock up now."

"Thank you, sir," the guard replies.

Adam turns to Christina. "Will I see you in the morning before you leave?"

"Yes, of course you will, every chance we get from now on." She quickly scans around. Not seeing anyone, she gives Adam another hug and a quick kiss on the lips. With that, she heads upstairs to her room.

Christina strides into the bedroom. Emily, sitting reading on one of the two beds in the room, sees

Christina walk in. She puts her book down. "Well, how was it?"

"It was beyond amazing. He does like me as much as I do him. I do not want to say love yet, but that is how I feel."

"I am so happy for you, Christina. He is all you have talked about since we left for school. I am glad your feelings were not wasted waiting to see him again."

"Thank you, but we both have very busy lives and duties keeping us apart, I'm afraid."

"Love always finds a way. I truly believe that."

"So do I. What about you and Connor? There may be something. He is very cute."

Emily shrugs. "We have never spent any real time together as you have with Adam when we were kids. While you were training with Adam and Connor, I was covering for you, but today we got time to talk and walk around. I think it would be fun to go out with him, but it will also have to wait since we are leaving in the morning."

"I will see how I can help when we have time."

"That would be great. I never wanted to say anything, but I have always had a crush on Connor."

"Oh, wow, really? Then I will have to help."

"I am so glad we have been friends all this time. You have made my life so much better."

"No, not friends, sisters, very close ones," Christina corrects her.

Emily stands up, walks over, and gives Christina a big hug. "Thank you."

Christina gazes at Emily with a big smile. "You're welcome. Maybe we should get some sleep. It has been a long and eventful day."

"Yes, you're right, it has been." They both get into their beds, say good night, then turn off the lights.

SHORTLY AFTER CHRISTINA GOES TO HER ROOM, ADAM follows, but instead of heading up to his room, he knocks on the door of his parents. Sara opens the door. "Adam, what is it?"

"Can I talk with you?" he asks.

"Sure, come in." They walk to the retreat. William sits on the couch facing the fireplace with a fire burning, and the light from the fire flickers on his face.

"What is it, my boy?" William asks.

Adam responds, "I have been talking with Christina again after you all left, and things have gotten very serious between us."

Sara smiles. "We have been hoping that would happen." She puts her arm in his. "And sounds like she feels the same way."

"Yes, she does, but we both have very active lives. She is leaving tomorrow. I don't know when I will see her again. I'm not sure how we can make this work."

William says, "Son, if she cares for you the way you do for her, anything is possible. Yes, they will leave, but she and Emily graduate in a few months, and the emperor will throw a big celebration, and we will attend. Then she will take on responsibilities with her father, the emperor. If you are here, that is only a two-hour flight with light speed between planets."

Sara adds, "With your father's help, we will try to keep you here as much as possible to help give you time with Christina."

Adam nods. "Thank you both. This makes me feel better about our chances. Glad I came to talk with you two. I could not imagine having better parents. I love you both." He gives each of them a hug.

William agrees. "We cannot imagine having a better son. We love you too. Why don't you get some sleep?"

"Thank you, I will. Have a good night." He walks out the door.

Sara strolls over to William and hugs him. "Remember what it was like when we first met?"

"Sure do. I was already working for Esteban and his father before Esteban became emperor and had come to your planet to work on a new contract for military support on behalf of the emperor. One day while I was there and saw you in the market, I had to talk to you. You were so beautiful it took me back a little. Then you smiled at me and spilled some fruit from your basket. I rushed over to help you pick them up and introduced myself. First, you did not want to tell me your name, but then you said, 'My name is Sara.' Then you rushed off. I was not sure I would ever see you again. Neither of us knew I had been working with your father, and he invited me to dinner later that evening. When I arrived, your father invited me in. We sat at the table. Then you came in from the other room and sat down. It took you a minute to realize I was sitting there. You then looked at me and said, 'What are you doing here?'

"Your father studied me with a puzzled look on his face and asked if I knew you. At first, I said no, but yes, since we just met today at the market. Your father said, 'So this is the man that helped you. You could not stop talking about him when you got home.' With your face all blushed, you said, 'Yes, he is.' It was then I knew we could have something special."

"Not sure I remember it exactly that way, but you're close."

"Well, something I am not sure you were aware of. Before I left that evening, when your father and I went off to talk, it was mostly about you. I asked if he would give me his permission to see you. At first, he said no, that I was from the Balcazar family, and our way of living was hard and dangerous. He feared for the life you might have with me. It took a little convicting, but I assured him you would always be protected, and if we did ever marry, I would provide you with a good life since I came from a wealthy family. I also reminded him who John and Eric were and they would be around whenever we were together, so he finally agreed."

"So that was why John or Eric and sometimes both went everywhere with us."

William starts to laugh. "Yep, it was your father's fault."

"I remember our life started out the same way Adam and Christina's is going to be now. I was trying to finish school, and the emperor had you busy and gone all the time. We also had a few adventures of our own before we got married. Remember the time on Termadrez? You had Eric bring me to meet you because of how beautiful the planet was, with the multicolored lakes and brightly colored sunsets, but then the three of us had to fight our way out because rebels were trying to start up again after the war had been won."

"Yes, it was a good thing your father taught you about weapons and how to fight, or we may not have made it out of there, having to hold our own until John arrived with backup troops. It allowed us to finally stop the rebellion on Termadrez once and for all."

"Yes, my father was so proud. He did not have any sons and did not think he would ever see that as part of his legacy."

"There was a big one that really did not directly involve you. It was with your father."

"His rescue, you mean."

"Yes," says William.

"We never talked in detail about what happened, simply that the three of you had to rescue him."

"Right, I know. At the time, I thought it was too gruesome to talk about, but where we are in life and everything you have been involved with, it would not be that bad if we talked about it now."

"Why, how bad was it?" asks Sara.

"Maybe we should start from the beginning, right before this happened with your father. This was before Esteban was the emperor. His father was still the emperor and had his finger in a lot of pies back then. We were all spread really thin, so I convinced Esteban to talk with his father to use your father and his right-hand man, Craven. We had worked with them on several campaigns, and they had been very successful, but they had only worked at either my or John's direction and never on their own. I had Esteban convince his father they could handle themselves. A rebellion rose on Ria 6 while we were trying to set up a mining colony, so the emperor sent your father, Bernard, and Craven with a battalion of men to shut it down, but the rebels had advanced weapons none of us were aware of. To this day, we still do not know where they gained them or from whom. Bernard and part of the battalion got cut off and while they put on a great fight and wiped out most of the insurgents that hit them, the rebels set off a bomb, leaving three men and your father alive. The renegades captured them before Craven could regroup his men, then go back for your father and the others.

"After two days, Craven could not make any progress rescuing your father. I had been cleaning up efforts on Troria and setting the new government up with Eric's help, and John was on Admis 3, settling a territory dispute; the emperor sent word about what happened. We put what we were doing on hold, but since Ria 6 was so far out, arriving took an additional day and a half, so the emperor sent word to Craven. We were on our way. By this time, Craven had received news. Your father and his three soldiers were being tortured, so we had to come up with a plan quickly. Since Craven had been on the ground there the whole time, we included him in the plan. Craven knew what building they were keeping Bernard in, so we waited till that night to move forward. We did not want to rush the building with the rebels, as we were concerned they may kill your father, so we sent most of our soldiers where we planned to exit and snipers in the trees.

"Then John, Eric, Craven, and I slowly moved toward the building. There were not too many lights, which helped. We only used our swords and daggers, so there was no noise as we took out the guards around the front of the building. Then we regrouped near the entrance and went in. We ran into several guards. One of them started to yell for help; I put my hand over his mouth, shoving him against the wall, and cut his throat, nearly cutting his head off. Blood squirted everywhere. Then we rushed down to the basement where they were keeping your father and the other men. There were several dark hallways, and it took us a little while to find the room. We also looked for where the other soldiers were but found them sliced up from torture, lying there dead.

"I am sure if we had waited much longer, they would have killed your father, too. By the time we got to him, Bernard was in rough shape, but we got him moving. I kept him with me as we moved out. We ran into several more guards and split up. John, your father, and I made it out the door after killing a few more guards along the way. I notified the snipers we were on the move and to cover us. Eric came out shortly after. Then we got to protection. Bernard and I kept going with the rest of our soldiers. John and Eric stayed near the building, waiting for Craven to emerge. They waited for a short time but no sign of him, so John and Eric went back into the building with a few other men. When they got in there, the building seemed to be empty. The rest of the rebels fled, but there was no sign of Craven. John, and Eric thought he may have escaped out the back and figured they would run into him at the camp. Just as they went out the front of the building, there was an explosion near the back. Then several rebels ran out from behind the building, and the snipers took them out, but still no sign of Craven.

"As we headed back to our camp, a large ship took off. We thought maybe Craven had taken off in it and we would see him land near our camp, but we never saw him again. After we all returned to our camp, I had John take your father home. Eric and I remained behind to finish what your father and Craven had gone there to do. We brought in another battalion in. With what your father had accomplished and with the rebels we already killed, it did not take much to eliminate the rebellion, or that is what we thought at the time. But we finished setting up the mining colony. Then I went back to Troria with Eric to complete things there. John went back to Admis 3. You know the rest as you were there when John brought your father home."

Sara says, "Yes, I remember when John brought Dad home, but neither of them would talk about what happened, and John left almost as soon as he got there. What I do not understand is—if so much was going on, why weren't Esteban and Lorenzo more involved?"

"Well, the emperor was sick. Esteban had stepped in and was really taking over, with his father giving final approvals. This was why we used your father, but unfortunately, after we rescued him, we were never able to use him again since he was never the same."

CHAPTER III

ESTEBAN AND LORENZO

William continues, "Maybe I should step back a little with some background for the two brothers and how our family came to support them. They groomed both Esteban and Lorenzo from the time they were born to conquer and settle the universe. After conquering their known world, this was their family legacy from almost the beginning of time. Then, when the family started space travel, they conquered new planets in the universe one by one for generations. This is how the Colon family came to be. As they expanded, they needed more help, someone to lead their armies. When they got to our planet Hmar 4 and discovered we had started our own space exploration efforts and the expanded armies we had, along with our knowledge of combat, the Colon family convinced our Balcazar family to join them and run their military, creating our legacy.

"I am sure you know pieces of this from our conversations over the years, but maybe after so long, I can put it all together for you. Leaping forward to

Esteban and Lorenzo. Esteban was the oldest who had a head for how the Colon family controlled and ran the known universe. This made him a perfect fit to become the emperor. Lorenzo did not have a warrior mind. He was more into sciences, so they put him in charge of the family R&D, manufacturing, and mining after he got out of school. Lorenzo has moved our sciences forward. Before he came on the scene, the family had been working on faster-than-light speed flights with little success. Then Lorenzo, while he was still going to school, brought the right people together to develop faster-than-light speed, making interstellar flight possible. This changed things drastically almost overnight. It was great Lorenzo's father could see this before he got so sick and died. When Lorenzo was put in charge of R&D, manufacturing, and mining, he discovered the mineral Zando Crystals, how they needed to refine the engine design, and build then the correct way to install them in the spacecrafts to make our empire possible. I am not saying Lorenzo did all the work, but he built the right teams with the creation and development.

"Before Lorenzo started working in the family R&D labs, there were rumors Lorenzo had been working secretly on a new style of weapons, but no one could ever prove it. Then, once he started in the family labs, no one seemed concerned, as he was helping further the family's exploration. In hindsight, that is why he developed the new weapons we used to dominate and shut down wars in some of the new worlds so fast. These allowed us to create the tactics we now use to capture the leaders of the incursions.

"Right before you and I met, Eric and I first tried the tactics Eric and Adam now use, like they just did on Castia, to test some of the weapons Lorenzo developed.

WILLIAM REMEMBERS THE FIRST TIME THEY USED THE sonic bomb. "When we first approached Sailaia 6, they were in the middle of several wars, mostly infighting between regions. Shortly after we made plans to work with them, several small hostilities exploded into one big one. It affected almost half the planet and, if left to run its course, could have completely annihilated everyone there. It took us almost six months of working with smaller factions to help control things, but one dictator was driving most of the larger war, so we came up with a strategy to capture him."

WILLIAM LOOKS AT ERIC, THEN SAYS, "WE SHOULD USE some of Lorenzo's new weapons, like the sonic bomb. If we can capture the dictator, President Nasco, we stop the war in its tracks."

Eric, thinking there is a target on his back, laughs. "Ok, but how? Let me guess. You want me to go in there and get close to him?"

William puts on a big smile. "You know me too well. Yes, that is exactly what I was thinking."

Eric now looks more serious about this. "So how are you thinking I can get close to him before you use a sonic bomb?"

"You fly in, make it look like you crashed, and let them capture you. We will have a tracker on you. Once your movement has stopped, then we can use the bomb to go in and retrieve you and Nasco."

Eric wears a concerned look on his face. "Crash my ship. Is that the best you can come up with?"

William grins. "Look, you are a much better pilot than I am, and you do not really need to hit. Maybe don't put out the landing gear or something like that."

"Ok, I get where you are going with this. I will figure something out."

Once the plan is confirmed, Eric takes off from their base and heads to where they believe Nasco is, but when he gets close, his ship is bombarded with missiles and crashes other than the way Eric planned. In the process, his arm is broken and then his ship is over run by Nasco's soldiers.

After Eric is taken to Nasco, something happened to the tracker, so all they have is his last location near the damaged ship, and it took them almost two days to find him. Unfortunately, during that time, since Eric is on a superior ship none of them had seen before, President Nasco wants to know more. He has him tied down in a chair, then says, "Who are you, and why are you here on a ship we've never seen?"

Eric glances around the room, then at Nasco. "Why would I tell you anything? Your reign will soon be over."

Nasco laughs. "I am winning the war here, and if we can get our hands on more ships like you have, it will all be over, and I will be the ruler. I need you to tell me where you got that."

Eric glares at him. "That will never happen. Nothing you can do will force me to tell you anything."

Nasco looks at one of his guards. "Take his coat and shirt off." He then looks at Eric. "This can be easy or hard. Are you going to tell me what I want to know?"

"It does not matter what you try to do to me. I will never answer."

Nasco looks at his guard again. "Ok, do it." The guard draws his sword and slides it across Eric's chest. As he does, blood starts to roll down.

Eric screams at him, "Is that the best you got?"

Nasco tells his guard, "Do it again." He does it two more times, only quicker. Then, all of a sudden, the building shakes, and everyone drops to the floor.

WILLIAM CONTINUES ON. "WITH MY MEN, WE RUSHED in, seeing Eric passed out, tied to a chair, and bleeding from the three cuts across his chest. I got help for him, and we captured Nasco. A few days later, after showing we had him, along with our superior weapons, the rest of his troops surrendered, thanks to the sonic bombs designed by Lorenzo.

"This explains why Lorenzo could not help us, with all that was going on between the different worlds. He was already busy developing new weapons and tools to end rebellions, excursions, and wars.

"While all of this happened, Esteban was learning how to do what his father, Esteban the third, had been doing as emperor, since he would take his father's place after he passed away or could no longer support the throne. Esteban was very good and picked it up quickly. He never finished school, as his father got sick and he had to take over for him. This is why Esteban could not help. I had to pick up the rest of the slack with the help of John and Eric, and your father occasionally. Back in those days, we developed two or three planets at a time while finding Zando Crystals and other critical minerals to help build interstellar flight. This was very profitable to the empire, making it profitable for all of us. This also helped us as we enhanced the other planets to help eliminate poverty for most, showing them how to mine without destroying. Stopping the need for war or rebellion within their own planets or between worlds.

"While Esteban was with his father, we collaborated with the king of one world we conquered, Sakair 6. Esteban fell in love with the king's daughter, Andres. Their romance went on for about a year. They were together, no matter what Esteban was doing or where they went. With the king's approval, they were married. Shortly after, Esteban's father got very ill and could not support the empire, and Esteban had to take over, which severely limited the time Esteban and Andres could spend together. This went on for almost two years before his father died, and Esteban the 4th was officially named emperor. Once it was done, Esteban brought John on as head of his security detail, and I took full control of the empire military with Eric's help. This allowed Esteban to focus more on expansion and gave him more time with Andres. Six months after this all happened, Andres announced she was pregnant, but there were complications, and she dies when Christina was born.

"This was so sad and pushed Esteban harder into the family business of expansion, making my life even busier than before, which was why John and Eric had to train the boys as they were growing up, since we spent more time living at Esteban's family home/palace. With Esteban focused on developing and expanding, he was not spending much time with his baby girl; she was over a year old before I got Esteban to slow down and concentrate on his daughter, but there was still a lot of moving parts. Eric and I had to take over. We were glad to, so that Esteban could get to know and bond with his daughter. This went on for a few years.

"I think Christina was about five when I helped shut down a war on the planet Diolara and found a young girl about the same age, Emily. Her entire family had been killed in the fighting, and no one could take care of her. It was amazing to me how much she resembled Christina, so I presented a plan for her to become a ward to Esteban and friend for Christina. This way Christina was not lonely when Esteban was away, letting him feel better when he was gone.

"Emily did not speak our language, but since she was so young, it did not take long before she and Christina, both with their blue eyes and blond hair, looked and sounded the same, like twins running around the family home. Esteban treated Emily as his own daughter, and she went to all the same schools and was given the best of everything, exactly like Christina. Emily was always grateful, knowing Esteban was not her father, but treated her as if she was. As time went on, Christina and Emily also grew closer, and Christina was happy to share her father when he was with them. While this was going on, John and Eric trained the boys. Adam and Connor were also working with Christina, teaching her how to fight, and Emily played the lookout, thinking we did not know what they were up to. That went on until the girls were about fourteen, about the same time Adam and Christina got in trouble. Esteban figured it was time Christina and Emily were sent away to school, and I had Adam leave with Eric for his intense training.

"At the same time, Lorenzo was in R&D fine-tuning space travel and new weapons, one of which was a sonic bomb. When detonated, it knocks out anyone outside a concrete building within a several-block radius, which has allowed us to shut down threats quickly.

"One thing that has concerned me is Lorenzo seems to do things none of us are aware of, and every time Esteban tries to find out, his brother shuts it down. Lorenzo thought he should have been able to take his father's place as emperor, but Esteban was older, and he spent more time with his father and knew how the family legacy has been followed for multiple generations. I truly think this has kept Esteban and Lorenzo from closeness.

"Esteban and I have had several discussions about how he and Lorenzo could work hand in hand, but Lorenzo never accepts what Esteban tries and accomplishes with him. That is why Lorenzo was not here for the celebration with our boys and the latest conquest. This has also been why Lorenzo has not spent time with Christina or Emily, their only uncle and only near family, and also why they have bonded more with us.

Since Esteban became emperor, Lorenzo rarely comes to the family home, even though this is where he grew up. I think if their mother had not died when they were both so young, they may have been better friends. Just like Esteban, his father focused on the family business to deal with the loss of his wife and left the boys to handle life on their own. So Esteban learned the family business so he could stay close to his father and Lorenzo dove into the sciences, causing the boys to drift further apart. They spent very little time with each other, and Esteban Senior did not help the matter any.

"My understanding is Lorenzo was very fond of his mother and could not remain where his mother wasn't anymore, so Lorenzo went away to school and would rarely come home to visit. It was like this until Lorenzo showed his father how smart he was and how he could help with the family business. Rumor is Esteban Senior put Lorenzo in charge of R&D at such an early age because he felt guilty for not spending much time with him when he was growing up, but I can say, by doing so, he really changed the face of space travel for us and our expansion in the universe."

Sara sighs. "That is all very sad and makes me feel bad for Lorenzo. Maybe we should have tried to reach out to him more."

"I have tried on several occasions over the years, but he was either too busy or was not willing to come out to our home for one reason or another. He is a very private person, and no one seems to know what he does when he is not at the labs or testing his inventions."

"Well, I have talked more tonight than all month. It is getting late, and I am ready for bed." With that, both William and Sara call it a night.

Early the next morning, Esteban informs William something serious has happened. He, along with John and the girls, must leave. Sara tries to wake Adam so he can say goodbye to Christina, but by the time she got back with Adam, Esteban and the girls had already departed. Sara says, "Adam, I am so sorry. I know you wanted to see Christina this morning, but Esteban was in a big hurry for some reason."

On the ship, as it flew away, Esteban asks, "How long before we get where they are going?"

The captain responds, "We should be there in two hours, sire."

"Ok, great. Thank you," says Esteban.

Christina is upset she could not at least say goodbye to Adam before they left. "Why did we need to exit so quickly?"

"Sorry, I know you wanted to see Adam, but there was an explosion at one of the labs where your uncle Lorenzo works. People died there. I have to find out what happened before the news gets out so I can respond."

"Oh no, I am sorry. This is terrible. Is Uncle Lorenzo ok?" asks Christina.

"Yes, he seems to be fine. He reached out to me, letting me know what happened. He said everything is under control, but I need to see what really occurred for myself."

"Is that why John came with us?"

"A lot is going on right now, and I need his help and protection."

"Why, Dad, what do you mean? What is going on?"

"There is a lot I want to tell you, but I really do not want to get you involved until you graduate. Then I will bring you in and let you see. Right now, you need to focus on finishing school and not worry about anything else. You only have a few months left."

"If you are sure, Dad. I just want to make sure you will be ok."

"If John is around, no matter what goes on, I will be fine."

"John makes me feel better, but I am still concerned about your safety."

"Please do not worry. Nothing is going to happen to me if that is your fear. There is simply a lot I need to deal with, so please focus on progressing. I will bring you into everything when you are back. It seems like we are here. John and I are getting off with some men, and the captain is going to take you girls home so you can get ready to go back to school. I will be there before you leave to see you two off. Don't worry. Everything will be fine. I love you both and will see you soon."

As Esteban and John leave the ship with his protection detail, Lorenzo stands there. "Why are you here?" he asks. "I told you when I called you—this was handled. You did not need to come. I would update you as needed."

"No, that is not good enough. Three people died here. I need to know what happened firsthand, not wait for some sort of report. Take us to the damaged building." They all get onto a transport, and Lorenzo's driver ferries to a completely obliterated building away from the main campus. As they get out, Esteban looks at Lorenzo, totally pissed off, and yells at him, "You told me there was not too much damage. What the hell do you call this? That was one of the main R&D buildings, now demolished. Looking at the building, I am surprised only three people are dead. If you had done your experiment during the day based on how many people work here, the numbers would have been horrible. I need to understand what you were experimenting on, and from now on, I need to know everything you are doing or working on. I have asked you several times about your projects. This is no longer an ask. As the emperor, this is now a demand for full disclosure."

Lorenzo screams back at Esteban, "I never had to do that with our father. This is all mine to share as I see fit."

"With this destruction, that all ends now. You either bring me in on everything that you have been and are working on, or you will be out, brother or not."

"I do not know who you think you are. Our father gave all of this to me to run and manage, not you!"

Esteban, fed up with his crap, shrieks, "ONCE AGAIN, I AM THE EMPEROR, AND OWN ALL OF THIS, SO YOU EITHER BRING ME IN, OR YOU ARE OUT!"

Lorenzo is now mad too. "FINE, you're right. You are not merely my brother. You are the emperor. I don't like it or agree, but I will have a report on what happened here by the end of the day. It will take me some time to package the rest of what I am working on. I have already reached out to the families of the people who have died to let them know how sorry we are and that they will be taken care of."

"Ok, thank you. Include in your chronicle what happened, then what it will take to rebuild what has been destroyed and how long it will take. You can have a few days for that piece of it if you need to."

"Yes, ok, will do. Well, I have a lot to accomplish, so I need to leave and get started. Talk with you later." Lorenzo and his driver then leave.

After Lorenzo disappears, Esteban looks at John. "That was way too easy. I don't like it."

John agrees. "Yes, in all the times I have dealt with Lorenzo, nothing has ever been that straightforward. I will have someone keep an eye on him."

"Yes, thanks, John. What is sad is Lorenzo and I used to be close until our mother died. Lorenzo took our mom's death hard. I did too, but could handle it better than he did. Our father threw himself into his work when Lorenzo really needed him, which made it even worse for my brother. I tried to be the bridge between them, but our father was gone more than he was home, and Lorenzo stayed locked up in his room when he was not at school. Then, when he went away to college, he refused to come home, which caused us to grow apart as well. Once our father seemed better about the loss of our mother and was home more, I spent more time with him and learn the family business. This was actually a fun season for me. I was able to spend time with my father, learn the business, and met new people all the time, then traveled to other worlds. That is when my father introduced me to you, William, and Eric, which made it even better. I finally had friends on the same path as I was. When my father sickened, if you three had not been there, I am not sure how I would have managed everything we needed to do and take over for him at the same time. When I got married while he was unwell, trusting you three as I do has made my life much easier. I do not want to downplay it. Life with my wife, while she was with us, was much better than I deserved, and I am grateful for the time you three allowed me to spend with her after my father passed. It was so painful when she died. If the three of you had not eventually reminded me I still had a daughter that needed me, I may have fallen into the same path as my father and would not have the relationship with her I have now. When William and Eric brought Emily to our family, things became even better for both of us. Sorry for the digression, but seeing what I lost with Lorenzo brings up all these feelings. Let's get back on track. Is Lorenzo really gone?"

"Yes, he seems to be. Why?"

"I want to take a closer look at the damage and see if we can figure out what he was really up to."

"I am not sure how safe it will be, but one of my men found something around back we should inspect."

"Ok, let's go." As they approach the back of the building, they can see a small part seems to phase in and out. Getting closer, they can see a big circle, and standing in front of it, they can see what appears to be another world disappearing in and out. "What the hell is this?"

"It looks like a portal to another planet, but I did not think that was possible."

"Can you make out where?"

"No, but I have seen this spot before. It seems very familiar. Let me get some images as it comes back so we can try to figure out where that is." John captures a few images. He then picks up a piece of debris, marks it, and throws it through. Just when he does, the window collapses, and the rest of the building falls into rubble as if that were the only thing keeping it up. John yells, "LOOK OUT." They all run back as everything crumbles in front of them.

Esteban looks at John. "Why did you throw that rock through the window?"

"I wanted to see if that piece would actually go through like it did, telling me there was a real opening to somewhere else."

"Sure, I get it. That makes sense. I am sure that is why Lorenzo agreed so quickly. He did not think we would check this out, is my bet. I really need to know what else he has been up to. I have seen enough. Call the ship so we can get home."

"Yes, will do."

"It will be interesting to see what is in the report my brother produces. If what we saw is not in the testimony, then we cannot trust anything my brother tells me from now on, and we will need to watch him closely."

As Lorenzo heads away, his driver, Andy, asks, "Do you think your brother suspects anything?"

"No, but my brother is very smart and likes to be in the middle of everything. He has been hands-on with everything except what I have been doing from the beginning, but he is going to ask a lot of questions about the destruction of the building and the three killed. I will need to come up with a plausible explanation to shut him down and only list the small things I have been working on. There is too much going on at this point to have him know everything before I am ready. With this exposure from my experiment, we will need to push up the timetable I laid out. Knowing my brother, I have six months to a year before he pushes for more information, if I cannot hold him off with what I give him over the next few weeks."

"What about any of the new weapons? Maybe one of those would suffice."

"No, all of those fall into my future plans, and I am not ready for him to know about those yet."

"Ok, he is your brother. You know better than anyone what you will be able to get past him."

"After we reach my other lab, I need you to return and make sure the reactor has been shut down. I could not do it since my brother showed up. I did not want to hang around to create suspicion. The portal to Zada 5 had shut down, but it could open back up if we do not turn the reactor off, and we do not want anyone to know or see that other than us."

"Ok, you got it. Will do."

After Andy drops off Lorenzo, he heads back to the destroyed building. Almost there, he sees Esteban, John, and the rest of the men riding to meet their transport home. When Andy arrives at the building and realizes more of it has collapsed and the reactor is completely smashed, he calls Lorenzo to let him know Esteban had been there for a while and had just left, but the reactor had been destroyed. Lorenzo replies, "Ok, thank you for taking care of it, but why was my brother there so long? I wonder what he was doing all that time. Do you think they were looking for where the actual explosion was?"

Andy answers, "I do not know. Everything had been destroyed, but I am not sure. It seems to me part of the building was still standing in the back, near where our lab was when we were testing after the main part of the building crumbled, but you can also tell it was not destroyed by an explosion like we have told everyone."

"If everything was wrecked, then there is really nothing for us to worry about. I now need to come up with what we were examining and a reasonable reason for what caused the explosion. With the building and the lab destroyed, we will have to build a new link, but let's craft it on Korbin. I still have a small lab there off the main one, so if we run into a similar issue, no one except us will know. We will also need to check nothing happened at the Zada 5 end. It was in an abandoned cavern, so I don't think there should be an issue. Reach out to Craven and have him check the portal platform at Zada 5."

"Ok, I will let him know what is going on and then obtain what I need before leaving for Korbin. I will get everything set up and regain some lost time from this failure."

Once Andy arrives at Lorenzo's other lab, he loads the equipment they will need for their next set of tests on Korbin. He also reaches out to Craven, tells him what happened and what Lorenzo needs him to do.

Craven responds, "Sure, no problem. I will let you know when I get ready."

Andy adds, "FYI, John was with Lorenzo's brother, the emperor."

"I wonder if he has any idea that I am still alive."

"I do not know, but I bet they will be shocked when they find out you are."

"Yes, and they will wish they never left me behind for dead back on Ria 6 when they came to rescue Bernard.

"They all escaped, but I got stuck with some rebels, and they did not return for me, so I had to flee out the back. I ripped open a gas line and set a fire just before getting out, creating an explosion which helped to cover my exit, with a freighter ready to leave I could climb into. But it was on an automated flight plan, and the explosion damaged some of the flight controls. I did not realize until after it took off and could not change its course. This was before interstellar flights, and it was set for auto-return to the home planet, a five-year flight, which gave me no choice but to go into hibernation sleep. The ship, being damaged, went off course, just drifting in space. After eighteen years, my hibernation pod failed, and I was awake on the ship for another two. If the ship had not been a freighter with food and water, I would have died. Losing my mind, being alone that long, despite most of the controls damaged, I slowly redirected it, forcing the ship to crash land on Korbin.

"Fortunately, Lorenzo was at his lab when the ship crashed. If he had not seen my landing, I would be dead now. He pulled me out before it exploded and burned up. Lorenzo then got a doctor to take care of me, helping me recover. I owe my life to him, so anything he needs me to do, I am there. I also owe him because, while recovering, he tried to find my wife and son, but a rebel, searching for me, broke into our home and killed them several months after they rescued Bernard. If they freed me, then my family would still be alive. Their loss eats at me every day. I've never been the same since. Eric, John, and William need to die for what they've done."

"I am so sorry for all you have suffered, and I am sure Lorenzo will assist you with whatever he can."

"Yes, he already has been a great help to me."

LORENZO, CROUCHED OVER HIS DESK, FEELS THE welling of irritation as he writes the report his brother ordered. While he ponders how to frame the explosion, he decides Zando Crystals will be the reason. They are a likely culprit, and his brother won't suspect. Lorenzo pulls some old reports on work with Zando Crystals and the issues. He then compiles the documents together and contacts Esteban. "I'll meet you within two hours with my information."

A LITTLE WHILE LATER, LORENZO AND ANDY ARRIVE AT the palace to meet with Esteban. "Just drop me off. I'll get back on my own."

Andy agrees. "Okay, let me know if there's anything else I can do."

As Andy departs, Lorenzo meets Christina out front, talking with Emily. "Uncle Lorenzo, is that you?

It has been a long time. I am so happy to see you."
She runs over and gives Lorenzo a big hug. "Do you
remember Emily?"

Lorenzo nods. "Yes, I do. Wow, you girls look so
much alike."

"Yes, we are as close as sisters could be."

"Sisters, really, that's beautiful. I'm so glad the two
of you are so close."

"Are you here to see my father? He told me about
the accident this morning. I am so glad you are okay."

"Thank you, my dear." He adds with a slight laugh
and a grin. "Me too. Well, I need to talk with your
father now."

"Can you stay for dinner?"

"I would really like to, but I am way too busy."

"Then maybe you can come to our graduation in
a few months?"

"Let me know when, and I will try."

"Great, I will make sure Dad gets you the
information."

"Sounds good. You take care. I will see you later."
Lorenzo then walks in the door and down the hall to
Esteban's office. As Lorenzo arrives, he sees Esteban
sitting at his desk. Behind him to the right, scanning
out the window, is John, standing there. Esteban glances
up, and John turns around, looking at Esteban. "Should
I leave?"

Esteban responds, "No, I have no problem with
you being here to hear this. Do you, Lorenzo?"

"No, I have no issue with it either," he replies.

John answers, "Ok, great."

Esteban looks at Lorenzo, holding something in his hand. "Is that the report about what happened early this morning?"

Lorenzo nods. "Yes, it is."

"Come sit down and show me."

Lorenzo obeys and opens the folder. "I was working on a new way to refine the Zando Crystals. It will increase interstellar flight speed by thirty percent, but something made them unstable, causing the explosion. I also have some historical data showing what I was working on to get this far. I still need to inspect the data from the test this morning to see what went wrong, so we can make corrections before I repeat the test."

"So, how much time do you think before you can run the test again?"

"Well, it will take time for the analysis, then to prep for a new test. I would think maybe another month, maybe two, before I am ready."

"Ok, I want to know when you are prepared to test and where the test will be. I want to be there."

John puts in, "But if there is another explosion, I do not want you anywhere near. I will attend with a few of my men."

Lorenzo smiles. "Sure, that works for me if you are ok with that."

Esteban consents, "Yes, that is fine. Now, how long is it going to take for you to fill me in on everything else you have been working on?"

Lorenzo gets red in the face over this. "I have been thinking about that all day. I still do not agree you should get access to everything."

"I understand it is your life's work, but after the issue today, I do not care. From now on, I need to know, or you will be out, and you will only get access through me. I really do not want you to force me. You are still my brother, and I would hate having to do that to you."

"Ok, but I am going to need time."

"That's fine. How much?"

"About six months."

Esteban, irate, knows he is dragging his feet but tries not to show it. "Six months, then I need monthly updates."

"I think I can manage."

"Good. Sorry I am being so tough on you, but what happened today puts us all at risk."

"It's ok. I get it; do you need anything else? I have a lot to accomplish and need to leave so I can get started."

"No, I am good. You can go. Also, I was glad nothing happened to you this morning and to see you again. It has been a while since the last time."

"Yes, it has been. I was happy to see you as well. Talk with you next month." Lorenzo then turns and departs.

John checks out the door to ensure Lorenzo has left, then looks at Esteban. "Do you really believe what he told you?"

Esteban demurs, "No I don't. It makes little sense based on what we saw."

"Then why did you ask about retesting and attending?"

"I didn't want him to know what we witnessed, and that I knew he was lying. Once he gave me that information, I knew he was not to be trusted. I was hoping he would tell me the truth, but the fact that he didn't, says my brother is truly lost to me. Now we need to find out what he is really up to."

"Ok, good. I had some of my guys return to the site and dig around to find anything to help. I am not sure if you saw the same things we did, but if there was an explosion, then debris should have surrounded the outside of the building. They saw more of the same, almost like the building just fell apart. They said parts looked like they had been crushed into little pieces, and there were trace readings of radiation where it collapsed. If it had been an explosion, as he said, you could get radiation readings from the entire building."

"This is why I tried to show Lorenzo I still cared about him. I do not want him to suspect anything, but we need to figure out from those images where we were seeing the opening. We also need someone he will not suspect to start searching through his labs to figure out what he is really doing. If he had nothing to hide, he would have told me the truth today. If we need to, maybe have several people track Lorenzo. He is very smart and cannot be underestimated until we have an idea of what he is working on. Sadly, I have to think this way about my brother."

"I will reach out to Eric and William to let them know what we have found today and what we suspect. Then we will come up with a plan. I will also send them copies of the images to see if they recognize where it is as well. Once we figure out where it is, I will send someone there to find anything that will help us understand his schemes."

"Ok, good, we will need to be quick about this. Knowing Lorenzo the way I do, based on what happened today and our interaction with him, he will up his timetable. Right now, he is way ahead of us. He is currently holding all the cards, so we have to kick over the table before we get caught with our pants down. We must be very careful he does not find out we suspect him and have to keep up the appearance. Everything is normal. I can give you until the end of the day tomorrow to draft a plan, as we have no time to waste."

"Yes, sir, it will be done. We will also try to get an idea of what location those images show to jumpstart our investigation. I will have Eric and William here; I think it is also time to involve both Adam and Connor."

"Yes, the more people around me I can trust, the better, and I will feel more comfortable about what we have to do. Also, the last time Lorenzo saw the boys, they were small, so we may be able to use them to track him, as he will not know who they are. Since we do not know who else is involved in this, they will not recognize the boys either."

"Yes, that is an excellent point. We will work them into our plans. There is a lot I need to do. I will leave you now. I have two of my best men posted outside your door just in case and several around the building, along with your regular security for your protection. Talk with you tomorrow."

CHAPTER IV

THE PLAN

A day after the explosion, in the afternoon, at John's request, William, Eric, Adam, and Connor land their ship. Since Eric, William, and his sons were still on their home planet of Hmar 4, it is a quick trip for the four of them to Esteban's home world of Markus 2, one of the largest and the most industrialized planet within the empire. Despite the large cities all over, the planet still has extensive areas of green forests with hundreds of lakes and rivers with four large oceans. The palace is several miles from any of the cites, which makes it easier to keep it and the emperor protected.

In Esteban's office, as they sit down, Esteban looks at them. "Thank you all for coming so quickly. As John told you, we have major concerns over what my brother may be doing. He lied to John and me yesterday about how the three people died. John also shared copies of the image of the world we saw. We need to figure out what world that was to discover what Lorenzo is actually doing."

Eric puts in, "I think I know where that is. It looks like one of the caverns on Zada 5. When we were negotiating with the warriors, this cavern had a motherlode of Zando Crystals we helped Lorenzo find. Something happened, and the entrance collapsed, leaving us trapped for almost a week, but it worked out, as we were there with their leader Mondo and convinced them to move from warriors to miners. We brought them the prosperity they had been seeking through war and came back with an agreement for the crystals. If that is where this cavern is, we will have to study the timing of getting to the planet through the asteroid field. The moon alignment creates a path in and out, which lasts about a day and a half. It only opens up every three months. The other problem is there's no communication in or out because of the asteroids."

John looks at Eric, "Once we figure out when we can visit, then you go there with Connor, introduce him to Mondo, and they can help us figure out what Lorenzo is doing there, if this is the cavern."

"Yes, you got it. Connor, this will be a good experience for you."

"Great, I look forward to it," says Connor.

William joins in. "Esteban, there was one thing I wanted to talk with you about before you left yesterday, but then you had to leave in a hurry. I have heard most of the minerals mined are slowing way down, forcing prices to go up. What makes little sense is this is happening from different worlds, including Zada 5. I suggest we audit these enterprises, but this is something else Lorenzo controls, so I am not sure how we get this done without letting him know."

Esteban nods. "That's easy. All I need to say is we are performing an audit across the board because finances are off, and mining is part of it."

"Sounds good."

John looks at Adam. "Ok, next topic, I have two of my best men tracing Lorenzo. Adam, maybe you can help. The last time Lorenzo saw you, you were about ten-years-old. I don't think he will recognize you. Maybe you can help track Lorenzo as well."

Adam agrees. "Great, yes, I would like to."

"I will set you up with the two guys."

Eric adds, "I just checked, and the window to get into Zada 5 opens in two days, but if we have to find Mondo, then the cavern, we may not make the window to escape in time. Connor, let's plan to be there for three months. Since this will be your first time, we can accomplish a lot."

Connor grins. "Sounds good. I look forward to meeting Mondo and his people, then exploring the planet."

Esteban takes over. "William, I need you to be in charge of the audit. Everyone, feed your updates to John and me, but the outlier will be what, Eric, you and Connor find out on Zada 5. If it takes three months to get an update, this whole thing could stall unless we get some good information tracking Lorenzo, or what we can discover from the audits."

Eric says, "I will try to send out as much as we can before the path closes, even if we have nothing."

"Ok, let's meet nightly to review anything that happened." With that, they all make their own plans to audit and track what Lorenzo is doing.

EARLIER THAT SAME MORNING, BEFORE ESTEBAN AND the rest met at the palace, Lorenzo, at his lab, calls both Andy and Craven back to talk about updating his plans. With and Andy and Craven in the lab, Lorenzo starts, "We have to switch the timeline from eighteen months to six months."

Before Lorenzo can say any more, Andy, in an excited voice, jumps in. "Six months? That is impossible. We were already pushing it at eighteen."

Lorenzo cuts him off before he can say anything else. "Yes, I know there is still a lot to be done, but knowing my brother the way I do, it will be very hard to stall him any longer. Esteban may suspect something."

Craven then says, "Do you have an updated plan if this is what you are asking us to do?"

"Yes, I do. Andy and I will go to Korbin to test at an accelerated pace while you work with the rebels to prepare them."

Craven is just as concerned as Andy. "I will do my best to get them ready by then and see what I can do to speed the process up."

Afterwards, Andy leaves for Korbin. Since the window for Zada 5 is two days away, Craven stays with Lorenzo to put together the equipment he will need to complete his part of the plan. Caven looks at Lorenzo and says, "If we are speeding up the timeline, then I need to leave in the morning. There are people I must meet with before taking off for Zada 5."

BACK AT THE PALACE, JOHN AND ADAM WALK OUT OF the meeting with Esteban. John tells Adam not only do they need to track Lorenzo, but anyone collaborating with him. "We also need to access to his lab files to see what he is working on." John continues, "We need an ally that works in the labs to help us."

Adam suggests, "The labs used to hire assistance from the academy near here. Maybe we can find an old student. My brother and I went to the academy here when we were staying in the palace. We can use that as a way in."

"Ok good, let's keep that in mind as we track what Lorenzo is up to. In the morning, we can meet up with my men tracking Lorenzo, see what they have found out so far, if anything, and then how we track him from now on."

As they both leave, Adam heads upstairs to Christina's room and knocks on her door. He hears Christina say, "Just a minute." She then opens the door and shrieks, "Adam!" Quickly pulling him into her room and closing the door, she gives him a big kiss. "I didn't know you were here."

"Yes, we arrived this afternoon, and I have to leave early in the morning with John." With a smile on his face, he adds, "I needed to make sure the kiss I gave you was lasting."

"Well, I think I need a better, longer one." Adam pulls her to him and gives her another like before, only longer this time, then several smaller ones. Again, her knees buckle while Adam holds onto her. "Adam, I do not want to scare you off, but I have fallen in love with you and cannot imagine my life without you."

Adam, leaning against the door with a smile on his face, regards her eyes, holding one hand and stroking her face with the other. "That is ok. I am not going anywhere, and I feel the same way, but you need to finish school, and I have a job to do for your father. Once you graduate, we can figure out where we go from there. I love you too, and we will make it work." He gives her a big hug and another long kiss. While clasping her hands, he gazes into her eyes. "I will see you at your graduation and will reach out to you when I can."

"I would love that." She then gives him another hug and kiss. Adam turns, slightly opening the door, and scans to see if anyone is around before he walks out.

Closing the door behind him, he goes back downstairs through the hall to his room to get some sleep.

As Eric and Connor leave the meeting, Eric tells Connor they need to get back to their home world of Hmar 4 to use Eric's ship to reach Zada 5. Since there is no exact time for when the path is clear, they will want to arrive as soon as they can for the most time possible to find Mondo, then see if they can find the cavern from the images John took.

Connor says, "Eric, I did not want to add anything in the room, but I have had visions of that cavern. There is something dark and ominous. I could not make out what it was, but I know it will be very dangerous. I saw people dying there, not us, but others will fall. I also see fierce bloody battles and things in there that will save us, but right now, it is only a feeling. Most of it, I still cannot make out what or why we need it."

"Ok. As your visions clear, let me know what you see. In the meantime, we will keep this between us. We will be home tonight, then leave early the morning after, so get some rest tonight, as I do not know how busy we will be when we land on Zada 5."

"Ok, I will try," says Connor.

Back in the room, Esteban looks at William. "I have an archive hidden with strict access. They passed it on from emperor to emperor, but I am locking Lorenzo out for now. I will make sure Christina has access when she gets out of school in the next few months. This location contains information with proof of her birthright. This is the documentation of Christina's dragon-shaped birthmark. Only a few people are aware of this. I made sure of it to protect her. We hold the information off-world with only a few people that know who and where it is maintained."

William asks, "Why are you telling me this?"

"I wanted you to know in case something should happen to me. The people that maintain this will know who has access, and only they are allowed to open it, but I am also putting a notification that, if anything were to happen to Christina, it will default to your sons. Your family will continue my family's legacy, should it come to that."

"Are you that concerned Lorenzo is planning to make a play for the throne? He would take both you and Christina out?"

"Yes, I am. If Lorenzo took over, all that we have accomplished would be gone. I know my brother; he thinks profits should be his, and every world would suffer under his rule. It is critical we find out what he is up to. We are in dangerous times here. We must be very careful about whom we trust. You, John, and Eric have had my back from the beginning. That is why I have you and them to help me. Something I discovered in the archive should help us access the files to audit inventories and accounts Lorenzo uses." Esteban hands William a file key from around his neck. "With this, you should be able to reach the information we need. Once you can, let's review the data."

"I will have Sara pull it and validate the information. Then I will let you know when she is done, and we can see what Lorenzo has been up to."

"Sounds good. Thanks, William," replies Esteban.

THE NEXT MORNING, ESTEBAN MEETS CHRISTINA AND Emily for breakfast. Christina looks at her father with a big smile on her face. "I heard Adam was here."

Esteban smiles back. "Yes, he was, but I gave him and John an assignment, and they had to leave early this morning." With a big grin on his face, he teases, "Why are you so interested in if Adam was around or not?"

"I have my reasons," responds Christina.

Emily, with a slight laugh, adds, "She sure does."

Esteban studies Christina, still grinning, "Good. I am glad Adam has grown into a good man, a great warrior, and I could not think of anyone better for you to be with."

Christina asks, "Whatever do you mean, Dad?"

Esteban puts his arm around Christina. "Did you forget I am the emperor? I see and know all, and I noticed how the two of you were the other night at William's Villa. Nothing gets past me."

Christina blushes. "I did not realize we made it so obvious."

"Only to proud parents," says Esteban.

"Do you mean Adam's parents also know?"

Esteban laughs again. "Of course they do, but there will be plenty of time for that later, after you and Emily graduate. Speaking of, are you girls packed and ready to go back?"

Emily admits, "Well almost, we still have a few things."

"Ok, good. The transport is nearly ready as well. I have a few things to take care of, but I want to see you two off. I am very proud of both of you and could not be happier. The next time I see you girls after you leave today will be at your graduation."

"Thank you, sir. If it had not been for you and the opportunities you have given me, I cannot imagine how bad my life could have been."

Esteban gives Emily a big hug. "It has been my pleasure. You have always been like a second daughter to me and a sister to Christina. It could not have worked out better for our whole family."

"Yes, I agree with Father." Christina hugs her as well.

A little later, the three of them meet in front of the ship that will transport Christina and Emily. "Goodbye, my loves," Esteban says as he embraces them both.

"Goodbye, Father," Christina and Emily say in unison. With the sweet farewell, they turn toward the ship, and the door closes behind them. Esteban's heart swells as he watches them take off and disappear into the clouds.

WHILE ESTEBAN AND THE GIRLS MEET FOR BREAKFAST on Markus 2, Eric and Connor are back on Hmar 4, preparing Eric's ship. They pack for possibly having to stay on Zada 5 for the second window to leave. After loading, they take off. It requires most of a day to get to Zada 5 from their home planet. When they approach the opening of the path, several ships are already there waiting for the path to open.

Eric explains, "The path should open soon. You need to keep watch. If you have never seen it before, it is almost unbelievable. When the three moons move into full alignment, they pull on the asteroids surrounding the planet. You can actually see the path appear like something is clearing the way." After sitting there for about an hour as they continue to look towards the planet, suddenly, the ship is pulled away as the path opens up, and they glimpse a clearing through the asteroid, then an opening towards the planet.

Connor exclaims, "Wow, if I had not seen this, I never would have believed it."

"Right, I know. We discovered this totally by accident. When we were searching for minerals to help Lorenzo in the early years, we had been told rumors about this world having potential, but when we visited the planet, we saw all the asteroids, so we had to hunt for a way in. It just so happened we arrived as the moons' alignment happened, and we saw what you witnessed." As Eric talks with Connor about the opening, he enters the path towards the planet, the same as several other ships. After making it past the asteroids, the ships split off and go separate ways toward the planet.

Eric continues, "As we talked about, with this planet, there is no way to communicate with anyone until you get to the surface. Even when the path is open, we have been unsuccessful at getting any message in or out, so there is still some sort of interference with the asteroid field. Even on the planet, interaction is patchy unless you are close with whom you are trying to talk with. I am going to land near an area where Mondo may be, and we will have to go from there."

As Eric communicates with the ground crew where he is landing, he also asks to speak with Mondo. The person on the ground asks who is asking, and he tells him, "I am Eric Aristo, on a request from the emperor."

The ground responds, "Yes, sir, we are not sure where he is currently but will try to locate him while you land."

"Ok, thank you."

Connor puts in, "Wow, sir, does everyone know who you are?"

Eric smiles. "Yes, mostly we spent a lot of time here first fighting, then helping them move from warriors to miners, making fighting no longer necessary and giving them a much better, profitable life. Most of the ships you saw waiting will take the mined Zando Crystals to refineries to convert to fuel for light-speed travel. There was another small ship I did not recognize, and we will need to investigate that as well while we are here."

As they land on the pad, several people nearby wait for Eric and Connor to emerge. As they do, one man comes up, "Mr. Aristo, sir, I am Captain Renaldo. Do you remember me?"

Eric shakes his hand. "Yes, of course I do. How have you been?"

"Good, sir."

"Renaldo, this is Connor, William's son."

Renaldo exclaims, "Oh wow, Connor, nice to meet you," as he shakes Connor's hand.

Connor grins. "Yes, I am glad to meet you as well."

Eric asks, "Why do you have these guards here with you?"

Renaldo responds, "There have been some problems with miners. They have become very upset, causing some problems, and are blaming the emperor, which is why Mondo is not here. He is trying to find out what was going on and stop it before it gets out of control. If the miners find out the emperor sent you, we are not sure how they will react."

"Then I guess it is a good thing we came when we did. Connor and I need to speak with Mondo as soon as possible. We have some issues of our own we need to validate."

"Ok, great, we have a transport to take you to him. Mondo is at another colony, about a day's travel from here."

Eric looks at Connor. "Well, it seems like it was a good thing we planned to be here for a while. I do not think we will reach Mondo, find the cavern, and get out before the window closes."

"What cavern are you looking for?"

"That is part of the issue. We only have an image John took. It looks familiar. I was thinking it was the one Mondo and I were trapped in."

"Can I see?" Eric shows Renaldo the image. "Yes, I think you are right. You are also right—that cavern is even further from Mondo, so there is no way you will make it back before the path closes."

"Ok, that is what I was afraid of. We will need to get a message sent out on one of the transport ships to the emperor to let him know the score."

"We can help," responds Renaldo.

"Thank you. I will work on the message after we meet with Mondo and have a plan for the cavern. I will also add to the note about the issues going on here once

I have an update from Mondo, after we speak with him and find out what he knows."

As they ride, along the way, Connor notices they moved from a lush green area to a total desert. Connor looks at Eric. "Why is there such a drastic change in the landscape, almost like there was a line drawn between the two?"

Eric explains, "Yes, I know when we first came to this planet, those green areas were a lot smaller, almost like a small oasis, but we have shown them how to increase the water supply and expand. We could not make the entire planet this way, as we need the Zando Crystals, and they are only found in the desert caverns. We tried to grow close to one area, but the cavern flooded and eventually ruined the quality of the crystals, making them almost useless. There are still deep desert areas that need to be explored, but as of now, there are still plenty in existing caverns to be mined.

"Maybe we should step back a little and talk about this planet. Zada 5 is the largest habitable planet we have ever come across. It has three moons. One is very large, almost the size of a small habitable planet, and the other two are much smaller. Asteroids completely surround the planet with no clear path to go through except, as you saw this morning, when the moons align every three months. That window allows us to retrieve the Zando Crystals. Other planets have Zando Crystals, but none have the same quality as here, and they do not produce fuel in the same way. In fact, on some of the other planets, the quality is so bad it has actually caused damage to the engines. Most of the mining for Zando Crystals has been abandoned on these other planets. Fortunately, the crystals are still very abundant on this planet, making mining for them not an issue."

Renaldo adds, "Yes, Mr. Aristo is right, but the cavern you are looking to go into has some issues and has not been mined for over a year."

Connor asks, "What kind of issues are you talking about?"

"I am not sure if I should say," responds Renaldo.

"Why not? What is really going on there?"

"Well, there has been a legend for centuries about the man who would tame the dragon, lead the clans out of darkness, and rule the universe. We have not seen or heard about any such creatures in a long time, but we believe that is what's hiding in the mine you are looking to investigate."

"A dragon? Really! I did not think they were real. Do you have any proof this creature still exists, or is it just some scared people making it up?"

"No, we do not have any proof. All we have at this point is what a couple of miners were claiming and why they will not go back to that cavern."

"Then I guess we will find out when we go there."

"Maybe, maybe not. This creature was only seen when they went down to lower levels that have not been mined for many years. Well below the cavern you are checking out, and I am not sure you would want to run into this creature. If the legends are true, they are ferocious with tough skin, almost like armor, and breathe fire. They can also communicate telepathically, causing anyone close to them to freeze with fear. But as I said, no one has ever really seen one for centuries, so they are all stories passed down through the years."

Eric looked at Connor. "Telepathy, you say, interesting, very interesting." Connor just smiles at Eric.

They travel towards the colony where Mondo is for several more hours, sporadically sleeping along the way. Nearly there, they see a large group of buildings, almost like they sprang up from the desert sands. It is almost dark by the time they reach their destination, parking near the building where Mondo is supposed to be. They get out of the transport, stretching before walking in. A tall, heavy-set man stands there, a large scar running down the side of his face, a face that has been weathered by years. He begins to speak. "Eric, my friend, I am very surprised to see you. I am glad that you are here, but why?"

Eric answers, "I have an image of a cavern. It looks like the one we were trapped in, but I am not absolutely sure. Please look at this and let me know if you think it is. Renaldo seemed to believe so. We are here at the request of the emperor. Things are stirring, and we need to get answers." Eric hands Mondo the image, and he inspects it.

"Yes, you are correct. It is the same one. We can go there first thing in the morning, but be aware there are issues with the cavern in that mine."

Connor puts in, "Do you mean the dragon?"

"Dragon, who said anything about a dragon?"

"Renaldo told us it was the rumor."

"And who are you?"

Eric puts in, "Sorry, this is William's youngest son, Connor."

"Oh wow, really, I am very glad to meet you." Mondo shakes Connor's hand. "Welcome to our world. Your father is a great man, and we will help you both any way we can, but like I said, we will have to be very careful going into that mine and exploring the cavern.

"Why don't you guys follow me upstairs? I have rooms you can use for the night. We also have food up there. I am sure you guys are hungry," says Mondo.

Connor agrees, "Yes, starving."

Eric laughs. "You young guys are always hungry."

Connor peers at him with a smile. "Yes, we are."

Mondo chuckles. "No worries. We have plenty, then you can get some sleep if you like."

"Great," says Connor.

As they walk upstairs, Eric looks at Mondo. "I will need to get a message to Esteban in the morning since we cannot get back before the path out closes tomorrow."

Mondo nods. "Sure, we have a transport ship nearby that can get a message out for you. We will go by there on the way to the mine."

"Ok, good. I was also told you were here because there has been trouble, and the emperor is being blamed."

"Ha, ha, Renaldo has been talking your ear off, it sounds like."

"No, he just seemed concerned about what you were dealing with and was also the reason for the additional men that came with us."

"He is correct. Things have gotten bad, but let's talk about that in the morning. The kid is hungry, and I am sure you are as well. Let's eat and relax for tonight, and we can discuss why I am here in the morning so you can add it to the message for the emperor."

"Sounds good. We will be here till the next window out, so as we discuss, let me know what we can do to help you as well."

"Thank you, Eric. Your help will be much appreciated." Once upstairs, they walk down the hall to a large room with all kinds of food and drink on the table in the center of the room. They sit down to drink, eat, and talk about when they first met.

Mondo says, "We had some wild times in the beginning, Eric. Do you remember?"

Eric laughs. "Remember? Yes, every time it rains, I feel it."

Mondo lets out a deep, loud laugh. "Yes, we had some fierce battles, lots of damage all around. Look at my face, but a warrior without scars is not a real warrior on my planet."

Eric snorts and says, "Then I guess you are welcome."

Connor looks at Eric with a surprised expression on his face. "You mean you gave Mondo that scar? Oh, wow, I am so sorry."

He reaches over and put his hand on Connor's shoulder, "No, do not worry. We are good. If not for this scar, we may not have become the friends we are now. It was a great fight. If Eric were not such an experienced warrior, he could be dead now, but because your father, John, and Eric were such great warriors and had superior weapons, we were willing to parlay with them.

"We had been fighting for what seemed like hours. Many were killed on both sides when I encountered Eric. I can honestly say I had never come up against anyone as good as I was in battle. Both of us inflicted about the same amount of damage on each other till Eric sliced my face, nearly taking off my head. Others from my clan saw what happened, as the battle was almost over and we were losing. Some of my clansmen grabbed me and forced me to retreat to the cavern to regroup and come up with a new plan, but Eric and the others followed us in. There was an explosion, and the entrance collapsed. This forced us to meet and discuss, as it took days to dig our way out. Already, we had great respect for them since they were defeating us in battle, and we had never been beaten before. We were the master warrior clan for over a century."

Eric agrees. "Yes, while we were trapped, it gave us the time we needed to talk rationally about why we had really come to their planet. I offered to repair the damage to Mondo's face. By the time we dug our way out, we had negotiated a truce with a plan to mine the minerals we needed and a way for them to stop warring between the clans. It took almost another year of battle with the other clans, but when they saw Mondo and his clan were fighting with us, we could finally unite all the Zandorrians, showing them a better way."

"Yes, Eric is right. Them coming here changed everything for us. We moved from being warrior clans to miners, making life better for all of us. Since I was the leader of our clan and we were the leading warrior clan, it made sense I would be the leader of our world—a count technically—but I prefer to just go by my name. That is why everyone calls me Mondo and rarely Count Mondo, even though that is my official title."

Connor exclaims, "Wow, this has been a lot to take in over a meal, but I have a better understanding of your planet and relationship with Eric. Not trying to be rude, but now that I have eaten, it has been a very long day, and I am ready for sleep."

Eric concurs, "Yes, that is a great idea. I am tired as well."

"Of course. Let me show you where you can stay for the night." Mondo shows them their rooms, and they all get ready to shut down for the night. Mondo then glances at Eric. "We will have to get up early if you want to talk about what is going on here and get a message out to the emperor before the freight ships leave."

"Sounds good. Thank you for all your hospitality."

Connor gives a big yawn. "Yes, thank you for everything."

Mondo smiles. "Absolutely my pleasure. You both sleep well. See you in the morning."

EARLIER THAT SAME DAY, AS ERIC AND CONNOR LAND, Craven is also landing, but near the mine Mondo would take Eric and Connor to the next morning. Craven enters the mine and heads to the cavern Lorenzo was testing, a dark secluded back corner of the cavern. Getting close using his light, Craven sees several pieces of tall lab equipment and a raised round platform big enough for two or three people to stand on, with some debris, including a baseball-sized piece of a building. Craven sweeps the debris to the side with his foot. He then runs several tests on the equipment, examines the readings, and makes some notes. This takes a few hours. Craven then shuts everything down. After he is all done, he hears some loud noises from the caverns below. Not wanting to either see what the noises were or be discovered, he quickly leaves the mine. As he returns to his ship, he sees a few people heading toward him. Not wanting to talk with anyone about what he had been doing in the mine or why he was there, he quickly gets onto his ship and takes off. Craven leaves the planet about the same time Eric and Connor arrive to meet Mondo.

Back on Markus 2, the same morning Eric and Connor are leaving for Zada 5, John and Adam leave the palace to meet with John's men, Matt and Dave, who tracked Lorenzo to his large lab complex just a few miles from the smaller destroyed lab building.

Just before John and Adam get to the complex, John hands Adam an ID. "I still manage security and can access any of the buildings owned or controlled by the emperor's family. This is a master pass and will get you in. On the back of your pass is the code you will need for any of the secure rooms. I can go with you to meet Matt and Dave since the building is so large, but after that, I will need to leave, as Lorenzo knows very well who I am, and we do not want him to become suspicious."

Adam nods. "Sounds good." They head into the building to meet John's men. All of them gather in one of the small conference rooms off to the side of the large greeting area in the front of the building.

John says, "Guys, this is Adam, the duke's son." Adam shakes both their hands.

Matt and Dave both say, "Glad to meet you."

Dave adds, "We have heard a lot of good things and are glad to be working with you on this. To that point so far, we have tracked Lorenzo to this building. He has been working here since he left the palace two days ago after meeting with two of his men. One was Andy, but the other guy I do not know, nor were we able to find out who he was. He was the same age as Lorenzo, but rough-looking, like he had been in many battles."

Matt puts in, "I tried to take his image, but they did not come out. He was moving too quickly from the building to his transport." Matt shows them to John, anyway.

John states, "It is hard to tell, but he does not resemble anyone I know."

Adam agrees. "If he shows up again, we will get a better image."

Dave explains, "Well, after Lorenzo came, he has been in one of the larger labs near the back of this building on the main floor. There have been only a couple of people besides Lorenzo inside, but he has been in there the whole time and has not left."

Adam takes this in. "Ok, Matt, do you want to go back and check that Lorenzo has not gone anywhere since we have been in here and is still in there before we come out of this room, so he does not see us together?"

Matt obeys. "Yes, will do." Matt goes to the back of the building. Lorenzo is still in the lab, visible through a long window near the door. Matt updates them so they can leave the room. When they go, Adam observes a young woman sitting at a table on the other side of the large entrance that keeps looking at him. He sees her tell the other woman she is with as she gets up that she will be right back. She then walks over to Adam and John.

The young woman stares at him. "Are you Adam Balcazar?"

Adam, with a puzzled expression on his face, studies her. "I am. How do you know me?"

She says, "I am Emma. Your friend from school, Roger's little sister."

Adam, smiling, now realizes who she is. "No way, little Emma, that's you. The last time I saw you, I think you were about six or seven."

She laughs. "Yes, that's me. How have you been? What are you doing here?"

"I am good. Very busy, but life has been great. I have some business here."

Dave nudges Adam and whispers behind him, "She is one of the people going into Lorenzo's lab."

Adam nods his head, then says, "So Emma, I need to finish my discussion with these guys, but would love to catch up with you. Can we meet for lunch later today?"

Emma gives him a big grin. "Yes, I would love that. Here is my info."

"Great, I will reach out to you a little later so we can meet."

"Sounds good. I look forward to it."

As Emma leaves, he waits a minute. Adam then looks at John and Dave. "There is our way in."

Dave asks, "Way in? What do you mean?"

"John and I were talking last night about finding someone that can get us information about what Lorenzo is up to. If she is working with Lorenzo, you cannot get any better or closer—if I can convince her to help us." Adam looks at John, "Why don't you take off, and we can rendezvous later so I can update you on what we find out?"

John agrees. "Sounds good to me. See you tonight."

WHILE ADAM TALKS WITH JOHN AND DAVE, EMMA GOES back to the table she was sitting at. As she sits down, she looks at the woman already there. "That was Adam Balcazar."

The woman responds, "Adam Balcazar, the duke's son?"

Emma still smiles. "Yes, the same. I have not seen him since I was a kid. He was a friend of my brothers. Adam is so handsome, and I had such a crush on him, but I do not think he ever knew it. He asked me to meet him for lunch later."

"Wow, I am glad for you," the woman says.

"Thank you," Emma says, "I better get going. There are a few things I need to take care of for Lorenzo before I go back to his lab this afternoon." Both women then leave.

MATT COMES BACK TO MEET WITH ADAM AND DAVE, just as John walks out of the building, Matt inquires, "So what did I miss?"

Dave peers at him. "Well, Adam knows that girl that has been going in Lorenzo's lab."

"Are you kidding me? Really? He knows her."

Adam nods. "Yes, she is the kid sister of an old friend of mine from school. She used to follow us around like a little puppy. We may be able to use her to help us get more information on Lorenzo."

"That is great. When will you know?"

"I am going to meet her for lunch and feel her out about helping us. In the meantime, why don't you show me Lorenzo's lab? Then I will reach out to Emma."

Dave and Matt show Adam that lab. They also work out a schedule, rotating around the clock to watch Lorenzo. They agree to four-hour segments, so as not to draw attention to themselves. Since Adam is meeting Emma for lunch, he tells them he will take the first watch. Matt agrees to come in to relieve Adam. With all of that resolved, Adam then reaches out to Emma, and they agree on when and where to meet for food. Adam makes several trips past Lorenzo's lab, and even though the window is almost as tall as the door, it is very narrow. Unless you actually stand in front of it and stare in, you cannot see a lot. Adam could only tell Lorenzo was still within, but not anything that he was really doing. Just before Adam was to meet with Emma, Matt comes over to talk with Adam. He lets

Matt know Lorenzo is still in the room and has not left. Matt then says he is good and ready to take over. Adam leaves to meet Emma.

Adam is the first to arrive at the restaurant. Just as he sits down, Emma walks in, all smiles. Adam gets back up, grins at her, and pulls her chair to sit down. Adam then sits down again, looking at Emma. "So, it has been a long time. How is your brother doing?"

Emma can't stop grinning. "He is great. He got married a couple of years ago, and they have a new baby. He also has a great job on Korbin managing the lab facility there."

"That is great. I am very happy for him. Tell him I said hello when you talk."

"I will," she says.

"Why do you seem to be so happy?"

"I am not sure how to say this, but I have had a crush on you since I was a kid, which is why I used to follow you and my brother around."

Adam says with a slight laugh, "I thought you just enjoyed hanging out with us because we were much older."

She then giggles. "Well, that too, but I just thought you were so cute and so nice when I was around. You were never mean letting this little kid hang out with you."

"No, I never had an issue. I thought of you as a kid sister."

Emma wears a smirk on her face. "A sister? I am crushed."

Adam chuckles again. "Sorry, that was when you were a little girl. You are definitely not a little girl now. You're an attractive woman."

"Well, thank you."

"Look, I have an ulterior motive for asking you to lunch today. I understand you have been working with Lorenzo in his lab."

"Yes, I have been. Why do you ask?"

"Since we have known each other for so long, I feel I can trust you."

"Yes, of course you can."

"Well, I am working with my father on behalf of the emperor."

"Ok, what do you need from me?"

"We believe Lorenzo has been hiding secrets. You are aware of the lab test he did and the three people killed because of it."

"Yes, I am. That was horrible. Lorenzo told me it was a complete accident. A power supply stopped regulating, causing everything to overload, and he could not shut it down."

"Well, he told his brother the emperor he was working on a new refining process for Zando Crystals, and they exploded."

"I know that was not what caused the explosion, and we are not even dealing with Zando Crystals. We are working with stuff that has already been refined, but what Lorenzo is actually doing, I cannot tell you; he only gives us a piece of what he needs accomplished, and we do not see what he is truly working on. We provide our finished parts, and he assembles everything."

"Ok, so you can see why the emperor is concerned and why I am here talking with you now."

"Yes, I can, but I am a little depressed. I thought this was going to be more of a romantic lunch."

Adam grabs her hand. "Oh, I am sorry, but this is very serious, and we are seeking your help."

"No, I get it, and understand. How can I help?"

"First off, I need you to understand this could be very dangerous if Lorenzo finds out what you are doing and that you are helping us. If you are concerned, we can stop talking about it right now."

"This is really to help the emperor and your father the duke?"

"Yes, absolutely it is. I would be happy to have you meet both of them when this is over. I am sure they would be pleased to thank you for your assistance here."

Emma demurs, "I was not looking for that, but it would be awesome to meet them both. Yes, I am in. Where do I start?"

"Outstanding. First off, see how much information you can get on what Lorenzo is really working on, with no one finding out."

"I will be with Lorenzo after our lunch today, so I will see what I can find while I am there. Then I'll search our files after my meeting with him."

"Perfect. Here is my contact information. We have several others monitoring him and will keep an eye on you also, so we can make sure you are safe. We will find a way for you to pass information and not get caught."

"Great, thanks, Adam. I will let you know what I find out tonight."

They both stand and Adam hugs her. "Thank you for your help. You do not know how much we appreciate it."

Emma smiles at Adam. "You are very welcome." Adam leaves money on the table for the bill, and they both leave.

Emma goes back to the complex and into her small lab near the front of the building, where she picks up two mini-drive chips for the meeting with Lorenzo. Down the hall, Matt watches her. She stops for a minute, nervous, thinking about what she needs to do, then takes a deep breath and walks into Lorenzo's lab.

He looks at Emma. "Hi, Emma, how are you doing this afternoon?"

Emma tries to stay calm. "I am doing great. How are you?"

"I am good. So, were you able to make the updates for your control system?"

"Yes, absolutely. Here it is. I will go ahead and load the updates."

"No, that is ok. I can do it."

Emma says, "No, it is not a problem. I already scheduled the time."

"That would be great. I have a lot to do if you have the time."

Emma walks over to the other side of the room. "Yes, not a problem, but I will need your access code to load everything."

"No, I cannot do that, but let me come over there and log in for you."

"Sure, that works" Lorenzo logs into the system, giving her full access to her program. Lorenzo then walks back to the other side of the room to continue working on the system he has been modifying for several days.

Emma watches Lorenzo as he goes back. Once he's there, and can no longer see what she is typing in, she takes out one chip and copies everything Lorenzo has been working on. After it loads the information on her chip, Emma then glances to make sure Lorenzo is not looking. Then she swaps chips to put in the one that has her program updates. While that is loading, she asks Lorenzo if there is anything else he needs help with, as the program will take some time. Lorenzo looks up at her with a smile on his face. "I would love your help, but this is secret stuff, and I would have to kill you if you knew what it was." Then he laughs.

Emma gives a nervous laugh. "Very funny."

"Yes, I thought so. All kidding aside, I am good, but thank you for offering." He then returns to what he was doing.

Emma says, "You're welcome." With Lorenzo not looking, she takes the copied chip out of her pocket and drops it in her boot. After some time, her program finally reboots. She pulls the chip out, then stands up and looks at Lorenzo. "All my updates are complete. You should be good to go."

"Great, please leave the program drive chip over there."

"Sure, you got it." She drops off the chip in the box, then looks at Lorenzo again and says to him, "You seem exhausted. Maybe you should get some rest."

Lorenzo responds, "Thank you for caring about me. I will as soon as I get my test platform ready to go later this evening."

Emma says, "Ok then, you have a good night."

"Thank you, I will," answers Lorenzo. Emma then leaves the lab. Matt sees Emma walk out of Lorenzo's lab as he is marching by. Emma then returns to her lab to validate what she copied from Lorenzo's system, but when it comes up, it asks for the encryption key. She watched the code Lorenzo typed when he logged her in, but it does not seem to work. Not wanting to risk being locked out, she pulls the drive chip free and figures she'll let Adam know what she did and what she had tried to accomplish.

LATER THAT AFTERNOON, ADAM GOES BACK TO THE complex about the time Dave meets with Matt to relieve him, wanting to tell them about the lunch with Emma.

Adam arrives just ahead of Dave. As he walks to the back of the building, he sees Matt moving his way, so he points to him and then to the room where they met that morning. Dave walks in to see where Matt and Adam are going, so he follows. When they get in the room, Adam then says, "I met Emma for lunch, and she is on board to try and help us. We will need to keep an eye on her as well and protect her while she deals with Lorenzo."

Matt then says, "I saw her go into his lab and then come out a little while later. She seems to be fine."

Adam replies, "She will reach out later tonight to let me know how her meeting went with him and if she was able to get us any information on Lorenzo. We will also need to invent a way for her to leave us any information while being tracked, so Lorenzo does not suspect." Matt points out a loose panel in the corner of the room they can place stuff behind. "Great, I will let her know when she calls me tonight, but one thing I think will protect her and you guys is if she does not know who the two of you are, so she is not nervous when you guys are near or watching her for a short time and will not blow your cover."

Dave agrees. "Yes, that makes sense to me. Plus, this gives her plausible deniability."

Matt nods. "Yes, good point."

Adam says, "Ok, it has been a long day, and I need to update John. Then I am going to get some sleep before my shift."

Dave responds, "I got some good sleep before getting here and can cover a full eight-hour shift if you like."

"No, that is not necessary. I can come back in four hours."

"No, really, I am ok."

"Well, if you are sure, that would be great, thank you. Then I will see you in eight hours. I appreciate it."

"No worries, it's all good. Matt, any issues I need to be aware of?"

Matt shakes his head. "No, he is still in his lab. Nothing has changed."

"Ok then, you guys get out of here and have a good evening." Matt and Adam then leave the room and the building.

Adam goes back to the palace. As he arrives, Emma calls him and tells him about her meeting with Lorenzo and that she could copy his files, but they are encrypted. Adam tells her about the loose panel location at her building and to put the chip in there. He will have someone retrieve it. He also tells her he made the rest of the team aware of who she is and that she is trying to help them and how much he appreciates her aid. If she gets anything else, let him know. If they have further questions, once they retrieve the chip from her and can break the code, they will inform her. Emma responds she will put the chip behind the panel before she leaves the building tonight. Adam thanks her, and they end the call.

Adam walks into the palace to meet with John and let him know how the day went. He walks over to the office that John uses. Inside, he sees Esteban sitting there with John. Adam says, "Oh good, you are both here."

John glances up at Adam. "Yes, I was just updating Esteban, but since you are here, why don't you take over?"

"Sure, so John may have told you we have found someone that works with Lorenzo willing to help us."

Esteban says, "Yes, he did. How did your meeting go?"

Adam has a grin on his face. "The lunch went very well. The woman, Emma, is the kid sister of an old school friend, and when I told her what we wanted was to help you, sir, she was very eager to do so. I just finished talking with her, and she told me she copied Lorenzo's files, but they were encrypted, so she was going to leave the chip for us to pick up. John, I know you have some great security experts who can crack the drive chip and get us the information we need out of it."

John agrees. "Yes, I do. That is a great idea. When will we get the chip?"

"I will pick it up in the morning when I go back to the building. Also, one more thing to add. Emma told me when she asked Lorenzo about the accident, he claimed a regulator caused it on a power supply that failed. It had nothing to do with Zando Crystals."

"So, this validates our concerns. What Lorenzo gave us was a lie, and we are justified tracking him."

Esteban adds, "This is great. Good work. You guys have seemed to accomplish quite a bit on the first day. I am very happy, and I hope you can continue this way."

Adam laughs. "Yes, sir, we will do our best to keep it up."

"I am sure you will. Now, to change the subject, I had the cook prepare dinner for us if you are hungry."

Adam beams. "Always. Let's eat." John and Esteban get up, and they all walk into the dining room to eat, have light conversation, and go to bed, as it had been a long day for everyone.

CHAPTER V
UNCOVERING THE TRUTH

Early the next morning, Adam heads to the lab complex, enters the building, and checks the loose panel location before meeting Dave. He looks around, just to make sure no one is near, before reaching in and retrieving the chip. He pulls it out and puts it in his pocket. Then he walks to the back of the building to relieve Dave. He gets there, seeing Dave come from down the hall.

"So, has Lorenzo been here for another night?"

"Yes, but I think he has been sleeping. All the lights have been off in the lab since about ten last night." They walk back down the hall just as Adam hands Dave the chip from his pocket.

"What's this?"

"I talked to Emma last night, and she copied Lorenzo's system files. I fetched them from the drop location. I think that will work out well for us, by the way, but the files are encrypted. Can you take this chip to John before you go home? One of his security techs will try to break into it."

"Great, will do. Anything else you need?"

"No, I am good. Get some rest," responds Adam. Just as Dave starts to leave, the lights turn on in Lorenzo's lab.

"Well, Lorenzo is awake now."

"Yes. Head out of here. I got this."

"Are you sure?"

"Yes. No problem. Get some rest."

"Thanks, I will." Dave then leaves for the palace to give John the chip.

Back on Zada 5, early that same morning, Eric and Connor head to meet Mondo. Then Eric can formalize his message and send it to the emperor on the Zando Crystal freighter ship. They return to the same room where dinner was served the night before. As they walk in, Mondo is already there. Eric and Connor greet him and sit down. Eric asks, "So what issues have you been dealing with here?"

Mondo sighs. "Well, there are two different mines here. The one we will go to this morning, is not being excavated at this time. The other one is very close to us here. Until about a year ago, we have set the pace on how many of the Zando Crystals we mine, but the miners tell me they are being forced to increase the rate to almost triple the amount. These demands have been coming from the emperor's brother, Lorenzo. He sent some guy named Craven with several soldiers to back him up."

Eric shouts, "Craven! Are you sure they said his name was Craven? What does he look like?"

"Yes, that is what they claimed. I have not seen or talked with this guy and do not know his appearance. Why? Do you know him?"

"I knew a guy named Craven. He helped us rescue Connor's grandfather. He went into the building with us but never came out. We thought he may have died when the building exploded. That was about twenty-five years ago, and we never saw or heard from him again, so we all assumed he was dead."

"Well then, maybe it was not the same guy. He just has the same bizarre name."

"Well, I guess that is possible, but not likely. We will need to dig into this more to be sure."

"Yes, you got it."

"But back to the actual issue. We were told mining was slow and creating more demand, causing the price of the crystals to rise."

"That makes little sense if we are mining three times as much. Where are the rest of the crystals going? They are mining so much it now requires two transport ships to ship them all off-world to the refinery, but this is not the only issue. The other one is because they have been drilling so much, they tried to reopen the other mine, but many people have died. Something or someone is killing them. The last time the miners went in there, only one came back. He was all torn up, talking crazy."

Connor asks, "Why? what was he saying?"

"This is where the story of a dragon comes from. The miner said it was huge and fierce and tore all the others apart. They discovered it in one of the lower caverns, looking for a rich vein of crystals. I heard stories when I was a kid, but no one has ever seen one in centuries. We always thought they were merely that— stories, not real. The miner died in the hospital, and no one will go back to that site now, as they are all afraid. That is why I am here. Since our communications here are so bad, I was getting rumors, so I had to come and find out what was going on for myself, then stop any fighting. The miners are ready to rebel against this guy Craven and his soldiers. They also say his soldiers have special armor, and they cannot be hurt. I was going to check out the freighters again this morning, thinking this Craven fellow might be there with his men to make sure the miners are delivering. Since yesterday, he has not been at the storage warehouse as they were loading."

Eric says, "Ok, let me put a note together for John and Esteban based on what you have told me and what we are planning to do. We will not be back until the next window out in three months. I am also going to put tracking devices on the transport ships and let them know so John and Adam can trace them to find out where the shipments are going."

"Sounds good. Thanks, Eric," says Mondo.

Renaldo comes into the room. "My men are downstairs by the transport. We are ready when you are, sir."

"Great, thanks, Renaldo. We will be right there." The three men follow Renaldo downstairs and get in the transport vehicle. Eric tells the driver to take them to the transport loading zone so he can put a message on it before they leave. Glancing at Connor, he hands him the two trackers for the ships and says, "You know what to do with these." It takes about twenty minutes to arrive at the loading zone. As the vehicle pulls up, the transports ships are getting ready to leave. Eric jumps out when the transport stops, with Mondo, Renaldo, and Connor right behind him. Eric waves at them to halt.

The door opens up on one of them, and the captain comes out. "What is going on? Why are you stopping us?"

"I am Eric Aristo, and I have an important message that needs to get to the emperor."

"Yes, of course, sir. I did not know who you were," says the captain.

"That is ok. I need this to go out before the next window." He hands the captain a chip with the message for Esteban and John, which included the tracking tag IDs so they can find them when the ships land again. Eric then tells the captain, "Sorry for holding you up. You guys can take off now."

"Thank you, sir. I will make sure the emperor gets this when we land."

"Thank you. Have a safe flight." Eric then peeks at Connor. "Did you put the trackers on?"

Smiling, he winks at him. "Yes, I took care of it."

Eric looks at Mondo. "Well, maybe it is time to go check out the cavern in the mine."

Mondo concurs, "Yes, that sounds like a good idea."

Connor puts in, "We need to be careful. All I see is blood and pain in my visions of that cavern."

"VISIONS?"

"Sorry, yes, I am still new to this, but I have had some psychic abilities since I was a kid, and they grow the closer we get to this mine and cavern."

"Sorry I have never believed in those abilities, but I will take you at your word. We will be cautious."

"Ok, thank you," says Connor.

Renaldo interjects, "My men are well armed, so we should be fine for anything we run into down there."

"Perfect. Connor and I have our weapons as well." They all get back into the vehicle and head toward the mine.

As they arrive, Eric and Connor notice a few men standing near the entrance. Eric looks at Mondo. "You placed guards by the mine?"

Mondo sighs, "Yes, I sent them here yesterday afternoon. Even before we talked, I was going to go in with some of my guards to see for myself and put the rumors to bed, hoping to help calm the miners down." As the vehicle stops and they emerge, the guards come up to Mondo.

One of them says, "We believe that guy Craven was here yesterday. As we walked to the mine, we could see a small ship by the entrance. Getting closer, we saw him come out. He seemed to be in a hurry to leave, like he did not want us to see or talk with him."

The other guard says, "That guy was real squirrelly. I swear we could hear him talking to himself as he was getting on his ship before he left."

Eric hears all of this. "Ok, what does he look like?"

The one guard adds, "We did not get a close look, but he seemed to be about your height and age, maybe a little stockier with dark hair."

"That sounds just like the Craven I knew, but how and why would he be working for Lorenzo?"

Connor says, "You gave his info on that note to the emperor and John. With any luck, they should be able to help uncover that while we are stuck here for the next three months with no communication."

"Yes, I hope so. He was very well trained and could be a problem for us to deal with if he is now working for Lorenzo."

Mondo asks, "How tough can he be? Not tougher than you or me, right?"

"No, he would not be, so long as it is you or I who deals with him."

"Well, we have three months to get ready for his next trip here, so we can be prepared if or when he comes again."

"Yes, good point. Connor and I can train some of your elite guards."

"Connor! You mean you and me, right?"

"No, I meant Connor and I; Connor and his brother were trained by John and myself, and I would put either of them up against you or I."

Mondo chortles, "Maybe we will have to test him while you guys are here." He grins at Connor."

"Sure, that sounds like fun. I am always ready to spar to help me stay on my toes," responds Connor.

"Perfect. We can set up something while you are here. It looks like we will have plenty of time for it."

At the end of the discussion about Craven, they all pull out their weapons and get ready to enter the mine, prepared for anything they may run into. As they get to the cavern in question, Eric holds the image up to compare. "It is very close, but it seems to be off with the direction it is facing." As they look around, then shine a light on a section in the back and see what looks like some large cabinets and a platform, they walk over. Once they get close, Eric looks around the platform and notices the debris Craven had brushed off it the day before. He continues exploring around and finds a piece about the size of his fist, part of a building. He picks it up and, as he turns it over, sees the initials JA written on it. "This is the spot. John told me before we left the palace to look for this piece, he had thrown it through the opening while the portal was still active. So Craven was here, but now the question is why."

Halting there, he points out towards the cavern and says, "When I stand on this platform and look out that way, this image matches perfectly."

Mondo adds, "I have a few technicians we work with, but they are back at the colony where you landed. Maybe I can have them come examine this equipment and figure out how to make it work."

"Yes, that is a great idea. We have three months."

Connor puts in, "We should get an image of this whole setup to take back with us as well."

Renaldo offers, "Sure, we can take care of that for you."

At the other end of the cavern, a large opening goes down to the mine below. As Renaldo has one of his men take the images for Connor, some loud noises come out of the opening.

Mondo looks at them. "We need to find out what that noise is." As Mondo is talking, they can feel cold and dampness from being in the cavern. Connor's head is pounding and a strong sense of fear overtakes him while hearing a voice, but he cannot make out what is being said, causing his head to pound even more, as if someone is trying to tell him something. The closer they get to the entrance, the stronger the sense gets for Connor.

Eric sees Connor holding his head. "What's going on?" he asks.

Connor admits, "I have a strong feeling of fear coming from down below."

"Maybe you should hold back a little. That may affect your fighting abilities, and I don't want you hurt."

"Ok, got it. But I can still hold my own. We need to be careful."

Eric and Mondo say at the same time, "Yes, agreed," as they both draw their swords and continue through the opening. When all of them get through, they find an even larger cavern on the other end. As they continue, the light progressively dims along with the dampness and cold. The voice in Connor's head pounds away relentlessly. Straining to make out anything in the darkness, the wall on the other side of the cavern appears to move. A loud roar rips through the chamber as a large creature appears. Its scales are immense and seemingly impenetrable. The men can just make out its large teeth and claws while it tears through one after another of them. It grabs one man and bites him in half, only to catch up to two more and tear them apart. Amidst the screams, everyone turns around and fires on the creature.

Mondo takes charge. "Fire at will!" To no avail. Everything bounces off. With that, panic takes over. Men run in every direction, except for Connor, who stands still in the midst of the chaos with his hands raised.

"We are not here to hurt you." As he tunes in, he can feel the creature's confusion begin to subside. At the same time, the pain in his head stops. Connor walks forward towards the creature as it simply sits there, sensing he is slowly communicating with it when he puts his hands on it.

Mondo barks, "What?! I can't believe what I'm seeing."

Eric says, "This is the first I've ever seen proof of what Connor said to me."

Mondo looks at Renaldo. "Let's get the injured men out here. Eric and I will stay with Connor. This should help keep the creature calm with fewer people."

"Yes, that is a good idea."

Renaldo says, "I would like to stay just in case."

Connor hears all the conversations. "That is fine. You can remain. She is calming down."

"She? How do you know it's a she?"

"She told me she has been killing everyone because she was afraid. When they used explosives to open up this cavern, they also killed some of her unborn children. I am thinking they were eggs, which makes her a she. I am still working on our communication, but I told her we are not here to harm her or her unborn kids anymore. Before this cavern was opened, she had been asleep for a long time, I am guessing centuries. Since there is no sundown here, she does not understand time the same way we do, but she is hurt from the explosion, so once the medic has finished with the hurt men, he can come and fix her up. That should buy us more goodwill with her."

Eric agrees. "Yes, that is good thinking. Do you know where the rest of her eggs are so we can make sure they do not get damaged?"

"Ok, yes, she is saying she moved them somewhere safe."

Mondo asks, "So, do you think we will be able to mine? I see a huge rich vein, right over there behind her."

Connor says, "I am not sure we want to do that yet. Perhaps when she feels safe and assured that we mean no harm to her or her kids."

"Good point. We can wait for a while as long as we can still drill in the first cavern. We have no idea about this Craven person and need to increase mining until we know more."

Eric comments, "I would think if we blocked the entrance to this cavern, the creature should feel safe and that we will not come in here to hurt it."

Connor concurs. "She agrees. I am telling her that at some point, we would like to take her out of here, maybe at night, so she can get used to daylight after all these years."

Mondo nods. "Yes, even create her own exit in and out."

"Yes, she is now telling me there used to be one on the other side of the cavern, but it collapsed, and she could not get it opened again and has been sleeping in here ever since."

Connor continues to communicate with the creature, and she tells him her name is Andorra, and all she had to deal with was humans trying to kill her. Every time she tried to communicate, they would freeze, and she realized she could not talk with them. Then the others around would attack her. That is why she would slay them all before they tried to execute her. This was the first time she could speak with a human. After the explosion and the destruction of some of her unborn kids and being hurt, she thought the humans were still trying to kill her after all this time.

As this discussion goes on, the medic comes in to mend the creature. Connor tells her it is ok and he is here to help her. With a lot of hesitation, the medic works on her injuries, but her skin is like armor, and the medic cannot stitch her up. He can spray healing medication over it that stops the bleeding and partially closes the wound. Andorra informs Connor she feels much better and to thank the human. Connor steps away and takes his hands down, then looks at Eric with a big smile on his face. "I can still talk with Andorra, and I am not touching her."

Eric exclaims, "This is amazing. If someone had told me a few days ago we would be connecting with this creature, I would have said they were crazy, but here we are."

"Yes, and on top of that, she told me she has seen a lot of bright lights coming from the path to the other cavern. She could not tell what it was because they were so dazzling it hurt her eyes, so she hid in the back of this cavern."

"Ok, that lines up with what Lorenzo was doing and the damage to the building back on Markus 2, along with what Craven was up to yesterday."

Mondo puts in, "I sent word to my technicians. They will be here later today to look at the equipment we found in the other cavern. Let the creature know others will come, but they will stay out of this cavern for now, so she is not afraid others are coming for her."

Connor agrees. "Yes, I told her that and only we will come to this cavern from now. Also, we will work on getting her out of here, or at least create an opening for her to escape on her own. We can leave now. I told her I would be back in a few days once we have the plan to create an opening. She can rest, knowing no one will come to kill her."

They all back away from the creature, then turn around as the creature lies down and goes to sleep. As they are walking back to the other cavern, Connor glances at Mondo. "I could not say this before as we came in, but that sword of yours is a magnificent weapon. I notice it seemed to light up as we got close to Andorra."

Eric asks, "Yes, I saw that as well. Why was that?"

Mondo explains, "Well, this is one of ten swords that have been made, and passed down, for the heads of the original ten clans on this world. At least, that is what I was told by my father when he handed the sword to me just before he died. From what I know, as all the clans fought and lost. The others were destroyed so a new leader could not take over the clan. There is only one other that an old friend of mine, Ramone, still held. He was the leader of his clan before we became the miners we are now. Unfortunately, he disappeared a few years later, and no one seemed to know what happened to him. I tried over the years, but could never find out any more about him.

"Recently, I found in some old archives how these swords were constructed. There is a special mineral that can only be found in the mines near the Zando Crystals. When melted and forged with the crystal dust in the correct amounts, it creates the metal for these weapons. It also states that it will light up as we wield it, and it seems to always do that as I wield mine. As I read more about them, it also stated it becomes more deadly as it strikes its enemies and is the only thing that can pierce a dragon's flesh. That is what they wrote about this weapon. It has always served me well and never failed me."

Eric asks, "So when you and I fought, that was not just my imagination. It really was lighting up?"

"Yes, that has always been the case, but until I read those archive notes, I never knew why."

Connor inquires, "So, if you have the book that tells you how to make those swords, could you make more?"

"I think so, if we can find all the right minerals. There is an old man that is rumored can still forge these, but why would you need a weapon like this with all the great armaments you have?"

Eric asks, "Yes, why?"

Connor explains, "Remember when I told you I see a lot of blood and fierce fighting in battles and things that can save us? Something is telling me that this sword is one of them, and the creature may be another."

Mondo considers this. "Ok, we will have to see if we can find what we need. Then I will send for the old man to help us construct these new weapons."

Connor shakes Mondo's hand. "Thank you for your help."

"If what you are saying is true, then this will help us all." As they reach the next cavern and continue to walk out of the mine, Mondo looks at Renaldo. "I need you to find the mineral to reconstruct the new swords. I can get you the list when we return to the colony. Also, let's continue to post the guards in front of the mine so no one but us goes in there for now."

Renaldo obeys. "Yes, sir, will do."

"Connor and I will get that cavern opened for the creature. Then we can mine those crystals we saw. Eric, you can train some of my elite guards just in case this Craven person comes back. I will send word and get them to meet us back at the colony."

Eric nods. "Sounds good. Will do."

With the guards posted outside the mine, the men get into the transport and head back to the colon they came from that morning.

Connor says, "I will need to sleep when we get back. Communicating with Andorra has taken a lot out of me, so Mondo, we will have to spar tomorrow."

Mondo laughs out loud. "You mean after all of this you still want to face me? Young warrior, no worries.

After today, I have no concerns about how brave you are or your skills as a fighter. You have definitely proven yourself this day, and I would be proud to fight alongside you if that is what it comes to."

"Thank you for your confidence and support. It means a lot to me coming from you."

As they get back to the colony and building, the sun comes down and the day ends. They all pile out of the transport. Connor yawns at them. "I am spent and will see you all in the morning."

"Great, have a good sleep." Mondo then looks at Eric. "The technicians are at the cavern and will look at the equipment and see if they can figure out what it is and how to make it work. The elite guards will arrive in the morning."

Eric says, "Ok, good. Then I think I am going to eat something and go to bcd as well."

"Sounds like a plan. We will join you as well to get dinner."

Renaldo looks at Mondo. "I will have a few of the head miners search for the minerals we need for the weapons in the morning."

"Perfect. I can get you the list of what we need after we eat."

"Great, thank you, sir." The three of them go upstairs to rest.

On Markus 2 that same afternoon, the captain of the transport ship from Zada 5, after landing, goes to the palace to deliver the message from Eric to John. When he gets there, he asks one guard to get the chip to John Aristo. The guard looks at him. "What is this?"

The captain replies, "I was asked to deliver this to John from his brother Eric, who is still on Zada 5."

"Very well. It will be done. I will deliver it myself. Thank you."

"No, thank you." The captain then leaves at the same time the guard walks into the place and over to John's office.

As he moves in, John is sitting at the desk and looks up. "Yes, what can I do for you?"

"Sir, I have a message from your brother, Eric. The captain delivered it from Zada 5," replies the guard.

"Excellent, thank you."

"You're welcome, sir." But right as the guard goes to hand it to John, he drops the chip on the floor and steps on it as he looks for it. He then picks up the chip and hands it to John. "I am so sorry, sir." He then sulks away, back to his post out front, embarrassed.

John loads the chip but is unable to read the message, not accepting any password. After trying several times with no success, John calls in one of his lead engineers to help, and he can finally read the message. John then gets up and goes down the hall to the conference room where Esteban is, with a large group of people. "Sorry for the interruption, sir, but I just received a message from Eric you will want to read."

Standing, Esteban looks at the people in the room. "I am sorry, but we will need to continue this discussion later."

One man in the room asks, "Sir, but we have a lot that we still need to review."

"Yes, I understand, but we have some serious issues going on that cannot wait. We can continue with this meeting first thing in the morning."

"Ok, thank you, sir, I will get it scheduled," the man responds.

Esteban then leaves with John, and they go back to John's office. Esteban sits down at John's desk and reads the note from Eric. "Do we know where the freight ships are?"

John answers, "Well, one of them is here. That is how I got the message, and I just loaded the tracking information for both of them. It shows one here, but the other is headed for Ria 6."

"That does not make any sense. We have no storage faculties on that planet, and there are still hostile rebels. We have not spent the time to stop them since there are no real minerals left to mine there. The people are still on our list to help, but we have had too much else going on."

"If that second freighter is headed to Ria 6, we will have to send a team there to find out what's wrong."

"We should be covert so we can find out what is really going on, while not stirring anything up or letting Lorenzo know we are aware."

"Yes, good idea. I have a team I can send in."

"Do you think we should send Adam with them?"

"Well, last time we were there, if you remember, we had to free his grandfather as the rebels had captured him. If you have read that whole note, he also mentions Craven. If this is the same guy, he came with us to get their grandfather, but Craven never emerged. We all thought he died in the building when it exploded. We saw a transport take off just after the explosion, but we thought if Craven was in it, he would have come back to our camp. We could never find that transport either. I guess he could have left with the remaining rebels and worked with them. At this point, I think we have a lot more questions and no real answers."

"William and Sara have been reviewing the files I could get from our accountants, and they are finding the same thing. Lots of stuff is being mined, but none of it is showing up at the refineries and warehouses, so supplies are down and demand is up, raising prices. If this is truly the case and the prices continue to go up with a lot of inventory hitting the market, that could cause prices to plummet, collapsing the entire market, and destroying everything we have built. We will need to find that other shipment of Zando Crystals and maybe everything else before it is too late. John, let's track that other shipment and see if it lands on Ria 6.

If so, send your team and have Adam join them while we continue to pursue what Lorenzo is up to."

"If that shipment is going to Ria 6, then they should land late tonight. I also talked with my tech working on the file Adam gave us. He should be able to get into it before the end of the day today."

"Excellent. Let me know when they do and what they can find out."

"Yes, sir, you will have it. I will also reach out to my team and prepare them to go to Ria 6. Adam will be back here later. I will update him on this note and what we are planning so he can get ready to join the team."

WHILE JOHN REVIEWS THE INFORMATION ON THE CHIP, Adam, at the lab complex, watches Lorenzo. He walks back and forth across the window like he is packing up to leave. It seems quiet for a long time. Then, sure enough, Lorenzo exits his lab and heads towards the main door. When he gets out the door, he steps into his vehicle and starts to drive. Adam rushes over to his vehicle to follow him out of the complex, trying not to be seen. While he follows, Lorenzo continues to the landing field, where there are multiple transport ships. Lorenzo parks, then gets out and walks over to one of the ships near the middle of the field. Adam quickly parks his vehicle and pursues Lorenzo again. Lorenzo seems preoccupied and not really paying attention to anyone around him. He then climbs into one of the ships. Adam rushes behind him, then waits for him to get in. As the door starts to close, Adam places a tracker inside the wing, then quickly hides behind another to not be noticed as Lorenzo takes off. While Adam ducks behind the ship, Matt comes running up, also trying not to be seen.

Matt asks, "What's going on? I was coming to relieve you when I saw you leaving, so I followed you but got stuck behind another vehicle, and it took me a bit to catch up."

Adam points to the ship Lorenzo is on just as it leaves. "Lorenzo is onboard. I put a tracker on it, and we will need to find out where he is going."

"No problem, I can do that."

"Good. I will go back to the complex and meet with Emma, then see if I can let her into Lorenzo's lab to see what else she can find out. We may have some time with him out of it."

"Yes, good idea. I will let you know where he lands, and we can go from there."

"Perfect."

Matt and Adam wait for Lorenzo's ship to fly out of sight. Then Adam leaves for the lab complex while Matt continues to track Lorenzo. Adam reaches out to Emma, asking her to meet him in the main room greeting area. Emma responds, asking for about twenty minutes to finish up. Adam sits at one table near the back of the room. A little later, Emma comes in and joins him. "Hi, Adam, what's up? I thought you did not want us to be seen together?"

"I was more concerned about Lorenzo, but he left on a ship just a little while ago. I think we are safe for now."

"Great, so what do you need?"

"If I let you into Lorenzo's lab, do you think you could find anything else about what Lorenzo is up to that may help us?"

"I would be happy to try, but all I have ever done is install our equipment and make updates as he requests them. But why don't you give me access, and I will see what I can do."

"Ok, great, let's go." They get up, and Emma follows Adam to Lorenzo's lab. With Adam's ID, he can open the door.

"Wow, you really are working for the emperor. Everyone here thought only Lorenzo could get in. Not even the janitors have access. He leaves everything for them outside his door."

Adam has a smirk on his face. "Yes, I can get everywhere."

"Ok, let me see what I can find. It might be better if no one observes you here. I can always say the door was open, and I was looking for Lorenzo if anyone sees me."

"Yes, good point. Call me later once you are done. Thank you very much for doing this."

"You are very welcome. Maybe you can buy me dinner."

Adam looks at her with a grin. "Let's discuss that when you call."

Emma grins back. "Great, will do." Adam then glances out the door to make sure no one is around. He walks out and heads to the main door to get back to his vehicle, then drives back to the palace to talk with John about how the day went.

As Adam arrives at the palace, a lot more security patrols around the complex. He drives in and parks, then goes to John's office. As he walks in, John asks him to come in and sit down. John then proceeds to tell Adam about the note from Eric, the discussion with Esteban, and the team on Ria 6. Adam then asks John if this was the same world they had to rescue his grandfather from. John confirms that is the case.

Adam then says, "Good. I would be happy to provide some payback to the rebels."

John then tells him no, not this trip. They need to be covert and try not to be seen or draw attention, as they do not want to make Lorenzo aware of what they know yet.

"Ok, they will not know we were even there for now, but we will have to reinvestigate this later if that is the case."

"Yes, Esteban said the same thing when we talked earlier."

"Perfect. We need to finish shutting the rebels down."

"Yes, agreed." Adam then tells John, Lorenzo spent most of the day at his lab and then left on a ship just as Adam was getting ready to leave, but he has a tracker on his ship. While he is explaining, Matt calls and tells him it looks like Lorenzo just landed on Korbin.

John states, "Ok, we know Lorenzo has other labs on that planet." Adam then points out he may know who is running that lab complex for Lorenzo—Emma's brother. "Wow, that is great. We will have to see if we can use him."

"Emma is going to ring me later, so I will get his contact information and reach out to him, but first, maybe we should send the guys to see what they can discover."

"Sounds like a good idea."

"I will reach back out to Matt and have him get Dave and go there." When Adam calls Matt, he tells Adam they were already on it, and he was just waiting for Dave so they could fly to Korbin. "You guys are great, but reach out to John if you need anything. I need to take a team to Ria 6 on another related issue."

Matt consents, "Ok, got it, good luck to you. We will talk when you get back."

"Good luck to both of you as well." Right after Adam finishes his call, Emma reaches out to him. "Hi, Emma, were you able to learn any more?"

Emma confirms, "Yes, there are some remarkably interesting things going on with Lorenzo. He has been working with quite a bit. I have information on several weapons. How about we meet for dinner, then give you all the data I have found?"

"Emma, I would love to, but I have to leave tonight on another mission for the emperor. Also, we have tracked Lorenzo to Korbin. Didn't you say your brother manages the labs there?"

"Wow, another mission for the emperor. You are busy, and yes, why? Do you need to talk with him also?"

"I would like to reach out to him to see if he has any information that could help us."

"Do you want me to ask for you?"

"No, I don't want to put you in the middle. You have already aided us so much and are already at substantial risk."

"I am happy to help however I can." Emma then gives Adam her brother's contact info.

"Thank you, Emma. If you want to leave the information behind the panel, I will have someone pick it up."

"Ok, then rain check on dinner?"

"Yes, rain check, and thanks again for your help."

Since Adam was still sitting in John's office, he could hear everything discussed between Adam, Matt, and Emma. John looks at Adam with a smile. "So, rain check on dinner."

Adam glances up with a grin. "Yeah, she thinks there could be something between us, and I am trying to find a nice way to let her know I already have someone."

"Do you mean Christina?"

Adam wears a puzzled look. "How do you know?"

"Kid, I have known you since you were born. Eric and I saw you and her the other night at your father's place, and we realized then."

"So, everybody knows then. What about Esteban?"

John laughs. "Of course, he knows. He has her watched all the time. She is the emperor's daughter, but you do not have to worry. He could not be happier. You have both grown up since your minor episode on Lucas 2. He is very proud of you both."

"Really?"

"Yes, it's all good. As for your other problem, be honest with her before it goes too far, and her imagination goes on about the two of you."

"Thanks, I get it, but in the meantime, Emma is going to leave the information from Lorenzo's lab in the loose panel. Can you fetch it since Matt and Dave are headed to Korbin and I need to go to Ria 6 tonight? Also, one more thing: can you remove the information about my accessing Lorenzo's lab earlier today in case Lorenzo gets suspicious?"

"No problem. I will go to the drop in the morning. Speaking of Ria 6, that transport ship landed there as we thought it would, and your team is waiting for you. They are at the last ship on the landing structure."

"Ok, great, then let them know I am on my way, and we can leave when I get there."

"You got it, kid. Good luck. Let me know what you acquire so I can update Esteban."

"Yes, sir."

Adam leaves the palace and heads to the landing structure. Once there, he parks his vehicle and goes to the ship. Seeing men standing outside the ship, waiting for him. When he reaches the group, he introduces himself to them. One of them says, "So you are the duke's son. We have heard a lot about you."

Adam questions, "All good, I hope."

The guy grins at him. "Yes, it's all good, and you are kinda famous."

"Famous, about what?"

"You have been in some big conflicts and helped settle them. We have been a tight group, but all of us are happy to work with you. We all know you can take care of yourself, and if it comes down to it, you will have our backs."

"You are right. I can and will. I take it John has already filled you in on what we are doing and where we are going?"

One of the other men puts in, "Yes, sir, we are up to speed and will follow your lead."

"Perfect, then let's get going." They all climb onto the ship and set a course for Ria 6. It takes a few hours. As they get close, Adam asks, "Is our radar jamming on?"

"Yes, sir," one of them responds. "I am considering someplace close, but secluded from where the transport ship landed. The good news is the freighter did rest in a fairly secluded location. There are several large warehouses, then another group of smaller builds, but not much else for miles around, so we should be able to enter without being seen."

The pilot says, "I see a small clearing over there." He points to his screen. "And with infrared, it seems there is no one around." He then turns the lights off, and they land in the dark. After docking, the pilot studies his screen. "I do not see anyone around, so we could exit without drawing any attention."

Adam exclaims, "Great, let's get close to the freighter and warehouse." They take off their IDs and change to dark covert dress attire, then leave the ship and head towards the freighter.

Getting near, only a few guards patrol around the warehouses, but not the ship. They move around to the other side by the ship. The side door is still open. Adam signals them to stay as he gestures he is going to the ship. Still not noticing any guards close, he quickly runs over to the side door and looks in. The shipment of Zando Crystals has already been offloaded, so he runs back to the rest of the men. "They have already delivered the shipment to the warehouse, so we will need to check them." They go back around to the other side of the buildings where the main doors are. Once there, most of the lights are off inside. They wait for the guards to walk to the opposite sides of the building. Then all but two of the men run in. The two outside watch to make sure the guards do not go into the building. Inside, the others slowly and carefully sneak around, looking to see if anyone is in there. The warehouse is completely filled with not just Zando Crystals, but other important minerals.

Adam states, "We need to get to the office and find an inventory list." They gradually move their way to the other side of the building. As they reach the office, Adam sees someone sleeping behind the desk. He checks the door to see if it is unlocked. It is, and he quietly opens the door, then rushes in, surprising the person behind the desk. As he jumps up and grasps for his communicator, Adam grabs him and quickly snaps his neck before the guard can alert the others. Two of Adam's men rush in as he kills the guard.

One man utters, "Wow, so the stories are true. You do not hesitate."

"No, we can't. No one can know we were here." Adam is rifling through the desk. "Here we go." He pulls up some paperwork. "They have been stocking this place for almost a year. This is crazy. We need to check the next building before we get out of here."

The men look at him. "Ok, let's go." They put the guard back in the chair and make it appear he is sleeping hunched over the desk.

As they leave the first warehouse, Adam tells them they may need to kill the other guards and make it seem like someone was robbing the warehouse. They all acknowledge him, then get to the exit and check with the men outside to make sure all is clear. Slowly, Adam opens the door. Not seeing the guards, they quickly leave, going back to the cover of dark, away from the building. As they get out of sight, the two guards march back toward the first building. Once the guards continue away from them again, Adam and his men move toward the second, even larger warehouse. They see a smaller door away from the main entrance. Once more, they leave two men outside while trying to enter the building, but the door is locked. Adam uses his tool to unlock it while the others watch for the guards. They enter the building. Just like the first one, it is also full of more minerals, but at the other end are boxes labeled armor. Adam breaks open one of them and sees thin, mesh-like suits. He pulls one out and hands it to the men. "Here, we need to take this back with us."

The one man says, "Ok," and puts it in his pack. Further down, they glimpse new-style fighter ships, four of them.

One man looks at Adam. "What are these? I have never seen anything like them."

Adam agrees, "No, me either. I thought I was flying our latest ships. Do we have images of all of this stuff?"

"Yes," replies one man.

"Ok, let's locate the office and see what else we can find out while we are here."

Another man puts in, "Sir, it looks like the office is up those stairs."

"Two of you stay here. The rest of you go with me." Adam and the two men left sneak up the stairs. As they get to the top, they hear men talking. Adam signals to the men behind him to wait. As he slowly looks over the stairs and down the hall, he sees two men walking towards him, unaware. He draws his sword, then runs up at them before they can warn anyone. He slices one man's throat, then runs his sword through the other. The two men behind him run up, and Adam continues into the office at the end of the hall with the two men behind. One looks at the other. "Wow, I thought I knew how to kill."

"Right. So did I. But he is quick."

"I would hate to be on the wrong side of him," the other one says.

Once in the office, Adam sits behind the desk. "There is nothing on or in here, but they never logged off this terminal. Let me see if I can find anything." After walking through a few of the files, Adam sees a larger inventory list. He plugs in his drive chip and copies the files, then shuts the terminal down to cover their tracks. "Ok, I think we accomplished our mission. Let's tear up the place a little downstairs to make it look like they were being raided, then head to the ship."

Back downstairs, Adam and the two men meet up with the other two. One of them looks at Adam. "Sir, we already tore up the place, so we can go."

"Excellent, then let's get out of here."

They get to the door, where one man outside tells them to wait. The guards have walked back almost to where they are, and one man inside asks, "Sir, should we just kill them?"

"No, they are not going in the building, just watching outside. That will buy us time to leave if they do not see us."

One man outside says, "Then sit and wait. Also, sir, there is another building further away, but the back door was open, and we could see it was empty."

"Great, thank you. What about the guards? Where are they now?"

"They are walking back the other way. Let's give them a minute." They sit there for a few, then get the all-clear sign, so Adam and the others open the door, peer around, then run out before they are seen. They look again. Not seeing the guards, they head back to their ship. Once back, they all strap in, then check their scanners if anyone is around to notice them leave.

The pilot looks at Adam. "Sir, we should be clear. I do not see anyone close enough if we head that way," pointing out in front of them.

"Perfect then, let's go."

As they leave, one man walks up to Adam. "Sir, we just wanted to say we now know those were not rumors, but the actual truth about you and your abilities."

Adam laughs. "Ok, thanks for the vote of confidence."

One of the other men adds, "Sir, also we would be proud to work with you anytime you think you may need us."

"I am always hunting for good men and would be happy to have you help me anytime."

A few hours later, they land back on Markus 2. Just as the sun rises, they leave the ship. Adam looks at them. "I was proud to work with you all. Glad I had you to cover my back. I am sure we will work together again at some point."

All of them concur, "Thank you, sir." Adam then leaves and heads back to the palace. Once he arrives, he heads to John's office with all the information, images, and the suit they took from Ria 6. At John's office, the lights are off, so John has not been there since last night. As he walks in, the lights go on. Adam places what they gathered on John's desk. He sits down on the chair next to John's desk, knowing John is always up early. If he waits for a few minutes, John will be there. Since Adam had been up early in the morning from the day before, being comfortable and knowing he's safe, Adam falls asleep. A short time later, John walks in. Seeing Adam is asleep, he quietly sits down at his desk and inspects what Adam places there. Suddenly, Adam jumps up and draws his sword.

John watches him and laughs. "Did we have a bad dream?"

Adam, still partially asleep, glances over at John, then smiles as he looks at his sword. "No, I heard a noise. It felt like I was still on Ria 6." Adam then puts his sword on the desk and sits again.

"It seems like you guys were successful."

"Sort of. I had to kill three. We tried to make it look like a robbery, and we do not believe we were seen by anyone else."

"Ok, good, I just got back from the lab complex and picked up what was behind the loose panel. I also chatted with Matt and Dave. Lorenzo is still on Korbin."

"Good, so let's discuss what we saw on Ria 6. Three warehouses were near the freighter. Two were filled to the max and guarded by the Ria 6 rebels. I thought you guys said there were not that many left. This place was in a remote part of the planet, and we do not know how many rebels there really are since we only observed five, and I killed three of them. Clearly, they must be working with Lorenzo if he is controlling how much is being mined and where the shipments are being taken to."

"No, you are right. We had not been worried about those rebels as we did not think they posed a threat, but we have a bigger problem now if Lorenzo is truly building special weapons for them, like what I see in the Images and what is listed on the inventories. What about this suit?"

"The box I took this out of was marked as armor, but the suit does not seem like more than very fine chain mail. But it is light, almost weightless. Also, if you notice, the pouch looks like it would be in the back with some small connectors. So, the question is what connects to it and what happens when it is connected?"

"Yes, these are all good points. I need to see if Esteban is awake and show this to him, but you need to sleep. You are no good to us the way you are now."

"Yes, you are right. I can barely keep my eyes open."

"Go. I will update Esteban, and the three of us can talk about our next steps when you're conscious."

"Sounds good." Adam then goes off to his room to sleep, and John heads to Esteban's office.

Not finding Esteban there, John walks down the hall to the main conference room. A large group of people is in there with Esteban at the end of the table. Seeing John standing outside, Esteban tells the people in the room to stop for a minute. He then waves at John to come in. "Is Adam back from his trip?"

John acknowledges, "He is, but we can chat when you are done."

"Are you sure?"

"Yes, sir, we have time. I told Adam to get some sleep."

"Very well. I will meet you in your office when we finish."

"Sounds good. Meet with you in a few." John then turns around and walks out the door, headed back to his office.

A few hours later, Esteban walks into John's office. He is still there, sitting behind his desk, writing notes on his terminal while looking down. He then glances up at the emperor.

"How did tracking the freighter go last night?"

"Very well. The list of questions keeps growing, but we have few answers still."

"What happened?"

"They found the ship on Ria 6 as we thought it was." John continues to apprise Esteban on his discussion with Adam from earlier, then shows Esteban the inventory list, the images, and the suit Adam brought back. "If you put this together with what I retrieved from the woman Adam is working with at the lab, that suit, when powered up, will be impenetrable to most weapons. Those ships in the Images will have stealth technology. You cannot see them on radar or visibly from the ground. According to those notes, Lorenzo is still having trouble making them work. It also mentions the platform Eric and Connor are looking for on Zada 5 and the failure here at the remote lab. So, everything he has been working on is not operational yet or finished."

"It appears we have three priorities. First, continue to track Lorenzo and see what else he is up to, and if we can track his progress. Second, understand why Lorenzo is hiding the excess minerals being mined and why he is showing less being delivered, causing the prices to rise. Then, last but not least, who is this Craven person, and if is he employed with the rebels on Ria 6, then how many rebels are actually left?"

While the two of them talk, Adam stumbles in, barely awake. They both turn and look at him. Esteban remarks, "You look like hell, and you got little sleep."

Adam says, "I got about three hours."

John exclaims, "You need more than that!"

With a smile on his face, Adam continues to wake up, rubbing his eyes. "I will get plenty of sleep when I am dead." John and Esteban both laugh.

John then says, "Yes, we both believed the same as you when were that young. Well, if you feel up to it, then let's discuss what we need to do next. I brought Esteban up to speed." John continues on their discussion.

"If Lorenzo is still on Korbin, then let me reach out to the guys to see if anything has changed. I also know who is managing the lab complex. I'll see if he'll help us."

Esteban responds, "We will have to be careful. He must be working closely with my brother."

"Yes, that is what I am hoping, knowing I will have to watch how he is approached and what he can do to help us till I know where his head is at."

John puts in, "We will need to figure out how many actual rebels there are on Ria 6, but we can deal with that later after we get more information about Lorenzo."

"Good, we can use the same team I went with last night. They were great. I felt they had my back the whole time."

"Perfect, I have utilized them for several other successful covert actions. They are my best squad."

"I told them I would be happy to work with them again."

Esteban asks, "To that point, John told me you had to kill three of the rebels. Are you ok?"

"Yes, I try to just look at it as part of the job. We are the good guys, trying to help people in the end. Then I do not bring it home with me, and it lets me sleep at night."

"That is a great attitude. You *are* helping and performing excellent work for us."

"Thank you, sir. I'll reach out to Matt and Dave and see how things have been going there, then call Roger on Korbin before I go. One more thing. Eric and Connor are completely out of the picture for almost three months?"

John sighs. "Yes, I am afraid so. There is no way in or out until the moons realign. We cannot communicate with them because of the asteroids encircling the planet. That is why Eric sent the note on the freighter ship for us, or we would have known nothing until they returned."

"I hope they will be ok then since we have no way to help them if they get into trouble."

"No worries. They found Mondo, so they will be fine. He was the head of the clans when they were warriors, before they became miners."

"Ok, great, I feel better about them being stuck there then. Let me reach out to the guys, and I will be on my way to Korbin."

"Sounds good. Take Esteban's personal transport so you can eat some food and rest while the pilot does all the flying. He can be discreet about where you land."

Esteban agrees. "Yes please. I would feel better if you did."

"Wow, really?"

"Yes really. I will let them know to expect you while preparing and waiting."

"Thank you. I truly appreciate it."

Esteban puts his hand on Adam's shoulder, then looks at him with a smile on his face. "Happy to do it." Adam shakes Esteban's hand, then walks out of the room.

Adam reaches out to Matt and Dave. They confirm Lorenzo is still at the building, and they can monitor him better, as he is using a lab in the back with a bank of windows, allowing them to see the whole room without being seen. Then he tells them about his plan to reach out to Roger, Emma's brother.

Both of them speak. "We hope he responds the same way that Emma has." Adam tells them he hopes for the same thing and he will be there in a few hours, then ends the call.

Before leaving for Korbin, Adam tries to reach Roger, but he does not respond, so he leaves him a brief message. He will be on Korbin this evening and would like to meet. Adam then leaves for Esteban's private ship to get to Korbin. Once Adam arrives, they are waiting for him. As he walks on board, the captain looks at him. "Sir, are you expecting anyone else?"

Adam responds, "No, we are good to go."

"Very well then, if you would like to take a seat over there." The captain points to a big comfortable reclining chair that looks like where Esteban would sit.

"Really? Are you sure, that one?"

"Yes sir, absolutely. It is the most comfortable seat on the ship." As Adam sits, the captain strides to the front of the ship to take off.

An attendant comes over to him with a tray of food. "The emperor told me to make sure you had something to eat. If this does not meet with your approval, I can bring you something else."

"No, this is perfect, thank you." As the ship takes off, Adam eats and then falls asleep. A few hours later, the attendant gently tries to wake Adam up. Suddenly, he looks at the attendant and jumps up.

The attendant is startled a little. "Sorry, sir, I did not mean to scare you."

"Not your fault. Too much going on, I guess."

The attendant says, "Well, now that you are awake, we are almost there. The captain would like you to join him."

"Very good. Thank you for everything."

"You are most welcome, sir."

Adam then goes to the front, opens the door, and sees the captain and his copilot. Adam rests in the seat behind them.

The captain comments, "Oh good, you're awake. You were sleeping hard back there."

"Yes, I have been going hard for a few days with not much rest."

"Then I am glad you could get some sleep on this trip, but we are almost there. Where would you like to land?" He pulls up a map of the area on his screen. Adam inspects the map and points to an area, which is a little secluded but not far from the labs. "Very well. We will be on the ground shortly." The captain hands him his information. "If you need a ride back, here is my contact information."

"Great, thank you for doing this. You have been very helpful."

"I was happy to do it." The captain shakes Adam's hand. Adam then gets up and walks out the door and back to where he was sitting. Just as they land, he grabs his pack. The captain strolls out the door. "Is there anything else you need before you leave?"

"No, I am good. Thanks again for everything." He throws the pack on his shoulder and marches off the ship.

CHAPTER VI
UNCOVERING THE TRUTH
PART II

ADAM, NOW ON KORBIN, WALKS FROM THE CLEARING for a while till he comes to the area where Matt and Dave are monitoring Lorenzo's lab. As he arrives, he sees Matt looking at the building. Matt is not aware of Adam, so he slowly sneaks up on him and points his finger in his back and says, "Hands up."

As Adam catches him off guard, Matt quickly swings around to hit who is behind him. Adam quickly ducks, laughing. "Man, you could have died."

Adam continues to chuckle. "Not if that was your best shot." Then they both laugh. "So, what is going on?"

"I sent Dave to the housing unit we secured to get some shut-eye, and Lorenzo has been working in that lab." He points at windows in the building and shows him the image from the scope. "Lorenzo has been in there since yesterday. He is sleeping inside as well. We've seen two other men going in and out of his lab. One of them has been spending a lot of time with Lorenzo. We sent images to John, and he could identify one of them as Andy like we thought. He has been working with Lorenzo for a long time, but we do not know who the other person is yet. We also know Lorenzo has a small place just outside the compound he stayed at in the past. If you go east of this compound, there are homes where most of the people live, then a lot of shopping and other amenities nearby. But on this side, it is more secluded, with a few units over here, one of which we are using thanks to John's help."

"I was able to rest before I got here, so I can relieve you if you like. It seems to be quiet for now and a good time to switch."

"Ok, that sounds good. If you need, we have a transport vehicle right over there." He points to Adam's right, then turns around and gestures in front of him. "You can almost see it the unit we can use for sleeping from here."

"Excellent. Then I am set for now. I will update you guys if anything changes."

"Sounds good. See you in a few hours." Matt then walks off to the housing unit.

Shortly after Matt leaves, Roger calls Adam back. Adam answers the call. "Hello."

"Adam, is that you? Wow, how long has it been? I think the last time we saw each other was when you left for break and never came back."

"Yes, you are right, but we can talk more about it in person. Would you have time to meet with me?"

"When will you be here?"

"Actually, I just arrived."

"Well, I am busy tonight, but how about breakfast tomorrow?"

"Yes, that works for me. Do you have somewhere in mind?"

"Yes, there is a place near my home. I will send you the information on it."

"Great, see you in the daylight."

"Perfect. I look forward to it."

The following morning, Adam visits Roger at the diner. As Adam moves in, he sees someone that may be Roger, but older and more mature. Adam walks over to his table. "Roger, is that you?"

The man stands and laughs as he reaches out to shake Adam's hand. "Yes, it is me. You don't resemble the same kid I remember, either."

With a big grin, Adam puts his hand on Roger's shoulder, grasping his hand. "It is great to see you again. It has been a long time."

"Yes, it has been." They both sit down at the table. Roger continues, "What have you been up to this whole time?"

"Well, after I left school, I was sent to take specialized training by my father so I could carry on with our family business, then started working for him."

"If I remember correctly, your father is the duke and provides security for the emperor, is that right?"

"You have an excellent memory. That is correct. We also settle new worlds to expand the emperor's universe."

"Wow, then you must be really busy. I hear about new worlds added all the time."

"Yes, I am very active working directly with the emperor."

"Then what brings you to my world?"

"In full disclosure, I ran into your sister back on Markus 2 a few days ago, and she told me you were managing the lab and R&D facilities here on Korbin. If so, how closely do you work with Lorenzo, the emperor's brother?"

"Actually, very close. He has a lot of special projects we have been occupied on together that are top secret, but if you are employed with your father and emperor, then you know all about them, I would think."

"Ok, this needs to stay at this table between you and me. We used to be close, and I always felt like I could trust you when we were kids."

"There has been a lot of time between us since then, but you can still have faith in me. Why? What's going on?"

"Lorenzo has been keeping his experiments from the emperor. I am sure you're aware of the accident on Markus 2."

"Yes, I was. Lorenzo told me right after. I understand Andy was there to help Lorenzo clean up the mess."

"Yes, he was, but he lied about what happened. The emperor and others got to the accident a little while after and saw some things once Andy and Lorenzo left the scene. The emperor launched an investigation of his own, which I am assisting with, and right now, we have lots of information but no real answers. Since the disaster, we have been tracking Lorenzo and trying to understand what he is up to. That is why I am here."

"Man, you are putting me in a bad spot. Lorenzo is my boss and the reason my family and I have such a great life here, but I also thought the emperor approved everything."

"No, which is the problem. The emperor does not know, but I can tell you that if you are worried about the life you have here, it will not be in jeopardy. The emperor knows you are helping us, and nothing will change for you or your family, and you will even have the gratitude of the emperor, which could lead to better things for you down the road."

"Boy, you have given me a lot to consider. I will need some time to think about it. Can you allow me till the end of the day?"

"Yes, as long as you do not say anything to Lorenzo. Also, he cannot know I am here, or you will blow our cover."

"No, my lips are sealed. I will not say a word. In fact, I need to meet with him next. He has simulated tests for us to run this morning."

"Ok, then I look forward to hearing from you later today. Either way, it has been great seeing you, and at some point, I would like to meet your family."

"Yes, I would enjoy that too." Then they stand up and shake hands. Adam leaves money on the table with the bill, and both walk out in separate directions.

After leaving the diner, Adam returns to Dave and Matt, monitoring Lorenzo's activities. They see someone walk into the lab with Lorenzo; it is Roger. Dave looks at Adam, then points to the monitor. "We still do not know who that guy is."

Adam says, "I do. That is Roger, the guy I just had breakfast with. He manages the labs here on Korbin for Lorenzo and is the older brother to Emma on Markus 2."

"Great, so is he going to operate with us also?"

"I gave him a lot to consider, and he asked if I could wait to let me know."

"Well, I guess that is fair, but you know even though he is a friend of yours, we cannot allow him to reveal our investigation."

Adam wonders how terrible he would feel if Roger said no, but what they are doing is too important. "I know, and if he tells me he cannot help us, I will take care of it."

"Are you sure? He is a friend of yours. Matt and I can do it."

"No, I tried to bring him in. This would be on me if he was not willing to help."

"Ok, but the offer is out there."

"Thanks, I appreciate it. I think I am going to get some sleep. I have been monitoring Lorenzo all night, but before I do that, let's see how Roger and Lorenzo interacted."

"Sounds good."

As Adam and Dave watch, Roger walks into Lorenzo's lab. Lorenzo and Andy are already there. Lorenzo glances up at Roger, then says, "Good morning. Running a little late, aren't we?"

Roger answers, "Yes, sorry I had breakfast with an old friend from school I have not seen in a long time and lost track of time catching up."

"No problem. Would it be anybody I would know?"

The question surprises Roger. "Well, er, no I would not think so." Quickly, he tries to change the subject, not wanting Lorenzo to know about his conversation with Adam. "Are you guys ready to start testing?"

Andy responds, "Yes, we were just finishing up the last adjustments. Do you want to validate against your specs?"

"Sure, let me take a look."

Lorenzo states, "If these tests go well, we will be able to do a live trial tomorrow."

"Great. I bet it would excite your brother, the emperor, to know."

Lorenzo smirks at Andy. "Oh, I bet he would."

Andy snickers, knowing Lorenzo has been doing all this work without Esteban aware of it.

Lorenzo then studies Roger. "Why would you bring up my brother?"

Roger answers, "Sorry, I just thought this is groundbreaking stuff, and you would tell him since he is your brother and emperor."

Lorenzo peers at Andy again with a puzzled look on his face. "Oh sure," then looks back at Roger. "You have never talked about my brother before. Why now?"

"Now that we are close to seeing our inventions function, we may get some recognition for it."

With Roger's back turned, Andy looks at Lorenzo and shrugs his shoulders while shaking his head.

Lorenzo questions why they are having this discussion now in a stern voice. "My brother gets all the updates he needs."

Roger tries to shut down the can of worms he has opened up. "Sorry, I meant nothing by it."

"It's ok. Let's just get on with the testing."

"Sure, you got it. I am almost finished checking the specs." In this conversation with Lorenzo, Roger realizes what Adam had told him is true. Lorenzo has not been informing his brother the emperor anything about what he is doing. Making Roger start to question why.

WHILE THE CONVERSATION IS GOING ON, ADAM HAS been watching, wishing he could hear what they were saying, concerned Roger may spill something to Lorenzo.

Adam continues to observe the three of them throughout the day, as they seem to be very busy moving back and forth inside the lab. Near the end, Matt comes to relieve Adam, who stayed to watch them, not wanting to leave, and had sent Dave back. Both looking at the screen monitoring the lab, Matt comments, "I wish we could hear them."

Adam laughs. "I thought that same thing this morning. The other problem is Lorenzo does not allow any cameras in his personal labs and only permits his people access here on Korbin. Even John could not get entry to them, which means I could not sneak in there like on Markus 2. If Roger will help us, we can bug Lorenzo's lab. Then we can get sound, and video, then not have to spend all our time trying to spy on what is going on from here."

"Which would be good. Winter is coming, and we will freeze if we have to stay out here. So, the other person in that lab is Roger? Dave told me about your conversation with him."

"Yes, it is."

Just then, Roger leaves the lab. A few minutes later, Roger calls Adam and asks if they can meet for a further discussion about the conversation they had that morning. Adam tells him sure, as soon as he is ready. Roger tells Adam to meet him in a secluded building on the far side of the complex. Adam can meet him there in about twenty minutes. Adam then glances at Matt. "I think I have him. He sounded very nervous and concerned."

A little while later, Adam meets Roger where he suggested, one of the largest buildings at the other end of the complex far away from Lorenzo's lab. It seems dark inside, and hard to see what is actually within from the office. Roger is already waiting. He looks at Adam as he walks in. Roger has a worried stare on his face, then says, "I tried to feel out Lorenzo based on our chat this morning, and I realized he does not want his brother to know anything."

Adam gasps, "What, are you crazy? You were putting yourself in a lot of danger!"

"I know, but I had to find out for myself before I betrayed my boss by helping you. I think I played it off fairly well. Nothing else was brought up after our short conversation when I first got to his lab."

"Ok, you are no good to us if Lorenzo does not still trust you, so does that mean you are in then and willing to assist us?"

"Yes, I am. If Lorenzo is doing all this work, and the emperor is not aware, I have concerns of my own about why he is hiding our business."

Adam hands him a small box with two small black round dots about the size of a small button in it. "What are these?"

Adam explains, "They are bugs, so we can see and hear what is going on in that lab. You will need to put them in a place where we can see everything between them, but you must also ensure they are concealed."

"Ok, I think I know where. Lorenzo told me he will leave the lab tonight to sleep at his apartment. We will do a live test in the next day or two. He needs to have a clear head. I should be able to place them while it is empty."

"Sounds good, but be careful."

"There was another reason that I asked you to meet me here." He points and walks to a door leading into the larger part of the building and then pulls a light out of his pocket. Adam follows him as they go through the door. Once inside, Roger points the light in front of them, then down the building. The building is full of stuff from end to end.

"What is all of this?" asks Adam.

"Lorenzo has been bringing in large quantities of Zando Crystals and other minerals. He has never said where they came from, and I could not find them on any inventory lists." They hike to the end of the building, where there are four more ships like the ones Adam saw on Ria 6. "These were built by our R&D labs, not at the manufacturing facilities on Markus 2. They are not on any inventory list either, and I am responsible for this complex and everything in it. You can see why I have had concerns of my own, but since Lorenzo owns everything, I had no idea where to go with my concerns. Since he is the emperor's brother, I did not think there was anyone higher I could speak to with this. Then you show up today, adding to my concerns.

Therefore, I had to test it with Lorenzo this morning. You coming has really been an answer to my prayers."

"Good, I am glad we can help each other here."

"Let's get out. I told security I had some work to do just in case they came around, but there will be lots of questions if they see you with me."

"Understood. Let me know when you have placed the dots and I will inform you if I can see them active."

"You got it. What else do you need me to do?"

"We will need all the data you can provide on everything Lorenzo is or has been doing. Then carry on with your normal routines."

"Give me a few days to gather everything. Then I will transfer it to you." They go to the door. Roger glances out to make sure security is not around, then signals Adam, and they both leave in different directions.

BACK AT THE LAB, SHORTLY AFTER ROGER LEAVES, ANDY and Lorenzo talk about him. Lorenzo states, "I am concerned about Roger, and his questioning whether my brother is aware of what we are doing. The last thing I need is anything getting back to Esteban when we are so close to the end here."

Andy demurs, "I don't think we need to worry about Roger. He has been very helpful. I am not sure we would have gotten as far as we have without him."

"Agreed. But once we have a successful test, then his work is done."

"Are you saying we need to get rid of him?"

"No, but we can push him off to something else and lock him out of the rest if we need to."

"Ok, good. I like Roger and would hate for anything to happen to him."

"Yes, so would I. But we can't let anyone impede what we are doing, or leak about it."

"Yes, I understand. You're right."

"As I said earlier, I need to rest. It has been a very busy couple of weeks, and I must sleep in an actual bed, not on the lab couch, for a few hours. I think we need to push the test out a few more days till I am fully rested before we do the live tests."

"Whatever you need. You want me to let Roger know we are going to wait?"

"Yes, please do." Lorenzo then leaves the lab, with Andy following him as they turn off the lights and lock the door. As Matt sees them go, he gets in the transport and drives around to the side of the building, looking for Lorenzo to come out. A short time later, Lorenzo comes out and gets into his transport, then drives away. Matt follows far behind him, after a bit, as Lorenzo pulls up to his apartment just outside the complex. He gets out of his transport and walks into his apartment. Matt parks a short distance away, observing the lights go on inside Lorenzo's apartment. Then, a little while later, they go out.

Shortly after Lorenzo enters his apartment, he reaches out to Craven. "I haven't heard from you since you left for Zada 5. I was concerned something happened."

Craven answers, "Sorry, no. I tested everything, and it all seems to work fine. There was a lot of debris on the platform, but I figured that was from the building collapsing before the window closed, so I just brushed it off."

"Yes, that makes sense. So where are you? I know clearly you must be off Zada 5, or I would not have been able to reach out to you."

"Correct, I am on Ria 6. I had to come back and meet with the rebels here. There was a break-in at the warehouses a couple of nights ago, and three of the guards were killed. The rebels could only track whoever broke in so far as the tracks disappeared. The rebels think it was merely thieves looking to rob the place. I had them step up security."

"Are the rebels almost ready to do what we need?"

"Yes, they will be prepared. That is why I was here making sure of it."

"Good. I have another issue. When can you come to Korbin? I want you here when we do the live testing."

"I need a few more days to finish here. Then I can join you."

"Ok, I will push the testing off. Let's speak tomorrow so you can tell me exactly when you can arrive."

"Fine, I will reach out to you tomorrow afternoon and let you know better on timing by then."

"Very good."

AFTER MEETING WITH ROGER, ADAM GOES BACK TO monitoring Lorenzo's lab. The lights are out in the lab. Also, both Matt and the transport vehicle are gone. Adam calls Matt, "Are you in front of Lorenzo's apartment?"

Matt responds, "Yes, how did you know?"

"I just left Roger. He told me Lorenzo was going there to get some actual sleep. He could not sleep in the lab anymore."

"Is Roger going to assist us?"

"Yes, he is. Roger is also placing our bugs in the lab tonight, so we will not have to hang out in that back area anymore as they continue to work."

"Excellent, so then do I need to remain to monitor Lorenzo here?"

"Just until I hear from Roger."

"Sounds good. Let me know when he is finished. Then the three of us can meet and talk about what's next."

"Yes, you got it. See you soon."

Adam goes back to the housing unit, where the three of them are sleeping. Right after walking in, Roger reaches out to Adam and tells him he has placed the bugs. Adam brings up the monitor and activates them.

"Yes, I can see both cameras, and I can hear you talking to me. We are good. Get out of there before anyone sees you. And thanks for your help."

"You're welcome. Talk with you later." Just as Roger walks out of the door, Andy comes walking up.

Andy says, "Roger, what were you doing in there?"

Roger, surprised, quickly thinks about his reason. "Oh, I forgot my coat when I left the lab. It is getting cold now. I needed it to go outside to the other building."

"I thought I heard you chatting with someone."

"It was just my wife. I was telling her I was going to be late for dinner since I needed to check on something. Why are you here?"

"I got a notice someone entered the lab."

"Oh, ok, but I am authorized, so why would you get a note about me?"

"You are right, but this is a secure lab, so I get one for everyone entering, even Lorenzo. All I have to do is log on and look up who accesses it."

"Why did you not do that with me?"

"I was not that far away and not near a terminal, so I walked over. If there was no one here, I would have had to look it up."

"That makes sense. Well, I am already delayed for dinner and need to go to the other building. You have a good night."

Seeing Roger start to walk away, Andy stops him. "Wait, one more thing. Lorenzo is pushing out the live testing a few more days, and he wanted me to inform you."

"Do you know why?"

"Lorenzo said he wanted to be fully rested before we do our live testing."

"Ok, I get it. Thanks for letting me know. I have plenty to do in the meantime." Roger then walks away.

Andy goes back into the lab, turns on the lights, then investigates around. Not seeing anything changed from when they left earlier, he turns the lights back off, then locks the door behind him.

Adam could hear the entire conversation between Roger and Andy. He waits, then reaches out to Roger, who answers as he is walking out the door. "Why are you calling? Were you able to hear all of that between Andy and me?"

Adam says, "Yes, I was. And I also saw Andy go back into the lab, snoop around, then leave again. Are you ok?"

"Yes, I was a little shaky. Andy caught me off guard, but it also lets me know they monitor anyone going in, so that will be helpful."

"Right, it will be. Thanks again. We will talk later. Have a good night."

"You as well."

Adam then reaches out to Matt to let him know the bugs had been planted. They were tested and working, so Matt could come back. Dave, hearing the whole conversation between Roger and Matt, looks at Adam.

"Then I take it, based on your conversation with him, he is onboard working with us?"

Adam concurs. "Yes, we are good to go with everything here. Roger is also obtaining all the information about what Lorenzo has been working on. They have a building here on the other end of the complex with a ton of material not recorded anywhere. According to Roger, he showed me tonight."

"So, you found one on Ria 6, and now we have one here. Why does he need so much, and why is it all off the books? This is clearly why the prices are going through the roof."

"You are correct. Again, more questions, but few answers. Hopefully, when Roger gets us what Lorenzo has been working on, we can acquire those answers."

"Yes, I hope so, for all our sakes."

Shortly after Adam's discussion with Dave, Matt walks in and glances at Adam. "So, what next?"

Adam answers, "I need to update John based on all that has gone on today." Adam then does so. John then reveals he did some investigation as well, and they could not find anything about the inventories from Ria 6 either, making the same statement. They have nothing but questions and no actual answers. Adam proceeds to tell him Roger will pass on all the information he can on what Lorenzo has been doing and his current projects, but it will take him a few days to pull it all together.

John then explains he went over all the information Emma provided, but it only backed up what Adam had found on Ria 6. It did not have any detail on how they worked, only stated that more testing was needed. It included talk about a sword-like weapon which could cut through anything when powered up, with incomplete blueprints, but not what the power source was.

Adam exclaims, "A sword! We found nothing like that on Ria 6. And Roger did not show me anything similar tonight, but I will reach out to Roger in the morning and see if he has any idea. One more thing, according to Roger, they are going to start live testing, then later, when I was listening to the bug, it was being pushed out a few days, but they did not say what they would be testing."

"Ok, let me know what else you find out tomorrow and when they will be experimenting."

"You got it. Will do."

The next morning, Adam reaches out to Roger to ask him what he knows about swords. Roger admits, "Well, I had heard rumors, but I have seen nothing myself. I will add that while I am pulling information on the rest, I am having trouble getting access, so it may take me a little longer to get everything on Lorenzo. I talked with Lorenzo this morning. He is still at his place, but has pushed out our testing to the day after tomorrow."

"So, what will you be testing?"

"This is game-changing stuff. We have developed a suit impervious to any weapon once it is powered up.

Then the huge one is a portal you just step through, and it will take you to another planet instantly."

"What? Are you kidding me? That must have been what John and Esteban saw on Markus 2 as part of Lorenzo's accident last week."

"It could be, but Andy told me he thought everything had shut down and did not think anyone saw."

"Yeah, not true. That is why I am here now. They saw the portal open for about a minute before the rest of the building collapsed. And Lorenzo has lied about what happened since then. Will you be doing the experimenting in Lorenzo's lab?"

"Yes, we have everything there, including a smaller version of the portal platform."

"What do you mean, a smaller version?"

"Once we can dial in on how much power is needed, then we control how long it stays open and how large we can make it. The test is for one person, but the plan is to allow up to five people at a time to step through, taking about two minutes per five. You can do the math. But how many people we could get through at a time will depend on how long the portal stays open."

"Wow, this is crazy. Why Lorenzo would want to keep this a secret is our concern. There is no telling what could be achieved with this technology."

"Yes, I agree. Well, let me get back to working to access the data."

"You got it. I guess we will communicate after you guys do your testing. We will watch and record, so we have proof."

"Ok, talk with you then."

Adam gets a message from Roger. Lorenzo has pushed out the testing two more days. The day of the test, Adam, Matt, and Dave sit waiting for Lorenzo and Roger to come in and start. While Adam and the others watch the lab, Roger walks in. Lorenzo stands there with someone else. As he strolls up, Lorenzo turns, looking at Roger.

"Good morning, Roger, this is Craven. I do not think you two have met." Craven puts his hand out to shake Roger's. Roger reaches out also as they shake hands.

Roger says, "Craven, is it? Nice to meet you."

Craven agrees. "Yes, nice to meet you as well."

Lorenzo explains, "I asked Craven to be here for our testing."

Roger smiles. "Oh good, we can always use an extra hand."

Craven says, "Great. Happy I can help."

They head toward the lab. Roger unlocks the door and walks in, turning on the lights and extra power sources on the wall.

Lorenzo states, "I think I want to start with the portal first."

Roger asks, "Really? That is going to take a while to get everything up and running."

"Yes, I know, but I want to make sure that is functioning. The suit is just an add-on. The portal is my priority for now."

"Ok, I understand. Give me a few to get everything in place so we can set up."

Just then, Andy walks in and sees Craven standing there with Lorenzo. "Oh Craven, why are you here? I did not think you needed to be for the testing."

Craven says, "Yes, Lorenzo reached out to me and asked me to come help."

"Then glad you are here."

Roger looks at Andy. "So, you guys know each other?"

Craven jumps in. "Yes, we have been working with Lorenzo for a while on some other projects."

Andy eyes Craven with a puzzled expression on his face. "Yes, other projects."

"Ok, good," Roger continues to move equipment around.

WHILE ALL THIS IS GOING ON IN THE LAB, ADAM WATCHES and hears their conversation. He looks at Matt. "Can you send a good quality image of that guy Craven to John so we can solve once and for all if this is the guy they knew?"

Matt agrees. "Yes, you got it. John will check shortly."

"Great."

BACK AT THE LAB, AFTER MULTIPLE HOURS, ROGER, WITH Andy's help, finally sets everything up. He then tells Lorenzo they are ready to begin.

"Great." Lorenzo then goes over to the main terminal and types in start on the platform program. The power supplies buzz from all the energy generated. Lorenzo then orders Roger to load the tubes. Roger opens a large steel box with six large tubes in it, about the same size as his arm, made of glass with a plugged opening at one end, lifting them out one by one. Roger pushes each of them into a channel open end first on the wall. As Roger pushes them in, a reading on the screen goes up until the last one is loaded saying 100 percent. Lorenzo then types in a few more commands. Suddenly, a window opens up over the platform. While Roger and Andy focus on the platform, Craven places something on the side of one of the power supply cabinets behind them.

ADAM LOOKS AT MATT AND DAVE, WATCHING WHAT IS going on in there. He then says, "Holy crap, look at that window. Can you see where that is?"

Dave exclaims, "No. But did you see Craven put something on that cabinet?"

Matt agrees. "I saw him. Can you tell what it was?"

Adam says, "No I could not. Do you think he's trying to sabotage the test?"

"Yes, it is possible."

"Dave, you stay here and continue to monitor things. Matt, come with me. I am going there just in case."

Dave acknowledges. "You got it. Be careful." Adam and Matt then head out the door.

Back at the lab, Lorenzo and Roger write down all the readings.

Lorenzo exclaims, "Everything is reading correctly, and the window seems stable. I am going to step through."

"Really?" Roger points to a stack of boxes in the corner. "I thought we were going to push these loaded crates through and make sure there were no issues."

"No. If I can make it, then we validate this is functional, the way we need it."

"I think it is a little reckless, but you're the boss."

Andy puts in, "I agree with Roger. This is reckless."

Lorenzo looks at Craven and nods his head, then steps through. Roger peeks out the window and sees Adam running towards the building. Then, suddenly, Craven squeezes a button in his hand. Both surprised, Roger and Andy watch him step through the portal just as one of the power supplies explodes, causing the other supplies to detonate, completely taking out the whole back of the building.

THE PERCUSSION BLOWS ADAM AND MATT BACK, HITTING the ground. Seeing what happened on the monitors, Dave comes running out and helps them both back to their feet. Adam stares at Dave. "What the hell happened there?"

Dave explains, "Well, Craven put an explosive device on the cabinet. First, Lorenzo stepped through the window. Then Craven squeezed his hand as he stepped through, and the room exploded."

"We need to get over there quickly and see if Roger survived." As they arrive, they can see the lab and other parts of the building were destroyed. Two mostly burned bodies lie lifeless on the other side of the lab, with a few small fires burning. "They murdered them both."

Just then, emergency services rush over. "What happened here?"

"It looks like something happened with the experiments they were working on, just like on Markus 2 last week."

One of the EMTs asks, "Do you know who those two are on the floor over there?"

"Yes, I think so. One is Roger, and the other is Andy. They both work here."

"Was anyone else involved?"

"No, no one that I know of. It looks like you guys have it now. We will get out of your path."

As they walk away from the destroyed building, Matt looks at Adam. "Why didn't you say anything about Lorenzo or Craven?"

Adam gives a slight laugh. "What should I have said? That they disappeared through a window before all hell broke loose?"

Matt laughs. "No, you are right. They would have thought we were nuts."

"Now we are even worse off. We have no idea where Lorenzo went or why he blew up the lab, and with Roger dead, we have no way to find out any information about that portal. We need to go to the building Roger showed me and see if we can find anything to clue us in."

They rush back to their transport vehicle, then ride over to the building on the other end of the complex. As they arrive, they notice a security guard nearby. Adam walks over to him and asked him to open the door. The guard wears a puzzled look on his face. "Why would I do that? Who are you?"

Adam pulls out his ID. "I am Adam Balcazar, my father is Duke Balcazar, and I am here on official business for the emperor."

"Sorry, sir, I did not realize who you were." The guard walks over and unlocks the door. "Here, but there is nothing inside."

"What do you mean? I was here a few days ago with Roger, and the building was full of stuff."

"Yes, sir, it was, but over the past two days, everything was loaded on transport ships and taken off-world. I was not given any information on where it was all going since it was approved by Lorenzo Colon, the emperor's brother." Seeing Adam is completely pissed off, he asks, "Is there anything else I can do for you?"

Adam takes a deep breath, then lets it out and says, "Sorry, no, there is nothing else. Thank you." The guard leaves. The three of them move into the building anyway and see for themselves: it is indeed barren.

Adam looks at both Dave and Matt. "This is insane. There were minerals and ships, and it's gone now. Where did they take it all?" At the complex, since ships were landing and leaving constantly, they had no way of knowing the building they were in was being emptied and shipped off the world.

They walk out of the building. Matt looks at Adam. "So now that we are totally screwed, what next?"

Adam still fumes over all that has happened. "I can't believe this. We need to reach out to John."

Just as he says that, John calls him. "I just saw the image you guys sent. That is the Craven we worked with. Do you still have eyes on him?"

"Well, no, not really."

"What do you mean, not really?" Adam then proceeds to tell John everything. John, in a loud pissed-off voice, demands, "Are you F'ing kidding me? How the hell could this have happened? We are now back to where we were when we started! Sorry, I am not mad at you guys. You did everything you could and had no way of knowing Craven would blow up the place. Do you think you can do anything else there?"

"No, we need to regroup."

"Ok, then you guys should come back here. We will work on a new plan tomorrow. I will see you in the morning."

"Sounds good. Talk with you then." Adam then stares at Matt and Dave. "Wow, I have never heard John lose it. No matter what has happened in the past, he has always kept his composure."

They both respond at the same time, "Right? Neither have we."

"Ok, let's pack up and get out of here." They ride back, pick up all their equipment, then journey over to the transport ship, load up, and leave for Markus 2.

AFTER LANDING BACK ON MARKUS 2, MATT AND DAVE agree to meet at the palace in the morning. Adam then goes to the palace to get some sleep. The next morning, as Adam is getting up, he gets a call from Emma, crying, "Adam, where have you been? I have been trying to get a hold of you. Did you hear about my brother?"

Adam says, "Yes, sorry, I was going to reach out to you this morning. I know about your brother because I was there."

"WHAT, YOU WERE THERE?" She gets hysterical, crying louder.

"It was Lorenzo. He murdered Roger. I saw the whole thing."

"What? Why would he have done that? Was my brother working with you too?"

"Yes, he was, but there was no way Lorenzo could have known."

"Then why would Lorenzo kill my brother?"

"The only thing we could think was Lorenzo had planned to do this. Right before Lorenzo and another person with him, Craven, stepped through that transport window, he blew up the place, killing your brother and Andy."

"So, Andy is dead as well?"

"Yes, they were both there when the lab exploded."

"Andy was here two days ago. And since then, all the files I had been exploring for you were erased. They have locked me out of everything related to anything Lorenzo was working on."

"What, so we cannot get any more information?"

"No, which is what I am saying. I am completely locked out, so there is nothing else I can do to help you."

"I am very sorry about your brother and getting you involved."

"Thank you, but it doesn't help. I can't believe he is gone. If Lorenzo was here right now, I would kill him myself. Please tell me you are going to make Lorenzo pay for this."

"Yes, you have my word. Once we find Lorenzo. I will also let the emperor know what happened here, and you and your brother's family will be taken care of."

Emma says, "I do not care about myself, but thank you for helping my brother's family."

"You're welcome. I will touch base with you in a few days."

"Thank you, Adam. You're a good man."

"I try to be." While Adam talks with Emma, he walks down the hall to John's office. As he walks in, John is already there, sitting at his desk.

Adam looks at John. "Did you hear all of that?"

"Yes, I did. So, Emma can't get us anything else, either?"

"Nope, she is locked out, and the files have been erased."

"I studied the video last night several times and could not get a good look into the window to see where Lorenzo went, but what concerns me, even more, is that Craven is working with him. He is a very dangerous person, so we have even more reason to be concerned about what Lorenzo is up to and where he went. And now we have no way of figuring out what else he is planning. I updated Esteban last night, so he is aware of all of this."

"The guys should be here shortly, and we can figure out our next steps."

"While we were waiting, I had one of my techs look at the files Emma copied on the drive. He could break the encryption. The files show the portal Lorenzo created. It talks about using Zando Crystals, but he was still controlling how long to keep the portal open. The experiments on Korbin would help figure that out. But unfortunately, when they broke into the files, some of them got corrupted, so there is still a lot of information missing. I have the team working to see what they can restore."

"Then we are back to square one with lots of questions, no answers, and no idea where Lorenzo is."

"Yes, that is right."

"Do you think they could have gone to Zada 5, where Eric and Connor are? That is what Lorenzo was working on before the remote lab was blown up here, right?"

"Yes, that is a good point, but we are going to have to wait for Eric and Connor to return before we will know. There is no way in or out until the alignment."

CHAPTER VII
ZADA 5, CONNOR

Back on Zada 5, the morning after their encounter with the creature "Andorra" in the cavern, Eric, Mondo, Renaldo, and Connor meet for breakfast in the main room. While eating, they talk about their plans. Eric and Connor have to wait for the next opening so they can leave the planet. Renaldo looks at Mondo. "Last night, I went over the list you gave me for the minerals needed to build new swords. Some of them are very rare and will be hard to find. I put the word out. Right now, there is not enough for one sword, but I have people searching for more, so we will require a few days."

Mondo agrees. "That's fine. We have almost three months before the window opens again, so we still have some time."

Connor states, "I want to go back to the cavern and see if we can find the blocked exit. Andorra is going to be a critical part of our support in a future battle. I saw visions of that last night when I was sleeping. I tried, but could not get a clear image of how yet."

"Sure, we can work on that. An engineer in town can help us figure out how to get it open once we locate it."

Eric looks at Mondo. "I heard you have a match happening tonight."

Connor perks up. "A match?"

Renaldo explains, "Yes, we call them clan wars. We are no longer warriors, but we still have matches between clans. The winning clan takes the title of head clansman for the year."

"Excellent. Can anyone fight?"

Mondo says, "No, first, you have to be part of a clan. Then you need to fight within the clan and win the honor of competing against other clansmen for the title."

"Then how do I become part of a clan?"

Eric asks, "What are you thinking? Would you really want to compete?"

"Why not? We will be here for three months. I cannot think of a better way to keep my edge and pass the time."

Renaldo and Mondo both look at Connor and then laugh. "This is no dance. We use real weapons. They wear some protection, but some have been seriously hurt," says Renaldo.

"I am not concerned. Ask Eric. I can handle my own. If you would let me, I would like to compete."

Eric concurs, "Yes, in some ways, he is actually a better fighter than his brother. But Connor, keep in mind, you could get seriously injured here."

"No, I get it. I am willing to take that chance."

Mondo says, "If you are sure, we can set you up to fight tonight against two from our clan. If you win, then we will officially welcome you in, allowing you to compete for the title."

Renaldo says, "This should be interesting."

Connor grins. "Yes, it will be fun. Thanks, Mondo, for your support."

Mondo replies, "Don't thank me yet. This will not be a cakewalk. The men you will fight will not be happy that a stranger is coming in."

"Perfect. The tougher, the better." The three of them eye Connor and laugh.

"It's your head," says Eric.

Mondo then looks at Connor. "We should get going. I asked the engineer to meet us at the mine if you want to check for that opening."

Connor exclaims, "Great, let's go."

Renaldo nods at them. "I will meet up with the three of you later. I am going to find the minerals we need."

Mondo agrees. "Sounds good." The three of them climb into a transport vehicle and head toward the mine.

When they get there, the engineer, near the opening, talks with the guards, waiting for Mondo to come. He looks at Mondo. "The guards would not let me in without your approval."

Mondo says, "Yes, that is correct. It is actually for your safety."

"Why? Are the stories true? Something is in there?"

"Yes, but with Connor here, we are safe."

"Why Connor?"

"Connor can communicate with the creature."

The engineer says, "You're kidding. Really?"

"Yes, really." They then start to walk in. "You will soon be able to see for yourself." As they enter the first cavern, two men sit near the equipment on the far end, working on the gear as they get closer.

Eric asks, "Have you guys been able to figure this stuff out?"

One man glances up. "Well, we have been working on this all night and are going to need a few more days, but so far, it seems like this is just a receiver. We could not find any way to activate a window, as you described. We think a sending unit must generate it, wherever that is. Give us a few more days to provide a better readout."

"Thank you for trying to figure it out for us."

"You are welcome. We are always up for a challenge," responds one of the techs.

The three of them, with the engineer, continue towards the second cavern. Connor is already hearing Andorra in his head, and says, "Andorra knows we're coming, and she is glad we are."

The engineer looks at Connor. "You are talking with her now? I do not hear anything."

Connor says, "We speak through our minds. Each day gets easier, and we can chat further apart."

The engineer says, "This is a trick. How do we really know you can communicate with it?"

"When we get into the other cavern, you will see." As they walk through the tunnel to the other cavern where Andorra is, she is standing, almost dancing, moving from one foot to the other, excited to see Connor again.

"Holy crap, it is real? What is it?"

"It is a she, and we are not sure what she is since it is so dark in here, and we cannot really observe her that well, but we think she may be an actual dragon."

"But if she is a real dragon, where are her wings?

"They may be folded on her back, but we cannot tell. She is telling me she was able to soar in the sky before she got trapped, and that is why you are here. She also told me there used to be a way out through the top of this cavern, over there, where that pile of rocks goes up the wall."

The engineer walks over. "Yes, there was a cave-in at some point, and we would need to use explosives to clear it."

"No, she will not go for that. She lost some of her children when they opened this cavern, and she is afraid of that noise."

The engineer says, "We could try from the top and come down first. Let me take some readings of where we are and find the opening from outside." The engineer pulls out his device and captures his analyses. "Ok, I think I have what I need."

"Great, I just let her know what we are trying to do and that we will be back to give her a way out." He walks over and pats her side, and actually talks, saying they will be back soon. She bends her head and rubs his, letting out a slight roar, her way of thanking him. She then communicates she knows he will do battle tonight and that he will need to be careful. If so, he should be victorious. If not, he will be badly hurt. "You mean you can see into the future?"

She responds, "Yes, I have visions of things that have not happened yet, the same way I have had visions of you for many years now. That is why when you came in yesterday with your hands up, I stopped, knowing you would not hurt me."

Connor, again actually speaking, says, "Then I am glad you knew that," patting her again. "We will be back in a few days once we know how to free you. In the meantime, is there anything we can bring you?" Andorra then communicates she has had no real meat in a very long time. "Sure, we can make that happen. I will have some sent back for you." Connor then glances at Mondo. "We need to get her some meat."

Mondo agrees. "Sure, just if she promises not to eat whoever brings it."

Connor laughs. "No, she will not swallow anyone. She now knows we are here to help her, not hurt her." They all then walk out. "We will be back in a few days. Enjoy the food we send you." As they leave, Mondo tells the guards that they will be send food for the creature and to let them through. The guards acknowledge.

The engineer then points up. The mine is at the base of the Desert Mountains. "I will need to bring some men back with me, and we will have to climb up there to find the spot where the cave-in was."

Mondo agrees, "Ok if you run into any issue, let me know." The three then get back into the transport and head back to where they are staying. Once they arrive, Mondo says to Connor, "You should get some rest. It is going to be a busy night for you."

"Ok. Wake me up in a few hours." Connor then goes up to sleep.

A few hours later, Eric wakes Connor up. As he sits on the bed, Eric studies him. "I think you are nuts. Are you really ready for this?"

"Absolutely." Connor jumps up.

"Ok. Mondo is downstairs waiting for us."

"Fine, give me a few. I will be right down." Eric then heads downstairs. Connor goes into the bathroom and looks in the mirror at himself. "Are you really ready for this?" He smiles at himself. "Good." He finishes getting dressed, then walks downstairs, meeting Mondo and Eric. "Ok, let's go." The three of them go outside and get into the transport. Mondo then takes them to the arena. They go into the door marked Clansmen.

As they get through the door, one of the two men monitoring it asks, "Mondo, sir, why are you here?"

He eyes them, then says, "I have brought someone here that wants to fight for my clan."

The man looks at a lean, 200-pound kid about six feet tall. "Really? This kid? Are you sure?"

"Yes, I have set up two qualifying bouts for him tonight."

"Yes, we heard all about it, but we did not think it was some young kid," responds the man.

Connor just watches them and grins. "You will not think 'young kid' when I am done."

The other man at the door responds, "Really? You sound pretty cocky. I hope you're right, or they will be carrying you out of here."

Right then, Renaldo comes walking in. "Good, you just got here. Mondo, you may want to stop Connor. The clan is not happy about an outsider trying to come in."

Mondo demurs, "The old rules say an outside clan's man has the right to challenge to join."

"Yes, you are right, but he is not from one of the other clans. He comes from off world."

"But he is part of the clan that conquered our world, the Balcazar Clan. That is how I am setting this up."

"Ok, but they have set this up for Connor to fight our toughest warriors together in one contest."

Connor says, "That's good. I would have expected nothing less. It would not have been a true test if they weren't."

"Well, ok. If you are sure."

"I am, so where do I go to get ready?" One man from the front door tells him they can use the second room on the right. They all go in and help Connor prepare. Mondo finds the leather armor, shaped like a clamshell, that pulls over the head. It covers the chest and back down to the waist and hooks on the sides. It also has covers hooked at the shoulders, down the outside of the arms to the back of the hands. They are all linked together in several pieces, allowing arms and hands to move.

Mondo hands it to Connor. "This isn't really armor, but it is what our warriors used in ancient times and what they agreed to for these tournaments." Renaldo helps Connor put it on. Mondo then hands him a sword. It has a cover on the tip, and the body is not very sharp.

Connor asks, "So is the tip guarded so we cannot stab anyone?"

"No, there is a sensor, so you can score points. It will also sense body hits, so keep that in mind as you are fighting them."

"Ok, got it. Anything else I should know?"

"The battle duration is thirty minutes, so if more than one person is standing, the clansman with the most points wins. We were able to set your fight to be first, so you would not have to wait long."

"Great."

After sitting in the room waiting for about thirty minutes, they hear announcements in the arena. One man, watching the door when they came in, tells them they are ready for Connor to come out. They all follow Connor to the main entrance, a round arena about fifteen yards across. As he walks in, two clansmen dressed like he is, stand in the middle. They gawk at this kid that comes walking in. Opponent 1 demands, "Are you kidding me? Can you even shave yet?"

Opponent 2 says, "Kid, this will be quick, and you will not remember it."

Connor just watches them with a stern face. "We'll see. Let's get started."

The first one replies, "Just waiting for the horn." They stand for another minute as someone announces the three of them. Three spots are set in the ground. The two warriors go over to each. Connor follows suit and makes his way over to the spot behind him. A minute later, the horn blares. The two warriors run toward him. He ducks to miss the sword of one, then elbows him, causing the first warrior to crash into the second. They both tumble to the ground. Connor drop-kicks the second, then rolls up and hits the first with the hilt of his sword, knocking him to the ground. He then rises back up and moves at Connor, who throws him to the ground.

Both of the warriors rebound, swinging their swords viciously, but he deflects their attacks. The first warrior oversteps his footing, and Connor pounds him in the head, knocking him out. The second warrior launches himself again and battles Connor relentlessly with his sword. Eventually, Connor knocks the blade from his hand and puts it at his throat, telling him to yield, to no avail. The warrior fights back, so Connor pounds him to the ground, shoving the sword into the armor on his chest and giving him a glare to yield. If the sword were real, the blow would have been fatal. The warrior surrenders, raising his hands in submission as the other warrior rises. Connor does a spin kick, hitting him in the head and knocking him out again.

Mondo is so excited he goes running in. They were all watching Connor from the arena entrance. When he gets to Connor, he grabs his hand, raises his arm, and starts yelling, "Winner, winner!"

The crowd, thrilled at the battle they just saw, all yell, "CONNOR, CONNOR, CONNOR!"

Mondo looks at Connor. "That was a great fight. You are an amazing warrior."

A little winded, Connor clearly had been in a fight. "Thank you. That was more fun than I thought it would be. So, when is the next one?" He laughs. By this time, both Eric and Renaldo had come up. Hearing Connor, they start laughing as well. Just then, the two men he had just attacked come over and shake his hand.

"We totally misjudged your fighting abilities. We will never call you a kid again. Congratulations."

"Thank you very much. I really enjoyed it."

They grin at him. "Well, glad someone did."

THE NEXT MORNING, CONNOR SLOWLY WALKS IN TO meet the others for breakfast. Mondo, Eric, and Renaldo are already at the table. They stand up and clap. Mondo declares, "That was quite a show last night. Looks like you are moving a little slow this morning."

Connor agrees. "Yes, I am hurting in places I did not know I had." He then comes and joins them at the table, and the others sit down as well.

Renaldo asks, "Well, what would you like to talk about first?"

"Um, where are we with opening the cavern up for Andorra?"

"The engineer will be here in a few to tell us what he found. I also have few people surveying for the minerals to build the swords, but one mineral is really rare, called Verbraso, and right now, we only have about a quarter of what we need for one sword. Apparently, this allows all the minerals to bond together as part of the process. The other minerals we will possess by the end of the day tomorrow."

"Do you have that mineral here with you?"

"Yes, I do. Why?"

"Maybe we can show it to Andorra, and she can help us find more."

Eric inquires, "Really? How could she?"

Connor, hearing noises in his head he cannot make out, manages to say, "I don't know, but something is telling me she can."

Renaldo agrees, "Well, ok, then maybe we can visit her later today and see what she can do."

Just then, the engineer strides in with a few of his men. "Gentlemen, I believe I found the remains of an old cave that had collapsed many years ago and filled in. We found it by digging around the coordinates I took from below, but we are going to have to blast. The creature should hear nothing till we get close to the cavern, but we wanted to check with you first and maybe warn it."

Connor says, "Ok, sure, we were discussing going back there anyway, so I will advise her."

The engineer says, "Great, then we will head over there now. May I also express that was one hell of a fight last night, and we are glad you are battling for our clan now."

"Oh, you saw." Connor smiles.

"Everybody either saw it or is gossiping about this morning. You took down two of our best like they were nothing. There are already rumors you are the one."

"The one what?"

Mondo chuckles. "You mean the legend?"

The engineer says, "Yes, sir, we are."

Connor starts to laugh too. "Well, we do not know what Andorra is yet, and we already have an emperor, Esteban. I am not really considering taking his place, and your world is no longer at war, but thank you for thinking it is possible."

"You are welcome, but be prepared. Everyone knows who you are now."

"That was not what I wanted, but thank you for letting me know."

The engineer shakes his hand, then leaves with his men.

Eric then chortles. "Well, Connor, you managed in a few days what took us months."

Looking at Eric, Mondo beams. "You're right. He did."

Renaldo steps in. "That brings us to the following subject, your subsequent fight. It will be next week, but now that everyone thinks you may be part of the legend, your bouts will get even harder."

Connor asks, "Why is that?"

"In our beliefs, if a warrior can defeat his enemy, they take on their powers. So, if you are the legend, then they will become the legend. You and I both know that is not true, but it is stronger encouragement for your opponent to compete harder."

"Ok, good."

Mondo exclaims, "Good! Kid, do you have a death wish?"

"No, I simply want to be challenged. The harder it is, the better I will become."

Eric asks, "Is this about your brother?"

"No—well, maybe a little. He is a real badass, and I want to be more like him."

"Well, if you continue like last night, when we leave, I do not think that will be an issue."

Renaldo is awed. "You mean there is another Connor out there?"

Eric laughs. "Oh yes, Connor's older brother, Adam, has been out there battling for a while now and has built quite a reputation for himself as well."

"I am glad we are all friends then."

With a laugh, Mondo puts his hand on Renaldo's shoulder. "Yes, so am I."

As their discussion ends, they go downstairs and climb into the transport to head back to the cavern and Andorra. When they arrive at the mine, guards are still posted at the front entrance. As they hike up to the entrance, one guard says, "We let the men in with the meat for the creature. They came out ok, but were a little unsettled when they realized who they were bringing it to." He then chuckles. "Since they came back out, I guess the creature enjoyed the meat and not the men."

They all laugh. Mondo agrees. "Yes, I guess so. Thank you for your help." They proceed into the mine.

Eric says, "Since we are here, let's see if the techs could find out any more about the equipment." The four of them head that way. Two men are still there, but this time, the equipment is running. Eric inspects them. "Well, have you been able to figure this stuff out yet?"

One of them gazes up at Eric. "Yes, we think we have, and we were right. This is a receiving unit only." He points to the platform. "This unit is activated when the sending unit either turns on or shoots a signal to it to turn on. We have never seen anything like this equipment before this all very new technology."

"Thank you for working on this."

Mondo muses, "Maybe we need to post men by this in case someone or something comes through."

"Yes, good point."

"I will talk to the guards outside about it when we leave."

Eric instructs the technicians, "When you guys are finished, put everything back the way it was. They may try to use it. If so, we might catch them on the other side."

One of them responds, "Ok, it will be done."

After speaking with the technicians, they go over to the second cavern. Once they get there, Connor hears Andorra in his head, telling him she was glad that his fight went successfully, and he was not really hurt. Connor responds, "You already know what happened?"

Andorra answers, "Yes, I knew you would be fine, but I could not be sure you were not really hurt until I saw you."

Connor kind of laughs. "Ok, so how was the meat last night?"

"Delicious. It has been a long time since I have had a meal so good."

"You are very welcome. We were happy to. The man from yesterday is working outside above us. He has to use explosives, like what opened the end of this cavern and broke your eggs, but they will not hurt you this time, so do not be scared."

"I will try."

"Good, one more thing." Connor glances at Renaldo. "Can you bring the mineral here?"

Renaldo hesitates. "Are you sure it is ok to come closer?"

Connor smiles. "Yes, absolutely. You're safe."

Renaldo then comes over and hands the mineral to Connor. He then opens the small container and shows it to Andorra. "We are surveying for this. Would you be able to help us unearth it?"

She smells it. "Yes." Ambling over to the other end of the cavern, she scratches on the wall, and they see something sparkling. "You will find some of that stuff there." Connor calls Renaldo to come over, pointing to the spot she scratched out.

Renaldo pulls a small hammer and chisel from his pocket, then digs into the wall. As he opens it up, a large vein of the Verbraso appears. "Wow, there is a lot, I think, more than we would need. Tell her I will bring some men back here to mine this. Once we have, we should have everything we need to build new swords."

"That's great. I will tell her." Connor lets her know what Renaldo said, then asks if she needs anything else before they leave.

Andorra responds, "Yes, I would like some more meat. I have been eating nothing but rats and bats for a long time, and that meal yesterday was wonderful."

He responds, "Sure, we would be happy to have more brought to you."

"Is there anything else I can do for you?"

"If you can watch the tunnel to the other cavern, we have stuff in there, and other people could come in."

"All right, I spend most of my time sleeping. Any change is welcome now that I know you are not coming to hurt me."

"You are correct. No one should come to hurt you anymore. If there is, one of us will come to warn you." They all then turn around and walk away.

As they reach the other cavern, Mondo says, "Oh, I forgot. I have something for you." Looking at Connor, he hands him a thick envelope.

Connor blinks at him. "What is this?" As he opens it, he sees a lot of currency.

"These are your winnings from last night."

"What? I did not fight for money."

"Yes, I know, but this is what the purse was for the winner. Since I entered you, they gave me the money."

"That is great, but again, I was not in it for the cash. Maybe it is a good thing, as Andorra wants more meat." He hands the money back. "Please use this to pay for a regular delivery for her."

"If you keep winning, she will eat like a queen."

Connor laughs. "What do you mean, if?" They all chuckle and exit the mine. Mondo tells the guards to place one sentinel by the equipment inside the first cavern, in case it gets activated remotely.

The guards frown at him. "What do you mean, activated?" Mondo tells them it is a portal that could connect to another world; they gawk at him and laugh. "Are you on some sort of medication to make up a story like that?"

Eric glares at them. "This is no joke. That brought us to this planet and that cavern."

"Ok, sir, sorry for laughing. We will get someone in there right away," responds the guard.

"It's ok. I would not have believed it either if we did not see proof."

They head back to the colony. Once they get there, Renaldo leaves to gather some men to take out the Verbraso Andorra found. Mondo also located a place nearby with the equipment Connor needed to train and get ready for his next fight.

After a few days, Renaldo, with help, mined all the Verbraso at the spot in the cavern. Then he reaches out to the old blacksmith, but he cannot travel, so Renaldo has to take everything to him to forge the new weapons. Arriving to the old man's village takes a few days. The blacksmith inspects the minerals and information about constructing the new swords. He tells Renaldo he heard Renaldo was working with Connor, as he had caught the allegations and how he won. Renaldo looks at the old man and laughs. "It has only been a few days, and you are already aware of the fight?"

The old man says, "Yes, but it's more so about the rumors that Connor is the one. Did you really find a dragon, and can he talk to it?"

"Well, we still are not sure what the creature is, but yes, he can speak to it."

"So, then, the rumors are true. If one of these swords is for him, it will take me about six months to create five new ones." After looking over the information, he tells Renaldo a few steps were missing, but his ancestors were the craftsmen that forged the original ten Clansmen swords, so he has the real instructions, passed down from generation to generation. The blacksmith tells Renaldo when he is close to finishing, he will reach out so Renaldo will have an idea when they will be completed and can make the trip to fetch them.

Renaldo gets back almost a week later, just in time for Connor's next fight. Normally, the bouts move and are hosted by the next clan combating, but because Connor is rumored to be the one, everyone wants to come to battle with him. All the clans agreed the fights would remain in the same arena Connor first fought at to honor him.

Renaldo walks in to where they are all staying and sees Mondo and Eric standing there. He looks at Mondo. "I got everything to the old blacksmith. He said it will take about six months to complete the swords. He also mentioned his ancestors created the original swords."

Mondo states, "Excellent, then the swords will be constructed correctly."

"Yes, that is what he said, as your instructions were missing critical information."

"Perfect. Thank you for taking care of it."

"It was my pleasure. Are we waiting for Connor to come down?"

Eric responds, "Yes, he should be here shortly."

"Good. I broke all kinds of speed records getting here. I did not want to miss his next fight." Eric and Mondo laugh.

Mondo adds, "You were not the only one. I am not sure the arena could hold any more people. I have never seen it this full."

"Right, I do not think anyone has not heard of Connor at this point. The blacksmith was almost two days away, and he has already learned the rumors."

Eric sighs. "This is crazy, but if anything happens to Connor, I will have a hard time explaining it to his father."

Mondo declares, "Well, his father trained him to be a warrior. This is what they do."

"True, but it would still be a difficult story to tell."

Renaldo agrees. "Very true, but I would not want to be the one to inform his father, either."

While the three of them chat, Connor comes towards them and hears the last part of the conversation. "None of you have to worry. I may get hurt, but I will not die."

Eric asks, "Why do you say that?"

"I have seen it."

Mondo appears skeptical. "Again with the visions?"

"Yes, some of these battles will be really hard, but I will make it through alive." Connor put his hand on Eric's shoulder.

Eric says, "If that is what you believe, let's go with it for now."

As they reach the arena, a large crowd waits to see Connor before he marches in. They all cheer him on, with several men standing by the door trying to keep them back so he can enter. Connor glances around, shakes a few of their hands, then says, "This is crazy. I was merely looking for a way to keep my edge, not draw a gathering."

Mondo says, "The word is out, and, wanting it or not, you are now famous." As they walk into the arena, more people fill the inside. Two of them are the men he defeated the week before.

One of the men he fought says, "Connor, sir, we are here to offer our services to help you train for future battles. We also wanted to warn you about other clansmen, very angry about an off-worlder competing and already being called the One. They will do whatever it takes to stop you."

Connor shakes their hands. "I appreciate you two letting me know. Thank you." He then paces into the room to get ready for his fight.

While they are in the room, helping Connor prepare, Mondo looks at Connor. "The opponent you're up against tonight is from one of the clans that does not want to accept you as the One. He will do whatever he can to take you down and prove you are not."

"Good. Then it will be a real fight."

Eric exclaims, "A real fight. Do you have a death wish? They will seek to put your head on a plate."

"Like I told you before, the conflicts may be tough, but I will not die. I need to do this to stay sharp for what's coming. I know you do not understand, and I still do not have a clear vision, but major danger is coming."

Renaldo hands him a leather helmet with partial face shields. "Ok, well, at least add this to your armor. It is a legal part of the uniform you can use."

Connor assesses it, then puts it on. "Okay, I will wear it." There is a knock on the door.

A man at the entrance walks in, glancing at Connor. "Sir, they are ready for you."

Connor looks up at him. "Ok, let's go." He then gets up, and they all head to the main arena floor. As they arrive, his opponent is already there waiting. Connor takes his place where he stood the week before. When he appears, the crowd goes crazy shouting his name. Calming the crowd enough to hear the announcer talk about his opponent takes a bit. Then he calls out Connor, and the crowd goes crazy again. As Connor is introduced, his opponent glares at him, lifts his sword, draws it across his throat, then points at him with it. The announcer fights to get the multitude under control again, telling them the fight cannot happen until they all quiet down.

The crowd finally settles down again. Then the announcer hits the horn to signal the start of the fight. Both opponents run to each other. Connor jumps up and hits his opposition in the chest with his knee, knocking him to the ground. As they hit the dirt, the opponent pushes Connor off, but not before Connor strikes him with his sword, scoring points.

Both men get up, swinging and striking each other, evenly matched, until Connor blocks. He leans in, hitting his opponent in the head with his elbow, then grabbing him by his arm and flipping him to the ground. As he hits the ground, the opponent rolls and pops up, punching Connor in the stomach. He then tackles Connor to the floor, but Connor flips him. When they tumble, Connor then jumps up, hitting his opponent with his sword on his side. His opponent swings around, trying to strike him in the head, but misses. Connor ducks and shoves him with his shoulder, knocking him off his footing. Getting behind him, Connor puts him in a headlock and shoves his sword into his opponent's neck, telling him to yield. He tries to pull out of the headlock, but Connor keeps him there. The other man finally nods his head, agreeing to yield.

The crowd jumps to their feet and screams Connor's name. He releases his opponent, who stands up, shaking Connor's hand. "Wow, I guess you could be the One."

Connor turns toward the exit. "Thank you for being such a great opponent." When they get to the doors,

Connor sees Mondo and the others standing with big grins on their faces. "What are you all smiling at?"

Renaldo explains, "That was another great fight, which will help feed the rumors about you." As they talk, the crowd in the arena continues to shout Connor's name.

Mondo says, "You will need to go back out there and calm the crowd down since they are looking for you." Connor agrees and walks back out there. As he does, the crowd really goes nuts. Connor moves to the middle of the arena and puts his hands up, trying to get the crowd to quiet. The noise slowly subsides.

"I want to tell you how much I appreciate you being here for tonight's fight. Thank you for your support. You honor me." He waves at them, circling around the arena, then walks out. They all clap, then disperse.

After Connor cleans up and readies to leave the arena, twice as many people are outside the exit waiting, trying to get a closer look at him as he emerges. They cheer again. Connor shakes as many hands as he can while trying to move forward, away from the arena. Just before he arrives there, a large man dashes at him with a dagger. The man slices Connor's arm, but Connor grabs the man, flips him to the ground, and pulls his arm with his foot on the man's neck.

Just then, several men come darting up to help Connor, including the man he just fought. They all grab the attacker from the ground, pulling him up to his feet. He yells, "You're an off-worlder. You cannot be the One."

Connor stares at him. "I did not ask for this. All I wanted to do was fight, but if you really want to match me, let's do it right here, right now. Let him go."

They release the man, then step back. The man runs at Connor just as he pulls his right arm back. Then, as the man gets close, Connor hits him between the eyes with all his might, knocking the man out. He falls to the ground. After a minute, someone throws water over him. The man sits up, trying to get his faculties back. He peers around, then asks what happened.

The man Connor fought earlier looks at him and says, "You just got your ass kicked with one punch." The rest of the men laugh.

Connor demands, "So do you still want to kill me?"

The man gets up. "No, I guess not. Since you won the fight, here is my dagger."

"No, you do not have to do that."

"Yes, it was a fair fight." He presses it into Connor's hand. "This is yours now." Connor takes it, then shakes the man's hand.

Then Connor stares at him. "We are all on the same side here, no matter how you feel about me."

"Yes, I guess you are right. Sorry I cut you." The medic who came out during the scuffle cleans up the wound on Connor's arm.

Connor replies, "No worries. We are good. I have had worse. What is your name?"

"Diego," he replies.

Connor says, "Well, Diego, you have a good night. Take care of yourself."

"Thank you. You are not the person I thought you were. You have a good night as well." He then walks off into the crowd while several men push the remaining audience out of the way so Connor and the others can leave.

As they get into the transport, Mondo comments, "See, Connor, I told you some would not be happy about you being from off-world. If you can handle them all like you did tonight, more rumors will fly."

Connor agrees, "I'm sure."

Renaldo comments, "That may help you in the long run."

"That is why I wanted to fight Diego, so I could halt his anger early."

Eric says, "Well, it seemed to have work. It was a good thing you put him down with one punch."

"Yes. I hit him with everything I had, trying to stop it as soon as it started. After already fighting tonight, I was not sure how much more I could do."

Renaldo inquires, "Was this part of your visions, as well?"

"No, not at all." Connor wears a stoic expression.

"So, there are gaps about your fights, then?"

"Yes, there seems to be."

Eric orders, "Then you need to be careful, as there could be more idiots out there, like Diego."

"You're right. I will be."

"I think we need to get you a bodyguard or two to watch your back, at least until you are done fighting. The two men you battled last week offered to help you."

Eric concurs, "Yes, that is a great idea."

Connor says, "Ok, I will talk with them in the morning, but I need to get some sleep. It has been a busy night."

Renaldo agrees, "Yes, it has been. I will reach out to the two men for you. I know them."

"Perfect. Thank you." He then goes up to his room to rest.

THE NEXT MORNING, THEY MEET FOR BREAKFAST TO plan the next few days. Connor again is the last one to join, moving slowly, full of new bruises and the cut on his arm. As he limps in, the three of them clap. Connor starts to laugh. "What is that for now?"

Renaldo explains, "Because of your second fight yesterday, even more rumors are flying, and you now only have two more left, not six."

"Why? What is going on?"

Mondo states, "No one realized it or recognized Diego because of how dark it was, but he would have been your toughest and last fight. Since you felled him with one hit, most of the others have agreed to drop their fights with you, truly believing you are the One. They could not win anyway, but there is a catch."

"I bet. What is it?"

"The last two want to challenge you at the same time, if you agree."

Connor snorts. "Sure, I am good with that, but can we push out the combat for two weeks to rest and get ready?"

"Yes, I am sure we can get them to agree."

Renaldo adds, "I will work out the details. Also, your two bodyguards will be here in about an hour. Last night, I looked at the dagger Diego gave you. It is ancient. I am thinking it has been part of his clan, going back almost to the beginning of his clan's creation. I have only seen one other like that."

Connor is awed. "Wow, that's crazy. If this is the case, why would he have given it to me?"

"This is part of the clan code. If you are defeated, you surrender your weapons to the victor."

Mondo explains, "That goes back to what I told you about the clan swords and why there are only two left."

Connor says, "Sure, that makes sense, but if it has been in his family forever, I do not feel right taking it."

Renaldo puts in, "He has no choice, and you would bring shame on his family to give it back."

Connor wears a sad expression. "Ok, I understand."

Mondo changes the subject. "All right, next piece of business. I talked with the engineer, and tomorrow they will be ready to open the cover at the top. They have been digging all week and made a massive crater into the mountain so the creature can climb out, but they are concerned about the last blast scaring the creature."

"Then we need to go see Andorra today and let her know. I can feel her, but I still cannot communicate with her this far away."

"Yes, we can. I would like to see the progress, anyway. Now, the last thing, I am still getting pushback from the miners. They are concerned they cannot meet Lorenzo's demands for more crystals to be mined, and Craven will be back with his men, causing pain for them."

Eric suggests, "Maybe we want Craven here trying to press for the extra amounts."

"I understand, but we are not warriors anymore, and fighting back could be a problem for us. We have merely a small security force and only a few weapons. There has been no need for them."

"Agreed, but I have been training your elite guards, and we have a plan if Craven comes with a small force."

"But you and Connor are looking to leave when the next window opens."

"True, but we have a day and a half, so we can wait until the next morning to see if Craven shows up to help deal with him. I will move our ship to the same landing pad as the freighter ships so we can leave right after they do if anything happens. We will have your guards there as well. Normally, isn't that where Craven shows up to check on the amount of Zando Crystals mined, anyway? If so, he would not expect us to be prepared for him."

Connor looks at Eric. "If this guy comes back and causes problems, maybe I should stay and let you go get help?"

"I am not sure your father would be thrilled with me if I did that. Plus, even if Craven shows up with his men, he will have to depart when we do, or they would be stuck here with no backup. If they are not expecting any confrontation, we will catch them off guard, forcing them to leave quickly. Then we could come back with men and weapons of our own after the next window to handle him and his men."

Mondo says, "Yes, that sounds like a good plan."

"Hopefully, by the time we get back, John and William will have figured out why Lorenzo is driving so hard to mine as much, and we will not need to come back with reinforcements."

Renaldo agrees, "Yes, we would like to know as well."

Connor states, "Either way, I will be back so I can check on Andorra."

Mondo laughs. "Then maybe you will make this your home and become a true Zandorrian."

"Yes, that may be the case now that I am linked with Andorra. I cannot imagine being away from her too long."

Mondo wears a big smile. "I am sure we can get something set up for you nearby."

"That would be awesome."

Eric chuckles. "You're thinking about living here now. I am going to hear it from your parents. But clearly, you can take care of yourself, so there is not much they could do to stop you. If that is really what you want, I will back you up."

"Thanks, Eric, but if I explain why I want to remain, they will understand. Plus, it does not mean I wouldn't want to still work with you and my brother for Esteban. Just when we are not, I could come back."

As they finish the conversation, two men march in, the two men that he had fought with the week before. He stands up as the two men come over to shake his hand. As Connor shakes their hands, he asks, "What are your names?"

The first one says, "I am Romano," and the second one adds, "I am Juan."

"Great. I am glad to know you both and appreciate you guys wanting to help."

Juan agrees, "We are glad to, anything for the One."

Connor laughs. "Is that what everyone is calling me now?"

Romano puts in, "It is. We all have great respect for you."

"We? Who are we?"

Juan explains, "The first warrior you fought last night, Ron, and even Diego, whom you knocked out. They also want to help protect you."

"I was not sure I needed protection in the first place, but have them meet us tomorrow and you can all help me train."

Romano says, "Yes, we would be happy to. I will let them know."

Mondo says, "Maybe we should get going."

Juan asks, "Great, where?"

Connor says, "We need to see the engineer's progress to open up the cavern in the mine and then meet with Andorra."

Romano asks, "Who is Andorra?"

"She is the creature in the cavern."

As they walk out to get into the transport, Juan excitedly exclaims, "You mean the dragon?"

Connor snorts. "Well, we are still not sure. It is dark in the cavern, and we cannot fully see her to know. That is what we are working on, so we can get her out of there. Do not worry. She is very calm now that she knows we are not going in there to harm her."

"Well, it does not matter. We are here to help cover your back no matter where you go, but it will be great to tell our friends we actually saw the creature and all the rumors are true."

They get onto the transport and take off for the mine. As they approach, they stop near the mountain pass and hike up to the excavation site. They take a little while to get to the work location. Once there, they can see several men busy around a large hole. When they get to the hole, they see the engineer. "Ah, you are here. We're just getting ready to set charges to blast in the morning. If you can, let the creature know what we are doing so she does not go crazy like before and tries to kill us."

Connor wears a smile on his face. "I am already communicating with her about what I am seeing. She is very excited to finally get out. I told her she will need to move to the far side tonight, so she does not get hit by any debris from the blast like before. I also told her it may be very loud and not to be afraid."

Eric asks, "You can talk to her from way out here?"

"Yes, it seems like the longer I know her, the further away I can reach her. I feel her from the colony, but I'm not able to communicate with her from there. I could start talking with her when we got about halfway. She asked me about the fights last night and if I was ok. She can see and feel things when I am further away, but I can't yet."

Renaldo comments, "Which must be why you feel her presence there."

"Yes, that makes sense." Connor looks at the engineer. "I just told her I would be here tomorrow morning before you blast."

The engineer says, "Very well, sir. We were planning for seven if that is ok with you."

Connor laughs a little. "Do not worry about me. If that is what you decided, then I am fine with it."

"Great. Thank you, sir."

Connor laughs again. "You do not need to call me SIR. You can call me Connor."

"Thank you, Connor."

Connor then glances at Eric and Mondo. "This fame is going to take me a while to get used to."

Eric and Mondo chuckle at the same time. "Yes, sir."

Connor now grins. "Ha, ha, hilarious." He then turns to Juan and Romano. "Sorry, I forgot about you guys following me everywhere. Does tomorrow at seven work for you?"

They both beam. "Sir, we are here for you, no matter when it is."

"Ok, enough with the sir stuff. Connor is fine."

Juan says, "Sorry, we meant no disrespect."

"None taken. I am just uncomfortable being called sir."

Romano explains, "We understand, but we are simply trying to be respectful of the One."

Laughing, Eric looks at Connor with his hand on his shoulder. "Son, let it go. You are famous whether or not you want to be, and the great respect they have for now goes with it."

Connor says, "Let's move on from that conversation then, and go see Andorra."

They all head back down the path of the mountain while getting to the front of the mine, where two guards still stand out front. Mondo looks at the guards. "Have there been any issues over the past few days?"

One guard says, "No sir, just the regular deliveries of food for the creature inside."

As they walk into the mine, Mondo states, "Excellent, keep up the good work." Lorenzo's equipment still sits at the far end of the cavern.

Eric looks at it as they continue to walk. "I sure hope John and William can find out about that stuff when we get back."

Renaldo adds, "Yes, I am very uncomfortable leaving that equipment there waiting for something to happen."

Juan and Romano ask, "Sir, what is that stuff?"

Connor explains, "We are not sure, but we believe it is a portal to other worlds."

Juan says, "Sir, no disrespect, but are you crazy? How is something like that possible?"

"That is the problem. We are not sure, but we have an object that came from the emperor's home world to this one. Eric's brother John threw it through when it was opened, just before the window collapsed."

"Sorry, sir—I mean Connor—but that is very hard to believe," says Juan.

Renaldo says, "Yes, we agree, but I saw the proof with my own eyes."

Romano and Juan keep staring back at the equipment while the group continues to the next cavern. As they enter, Andorra stands there in excited anticipation to see Connor; she lets out a loud roar, and all but Connor jump back. Then she says to Connor,

"Sorry, I was excited to see you." Connor tells them all it is ok. She is just happy.

Juan says, "Oh wow, it is real. I never would have believed it if I did not see it for myself."

Romano exclaims, "That roar was very scary. I am glad she is happy. I would hate to see her mad."

Renaldo comments, "Oh, we did when we first met her. She killed and hurt several of my men, but it would have been worse if Connor had not stepped in front and stopped her."

Juan says, "So then, all the rumors are true. You have no fear and tamed the dragon."

Connor shrugs. "I cannot say I was not afraid. It was scary for me as well, very, but I knew she would not hurt me, and now we have a bond I cannot explain. We trust each other. Also, not sure how, but she understands you are the first two men I fought, and now she wants to know why you wanted to hurt me." Both men step back. Connor waves his hands down, trying to calm them. "It's ok. Breathe easy. I just told her it was just a test for me. I passed. You did not want to hurt me, and now you are here to protect me."

Juan says, "Well, thank you. We do not want to see her mad at us for any reason."

Connor laughs. "You're safe. She thanks you for having my back."

Romano comments, "I have not heard you say a word. You talk to her with your mind?"

"Yes, I could speak out loud, but this is much faster. Mondo, she also wants to thank you for all the meat. I told her you have been the one making sure she gets it. She is now almost back to full strength and should be able to escape through the top when it is open."

Mondo says, "Good, then we can start mining operations in here soon, since I have seen all those new rich veins."

Eric agrees. "Which is a good point. I wonder if that is why Lorenzo built that platform here, so they could get the crystals quicker."

Renaldo agrees. "That would make sense. They could mine and send it the same day, and we would never have known if you had not come here searching for that platform, if the device works the way you say it did."

Mondo mutters, "Which reminds me. I did not see a guard by the equipment when we came in."

Connor tells Andorra he will see her in the morning, and they all turn around and walk out. As they get back to the entrance, Mondo asks the guards what happened to the man he had asked to be posted by the equipment inside. The guard tells him they are having trouble keeping someone in there as they hear noises from the creature in the other cavern.

Mondo comments, "I understand. It may be scary, but it will harm none of you. If that is the case, then do hourly checks."

Eric agrees. "Yes, that should be fine, especially if they are looking to mine and then remove it. That should take longer than an hour." The guards make the changes and add the rotation. The men then leave and head back to the colony to help Connor work out.

THE NEXT MORNING, CONNOR IS BACK WITH JUAN AND Romano in the cavern to support Andorra. When they get in, they find Andorra on the far side, waiting for Connor and the explosion. Minutes after they arrive, they hear the explosion and a large rumbling from above. Suddenly, part of the cavern ceiling comes falling. Then a huge dust cloud fills up the cavern. They all drop to the ground so they can breathe, including Andorra. After a few minutes, the dust settles, but there is still no light from above. Andorra asked Connor what happened. Connor tells her he does not know. They climb up on the rubble as far as they can to the ceiling, but still no sight of an exit. As they climb down, the engineer with a few of his men comes hiking in. Connor looks at him. "What happened? I thought we would see an opening, or at least a part of one."

The engineer explains, "I know, sorry, but the explosion caused part of the tunnel from above to collapse. We think we can get it all out, but it will take another week of excavating,"

Connor smiles at the engineer. "She told me she has been in this cavern for a long time. Another week will not be a problem as long as we can keep sending her meat. I told her that is the simple part."

"Sorry, sir, I did not want to disappoint you."

"It is ok. Things like this happen often."

"Thank you, sir, for understanding."

"You're welcome. I told Andorra I would be back when you are ready to finally open it up."

"Yes, sir, I will let you know."

Connor then glances at Juan and Romano. "Let's go back to the colony so I can get ready for my next fight." He then looks at Andorra and responds, "Yes, I will be careful. Don't worry."

Juan asks, "What did she say?"

"She told me this battle is going to be very hard for me, and I could get badly hurt if I am not careful."

Romano states, "Then I guess we need to push your training even harder."

For several days, Romano and Juan help Connor train. On the fourth morning, as they walk into the makeshift gym, several men stand there with Eric. Connor looks at Eric. "What's this?"

Eric explains, "These men are Mondo's elite guards. I have been training them, and I thought maybe you can help. They also wanted to meet you."

"Ok, great. I could use the extra assistance exercising, especially if I will be fighting two men again.

Romano and Juan have been a great help already, but more people with different styles will keep me on my toes." As Connor speaks, they all come up and introduce themselves to him.

"Yes, I thought so. Plus, I figured your guys would join them as guards once you are done with your fights."

Both Romano and Juan shout, "YES, we want to!"

Connor, looking at Eric, starts laughing. "It seems like you have your answer."

Juan adds, "I think Diego would like to join as well."

Eric says, "The more the better."

"Do you think you can get a hold of him?" Just as Connor says that, Diego walks in.

Pointing at Diego, Juan laughs. "Ask him yourself."

Diego wears a shocked look on his face. "Ask me what, sir? I hope it is ok that I am here. Juan told me to come."

Connor walks over and shakes his hand. "We are good. I am glad Juan did, but to your question, we are looking for you to join the elite guard under Mondo."

"Yes, I would love to."

Eric says, "Excellent. We can help with Connor's training and, at the same time, prepare in case Craven comes with his men."

Romano asks, "Who is this Craven?"

"We believe he was someone I had fought with many years ago, but who is now working for the emperor's brother Lorenzo. He is pressing the miners to deliver much more crystals than they have in the past, causing hardship. Craven has been here in the past with some of his men pushing the miners to deliver more. I am organizing these men to help us deal with him and his men if he returns."

Connor then begins his training for the day and shows them the moves he has learned and how they can be quicker and smoother with a combination of actions that have helped him defeat his prior opponents, like Romano and Juan.

About halfway through the day, the engineer walks in and over to where Connor works out.

The engineer says, "Sir, we should be able to finally open the cavern in the morning if you want to be there."

Connor says, "Yes, I would. Thank you for letting me know, but I feel like Andorra is aware of it, too."

Hearing what he just said, Eric looks over at Connor. "Are you able to communicate with the creature from here now?"

"I think so. It is weak." He then glances at the engineer. "Thanks again for letting me know. I will attend. Are you going to be starting the same time as last time?"

The engineer says, "Yes, sir, we will be."

"Great. See you in the morning." The engineer shakes Connor's hand, then walks away.

CHAPTER VIII
ZADA 5, CONNOR, CONTINUED

Late in the afternoon, Mondo comes marching in. All the men are training and working out with Connor. As he walks over, he looks at Connor. "Wow, you are looking good. You seem even bigger than when all of this first started." Mondo was correct. Since Connor was from another world and now on Zada 5, his muscles grew at an increased rate and gave him quicker reflexes. It even caused him to grow another few inches taller, making him six foot three.

Connor says, "Thank you. I feel better and quicker."

"Good, you will need it for your next fight. They are the best of all the men you have battled till now. But that is not why I visited; we have something I need to show you. Can you come with me?"

"Sure, I was just about done for the day. Let me get cleaned up, and I will meet you outside. Do the guys need to come?"

"No, you will be safe."

"Then I will let the guys know to hang out here and I will see them later." He walks over to talk with them but must convince them he will be ok.

Mondo then glances at Eric. "I think you should come as well."

"Ok, I would be happy to."

A few minutes later, Mondo meets Eric and Connor out front. They all climb into the transport headed outside of the colony, past the landing area for the transport freighters, then turn before heading to the mine. They pull up in front of a ranch-like area with three buildings, one of them a large barn-looking building, the other two smaller, but one larger than the other. Renaldo is standing in front of the larger of the two smaller buildings. They get out of the transport. Connor looks at Mondo. "What is this?"

Renaldo beams at them. Then Mondo says, "We did some looking around, but if you are ok with it, this is your new home."

"What, are you kidding, really?"

Renaldo and Mondo both laugh, then Renaldo says, "Mondo and I met with the other clan leaders. We all agreed to provide this. There is a main house, a guest house, and a large building that could support the creature when it is free from the cavern."

Connor cannot believe his eyes. "This is amazing, but I do not know how I could afford something this size."

Mondo explains, "No, you do not understand. This is a gift from all the clans to you as they believe you are the One, and if you really want to live here, everyone, including Renaldo and myself, want to give you a home to help feel you comfortable."

"But I still have one more fight to prove I am the One in their eyes."

Renaldo says, "It does not matter if you win or not at this point. Everything you accomplished has proven it in everyone's eyes, so this is yours regardless."

"I really have no words. I just hope I am worthy."

Mondo puts his hand on Connor's shoulder. "Son, you already are. Before you and Eric came, I was dealing with upset miners ready to rebel, but you have given them a feeling of pride and togetherness we have not seen since the emperor was here many years ago showing us a new way to live and prosper."

After walking around inspecting the buildings, Connor says, "This is all amazing and hard for me to believe. This is going to be my place to live. There is plenty of room if you all want to stay here. Romano and Juan can remain in the other building until the fight is over and things calm down."

Eric agrees. "Yes, I would like to stay away from the craziness."

Renaldo adds, "I think Mondo and I would also like to stay here, but just until the fight is over. Then I would like to go home, but I will return before the freighters arrive."

Mondo concurs. "Yes, same here. I need to go home for a while as well."

Connor says, "Great, I am happy to have you here. I can also communicate with Andorra, and she is excited to see this place as well when we can get her out of the cavern tomorrow." They go back to the colony and pick up their stuff. Connor meets with Romano and Juan, and they head to Connor's new home for the night.

The next morning, Connor and the guys meet with the engineer at the top of the mountain path. A crane-type system is going into a large deep hole below. The engineer says, "Good morning, sir. As you can see, we are almost through to the cavern below. We think it will be another hour and we should be there. If you want, go in and let the creature know and be there when we open it up."

Connor says, "Yes, it looks great. Thank you for all your hard work. We will wait with Andorra for you to open the cavern up from above."

Connor and the guys descend the mountain to go into the mine. It takes a little less than an hour to reach the front. They see the guards standing out front. Connor asks, "Hi, guys, any issues?"

The guards answer, "No, sir, it is still quiet. We have also been checking the equipment inside but have seen nothing in there, either."

Connor says, as the three men walk in, "Excellent, thank you all."

"Thank you, sir."

Then the men continue into the mine. Juan and Romano can hear Connor, like he is muttering to himself.

Juan asks, "Sir, are you ok?"

Connor laughs. "Sorry, guys, I was talking to Andorra."

Romano chuckles. "Ok, good, we thought you might be losing it."

Connor smiles. "No, I am good." They continue on through the mine to the next cavern, where Andorra waits for Connor. Juan and Romano are still a little uneasy being that close to her. Connor looks at them with a big grin. "Guys, relax. It's ok. She will not hurt you." Just then, rocks fall with crumbling noises. After a few minutes, the machine pulls rocks out. Andorra getting excited, pacing a little, bouncing from foot to foot and her tail whipping around.

Juan asks, "Is she ok?"

"Yes, she is just getting happy to see progress. She has been down here for many years trapped in this cavern. I told her to calm down. We are nearly there." It takes almost two more hours to finally open up the cavern all the way.

Right about the time the hole appears, the engineer comes in and addresses Connor. "Sir, we are almost done, but it will take us a little time to get the equipment out of that hole."

"That is outstanding. Thank you so much for all your help to get this done. By the way, I feel bad. All the time that we have talked and I still do not know your name."

The engineer says, "It is Donovan, sir."

"Well, Donovan, we appreciate all of your efforts here to make this happen, Andorra thanks you as well."

"Can she understand me?"

"Yes, she can."

"Well, then," Donovan looks at Andorra, "I am glad that we could help you get out."

Connor then looks at Andorra and explains they are going back to the top of the mountain pass so they can be there when she escapes. He tells the guys the same thing, and they head out of the mine. By the time they get back to the cavern opening, Donovan's men are removing the last of the equipment in the hole. A short time later, all the equipment is out, and Connor tells Andorra to come up. As they all stare down the hole, movement emerges suddenly. Andorra pops up out of the hole, and they all cheer as she walks over to a clearing and stretches out. She arches her back, and huge wings unfold. She tells Connor how great it feels airing them out; she flaps them and then takes off. They watch her fly around for a few minutes, then come back to the clearing. She then asks Connor where his place is so she can inspect it. Connor points over to the direction of his place. She takes off, telling him she will see him when he arrives.

After she takes off, Donovan informs Connor they hit a large vein of crystals, and part of the vein is in the pile of rubble they excavated from the hole. Connor tells him he will let Mondo and Renaldo know so they can have the miners fetch it.

Romano laughs out loud. Both Connor and Juan look at him; then Juan says, "Do you want to include us in the joke?"

"I was thinking how scared the guys are going to be when your dragon flies overhead and then lands." Right then, both Connor and Juan chuckle as well.

Then Connor says, "Man, we better hurry and get there before the three of them freak out." They dash back down the path to get to the house.

In the meantime, at Connor's new home, Andorra circles, searching for where she should land. As she does, Eric, Mondo, and Renaldo come running out, hearing the noise from her wings, and gaze up to see this large creature heading to drop right in front of them. As she rests, they immediately run back into the house and reach out to Connor. Because of the issue with communication resistance, they cannot get a hold of him. It would normally have taken the guys about an hour, but because they ran down the mountain and broke all speed records, they make it there in about half the time. Andorra lies in front of the large building, as Connor asked her to do. She tells him she saw the men run into the building. As the guys pull up in front of the main house, they exit and start laughing, then pointing when they see Eric, Mondo, and Renaldo emerge.

Eric demands, "What the hell is so funny?"

Connor says, "Andorra saw you guys run into the house when she landed."

Renaldo barks, "What did you think was going to happen?"

Mondo agrees. "Yeah, do you think you could have had her wait until you joined her or give us a heads up?"

Connor shrugs. "Actually, I didn't think about it. It wasn't until Romano mentioned it. Then we busted all the speed records. I am sorry, but it is funny, as she would not do anything to you three. She was just so excited to be out of the mine and wanted to see where she could come while still being outside."

Eric says, "I do not think any of us really thought about her being here with us, so this is going to take some time to get used to."

Renaldo agrees. "It really is, but she will be much better than a guard dog or security system." They all laugh.

Connor agrees. "Yeah, think about it. We will never have any problems with her here."

Connor spends a few minutes chatting with Andorra. She then goes into the big barn-like structure, then turns around, and lies down. He looks at the guys and says, "She is very happy to be here and likes her new home, but asked me what happened. Before she got trapped, everything around here was lush and green with only a few small areas of desert."

Mondo exclaims, "What, really? It has been this way for centuries. How long has she been in there?"

"Since it was dark and with her asleep most of the time, she has no way of knowing."

Renaldo says, "All we have is stories, but what was passed down was that there used to be four moons in the sky, but something caused one of them to explode, which is why we now believe the outer atmosphere is covered with debris." While they are talking outside, it gets dark. Then Andorra informs Connor one moon is missing.

Connor glances at Renaldo. "Ok, well, according to Andorra, there used to be four, so the stories are true."

Eric whistles. "Wow, then she is even older than we thought she was."

"Yes, I guess so."

The conversation goes on for a while; then they decide to go inside and relax. As they all sit and talk about the day's events, then a few stories about each of them, Connor just listens to them while he looks around, then thinks to himself, *Is this really my future life?* As Eric turns and looks at Connor, a big smile fills his face.

Eric asks, "What are you so happy about?"

"I cannot believe how my life has turned out so far. If this is how my future has rolled out, I could not be happier."

Eric emits a slight laugh. "I think you are rushing things. You are still young and have a lot of experiences left to live."

"No, I get it, but things are great right now, and I would be happy if it stayed this way, at least for a while longer."

Hearing their conversation, Mondo looks over at Connor. "You're right. Enjoy life when you can, as it always changes."

OVER THE NEXT FEW DAYS, CONNOR WORKS OUT AND trains with Juan, Romano, Diego, and elite guards, then spends time with Andorra in the afternoons. But after a few days of Andorra flying over the colony, Mondo comes in, telling Connor people are getting scared, so Connor asks her to fly more over the mountain range while avoiding the colony. She is ferocious, with horns on her head, big claws on her hands and feet, huge wings with points on the ends, so the way she looks feeds their fear in the colony. Connor suggests allowing them to meet Andorra after his last fight at the end of the week. As Connor gets closer to the day of the fight, Andorra gets more and more concerned. Connor continues to assure her he will be ok.

The day before the final contest, Mondo and Renaldo, when they come back to the house, tell Connor that they need to change the location. So many people want to see it, the current arena cannot support all of them, so they agreed to move it to the next colony of Vernoda about thirty minutes further away. The arena there is almost three times as large. Mondo tells him his elite guard will work security, so there should be no issues, and Connor will have his four guys, Juan, Romano, Ron, and Diego, with him as he enters.

On the day of the fight, Eric leaves with Connor and his bodyguards, as Mondo and Renaldo had already left to work with the elite guards to set up security. As they leave, Connor can hear in his head how agitated Andorra is and tells her to stay. He will be ok. She reluctantly agrees.

As they arrive at the arena in Vernoda, enormous crowds swarm everywhere. As they try to get in, they also wait outside the fighter's entrance to see Connor. Mondo's guards try to keep the entrance clear so Connor can enter. As he gets out of the transport vehicle, several people recognize him and push to get close to him. Then the crowd yells his name. The rest of the guys rush out to surround him and help get him through the crowd to the guards and into the arena. Once they enter, Connor thanks them all for their help, then sees Mondo and Renaldo there waiting. Eric and Connor walk over, and Connor then looks at them. "This is insane. I was not sure we were going to get into the building. I am glad this will be the last fight. I am getting way too much attention, and it needs to calm down. In starting all of this, I just wanted a way to keep my edge."

Renaldo says, "Just so you know, the two men you are about to face have reputations of their own, and we all think this will be your hardest battle ever."

"Maybe that is why Andorra was so agitated when we left."

Mondo agrees. "I am sure it was." He then points over to one room. "Let's go in there and get you ready." They walk in.

Connor sees all his armor and sword set up on a table waiting for him. His name was etched into the bottom of a new chest plate. "Wow, who did this?"

Renaldo explains, "The people in this colony wanted to honor you with this gift from them."

"Please tell them how much I appreciate it." He then does several stretches, and they help him put his armor on. Once he is dressed, he grabs the sword and wields it around to get ready for the fight.

After warming up, he sits there for a minute, gathering his thoughts. They tell Connor they are ready to start; he paces out to the main floor of the arena, goes to one of three spots, and waits for the notices to start. Then a horn goes off and they run into the center, Connor waving his sword back and forth between the two men. Spinning around behind one of them, he pushes his opponent Dutch into opponent Kass. Kass falls to the ground as Dutch pushes off of him to spin back around, swinging his sword at Connor's chest. Connor partially deflects Dutch's sword, but Dutch slices down Connor's side, cutting off the latches on the side of his armor, leaving him exposed. Connor leans into Dutch, hitting him in the head with his elbow, knocking Dutch off balance. Kass swings his sword at Connor's head, but he perceives Kass just in time to duck while pushing Dutch to the ground, then shoves his sword into Kass's chest plate, forcing him back. Connor steps away as Dutch rises, lunging at him.

Connor swings his sword up, deflecting Dutch's away. Then Kass swings his sword into Connor's arm, hitting his leather armor. Connor spins around, hitting Dutch in the chest with his sword. He continues around, hitting Kass in the head, causing Kass to slam into Dutch, forcing both of them off balance. Connor then dropkicks Kass, who again slams into Dutch, already being off balance, and they both fall to the ground. All three men pop back up. Kass and Dutch both wield their swords at Connor, and he deflects several times, going back and forth. As Dutch loses his footing, Connor grabs Kass's arm, deflecting his sword, and hits him as hard as he can with his elbow, driving him to the ground and knocking him out.

With Connor partially turned away and one opponent downed, Dutch pulls a dagger from his boot and lunges, trying to stab him under his armor, but Connor, out of the corner of his eye, sees Dutch coming at him and moves just in time. Dutch still slices Connor where his armor was opened earlier. Shocked Dutch has the dagger, Connor now realizes Dutch wants to kill him. Connor spins around, hitting Dutch with his sword. With Kass on the ground knocked out, Connor can focus on Dutch. At that point, Connor realizes Dutch is also using a fully sharpened sword.

BACK AT THE ENTRANCE TO THE RING FOR THE ARENA, all the guys see Dutch tried to stab Connor. Renaldo looks at Mondo. "We need to stop this fight."

Mondo shakes his head. "No, you know the rules. We cannot, no matter what, until the contest is over."

CONNOR, AFTER SEEING DUTCH HAS A LIVE SWORD AND dagger, realizes his life is now at stake, and he needs to end this contest as soon as possible. Connor swings his sword, deflecting Dutch's attacks. After several more swipes between them, Connor knocks the dagger out of Dutch's hand, then swings around, hitting Dutch in the head as hard as he can with his sword, dazing Dutch. Then he slams Dutch to the ground while holding his arm. He then pulls it while putting his foot on Dutch's throat and orders him to surrender, or he will snap his neck. Dutch struggles to pull away at first, but not being able to, finally agrees. Just as Dutch concurs, the whole arena hears a loud roar, and Andorra lands in the center near Connor.

As Andorra arrives, Kass wakes up and jumps back. Connor quickly releases Dutch, then runs in front of Andorra, swinging his hands in the air and yelling, "No, I am ok. It's over. I am ok."

Meanwhile, everyone in the arena screams and starts to run out. Connor then goes to the middle of the arena and repeatedly yells at the crowd, "It's ok. She will not hurt anyone. She is here for me." People, finally hearing Connor, stop and just stand there. At the same time, Connor's bodyguards come barreling out and grab Dutch. Connor looks at them. "Let him go. The fight is over."

Juan says, "But he tried to kill you."

"Yes, but so did Diego at my last fight." Connor orders Andorra to go back home, since he is fine. She then leaves.

The crowd goes crazy, and, like the last fight, starts to yell, "Connor, Connor, Connor!" Then they yell, "He's the one!" several more times. Connor raises his hand and tells them thank you all. The guys then walk him out, as he is bleeding badly from the dagger wound. They take him to the room where the medic is waiting and seal him up.

Mondo comes up. "I am so sorry. We looked over everyone, but the two men you fought. That should never have happened."

Connor says, "It's ok. This was not your fault. Andorra knew the whole time. I do not know why I did not suspect it."

Eric asks, "Right, why didn't you see this?"

"I do not know. I should have. Maybe I am too focused on Andorra. Speaking of that, does anyone know why Dutch wanted to kill me?"

Diego puts in, "Yes, I do. I talked with him after you all left. He felt like I did and thought this would be the last chance, so he had to try it in the battle with you, but after seeing the dragon, he now realizes he was all wrong and is very sorry. He also handed me his sword and dagger to give to you." Diego places them on the table next to Connor.

Connor looks at Diego. "Can you see if Dutch is still here and ask him to come see me?"

"Yes, sir." Diego then turns and goes out the door to find Dutch.

A few minutes later, Diego returns with Dutch, who stumbles over to Connor. "I am ashamed. Why would you want to talk to me?"

Connor says, "No, you do not have to be. I was not born on this world, an outsider coming in and taking over your clans' beliefs. I did not ask for this, but this is where we are. I wanted to make sure you knew I understand why you tried to kill me. It was a fair fight. I won and hold no ill will towards you."

"I talked with Diego. He told me that is how you would feel. That is why I am ashamed about my behavior; you are clearly the One."

"I am not sure I will ever get used to being called that, but I am learning to accept it."

"Sir. you are. I will make sure that everyone else in my clan knows it. You will not have any more threats on your life." Holding his wounded side, Connor gets up from the table and shakes Dutch's hand, then asks if he would like to join Mondo's special guard since they need as many men as they can get. Dutch agrees;

Connor points him to Eric and Mondo to talk with them about the next steps. Dutch thanks Connor for sparing his life and obeys.

Renaldo comes back into the room and heads over to Connor. "You need to come outside and see this." With his guards, Connor follows Renaldo out of the building. The whole town, along with everyone that came to see the fight, stand outside the arena, waiting for Connor. Connor steps out.

Seeing the heads of all the clans in front of the crowd, Mondo walks over with them. "Connor, they have asked me to speak on their behalf. With your abilities to talk with the dragon, and now your victory in the Clan fights and willingness to live here, we want you to become an official Zandorrian."

Connor is stunned. "I do not know what to say, other than I am very honored and would be very proud to be called a Zandorrian." For winning the final contest, Mondo places the chain with a medal over his head, and the entire crowd cheers.

Mondo declares, "You are now an official Zandorrian." The crowd cheers again.

"Thank you for your willingness to accept me as one of your own." While clutching his injury, he shakes hands with the heads of each clan, then tells them what a great night it has been and what a wonderful experience it has been for him.

Eric looks at all of them. "I think this has been a lot for Connor to take in, but we should get him home, as his injuries were severe and he needs some rest." As the crowd applauds, Connor gets into the vehicle and leaves with the rest of the guys.

When they reach the house, Connor goes over to Andorra, still not sure why he did not see it. "So, you knew I would get hurt and that one man wanted to kill me?"

Andorra agrees. "Yes, I knew. That is why I was so concerned and could not wait here to find out what happened. You are the first human I could talk to or care about my entire life. I was used to being hunted and having to kill those that came after me, so this is all new, giving me feelings I never had before."

Connor laughs. "This is really new to me too. I could never communicate with anyone without speaking. But I care about you too."

"I can tell you are hurting, so please go in and rest. I am ok now that you are back." Connor thanks her, then goes into the house and his room to sleep.

CONNOR TAKES A FEW DAYS TO RECOVER, BASED ON HOW severe his wounds were. On the third day, Connor returns to working out with all the men, then spends the afternoon with Andorra; she convinces Connor to climb on her back for a ride. As they take off, Eric and Mondo witness the event. Andorra takes Connor over the colony and then back over the arena. Most people living in both colonies see the two fly overhead. Connor waves at them below, and they wave back, excited little kids waving and laughing. Boy and dragon then head back home. After landing, Connor climbs off, telling Andorra how great it was. Both Eric and Mondo come up to him.

Eric asks, "So how was it?"

Mondo adds, "Yeah, how was it?"

Connor says, "It was a lot of fun. I have flown a few crafts, but this was totally different. We also flew over the colonies, and the people seem to be more accepting of Andorra when I was riding her. I think if we do this a few more times, they will not be so afraid."

"That sounds like a good idea, and maybe land in a few places and let them get close and see she will not hurt them."

"Yes, we can do that. She is ok with it." Over the next few weeks, Connor and Andorra fly around to other colonies, allowing the local people to meet them.

With only a short while left before the moon alignment, the landing of the freighters, and the possibility of Craven showing up with his men, they kick the training into high gear, preparing for a possible confrontation.

A few days before the event, Eric and Connor, with Mondo, Renaldo, and the guards, decide where everyone will be placed to support any issues if Craven and his men appear. They also agree that Renaldo will take the lead as head miner to face Craven about the inventory, keeping the miners out of harm's way if any fighting breaks out. That afternoon, Connor explains to Andorra that he will be leaving for a few months and they will continue making sure she is still fed while he was away. Andorra will try communicating with him while he is away, and she is teaching him about his powers, with ways that he can focus on his visions for better skills.

THE NEXT MORNING, THE FIRST DAY OF THE ALIGNMENT, as everyone prepares for the freighters to land, Connor, Eric, and Mondo wait in the warehouse with the crystals. After a little while with no sign of Craven or his men, they emerge from the warehouse as the crystals are being loaded by the same captain Eric gave the note to on his last trip.

He walks up to Eric. "What's going on? I am seeing many people here, more than before."

Eric explains, "We were waiting to see if the guy Craven was going to show up."

The captain says, "I do not think he is coming this time; I did not see any sign of his craft waiting for the alignment to fly through as we had in the past." Eric then waves at the other men stationed around and tells them to come over. "Wow, you had everyone waiting? For what?"

Mondo puts in, "Craven has been forcing the miners to produce more product and had his men intimidate them. We were here to find out why, then push back."

The captain, "Then I do not think you will have any issues this trip."

Eric looks at Mondo. "Let's short the load, forcing them to come here with the next alignment."

Renaldo says, "But you and Connor will not be here when they return."

Connor explains, "True, but we plan on coming back with the next alignment to help."

Mondo consents, "Ok, if you guys will come back, then yes, let's short the load and see what happens."

The captain hears all of this. "What do I say when we deliver this freight?"

"Tell them the miners could only provide the normal amount and they will need to discuss it with the workers here on Zada 5. You are merely delivering the message they gave you."

"You got it. Will do. I hope you guys know what you will be stepping into. He seems to be a little off to me."

"Yes, that is what I heard, but we will be prepared for him no matter what."

Eric and Connor load their ship, then discuss with Mondo and Renaldo what they need to achieve before the next alignment, then what Eric and Connor will do when they come back. Then leave early the next morning.

CHAPTER IX
ONE STEP FORWARD?

ON MARKUS 2, IN ANTICIPATION OF ERIC AND CONNOR returning, they agree to meet at the palace, but after checking the first day of the alignment, everyone finally realizes they will not see them until the next. William, John, and Adam agree to meet back in John's office the following morning to update Esteban and learn what the guys discovered on Zada 5.

The following morning, they gather in John's office, waiting for Eric and Connor. They discuss what went on while the guys were gone. William and Sara had been working on the audit. They realized Lorenzo had been hiding a lot of money that should have been going to the empire, but was not showing up on the books anywhere. By reverse-engineering the transactions, they could see where the money should have been coming in. With Lorenzo causing a shortage of the Zando Crystals, forcing the price to raise, it has been clear Lorenzo is hiding the excess crystals. If he keeps this up, it could cause financial issues for the empire.

They agree more information is needed to understand what Lorenzo is doing. They still need to hide tracking Lorenzo, but after the lab explosion and the disappearance of Lorenzo and Craven from Korbin, no one has any idea where they are.

Adam states, "We reran the video up to the time of the explosion, but no matter how we expanded it or moved the angle in the view, we could not get a clear vision of the portal opening. The explosion destroyed all the files in the room. And with access to the system locked up, Emma cannot provide any more information either." Adam looks at John. "Was anyone able to crack the rest of those files on the drive?"

John sighs. "No. As the techs tried, the files increasingly corrupted. Lorenzo had some kind of virus built into them if they were copied and the encryption broken without the correct key."

A little while later, Esteban enters and addresses John and William, "Have we heard from the boys yet?"

William demurs, "No, not yet, but it takes several hours to get here from Zada 5, so we may not see them for a while."

"Ok, then I guess let me know when they get here."

Adam chimes in, "Yes, sir, will do."

LATER THAT AFTERNOON, ERIC AND CONNOR FINALLY arrive. Esteban walks into John's office at the same time they do. Connor is noticeably taller and larger. Adam is the first to comment, gawking at him. "Holy crap, what happened to you? The two of you were only gone three months, right, not three years?" They laugh.

Connor is a little embarrassed. "Yes, yes, I am bigger. I made the most of being there."

Eric puts in, "You guys have no idea what went on in those few months we were there."

William asks, "Why, what do you mean?"

John interjects, "Wait, first, I have a question: did you guys run into Lorenzo?"

Eric wears a puzzled look on his face. "No, why would you ask?"

Adam explains, "Well, he stepped through his portal on Korbin and disappeared, and since you went there to possibly check out a portal, we thought maybe that is where he went."

Eric says, "You were correct. There was a portal in the cavern we were trapped in." He glances at John. "Also, we found the building piece you threw with your initials on it."

John turns to Esteban. "Now you know why I did what I did."

Esteban laughs, "Yes, it was a smart move, so we have actual proof."

Eric continues, "After we discovered it, Mondo had it checked out. You need two devices to work the system, and the one on Zada 5 is a receiver, so the one here must have been a sender, based on what Mondo's guys could figure out."

After Eric finishes explaining their time, all stand there with their mouths open.

William starts off, glaring at Eric. "What were you thinking, letting Connor compete like that?"

Connor jumps in. "Dad, that was not Eric's fault. It was my call. Eric warned me you would not be happy about this if I got seriously hurt, but if you think about what I went through, going after Adam on Castia was just as bad. None of us thought anyone would want to kill me while I was competing, either."

Eric faces down William and John. "Connor also accomplished in a few weeks what took us almost a year. The one thing I left out is that Connor has officially been accepted as a Zandorrian."

Esteban exclaims, "What? So, he is officially a dual citizen now?"

Connor wears a big smile on his face. "Yes, sir, I am."

Adam says, "Let me get this straight. You now have a pet dragon and are a clan leader on Zada 5?"

Connor beams. "Well, she is not really a pet, more like a friend."

They all laugh; then John says, "So, Connor is officially a dragon tamer and world conqueror."

William asks, "Then what happened to you? How did you get so big?"

Connor shrugs. "All I was doing was working out every day, but because I was not born on that planet, it sped up my growth. That is all that Eric and I could figure out."

After Eric and Connor update the guys, John jumps in about what they missed. Eric clarifies, "So, the Craven they were talking about on Zada 5 is the same one, now working for Lorenzo?"

John concurs, "Yes, it appears that way, and now no one seems to know where he and Lorenzo are."

Adam agrees. "Correct. We hoped Lorenzo had jumped there to Zada 5. We have been waiting for you guys to return to find out, but now that we know you didn't see him, we need to search even harder."

"Ok, I think we need to go back to Ria 6 for two reasons. First to see if Lorenzo is there with Craven, then try to determine how many rebels are there, and how to deal with them, since that seems to be where the hidden crystals are."

Adam jumps in. "I will go back with the team I used last time."

Connor says, "I am going with you." They all laugh. "What's so funny?"

John explains, "It seems like you cannot get enough."

"Yes, that may be true, but I feel most alive when I am in the middle of it."

Adam soothes him. "It is fine. I will keep an eye on him when we are there."

Connor is a little annoyed at his response. "You do not need to watch me. I can take care of myself."

"True, but you have never been involved in a covert operation like what we will step into."

"Good point. You're right. I will follow your lead."

William says, "You boys make me very proud, but I am not sure I like you involved in the same mission. If anything happens, we could lose you both at the same time."

Eric assures him, "After seeing what Connor could do and knowing what Adam is capable of, I would be more concerned about who will run into the both of them with backup."

The next day, Adam and Connor meet Adam's team. As they walk up, one guy looks at them. "So, who is this with you?"

Adam, putting one hand on Connor's neck, the other on his shoulder, shakes him a little. "This is my little brother, the dragon tamer." They all laugh. "No, really, my brother tames dragons in his spare time." They continue to chuckle.

One of the other men says, "Yeah, right, and I am a lion tamer."

Connor smiles at them. "Where do you keep your lion? I keep my dragon near my home on Zada 5."

Another one of the men tries to shut him down. "Ok, all fun aside, dragons are not real."

"Until a few months ago, I would have agreed with you, but Andorra exists." He shows them a few images of her. "I knew no one would believe me without these."

The first man who asked Adam about Connor says, "If he is your brother, is he a true warrior like you?"

Adam responds, "He just came back from Zada 5 after winning a warrior competition with Zandorrians. If you heard anything about them, then you know what it would take to win."

One of the other men exclaims, "Then, when we thought there was only one of you, there are two. I feel much better about our chances."

A few others chime in, "Yes, me too."

Adam surveys all of them. "We are going back to Ria 6, and our plan is to locate these two men." He displays images of Craven and Lorenzo. "We also need to see if we can figure out the rebel numbers, and then if more crystals are being stored. Like before, we need to accomplish everything without being seen."

Laughing, one man looks at Adam. "Then I guess we need to take your sword away to keep the body count down."

Connor peers at Adam. "What is he talking about?"

Adam says, "Nothing, he is joking."

One man responds, "Yeah, he only killed three, but we did not get caught."

Connor says, "Three, huh?"

Adam admits, "Yes, ok, they saw us, and I needed to make sure we could get in and out. Let's move on."

They all get on the transport ship and take off for Ria 6. A few hours later, they arrive. Ria 6 is a minor planet, mostly covered by jungles, a few large lakes, and several rivers. One runs almost the length of the planet on one side, feeding into one of the two oceans and a few small deserts.

Prior to landing, they set the ship into stealth mode to avoid detection by anyone on the ground with their radar. Getting close to the warehouse location, they notice several large groups of people near the warehouse clearing. They land near the same spot as last time since it appears to be far enough to not be spotted when they get on the ground. By this time, it is almost dark.

After settling and before leaving the ship, they all change to dark gear and remove their IDs just in case they are detected or captured, so the rebels will not know who they are or why they are there. With their weapons drawn, they slowly come out while surveying around to make sure no one is near. After a while maneuvering through the jungle, now close to the warehouse, getting there undetected, they notice several more guards than before. This time, they wear the suits Adam discovered from the last trip, but the suits have a strange glow with only their face and hands exposed.

Connor looks at Adam. "What the hell are they wearing?"

Adam answers, "I am not sure. It seems like the suits we saw here last time, but those are powered up somehow."

"Were there this many guards previously?"

"No, and I only killed the guards in the building, not outside. Let's go around to the other side to see if there is a way in without being seen." They go back into the jungle and back around to the opposite side of the warehouses. The large main doors are open, and this time, all three buildings are full.

One man gapes at Adam. "Why are the doors open? Either they just loaded something, or they are getting ready to unload."

"Yes, that was my thought as well. Maybe we need to inspect where we saw people gathered."

Connor suggests, "Maybe we need to grab a guard and nab one of those powered-up suits."

"Yes, but that will need to be one of the last things we do. When we grab the guard, the others will discover us shortly after."

"You're right, good point."

"You'll learn, little brother."

Connor just studies him and smiles.

One of the other men looks at Connor. "How many missions have you been on with your brother?"

"Counting this one, two. But my first mission was to save my brother's ass after being captured."

"You saved Adam? Yeah, right."

Adam counters, "No, he is correct. My ship crashed behind enemy lines, but it was part of a bigger plan to capture their general, which we could do. We are getting off topic. We came here to find Lorenzo, Craven, and the rebels. We have already seen the crystals are here, so let's move closer to where we spotted the people on radar." As they approach, they observe several troops wearing the same suits as the guards, but they look more like uniforms with the same insignias the rebels were wearing. However, they are not glowing like the guards' suits were.

They spot one man, glowing but far away from the troops. Adam signals for the others to hold back. When Adam goes to stab the man with his sword, it bounces off like he hit a wall. The man turns around with a shocked look on his face, swinging his sword. Adam repels the first swipe, but the second time, the man's weapon cuts through Adam's like cheap metal, then slices Adam across his chest.

Seeing this, Connor runs up and dropkicks the man, knocking him to the ground. Adam snaps the man's neck before he can get back up. He then stares at Connor while holding his chest. "Quick, take off his suit and grab that sword. We need to get out of here before he and we are discovered." Connor does as Adam asks. When he removes the suit, it turns off. He then picks up the sword along with the broken piece of Adam's, not wanting to leave any evidence behind, while one man helps Adam with his wound. Then they run back to the ship.

Getting in, Adam looks at them. "This is not the mission we had planned, but we know the rebels have a lot more men than we thought, and we can't fight them with the armor and weapons they have. We need to go home and figure out a new plan."

As they fly back, one man on the ship, also a medic, seals up the wound on Adam's chest. Connor smiles, then pulls up his shirt. "Well, you now have one like mine." He shows Adam the scar on his side.

One man gawks at both of them. "Man, I am glad we are on the same side. I would really hate to run into both of you at the same time." He then turns to Connor. "You are just like your brother. Neither of you hesitates. You jumped in the very second you saw your brother was in trouble."

Adam agrees. "Yes, and I am glad he did. It surprised me when that guy's sword cut through mine like butter. If we cannot combat those new weapons, we will be in big trouble."

Connor puts in, "Mondo on Zada 5 should be able to reverse-engineer how they work, but the window will not be open for a few months."

"I know someone a lot closer that should be able to help us. I will reach out to her when we return."

"Great, the sooner the better."

"I agree."

One of the other men on the ship asks, "What should we do in the meantime?"

"Just hang tight and stay tuned until we can figure out what we are dealing with here and how to fight them."

"Ok, sir, you got it," replies the one man.

They get back to Markus 2 very late that evening, almost early in the morning. As Adam and Connor head back to the palace, Connor says, "Should we wake up John and Dad to let them know what we ran into?"

Adam demurs, "No, let them sleep. We can update them in the morning. There is nothing they could do anyway until we know more."

LATER THAT MORNING, ADAM AND CONNOR RISE EARLY after only a few hours' sleep, then walk into John's office just ahead of John and William, who are both surprised.

John asks, "Why are you guys back already? What happened?" Adam explains his interaction with the rebel. William questions if he is ok, and Adam assures him. They sealed him up, but will be fine in a few days. Adam then tells them about his plans to have Emma inspect the suit and sword to learn how they can fight against them.

Just as they finish the discussion, Esteban and Eric walk in, so Adam has to repeat what happened. Esteban voices his concerns. They still do not know where Craven and Lorenzo are, but agree they need to tackle the new weapons before going further. They then discuss Lorenzo's plans and the prospect of locking down the labs. However, John and Eric point out Lorenzo would not have disappeared without putting his plans in place. If he got wind of closing the labs, he might realize they're tracking him. Adam then points out that one person who helped them was dead, and they locked the other out of Lorenzo's files. Not knowing who else they could trust may just help Lorenzo if the wrong person finds out.

AFTER THE MEETING, ADAM REACHES OUT TO EMMA, who is more than willing to help them after Lorenzo killed her brother. He arranges to join her at the labs that morning. As Adam leaves, he invites Connor to meet Emma. When they walk into the building, Emma is already there, waiting in the reception area for them. Adam reaches out, giving her a hug as she hugs him back. "Emma, I am so sorry about your brother. Are you doing ok?"

Emma says, "Thank you, yes, but I really want Lorenzo to pay for his death."

Connor assures her, "That is why we are here."

"I am sorry. Who are you?"

Adam explains, "Sorry, Emma, I forgot. This is my little brother, Connor."

"Little brother?"

Adam laughs. "Well, not so little anymore. I guess I need to stop saying that."

Emma shakes Connor's hand. "It is a pleasure to meet you."

Connor agrees. "Yes, same here. Adam tells me you are really smart and may be able to help us."

"I hope so. Why don't you guys follow me to my lab, and I can study what you have?" They all go. She unlocks the door; then they head in. Once inside, she locks the door again. They both glance at her, a little puzzled. She realizes what she just did. "Sorry, but after Lorenzo killed my brother, I do not trust anyone around here, so I keep my lab secured even when I am in here."

Adam says, "No problem. We get it."

Connor agrees. "Absolutely."

Emma takes the bag and weapon from Adam. "Let me see what you have here." As she studies it, she pushes something on the sleeve, and it powers on. "Wow! Ok, I heard rumors of these suits, but this is the first time I have actually seen one. In the files I sent you, there was some chatter about these, but no actual information. There is a microswitch at the end of the sleeve here. That is how I activated it." As she continues to inspect the suit, she opens up the back pouch, pulling out the compact power unit, and unplugs it. "Ok, this must be what powers it."

Adam explains, "Once this is powered up, it works like a force field. I could not get through it with my sword."

"So, someone was wearing the suit?"

Connor says, "Yes, I took it off of them."

"What happened to that person?"

Adam admits, "Well, I killed him. Then Connor stole the suit."

"Good. One less person working for Lorenzo." As Adam and Connor both grin at her, she continues looking at the power unit. "It looks like this is also using a more refined version of Zando Crystals, but there are some other minerals in here as well. Based on what I can tell so far, this suit will work with the power supply for about six hours before it would need to be replaced, but that is just a rough guess. I would need more time testing this to know for sure."

Connor says, "You said there is a switch. I must have bumped it when I took the suit because it shut off."

Emma holds the sleeve up. "Yes, it is right here."

Adam inquires, "Could we hit it and power down the suit as we are fighting them?"

"Not sure. I will need to experiment. Can you leave this with me, and I can work on it?"

"Absolutely, if this will help us figure out how we can fight back."

Connor asks, "What about the sword? It cut through Adam's almost like paper."

"Let's take a look." Emma inspects it. "You said it was powered up somehow."

Adam agrees. "Yes, it had a strange blue glow."

Emma says, "I don't see any way to really turn it on. Did you notice anything in the dead guy's hand?"

Connor reaches into his pocket. "Well, he had this strange-looking ring on his finger."

Adam laughs. "You took it off him."

Connor has a smile on his face. "Zandorrian warrior rules. All goes to the winner of the fight."

"But I killed him."

"True, but you would not have been able to if I had not dropkicked him to the ground. But we are backtracking." Looking at Emma, he puts the ring on. "Hand me the sword." As she does, it activates.

Emma asks, "Can I see that ring?"

"Sure." He puts the sword on the table, then removes the jewelry and hands it to her. As she puts the ring against the handle of the sword, it turns on.

She then takes a closer peek at the ring. "I think this ring is made of Verbraso."

"Verbraso? Are you sure?"

Adam asks, "What is Verbraso?"

"On Zada 5 it was used to make the ten head clansmen swords, and in the hands of the right person, the sword glows like this one, but it is also very rare."

Emma agrees. "Connor is right. If this is indeed Verbraso, then it is very hard to find. I will need to do some assessments on this ring and sword as well."

Adam says, "Let me see if I have it now. We will need to hit the power switch on the suit to turn it off and cut the ring away to shut down the sword?"

Connor laughs. "Sure, piece of cake."

Emma says, "Give me some time to see how I can help."

Connor shakes her hand. "Emma, it is nice to know you. Thank you for helping us."

She gives him a big smile. "Um, yes, I am happy to have met you as well. Anything I can do to help you take down Lorenzo, I am there. I will reach out to you once I have figured out a solution."

Adam declares, "Emma, thank you."

She then walks over and unlocks the door to let them out. They both give her a hug, then stride out of the lab. As they go out, she relocks the door behind them.

After they leave, Connor grins at Adam. "Wow, she is cute. Where have you been hiding her?"

Adam laughs. "She is all yours. She was the kid sister of my friend that Lorenzo and Craven killed on Korbin."

"Yes, I grasped that from her conversation about the door. We may need to get her some protection."

"Yes, already on it. Matt and Dave will keep an eye on her."

"Who are they?"

"They were working with me to monitor Lorenzo before he disappeared, and they have been in this building and know the layout."

"Perfect."

THE NEXT DAY, MATT AND DAVE MEET ADAM AND Connor at the palace. Adam introduces them to Connor and tells them what they found and their meeting with Emma. They both agree keeping an eye on her to make sure she does not run into any trouble is a good idea. Then they head to the lab complex and start watching her.

SEVERAL DAYS LATER, EMMA REACHES OUT TO ADAM. She thinks she may have a way to help them deal with the rebels and their new weapons, but will need to run some more testing. She will reach back out to him in a few more days.

A FEW DAYS LATER, MATT WALKS BY EMMA'S LAB. SEEING her lying on the floor face down, he tries to open her door, but it is locked. He reaches out to Adam to get help. Just as Adam answers, he hears Matt say Emma is on the floor, a loud explosion, and then nothing.

Adam is in John's office when he receives the message from Matt. Connor is just strolling in. Adam stares at him. "We need to head to the labs right now! It's Emma." They run to Adam's vehicle, getting to the building as quick as they can. When they arrive, part of the main building has been destroyed, with part of it burning. They try to break into the building but are held back, told they cannot go in until the fire is out. While waiting, Adam calls Dave and informs him what is going on. With the fire almost out, Adam and Connor walk back up, showing security his ID, then explain they are supporting the emperor and need to be one of the first in the building. They agree. While waiting, Dave comes up.

After another thirty minutes, security gives them the all clear. When they enter, several bodies lie dead and burned on the floor. The three men run over to Emma's lab. A burned body a few yards from her door lies face down, dead on the floor. Dave turns it over. Only part of the body's face was burned; it was Matt. They move through the hole where the lab door used to be. Seeing a female body in the middle of the floor, they turn her over. Emma; it looks like someone hit her on the back of her head with her skull partially caved in. When they pulled her over, a ring rolled out of her hand, the Verbraso ring Connor gave her. They look around for the sword and suit, but they are nowhere to be found.

Adam looks at Dave. "Did you talk to Matt this morning?"

Dave says, "Yes, we touched base just before noon. A guy knocked on her lab door. They talked for a few minutes, but he left, according to Matt. He tried to get an image, but he turned the other way. Matt said he had not seen the guy before. He was older, from what Matt could tell."

Connor says, "I wonder if whoever it was blew up the place because he could not find this ring."

Adam agrees. "Yes, that would be my bet. This work was very sloppy."

Dave asks, "What do we tell security out there?"

"Just what it was, a gas explosion, but that it appears to be an accident. Put Emma back the way she was and place this debris here by her, so it looks like it hit her in the head. It's close enough to the damage on her head. We need to leave and let the guys know what happened."

Connor demands, "So now what? We still do not know how to deal with the new weapons."

"You're right. Every time we take one step forward, we end up two steps back. Let's reach the palace and talk with John and Eric about it."

Dave asks, "What do you need me to do?"

"Why don't you follow us? You should hear what we plan to do next. This will affect you as well."

After the three get back to John's office, Adam asks for everyone else's presence as well. After a few minutes, all but Esteban walks in. Adam frowns at John. "Where's the emperor?"

John explains, "He is finishing up an important meeting and will be here shortly."

Eric asks, "So what's going on?"

Adam says, "I would like to wait for the emperor, so I do not have to repeat myself."

John replies, "Is it that important?"

"Yes, I think so."

A few minutes later, Esteban strides in. "What did I miss?"

"Nothing, sir, we were delaying for you."

"Well, then let's get to it."

Adam explains about the suit and sword and Emma had found out so far. She had just been killed for helping them, exactly like her brother, but she could not finish her analysis on either of the items or how to defend against them.

"How did someone find out about her research?"

Dave jumps in. "Sir, we do not know. We had been watching over her the whole time. Earlier today was the first time we saw anyone talk with her at the labs. According to Matt, it was an older gentleman, but he could not get an image of him before he walked away."

Adam adds, "Yes, and then later someone got into the lab and hit her in the back of the head. We believe that killed her, not the explosion."

Esteban says, "You mean the explosion that killed several people at the complex?"

"Yes, sir, we think they set it off to cover their tracks. Unfortunately, we could not get access to any video either."

John declares, "Let me get my team on it to see what they can dig up."

Connor states, "The bigger problem is, we do not know how to fight against the suits or their swords. We cannot go back to Ria 6, even if that is really where Lorenzo and Craven are, especially not knowing how many men they have backing them up. We saw on the radar quite a few people there, but no idea the amount of rebels."

Esteban says, "We must assume at this point that Lorenzo knows we are trying to find and track him, so we need to lock down the labs here and on Korbin, killing any remaining access."

John agrees, "No problem. We can have him locked out before the end of the day."

"We will need to add additional security here, but the other problem I have is Christina and Emily graduate in a few weeks, and we already have a party planned next month."

Connor asks, "When is the party?"

"It is on the eighteenth. Why?"

"That is when the window opens back up for Zada 5 and we have to return in case Crave shows up with his men."

"That's ok. We will leave early the next morning. The window remains open for about a day and a half. We will also bring a company of men with us."

Adam declares, "I am going too."

Dave adds, "Yes, I want to come."

Connor agrees. "I was going to ask if you would come, brother, but thank you both."

Smiling, Adam looks at Connor. "You bet. We are a team now."

"Then, at this point, we need to stay put and be on our guard until after the party." William reaches out to Sara, asking her to come to the palace along with more of his special security team, and plan on staying until after the party for Christina and Emily.

CHAPTER X
ON THE OTHER SIDE

Back on Korbin, Lorenzo and Craven step through the window from Korbin to Ria 6, which closes suddenly behind them. Carven stares at Lorenzo. "You were right. Twenty seconds was enough time to get through before the explosion shut the portal down, but why did we have to kill both Roger and Andy?"

Lorenzo replies, "Roger was asking too many questions, and I could not take a chance on him saying anything to anyone before we were ready."

"Ok, I get that, but then why Andy? He has been working with us."

"Yes, that's the point. He knew everything, including where we are now and our plans. I could not take the chance if my brother picked him up, he would tell them anything."

"I understand that, but felt bad having to. At least he did not know it was coming."

"The accident on Markus 2 almost exposed what I have been working on to my brother, causing him to look for proof and demanded I show him everything. I needed to disappear. My brother wanted regular meetings with him and to see all my new projects and weapons."

"But we are still not ready."

"You're correct, but now that he doesn't know where I am, and we have a makeshift lab setup here, I can finish."

Lorenzo and Craven walk out of the building just as Major Johnson comes walking toward them. Johnson looks at Lorenzo. "Sir, why are you here? We were not expecting you for several months."

"My plans have changed. I will need to complete what I was working on here on Ria 6." He then looks at Craven. "Were you able to get the rest of the minerals and equipment delivered from Korbin?"

Craven says, "Yes, they have been shipping for the past couple of days. The last of it should arrive later today."

Lorenzo frowns at Johnson. "What about the break-in a few days ago?"

Johnson says, "From what we can tell, it looks like local thieves looking for money or anything they could sell. They broke a few boxes open, but since it was only the suits, they left them alone. We have doubled the guards and dealt with the ones that let them through in the first place. The additional guards will wear the new protective suits, so even if they are caught by surprise, they will still deal with whomever. Those new swords are amazing. They cut through everything, but they only last five hours."

"Yes, I need to work on the mineral combination to extend the sword life to eight hours to match the suits."

"We could also use more blades."

"I agree, but we need to find additional Verbraso, or they will be useless."

After talking through a few things with Craven and Major Johnson, Lorenzo marches into the building, which is also his makeshift lab. After a while, Craven arrives with equipment shipped there from Korbin.

He looks at Lorenzo. "How long is it going to take to convert the platform to a sending unit from a receiving one?"

Lorenzo mutters, "Well, if I could have trusted Roger and used his help, it would have been about a month, but since I am on my own, it may take me three months."

"Ok, good, that should give us enough time to meet your schedule. Does that include building the new receiving platform?"

"It should, but I will need a few weeks to test everything. Will you and the rebels be ready?"

"Yes, they will be for what you'll need. I still have them manufacturing more power supplies for the suits, and we continue to search for Verbraso."

"Yes, we will also require it for further swords down the road. If Ramone let us melt down his sword, we could have done a better job of ones that last, but he will never allow that to happen. It has been in his family for centuries and proves he is the head of his clan. Once I get the sending portal working, we should be able to enter the cavern on Zada 5 and locate more of the Verbraso, with none of the local miners knowing we are there. It should also allow us to travel there anytime we want and not wait for the alignment."

"I never asked, but how did Ramone come into the picture?"

"He has been around for a long time now. For years, I had been slowly sending Zando Crystals to Korbin for use at the labs. One day, he wandered out of one of the small freighters, ready to fight the guards. I was on Korbin, so one guard fetched me to talk him down, but getting there, I could see him swinging his sword, and it had a strange red glow. I convinced him to stop and trust me. He was seeking a way to end his life by combat. I told him we could come up with a better solution, but needed his help once I saw his sword and realized what could be done with it. I needed to build new ones like his. It took years of trial and error. Then I invented the ones we have now. While working on them, I brought Ramone here to work with the rebels."

"Wait, was he around when we rescued Bernard?"

"No, I think it was much later. I was using the rebels to test all my new weapons, and Ramone formed them into more of a tight unit and grew. I think if he had been here before, you guys may not have got out."

"That would make sense, as they seemed to be fiercer and better organized when you brought me back after the crash. With my training, they will be an unstoppable army for you to control."

Lorenzo smirks. "Good, they will need to be for what I have planned."

OVER A MONTH LATER, RAMONE, A TALL, OLDER MAN with several scars across his face and a clan sword strapped to his back, walks into Lorenzo's lab and over to his workspace. "When will we be able to get to Zada 5 with your machine?"

Lorenzo laughs. "Machine, you mean portal?"

"Okay, whatever it's called."

"Well, we need to do trials, then complete a new one. So, we will be able to after we use the new one in about two more months."

"Good. I have been training for months now to face Mondo. As it gets closer, I find myself getting antsy to take my rightful place as head of all clans. If the emperor had not invaded, I would have been able to defeat Mondo."

"I understand how you feel. I should have been the emperor, not my brother."

"But I thought the emperor was your older brother?"

"Yes, but when my mother was alive, she told me I was so much smarter than Esteban, which would make me a better ruler. She was going to convince our father how much better I would be, but she got sick and died first.

"Then, while I was performing my early testing for interstellar travel and crash landed here, one of the original rebel leaders found me. He helped me recover from a broken leg and arm, so I built them new weapons, which would give me an opportunity to test everything I was developing. While I was doing this, my brother worked together with our father. Then when my father got sick, he made me the owner of labs and manufacturing, but he still declared my brother the emperor when it should have been me. I have never forgotten that. We all have people we need to face, and once I am done here in the lab, we should all be able to."

"Agreed. I am going back to my training, so I will be ready."

"Once the trial is complete, I will have Craven let you know."

"Thank you."

EARLY ONE MORNING, ANOTHER MONTH LATER, MAJOR Johnson rushes into the lab hunting for Lorenzo, who is in the back sleeping after working most of the night. Waking him up, the major says one of his men had been killed and all his weapons taken from him.

Lorenzo glares at him. "Why are you waking me for this? It sounds like a local issue that you should deal with."

Major Johnson explains, "Yes, normally, I would agree, but if they are wearing the suit and wielding the sword, they will be as unstoppable as the rest of my soldiers."

Lorenzo, still half asleep, mumbles, "No problem. Have one of your soldiers slice off the right hand, then knock them down and stomp on their right wrist, shutting down the suit."

"You mean it is that simple? I hope our enemies do not find that out."

"Agreed. I had to take a few shortcuts to make everything work."

"Thank you. Go back to sleep. I will find the weapons."

LATER THAT DAY, MAJOR JOHNSON ROUNDS UP SEVERAL people from the local town because they could find none of the weapons taken from the dead sentry. After torturing and killing two, they still could not get any information.

That evening, Lorenzo checks in with Major Johnson. "Were you able to find the suit or sword?"

"No, sir, we were not. Do you think the emperor could have sent someone here?"

"I do not. There would have been an actual battle, not merely one sentry killed. I would suggest you double the guards, if that is the case."

"Yes, sir, it has already been done. We also have installed video cameras around the outside of our base, so we will see anyone who tries anything like this next time. After torturing and killing some locals, we made it clear what would happen, so they will not attempt it again."

"Very good. I am getting close to finishing. We cannot afford any further interruptions."

"Yes, sir, you got it. There will not be."

"I will send Craven and Ramone to the lab on my home planet of Markus 2 after they finish assisting me to see if they can find out anything. I still have a few people there I can trust."

Headed to Markus 2 a few days later, Craven and Ramone take off. Once they arrive, Craven leads the two of them into the lab complex through a back entrance, so as not to be seen. Inside, Craven reaches out to a woman, Rita, who is still loyal to Lorenzo and friends with Emma. Rita tells Craven she has seen Emma talking with Adam Balcazar, the duke's son.

Craven says, "Oh yes, I know the duke very well. He cost me my family."

Rita exclaims, "I am so sorry. I did not know."

"No one but Lorenzo is aware, but he will help me get even one day."

"So, what else do you need from me?"

"If Emma was with Adam, then she must be aiding him. Wait, isn't she the sister of Roger, who died on Korbin?"

"Yes, she is, or, should I say, was. We were all very sad to learn about the accident."

"We all heard the same thing." He asks her if she has been in Emma's lab.

She says, "Yes, I have, several times."

"Can I get in any other way than through the main door so I can learn what she is currently working on?"

Rita tells him, "There is a window in the back of the lab that cannot be seen from the front. If you distracted her somehow in the front, then you could enter."

The next morning, Craven sends Ramone to Emma's lab. Ramone tells her he is part of a new security team, then asks her a few questions about her lab and her experiments to be safe. While he does, Craven breaks the lock on the window and sneaks in. Ramone and Emma finish their conversation. He walks away, being careful to hide from any cameras so as not to expose his face. Emma locks her door again, then returns to the table with the suit and sword. Craven sneaks forward to see what she is working on. After a bit, he glimpses the suit and sword.

Then, as she picks up the ring, Craven comes from behind and hits her in the head with a pipe he took off the shelf. He hunts around for the ring, but cannot find it anywhere. He quickly grabs the suit and sword off the table, then turns on the gas, setting a small fire as he slips out the window. As Craven walks away, an explosion sounds behind him.

Ramone meets him in the back of the building. When he walks up to Craven, he demands, "Did you have to kill her?"

Craven responds, "You may not understand, but she had the missing suit and sword, so she had to be working with the duke or emperor, possibly exposing us."

"What could she have told them if you took the equipment? All you had to do was knock her out."

"Whether or not you what to accept this, we are preparing to fight a war here. You will need to pick what side you are on. If you want to reach Zada 5 and fight Mondo, then you will need to trust Lorenzo and me."

"Yes, I do, but our clan has a code. We do not hurt women or children."

"I understand and used to feel the same way, but when my family was murdered, all of that changed. Now anyone that is not with us is against us, including you, so which do you choose?"

"I am with you."

"Ok, good, then let's get back to Ria 6 so I can update Lorenzo on what we found out."

LATER THAT EVENING, THEY GET BACK TO RIA 6 AND Lorenzo's lab. Finding him still working, Craven walks over, handing him the suit and sword. "We got this from Emma's workplace."

Lorenzo groans, "No, not Emma. So, she was working with my brother?"

"According to your friend, she was with Adam, the son of Duke William."

"Well, I am not surprised. I have been hearing Adam was getting more involved with my brother's expansion efforts, creating quite a reputation for himself already. But if they came here, why did they kill the sentry and leave?"

"Maybe they saw what they needed to and left."

"My bet is they stepped into more than they thought they would but found a way to kill the sentry, then take his suit, sword, and the ring. That reminds me—where is the ring?"

"I could not find it. That is why I blew up the lab."

"So, did you have to kill Emma, too?"

"Yes, we could not have her giving your brother or the others any more information. Just like you had me do with her brother."

"No, I understand, but it is a shame. She was very sharp; it was just too bad she had to pick the wrong side."

"One more thing will work to our advantage. Your friend told me your niece and her friend are graduating.

There will be a celebration on the eighteenth of next month. Everyone will be at the palace at the same time for several days."

"Yes, I was aware. Christina invited me, but that was before we disappeared. Why do think I have been in such a hurry to finish? This could not have worked out more perfectly for us, but we have one problem. I need more Verbraso. Right now, the only place we know where to find any is on Zada 5."

"Well, the window closed about a month ago, and the next will not be until the eighteenth of next month, but we will already be busy then."

"I have enough to open two windows for the portal once I have completed my testing."

"When we are done on the eighteenth, then we should be able to do whatever we want, when we want."

"You are right, but we had agreed when we were ready, we would send Ramone back to Zada 5 to gain his rightful place."

"Then we will need to explain to him the reason for the delay. He has been waiting this long. What is another few months? He also voiced his concerns about killing Emma. I had to make it clear to him."

"He comes from an old school of thinking, but we cannot let him get in the way if that is the case."

"He seemed to understand, but I know what you are saying, and he will not stop us, no matter what."

After their discussion, Lorenzo tells Craven to have Major Johnson come meet with him. A short time later,

Major Johnson walks into Lorenzo's lab and over to Lorenzo. "You sent for me, sir?"

Lorenzo says, "Yes, you can let the remaining locals go. They did not take the suit or sword."

"Well, then who did?"

"One of the duke's sons."

"*The duke's sons?* Why would they be here?"

"Remember the warehouse break-in? I suspect it was them as well."

"Why? It was locals looking for money or something to sell."

"No, I am sure it was those brats. I think somehow they found out we are storing the excess crystals and the suits. You said they opened one box, but it did not look like anything was missing, right? My bet is if you inventoried that box, one suit would be absent. With that said, they have no power supplies to make it work. I think Roger, my lab manager on Korbin, was allied with them. That is why he asked so many questions. He likely showed them the equipment. When we killed Roger and I disappeared, they came back searching for more. Which makes me glad we killed Roger before he could tell them anything else about us."

"That is a wild theory."

"Do you have anything better? None of the locals confessed, right, even after torture and killing? I think someone would have. Then, on top of it, Craven went back to Markus 2, finding the suit and sword in one lab, owned by Roger's sister Emma. She was working with Adam, the duke's son."

Major Johnson now thinks they could be overrun. "Then we have to get ready for an attack. They can come back anytime."

"Relax. I know my brother. Until he knows how to combat our suits and swords, he will not risk killing a lot of his men. In addition, he cannot bomb us since I control manufacturing, disarming anything that may hurt us. Lastly, we are too close to the locals. He will not risk killing any of them either. Just stay on your toes until the nineteenth of next month."

"Why then?"

"Then we will activate my plan, and if all goes correctly, you will not have to worry about anything again."

"Everything will be ready?"

"If I can stay on schedule, yes, it will be."

MAJOR JOHNSON COMES BACK THE NEXT DAY. "YOUR new ships are up and flying now. We have been testing them to patrol the outer areas. No one will perceive them from the ground, and it will give us more time if anyone else does come surveying to attack us."

Lorenzo orders, "Go ahead, but limit flying time to an hour. There are still heat issues with the stealth functions, and that has not been a priority for me."

"Yes, sir. You got it. I also released the locals we were holding last night."

"Did you give them a reason?"

"We told them we had found the person responsible, then threw them out of the building."

"Good. We need them to stay scared, so we do not have to deal with anyone looking for revenge. We have enough to manage right now."

A FEW DAYS LATER, LORENZO ASKED CRAVEN TO TAKE equipment he marked in his lab out to the large warehouse the rebels used for storing vehicles and equipment. A few days after that, Craven lets Lorenzo know everything has been set up and prepared. Lorenzo then orders Craven to wait there for him to show up. Just like Roger had done on Korbin, Lorenzo loads the tubes holding the refined Zando Crystals and the other minerals, including Verbraso, and powers up the platform in his lab. A few seconds later, a window opens up in front of Craven. Right after the window appears, Lorenzo steps through, but just as he steps out, the window disappears.

Craven gawks at Lorenzo. "Was the window supposed to close as quickly as it did?"

"No, it should have stayed open until I closed it from this side." After spending hours going over the equipment, he looks at Craven. "Everything seems good here. Take me back to my lab so I can inspect the sending unit." Craven obeys, and Lorenzo spends multiple days going over all the equipment. Finally, he uncovers a control card in one of the power supplies with some burned-out spots. He goes through his spare parts but does not find that same card anywhere. Lorenzo glances at Craven, holding up the defective card. "You will need to go to Korbin and get a couple of these." Then he hands Crave the name and location of a person who can provide Crave with the replacements, along with some other parts he wants, but tells him he needs to be covert.

Shortly after talking with Lorenzo, Craven leaves. He takes until early the next morning. Just before the sun comes up, Craven lands back on Ria 6 with the parts. Craven marches off the ship and has a few of the rebels unload, then takes the parts to Lorenzo's lab while Craven goes to his room to sleep. Several hours later, Lorenzo wakes him up. "I have made all the repairs. Now I need your help to test one more time."

Craven yawns. "Give me some time to wake up."

"When you are ready, go back to the storage building again, then let me know when you are there." Lorenzo walks away.

"Will do." An hour later, Craven reaches out to Lorenzo. "Ok, I am here."

"Great, give me a couple of minutes to turn everything on." As Craven observes, a window above the platform opens, and Lorenzo walks through. He stands there for a few minutes, then walks over and shuts the window down. Excitedly, he beams at Craven and shakes his hand. "It's working. The test was successful. We are almost ready. Now all we need to do is place this equipment on Markus 2."

"Finally, I did not think this time would ever come."

Lorenzo now wears a big smile, thinking everything is ready and they can finally execute the plan. "Right, I know, neither did I. That is why I have been killing myself to get this completed and working correctly."

"I have something to tell you, though."

"What?"

"When I set the explosion to kill Emma and destroy the evidence, it actually killed ten people, not just her."

"That is sad, but I cannot care at this point. In a few weeks' time, it will not matter."

CHAPTER XI

THE GRADUATION

At the palace a few days after Emma died, Esteban and the team are still trying to find any signs of Lorenzo while keeping the palace safe and getting ready for the girls' graduation and palace celebration. Continuing to work on security issues, John had his team pull video from the lab complex the day they killed Emma. He asks Eric and Adam to join him in his office. Connor paces in with Eric. Adam comes in a few minutes later. John says, "I have the video feed from the day that Emma was killed."

As they watch it, Adam comments, "Where is this camera?"

"There are actually two, and the video was streaming to a central location."

As it starts, a split screen appears with one feed outside the door on the opposite end from where Dave and Matt monitored Emma, then another one from inside her lab. "I had them installed right after they killed Roger on Korbin. We needed to make sure if there were any more issues, we had better video."

While they fast forward to when the older man knocks on her door, Eric interrupts, "Wait back that up. I think I know who that guy is." As he comes up to the door, they pause it on a full view of his face. "That's Ramone!"

Connor exclaims, "Wait, you mean one of the clan leaders Mondo said disappeared many years ago?"

"The very person, but how did he end up there?"

"That is an excellent question. Let's go forward with the video." As John starts the video again, some movement flickers in the back of Emma's lab, but they cannot tell who it is. She closes and locks the door, then goes back to the table to continue working. A short time later, someone moves forward.

Adam shouts, "That's Craven, the guy in the lab on Korbin." He hits Emma, knocking her to the floor, then looks around the area for a few minutes before grabbing the suit and sword. He turns the gas on; then he goes to the back of the lab where they cannot see him anymore. A few minutes later, Matt tries to open her door and call Adam, and they witness part of the explosion before it destroys the cameras.

John says, "So this means both Craven and Ramone are working together with Lorenzo, but how did they find out about Emma having the suit and sword?"

"My guess would be Emma talked with someone or they suspected her since she was Roger's sister. We were very careful on Ria 6, so I know they did not know we were there."

"There is still an investigation going on at the lab, so we will see who knew Emma or if anyone recognized what she was doing in her lab."

A FEW DAYS LATER, JOHN SENDS A MESSAGE TO ADAM to meet in his office. The young man walks in a little while later, followed by Connor right after him. "Have you seen Eric?"

John answers, "No, but I think he was going to be busy with Esteban today."

Connor asks, "So, what are you two up to?"

"I received some more news about what happened at Emma's lab and was going to update your brother."

"Well then, I guess it was good timing for me. I would like to hear as well."

Adam agrees. "Sure, that is fine with me. So, what do you have?"

John says, "We found a woman. Her name is Rita. She was very upset from the time we questioned her. She started by saying she did not think they were going to hurt her; they were just searching for something, but when she told them she saw Emma and Adam talking, they got very interested in her, wanting to know what she was working on and how to enter her lab without being seen. Then she said, 'I told them about a back window they could use.'"

Adam now feels horrible for getting her involved. "So, this was all my fault. *I got her killed, just like her brother!*"

"No, it's not. You did nothing wrong here except ask someone to help us. Lorenzo's the bad guy here, killing people to cover his tracks."

"But we get paid to do this kind of work, not them."

Connor states, "She knew the risks and was willing to assist if it meant getting to Lorenzo. You heard her say so when we last saw her."

John agrees. "Connor is right. After they killed her brother, she would have done anything to pin Lorenzo to the wall."

"And Craven too."

Adam sighs, "You are both right, but it still hurts because I basically recruited her."

John assures him, "I am sure it does, and I would be concerned if you did not feel badly about it."

"The way I see it, we need to get everybody through the girls' graduation and celebration, then head to Zada 5 where we could run into Craven, capture him, and get him to lead us to Lorenzo so we can end all of this." As Connor is saying this, Eric and Esteban walk in.

Esteban comments, "It sounds like you guys are working on a plan to take down my brother?"

John looks at Esteban. "Yes, I think we are." John then updates both him and Eric on what they discussed.

Afterwards, Esteban walks over to Adam and gives him a hug. "John was right. None of this was your fault. My brother caused all of this, and we will have to stop him."

Days later, it's the girls' graduation and everyone gets together, along with a small security detail, to fly to the girls' school several hours away. While everyone else is flying, the girls are at the school getting ready.

Christina wears a big smile, looking at Emily. "I cannot believe how excited I am. It has been over three months."

Emily says, "Wait, I thought you were talking about graduation, but you mean since you last saw Adam, right?"

"Ha, ha, ha, sorry, yes. I am excited about commencement too, but more so about Adam. I cannot believe how much I have missed him, and am so glad I will finally get to be near him today. He may not know it yet, but I am going to marry him."

Emily laughs. "Well, doesn't he have something to say about that?"

Christina starts to giggle as well. "Yes, he does, but if he really feels the same way I do, it will not be that hard to convince him."

Emily grins at her. "Yes, I am sure you are right. Not to change the subject, but I wonder if your uncle is going to be here. Since we now have degrees in the sciences, I was hoping he would let us work in his labs."

"Well, I saw him before we left and invited him. I agree, it would be exciting to work on all the new technologies."

"When is everyone going to arrive?"

"According to the message I got from Father, they will be here around one this afternoon."

WITH EVERYONE ON THE SHIP FLYING TO SEE THE GIRLS, Adam pulls Esteban to the back for a private conversation. The emperor responds, "What is it, son?"

Adam states, "I want a moment alone with you, as I have something I wanted to ask you."

I think I know, but sure, what is it?" Esteban smiles at him. "

Adam remains a little hesitant. "Well, sir, if your daughter agrees, I would like your permission to marry her."

Esteban gazes at him with a slight laugh. "I knew that is why you asked."

Adam wears a puzzled look on his face. "How did you know?"

Esteban laughs out loud. Hearing the laugh, everyone at the front of the ship turns and looks back, seeing the two of them talking. William and Sara stroll to the back.

Now Adam turns a little embarrassed. "Mom and Dad, this was kind of a private conversation."

"No, they should be here to hear this. Adam, I have always wanted someone brave, strong, and smart to marry my daughter, and I wanted it to be you from the time the two of you got into trouble together. But you both had to grow and mature first, which I am proud to say I have witnessed in the two of you. Yes, you have my permission."

Sara exclaims, "Adam, did you ask to marry Christina?"

"Yes, Mom, I did." Adam is still a little embarrassed.

She comes over, giving him a big hug. "I am so happy for you."

"Wait, you are all celebrating, but I have not even asked her yet!"

The three of them laugh; William puts his hand on Adam's shoulder. "Son, we have all seen the two of you together, and we do not think she will say no, but you are right. We need to let the two of you meet and talk before we say or do anything."

"Thank you, sir, for your support." Looking at Esteban with a big smile, Adam shakes his hand.

Sara says, "When do you think you will propose?"

"I wanted to wait until after they graduate, so maybe before we all fly home tonight."

"Do you have a ring?"

"No, I was going to tell her we would pick one out together if she said yes."

"You cannot do that." She pulls a ring off her left hand and hands it to him. "This was your grandmother's. She would have wanted you to have it for your wife."

Adam holds it up. "Wow, Mom, are you sure? I always thought it was beautiful."

"Yes, I have been wearing it since she passed away, waiting for this day to give it to one of you boys."

Adam gives her a big hug. "Thank you, Mom."

Connor and Eric come walking back. "Is this a private party?" asks Connor.

Sara puts her arm around him. "No, we were talking about the graduation and celebration in a few weeks."

"Really? That is what everyone seems to be so happy about?"

Esteban laughs, "Of course, what else would it be?"

"Not sure, sir, but it seemed to be more."

"You do not need to call me sir. I think we have been working together long enough."

Eric laughs. They all look at him. William inquires, "What was so funny?"

Eric explains, "Your son had the same conversation with several people on Zada 5."

Esteban asks, "Really?"

"Oh, yes. He has become highly thought of there and everyone wants to call him sir, but he keeps telling them they do not have to."

Sara, with her arm still around Connor, squeezes him. "I am so proud of how much you boys have grown."

At that moment, John comes down to the end of the ship with everyone else. "I hate to break up the party, but we are about to land." Adam puts the ring in his pocket, and they all sit down just before the ship lands. The pilot lands near the back of the airfield, away from the other ships to keep it secure.

After they arrive, the security detail asks them to stay on the ship until they validate that all is secure. As they get off, Adam and Connor go out with them. The captain of the security detail asks, "Sirs, we know about both your reputations, but are you armed?"

Connor states, "Yes, of course, with everything that has been going on, we always are."

"Very well. You may come along."

Adam laughs while putting his hand on the captain's shoulder. "We weren't asking." After quickly patrolling around, they come back to the ship. Adam leans in, looking at everyone inside. "It is all clear. You can come out now. Let's go see the girls graduate."

They stroll into the auditorium, where there is a clearly marked spot for the emperor and his guests with a small security detail behind them. The rest standing at the doors. Just as they sit down, the girls stride in with the rest of their graduating class. The group waves, and the girls wave back.

After a few hours of the graduation ceremony efforts and the names called, then the final announcements, the girls come running over and hug everyone. Then Christina grabs Adam's hand and yanks him over to the side of the stage where they cannot be seen. Then she gives him a big kiss. "This is all I have been thinking about since I saw you as we came walking out. I have missed you so much." Then she kisses him again.

"Well, I was going to wait until a little later." Adam pulls the ring out of his pocket and gets down on one knee holding up the ring, but before he can ask, "Will you marry me?" she squeals really loud, then screams,"YES!"

Still near their seats in the auditorium, everyone hears Christina squeal. They all laugh. Sara says, "It sounded like it is official."

Both Connor and Emily, at the same time, ask, "What is?"

William explains, "Your brother asked Christina to marry him, and you just heard her response."

Both have a surprised look on their face. "He did?"

Emily giggles, "Too funny. She was saying earlier today she would convince Adam to wed her. I guess she did not need to push him. He must have missed her as much as she did him."

Sara agrees. "Yes, I am sure he did."

A few minutes later, the couple strides back hand in hand with big smiles on their faces to everyone else. As they appear, everybody claps. When they get close, Christina says, "Did all of you know he was going to ask me?"

Eric admits, "Well, most of us did. I think Emily and Connor were the only ones not aware." Then they congratulate the both of them.

Esteban walks over and hugs Emily. "I know the spotlight has moved a little, but I need to say I am so proud of you and all you and Christina have accomplished. I could not be happier with my two successful daughters."

Emily says, "Thank you, Dad, and I truly mean Dad. I really cannot remember any other family but this one. I have always felt accepted by both you and Christina."

"I am glad, but I am sorry that you have no actual memories of your birth family. I hope we have honored them with how you have been taken care of."

"From my point of view, you definitely have, and I could not be happier for Christina, but one thing is on my mind. I thought Uncle Lorenzo was going to be here. We are interested in working in his labs since we have degrees in the sciences."

"Well, he has kind of fallen off the map, but we can talk more about that when we get back. This should be a happy time."

"Oh sorry, I did not realize there were any issues. We saw him at the palace the day before we left, and Christina invited him."

"Yes, that was the last time I talked to him as well. There is a lot going on, and I will update the both of you tomorrow, but for today, we have a lot to celebrate."

He then paces up to the rest of the group. "I was just telling Emily we have a lot to commemorate, so we need to get home."

Christina agrees. "Thanks, Dad. Good point." They all stroll back to the ship where security already waits after patrolling the path.

On the ship, Christina and Adam almost sit on top of each other, still with big smiles. Connor comes over, peering at the both of them. "I did not say it before, but I am very happy for the both of you. But as you guys will have a long lifetime together, can I talk with my brother privately for a minute?"

Christina says, "Absolutely."

Adam follows Connor to the back of the ship, where they can talk without being heard.

Connor states, "I could not be more delighted for you, but do you think this is the right time?"

Adam demands, "What do you mean?"

"We still have a lot of dangerous stuff to do, and being overcautious could get you killed and me along with you."

"What are you talking about?"

"When we are out doing what we have to, I want to make sure you are focused on what we need to accomplish, not back with your soon to be wife."

Adam turns a little stern. "You do not need to worry. I am always focused on the job."

"Sorry, I am not trying to upset you. I would not want to lose you—that is all I am saying."

Adam puts his arm around Connor. "I get it. I am sure I would say the same to you if things were reversed. I promise my attention will be on our mission when we are away and appreciate your concern."

With their conversation finished, they go back to the group. Adam sits down with Christina, then grabs and squeezes her hand. She looks at him. "So, what was all that about?"

"It was nothing. He was just concerned."

"About us?"

"Sort of, but we can talk about that when we are alone."

She smiles at him and then squeezes his hand back. "Ok."

Meanwhile, Emily moves over to Connor. "So, what happened to you? It has only been about four months, and it may be my imagination, but it seems to me you are taller and bigger." Hearing her, Eric and John start to laugh. She glances at them. "What is so funny?"

Eric pats Connor on the back. "No, it is not you. He is bigger all over, thanks to working out on Zada 5."

"Don't get me wrong. I think you look great. I was surprised to see the changes in you, and I am not sure how to pinpoint it, but it also seems you have grown up."

"Yes, you are right. Zada 5 changed him for the better."

Then John nudges Connor. "Maybe you should tell her about your dragon." Everyone else hears that all, but Christina and Emily laugh. Connor is completely embarrassed with his cheeks turning red.

Then Emily and Christina both at the same time say, "DRAGON?"

Connor agrees. "Yes, I have a dragon that lives with me on Zada 5."

Emily says, "You're not talking about an actual dragon. I did not think they were real, just a myth in stories?"

"No, a real dragon. Her name is Andorra."

Emily teases Connor a little. "Oh, a GIRL dragon. What did you do, lift up her skirt?"

Connor lets out a slight laugh. "No, she told me she had eggs, which means she was the female."

"Wait. You talk to it? Really talk with it and she responds?"

Eric agrees. "Yes, I have seen it for myself, and he can do it, saying nothing."

Christina asks, "How?"

Connor explains, "With my mind. She is telepathic, and so am I."

Emily says, "Wow! I would like to hear more about it. Maybe we can sit down and talk about your abilities at the palace." Eric winks at Connor. He smiles back.

Connor looks at Emily. "Yes, I would be happy to."

As the flight continues, they share a lot of small talk with laughter as, for the time being, they try to forget what they endured tracking Lorenzo and all that he had done and the people he killed.

The flight soon lands near the palace. The security detail checks the path to the palace, with Connor and Adam behind them. They come back to the ship, and Adam enters, reaching for Christina's hand. "It is all clear. We can go in." They walk out with Connor outside by the door.

The last one off the ship, Emily comes over to Connor, then puts her arm through his. "Would you escort me to the palace?"

Connor studies her with a big smile. "Yes, it would be my pleasure,"

"Why is there so much security here? We saw more at school, mostly focused on us."

"What did Esteban tell you?"

"I did not ask him anything about it. He mentioned Lorenzo was missing."

Connor laughs. "That is an understatement."

"Connor, what is going on?"

"I think your dad should really tell you. We have been dealing with some things involving Lorenzo, and we need to make sure everyone is safe until we can find him."

"Ok, I will accept that for now, but I think we have a right to know."

"You're correct, but now should be a happy time. I am sure your dad will let you in on everything when he is ready."

"You are correct. We just graduated, and we need to celebrate. Will you dance with me later?"

"Yes, I would be happy to."

By this time, they have made it to the palace with guards outside. All walk in to the main room with music playing. A long table at one end has all kinds of food just placed on it. The group sits down, Esteban at the head of the table with Christina, Adam and his parents on one side, Emily, Connor, Eric, and John on the other.

Esteban stands with a glass in hand. "I would like to make a toast to my two beautiful daughters. You have both made me so proud to see my little girls grow and mature into the women you are now, very smart, both graduating with honors. I am sure you will be successful in your own right. I have never been happier than I am now. To Christina and Emily."

They all raise their glasses and say, "To Christina and Emily."

Both blushing, the girls get up to hug and kiss their father on the cheek, saying at the same time, "Thank you so much, Father."

Holding their hands as they sit back down, he continues to stand, picking his glass back up, then turns and look at both Christina and Adam. "Now for Adam and Christina. This has really been an emotional day for me. I have always wanted the best for you girls, but Christina, you were a little more on the wild side. I knew eventually you would settle down, but wow, I did not think it would be so soon. When you two got into trouble, I knew then there was something special between you and always hoped it would grow. Boy, did it. Now that it is official, I would like to say how happy we all are for the both of you. Emily, if you are ok with it, I would like to turn the celebration on the eighteenth to a joint Graduation/Engagement."

They all look at Emily, making her a little embarrassed. With her red cheeks, she gets up and runs over, giving Christina a hug. "Absolutely, I would love that."

Eric glances at John. "This is going to be one hell of a celebration."

John says, "Yes, I agree, but security is going to be a nightmare."

"No, you are right, but we had already planned on bringing a team to Zada 5 with us. We will simply bring them earlier to help."

"Yes, I like that plan." They then clink their glasses together.

Esteban gazes over at them. "Are you already celebrating?"

Eric replies, "No, just making plans to cover this big event."

"Excellent, I can always rely on you."

John concurs, "Yes, sir, you can."

"Well, I think I have done enough talking. I know we are all hungry, so let's eat and enjoy."

Connor says, "Hear, hear." Everyone laughs.

Eric puts his hand on Connor's shoulder. "Yes, he is always hungry."

Emily looks at him and smiles. "I am sure it takes a lot to fill his big body."

"Yes, you bet it does." Connor winks at her.

Everyone eats and drinks. Adam, seeing Christina, keeps peeking at the ring he placed on her finger, leans over and whispers in her ear, "It belonged to my grandmother."

She grabs his hand. "It is beautiful. I love it. Adam, I am going to make you so happy."

He looks into her eyes. "You already do."

"I am not hungry. Are you?"

"No, not really."

Still holding his hand, she stands up. "Do you want to take a walk with me?"

Adam gets up. "Yes, I do." They hurry off.

Connor hears Eric say to John, "There they go. That did not take long."

He laughs and says, "What do you mean?"

John leans forward to see Connor. "What happened last time they were together at your father's home?"

"Oh, right."

Eric explains, "Young love. They will want to be alone as much as they can. Get it?"

"Yes, I get it."

They finish eating. After a few minutes, Emily looks at Connor. "Would you like to dance with me? I enjoy this music."

"But it would be only you and I."

"Yes, but you know everyone here. They won't care."

"You're right. Let's go." They walk to the other end of the table and the dance floor. While they are dancing, Eric and John move closer to Esteban; then William and Sara do the same. Esteban sees Sara smiling while looking at Emily and Connor together. "Why are you grinning?"

Sara sighs. "Oh, I was just thinking how nice it would be if those two hit it off like Adam and Christina did."

Esteban smiles as well. "Yes, I could not dream of a better match for her, to have my two girls marry your two boys. Just thinking about it does my heart good, but we cannot get ahead of ourselves."

"No, you are right. It is their call, not ours, but it would not hurt to give them a little nudge."

William says, "No, stay out of it, MOM."

"What?"

Eric and John both laugh. "We know what he means."

She laughs. "Ok, ok, I get it. I will leave it alone for now."

William asks, "For now?"

"Yes, for now."

After a few minutes, a slower song plays, and Esteban walks over to the dance floor and looks at Connor. "May I cut in here?"

Connor shakes his hand. "Yes, you may."

Esteban waltzes with Emily while Connor sits down with his mother. She puts her arm around him. "Are you having a good time?"

"I am. Emily is a lot of fun."

"I am glad. You two look good together."

The three men hear her and laugh. Then William says, "I thought you were going to leave it alone?"

Connor asks, "What is Dad talking about?"

Sara says, "It was a private joke."

"Are you sure?"

She just smiles. "Yes, it is nothing."

While they chat, Esteban and Emily finish their dance. She gives him a big hug and kiss on the cheek. "Thank you, Daddy, that was nice."

"Yes, I liked it too." While holding her hand, Esteban walks her back to the table next to Connor. "She is all yours." He goes back to where he was sitting.

Emily looks at Connor. "Would you like to take a stroll outside and get some air?" Connor stands up. Once he does, she puts her arm in his.

As they walk away, he responds, "Yes, that sounds good."

John looks at Esteban and Sara. "They do not have a chance with you two working them."

Esteban has a smile on his face. "I do not know what you are talking about."

Eric says, "It is clear to me Emily would like there to be more. Connor will not understand what happened to him with the three of you against him." All but Sara laugh.

Sara asks, "Why are you all laughing? This is how it really works."

William points out, "That is not what happened with Adam."

"Oh, you think so?"

"Wait, what are you saying? How did you have a hand in that?"

"What would have happened had I not pushed you to send Adam off to work with Eric, then done the same with Christina after they got in trouble together on Lucas 2?"

Esteban laughs. "So that is why you convinced me to send her away to school."

"When that happened, I already knew they had feelings for each other. Splitting them up like we did increased those feelings. Now here we are." The men chuckle again.

Esteban smacks William on the shoulder. "You are married to an evil genius."

"Hey, evil genius?" Sara questions.

Eric agrees. "Man, I am glad you plotted nothing for us."

"Well, if you guys had been with anyone serious, I may have."

"Why is that?" Esteban gazes at John and Eric.

John explains, "Because of the life we chose, there was very little time for it. Not to say there was no one.

We both had a few women we thought were special, but none of them were willing to be second, so they always ended. Some quicker than others."

"You guys never wanted a family or kids?"

Eric shrugs. "We have all of that. You guys are our family, and we both feel like Adam and Connor are our boys and would do anything for them. We helped raise them into the men they are now and could not be prouder of them."

"I get it. They are great boys. Anyone would be proud to say they were theirs."

Out in the back garden, Adam and Christina walk. They embrace, kissing and caressing each other. After a minute, Adam stands up. "We need to stop, or I am going to have to take you right here on the bench."

Christina smiles. "Okay, what's wrong with that?"

Adam grins in return. "Well, there are guards that keep walking around."

She starts to laugh, "Oh, yes, them. I forgot they were here. Well, if we are taking a break, I have a question. Why are you are still wearing your weapons?"

Adam becomes grave. "There have been some issues, and we need to make sure everyone is safe. That is why there are so many. They have been trying to give us some space, but the guards need to be active, making sure all areas stay safe."

"Why, what's going on?"

"I am not sure this is the right time to be talking about it. I think your father should be with us."

"Adam, I do not want there to be any secrets between us."

"I understand that, and agree, but like I said, your father should be here."

"Ok, that's fair. So, do you want to go back to making out more or go get some food?"

Adam laughs. "Just making out."

Christina laughs too. "Well, not just."

"Maybe we should pick up some food, then come back to what we were doing."

"I like that plan."

Adam grabs her hand and pulls her into a hug. They kiss again, then walk back inside.

WITH ADAM AND CHRISTINA IN THE MAIN GARDEN OUT back, Connor and Emily walk out to a smaller garden on the side of the palace. While they move around, Emily reaches down, sliding her hand into Connor's. He looks at her and smiles.

"I have a confession to make."

"Oh really? What is it?"

"I am not sure how to say this." Emily pauses. "I have had a crush on you for a long time. Basically, since we were kids, I always wanted to be in the room training with you and Adam like Christina was, so I could spend time with you."

"Wow, I never knew. I would have enjoyed having you with us as well." He gives her a kiss.

"That was nice. Can we do it again?" This time, Connor puts his arms around her. "Wow, I am a little lightheaded. I like that one even more."

As he grabs her hand, they walk over to the bench nearby. The two fall into another kiss, this time deeper and more passionate. By this time, it has been dark for several hours.

One guard comes up to Connor and Emily. "Sir, I am sorry to interrupt, but we need you to go back. We will be locking it down and must have everyone inside the building."

They stare up and laugh. "Sorry, we got carried away."

"Yes, sir, maybe a little bit." As he walks away, they both head inside the palace.

At the same time, Adam and Christina return to the main room hand in hand, grinning from ear to ear. Eric and John turn as they hear the two of them. Eric teases, "So, do you need food now after working up an appetite?" They both turn red. Everyone at the table laughs.

Adam says, "I do not know what you are talking about, but yes, we are hungry now."

John winks at him. "Sure, you don't." They both come over and sit down to eat.

William looks at them. "I guess you were hungry." Adam returns the gaze and grins.

As Adam and Christina are almost finished, Connor and Emily walk in from the other side of the room, also hand in hand. Connor's parents, Adam, and Christina turn and gawk at them. Sara squeezes William's arm, and Esteban says, "Well, well, what is this?" Christina excitedly claps.

Connor shrugs. "What can I say? We were outside talking and really hit it off."

Sara says, "Well, I am happy that the two of you have."

Christina stands up, goes over to them, and gives Emily a hug. Then Emily leans in and whispers in her ear, "I really need to talk with you tonight."

Christina responds, "Yes, I need to talk to you too." She settles back down with Adam.

Esteban declares, "I think this has been a busy, eventful, and happy day. I am glad we have been able to share in it together, and I just wanted to say I love you all and consider everyone part of my family. I hope you feel the same way about us."

William stands up. "Esteban, I am sure I can speak for my entire family. We feel blessed to be accepted this way and believe you are part of our family as well." They get up and hug each other.

Esteban then says, "Not sure about the rest of you, but I am ready to get some sleep."

William turns to him. "Yes, this has been a very long and busy day." He reaches for Sara's hand. "We are ready as well." The rest of them agree and head to their rooms.

Connor looks at Adam. "I need to talk with you."

Adam kisses Christina. She squeezes his hand and whispers, "I will see you later."

Connor kisses Emily and says, "Have a good night."

She kisses him back. "I will. You too."

The girls both go into Christina's room, while the boys head to Adam's. In his room, Connor and Adam talk. "So, you and Emily, how did that happen?"

"I do not really know. She asked to walk with me back here to the palace, and it seemed to go from there. While you guys were outside, we danced a little, and then we also went for a stroll. She told me she had a crush on me since we were kids, and it got physical from there."

"Physical, really, how so?"

Connor laughs. "No, nothing like that. Just hugging and kissing, but it felt like we belonged together. It may end up being nothing, but then again, it could be something. I want to see where it goes."

"Now I need to ask you the same questions you asked me about where your head will be during the mission."

"You're right. I need to be like you when we are out there. I get it."

"Good, because I need to depend on you too."

"You can. I really was not looking for this, but it was a nice way for the day to end."

"Well, if I know these girls, your day is not over."

"Sure, it is. This has been a very long celebration, and I am going to my room to get some sleep."

WHILE THE BOYS DISCUSS IN ADAM'S ROOM, CHRISTINA and Emily walk into her room. Emily grabs her hand and looks at her ring. They jump up and down, screaming. "This is amazing. You said you were going to marry him, and he asked before you had a chance to put the idea in his head."

Christina replies, "I know. I could not believe my eyes when he bent down and showed me the ring. I was so excited and just lost it. I could not say YES fast enough. This is all happening so fast. *Is this really my future life?* I cannot believe how happy I am right now."

"I know, and I am so glad for you."

"What about you and Connor?"

"Well, I really started it, but when I saw him on the ship up close, all those muscles and how tall he got, I knew I had to try something. I made him walk with me to the palace, placing my arm in his. Then we danced after eating, and I asked him to come outside with me. I took him to the side garden so we would not run into you guys like last time at their place. Then I told him about my crush, and he did the rest."

"I am thrilled it is working out for you. Maybe we can have a double wedding."

"Yes, that would be amazing, but I do not want to scare him away either."

"Well, Connor wanted to talk with Adam, so I will gauge where his head is when I see him in a few minutes."

"What do you mean?"

"I mean, tonight is the night. I cannot wait any longer."

Emily grabs her hand tight with a screech. "Really?"

Christina responds, "He does not know it, but oh yes, and you should do the same thing."

Emily's eyes open wide. "Really? You think so?"

"Oh yes, how long have you been waiting?"

"As long as you."

"Trust me, he will be more than willing and happy you did. Give me a few minutes, then go to Connor's room. If the guys have not finished talking, they will be when I show up." She goes down the stairs, then through the hallway to Adam's room and knocks on his door. At that very moment, Connor turns toward the door after finishing his conversation with Adam. He opens it. "Is Adam here?"

With a big smile on his face, Connor looks back at Adam on the other side of the door, then back at Christina. "Who should I say is asking?"

She giggles, "His soon to be wife."

Connor smiles. "Oh, in that case, yes, he is here." He gives her a hug. "I am very happy for the both of you. I am going to my room. He is all yours."

"Back to your room, you say?"

"Yes, it has been very busy."

"Your day is not over yet."

"It is for me."

"Ok, if you say so. Have a great night."

"I will. Thank you."

"Oh, I know you will."

As he leaves, Connor gives her a puzzled look.

Adam inquires, "What was that all about?"

Christina says, "Nothing."

"I did not think I would see you anymore tonight."

"Really, did you think we were just going to stop after this evening in the garden?"

Adam laughs. "Well, I wanted more, but we are in your home with your father here, so I did not think it would be a good idea if I got caught in your room."

"No, you are right. That is why I came to you. We really need to finish what you started."

Adam laughs again. "What I started?"

Christina takes off her clothes and leans up against him, wearing nothing but her lacey panties. "Yes, what you started."

Just as Christina and Adam lose control, Emily knocks on Connor's door. He opens it, seeing this beautiful voluptuous women with amazing long, blond hair standing there in her robe partially open, showing nothing under it but her panties.

Connor wears a surprised look on his face. "What are you doing here?"

Emily asks, "Why don't you have a girl in there?"

He laughs, grabs her hand, and pulls her into his room. "You're crazy. Get in before someone sees you." After pulling her in, he shuts and locks the door. Emily slips off her robe, puts her arms around him, and moves them towards the bed. They fall on to it with her on top of him. She reaches down, unzips his pants, and pushes them down and off. She then slips off her panties and climbs under the covers on the bed. Connor pops up and slips under the covers, too. She reaches into his shorts, feeling his large member. "Oh wow, everything on you is big."

He rolls towards her. "I need to tell you something."

"What? You can tell me anything."

"I have never been with a woman like this before."

She strokes his face and kisses him a few times with soft kisses, then looks him in his eyes. "It's okay. This is my first time too." She pushes down his shorts and climbs on top of him. She is so wet he just slides inside her, and she almost comes as soon as he is inside of her. As they continue, she gets so worked up she screams.

He pulls her down to him, putting his hand over her mouth. "SSSH, my parents are down the hall." They both laugh, then go at it several more times before falling asleep.

In Adam's room, Christina says, "I am glad you are not wearing any of your weapons except that one between your legs, but you still have on too many clothes." She pulls his shirt over his head, then undoes his pants, leaving him in his underwear. "That is much better." She reaches into his shorts. "I like this weapon."

Adam says with a slight laugh, "You keep doing that and we will be done sooner than you think."

"That's ok. We can start again, and again." Adam then picks her up, lays her on the bed, and pulls off her panties. She tugs the covers and climbs under, lifting part of the covers. "Get in here and let's finish this— well, the first one."

Adam climbs on top of Christina, and shortly after, she screams too. Adam, just like Connor, puts his hand over her mouth. "SSSH, my parents are down the hall." They both laugh as well.

"Wow, that was a nice finish." They continue to kiss, then finish again several more times before falling asleep.

THE NEXT MORNING, CHRISTINA WAKES UP, LOOKING at the time, and jumps out of bed. "Oh crap, oh crap, it is late. Everyone will be getting up soon."

"Okay, let me look out the door first." Adam does, and no one seems to be around. He turns back to Christina as she's getting dressed and gives her the okay.

She puts her hand on his face, gives him a quick kiss, and knocks on Connor's door. "Emily, are you still in there?"

Emily leaps out of bed, peering at the time. "Yes, I am." She steals a kiss from Connor, grabs her robe, and puts it on while opening the door.

Christina sees her in only her robe. "That is all you wore here?"

Laughing, Emily ties it closed and laughs. "Yes, it was."

Christina giggles. "Oh, you slut."

"And what were *you* doing?"

Emily grabs Christina's hand. Just as they head back to their rooms, they hear a noise behind them. Sara walks out of her room from down the hall, sees them, and waves. "Hi, girls." They sheepishly wave back, then flee before anyone else wakes up.

CHAPTER XII

LOVE AND FEAR

LATER THAT SAME MORNING, THE GIRLS ARE ALREADY down for breakfast as Sara enters with a big smile on her face. The girls are embarrassed and can barely meet her eyes. "Girls, did you have a good evening?" They both pop their heads up and look directly at her as she comes over and sits next to them. "It's okay, girls, I will not say anything. I'm on your side, for both of you." They reach over and grab her hand. "Emily, the men already know that I am pushing for you and Connor to follow the same path Christina and Adam just stepped into."

Emily blushes. "Oh, well, thank you."

"You girls can both call me Mom. If you ever need to talk, I will be there for you. I know your father loves you both, but I am sure there are times you would rather talk to a woman."

Christina says, "Thank you, Mom, we would love to."

Emily asks, "So, where are the guys?"

Sara explains, "They are still asleep. I think you two wore them out." The girls both titter.

Just then, Esteban comes walking in. "What were you ladies laughing about?"

Sara winks at the girls, then turns to Esteban. "Oh nothing, just some girl talk."

"Emily, I did not say anything, but it looks like you and Connor hit it off last night."

"You bet she did," Christina utters just loud enough for Emily and Sara to hear. The three of them giggle again.

"Sorry, what was the joke?"

Emily says, "No joke, Daddy, we are just happy this morning. Yesterday was great for us."

"Excellent. But I am sorry to say we will need to talk about more serious matters. I have some meetings this morning, so let's meet after lunch today in John's office."

Sara asks, "Do you think it is big enough for everyone?"

Christina adds, "Everyone? What is going on?"

Esteban agrees. "A good point. There is a larger conference room right down the hall. We can use that." He reaches for Christina's hand. "That is what we will talk about later today. I need to get to my next meeting. I will see you girls after lunch so we can catch up."

Sara informs him, "I will let the boys know when they come down."

"They are still sleeping. I guess they were not done celebrating last night after I went to bed."

"No, I guess not." Emily has a big smile on her face. Esteban continues to walk away.

Shortly after Esteban leaves, the guys enter, seeing the girls sitting with their mother. Connor beams at them. "So, girls, what did you end up doing last night?"

Emily laughs. "We did you guys."

Connor and Adam stand in shock. Christina reassures them, "Relax, your mother knows. She saw us leave your rooms this morning." The guys' faces change from shock to embarrassment.

Sara gets up and hugs the boys both at the same time. "It's okay. I love you, and I'm happy for you two." She steps back and turns. "Actually, I am happy for all four of you."

Connor says, "Now that all of this is out in the open, I am hungry and need food." He sits down beside Emily.

"Aren't you the romantic one." Adam pulls Christina up to him, giving her a big hug and a kiss.

Connor puts his arm around Emily and kisses her on the cheek. "What can I say? She exhausted me. Now I need food."

"It's okay. I know he is still a growing boy." Emily winks.

Connor whispers to Emily, "Save it for later."

She turns, putting both her arms around him. "I will try, but I am finding it hard to maintain myself." She kisses him on his cheek.

"Well, can I eat first?"

"Absolutely, I want you fueled up and ready to go." Emily then kisses him again. Just then, they realize everyone is watching and listening.

Connor and Emily both ask at the same time, "What?"

Sara says, "We are all just happy you two are enjoying being together."

They both then gaze at each other, and Connor says, "Yes, we are."

"Esteban was here before you boys came down, wanting to meet with all of us in the large room by John's office after lunch."

Emily gets serious. "Right. What is this all about?"

Connor says, "Like I told you yesterday, we would be happy to tell you, but it is not our place. It really needs to come from your father."

Sara agrees. "The boys are right. You will know soon enough. Then all your questions will be answered."

Christina nods. "Ok, that's fair. Thanks, Mom."

Adam sputters, "Mom?"

Sara says, "Yes, Mom. I told the girls that's what they can call me."

Emily adds, "Yes, Mom. Do you have a problem with it?"

"No, I don't think so. It sounds nice to me." Connor continues to eat.

Adam watches him. "You might want to slow down, or you might eat your fingers." They all laugh.

"Sorry, I am hungry."

Emily strokes his face. "It's okay. You keep eating."

Adam whispers to Emily, "Look out, he might chomp your hand."

Sara interjects, "Leave your brother alone. He just has a healthy appetite. You should eat something. I am sure your night was equally busy."

"Oh yes, it was." Christina kisses Adam's cheek.

BEFORE THE MEETING, THE FOUR SPEND THE MORNING walking to town and back. As the time draws near, they all head to the office. Eric and John are already there. John asks, "How are the two happy couples doing today?"

Christina says, "We have had another good day."

Eric replies, "Well, I hope this meeting does not dampen that for you."

Emily says, "Okay, now I am a little nervous about all of this."

Connor lightly squeezes her hand. "It will be okay."

Emily leans next to him. "It will be if you are here."

The four of them sit down on the other side of the table from John and Eric. Then William and Sara come in and sit down next to John and Eric. As they do, William winks at the boys.

Adam laughs. "So Mom told you?"

William asks, "What do you think?"

Leaning over, John looks at William. "Told you what?"

He chuckles. "Nothing, it's not important."

At that same time, Esteban enters and sits down at the end of the table. "I am glad you are all present so we can get started right away. Girls, I know you asked yesterday about your uncle Lorenzo. The answer is we do not know where he is. The bigger issue is he has been working on weapons we have had no idea about. One of them is a portal that would allow us to move between worlds. Another is a suit that is impervious to anything, a sword that cuts through anything, including other weapons, and, lastly, a new ship, invisible from the ground. He has been doing all of this secretly. In addition, he has been hiding massive amounts of minerals, including Zando Crystals. This has caused the price to increase." Esteban outlines the lab explosions and all the people Lorenzo has killed, including the two helping them.

Christina then asks, "Can we get another suit and sword to evaluate? This has been what Emily and I have been studying for."

Emily chimes in, "Yes, she's right."

John says, "Well, right now, all we have is the suit Adam first took from Ria 6, but it is missing the power unit."

"Then let Christina and I study it and see what we may be able to do."

Christina asks, "What about this portal? Is there one we could look at?"

John shakes his head. "The only ones we really had access to were blown up. There is one on Zada 5, but the window to get there is about every three months."

Eric adds, "He's right, but when it was checked out, they figured out it was a receiver only. It needs a sender to work."

Emil asks, "When is the next window to get there?"

Connor explains, "It starts the eighteenth. We will be leaving early on the morning of the nineteenth, just before the window closes. Adam, Eric, and I, along with a group of men from our home world."

Christina declares, "Then one of us should go to check out that portal."

Adam shuts her down. "No, that will not be happening. We expect to battle Lorenzo's men and their new weapons. We cannot be confident about keeping either of you safe."

Esteban adds, "Adam is right. Neither of you are coming. If need be, they can bring their discoveries back here when they return."

Emily stammers, "Wait, you guys will be gone for three months?"

Connor says, "Yes, I know, but we did not see you for four months."

"Yes." She squeezes his hand. "But that was before yesterday."

Eric states, "Once we solve all these issues with Lorenzo, you guys can spend plenty of time together."

"Yes, I guess you're right." Christina leans on Adam.

Esteban adds, "Now that you girls have graduated, we can focus everything on our issues with Lorenzo. Anything you girls can do to help will be very much appreciated, but I want the work done here in the palace. We can set up a remote lab if needed. You can give John a list of everything. He has people who can obtain what you need and bring it here."

Emily says, "That sounds good. We can write a list by the end of the day."

Eric steps forward. "To Connor's previous point, we will have extra security here starting at the end of the week to get ready for the celebration. With all the additional people coming in and out of here, I am glad you girls have personal security. They can help keep you safe since they will not be going anywhere until after, and you girls can put them to work."

Emily shouts, "*Great.*" They all laugh. "Oh sorry, that was too loud." She turns red from embarrassment.

Connor leans against her. "It's okay."

William states, "Ok, I think we are all on the same page now, but we all need to be diligent until after the celebration."

As everyone leaves, Esteban addresses the girls. "Can you two stay for a minute? I need to talk to you."

Christina says, "Sure, Dad."

"You know I love you both, and you are grown women, but I need you to be a little more discreet."

"Why? What do you mean?"

He laughs. "Do you really think I do not know what goes on around here? I am happy that you have both found someone. Just help me and be more subtle is all I am saying."

They both hug him. Emily says, "Ok, we will."

"Thank you, girls." Esteban walks out first. As he does, he winks at the boys.

The girls come out right after.

Adam asks, "So what happened?"

Christina explains, "He knows about last night."

Connor asks, "What? How could he have found out?"

Emily puts in, "He would not say, just that he knew, but asked us to be more prudent. So, if we come to your rooms, we will need to set an alarm and leave much earlier."

Christina agrees. "Yes! We will need to." They then walk out to the front of the palace where William and Sara sit on one of the benches.

Adam looks at his mom. "Did you say anything to Esteban?"

She studies him. "About what?"

Connor says, "You know, about last night."

"No, did you really think I would have?"

"Well, he knows."

William asks, "Was he mad?"

Adam says, "I don't think so."

Christina concurs, "No, he just asked us to be more discreet."

Sara shrugs. "Then what's the problem? It does not matter how he caught you. You four simply need to be careful about your late-night activities. Right, girls?"

"Ok, Mom," they respond.

William inquires, "Mom?"

Sara replies, "Yes, Mom, do you have a problem with it?"

"Not at all. I always thought it would be nice to have a daughter. Now I guess we have two."

Connor starts to realize how serious things are getting already. "Wait, I think we might be going a little fast here. Not saying I am not happy being with you, but we have only been together two days now, and you are calling my mother mom, and now my dad is saying he has two daughters. I get it with Christina, as Adam asked her to marry him, but we are not there yet." With his back to Sara, she looks at Emily, signaling that she will work on him.

As she does, Emily puts her arm in his and leans against him. "Would it be so bad to be married to me?" She looks up at him, batting her eyes.

"No, it would not. I already have a house."

Sara, Emily, and Christina gawk at him, amazed. "WHAT?"

"Yes, back on Zada 5. The leaders there gave it to me with a guest lodge and a large building for Andorra."

Emily asks, "Which is the dragon, right?"

"She is. But back to what we were talking about. I have no problem with the subject, but I think we should get to know each other a little better."

"That's fair. I cannot argue with that."

Adam interjects, "Before this conversation gets any deeper, let's continue our walk."

As they walk away, William looks at Sara. "You will not let this go until you get him to marry that girl, will you?"

Sara says, "What do you think? Between the three of us, we will have him asking her by the time the celebration is over."

"The three of you?"

"Yes. Christina, Emily, and I."

William laughs. "My poor son. He will not know what hit him until it's all over."

"Nope. Come on. You know she will be good for him."

"Yes, I know, but I am staying out of it."

"Good, you would just mess it up."

William chuckles again.

As the four walk away, both Emily and Christina glance at each other at the same time. "We should work on the list for John."

Adam agrees. "Okay, let's go back." When they return, Connor suggests they head to John's office. As they walked in, Eric is sitting there.

John asks, "What can we do for you kids?"

Adam says, "Kids?"

Eric points out, "Well, you're not old folks, are you?"

"No."

"So, what's up?"

Christina explains, "We were going to build a list, but wonder how big our potential room would be."

Eric looks at John. "Do you think they could use the one storage area on the third floor?"

John agrees. "Yes, that would be good. It was just cleared out a few weeks ago, so it should be empty."

They all go check it out. As they walk through, Emily says, "Yes, this will do. We will have a list to you shortly. How long will it take to obtain everything?"

"If the list is not too big, a few days, I would think."

Christina asks, "What about the suit you said you had?"

Eric says, "Yes, no problem. We will have it delivered with the rest of the stuff."

"Great, thank you." The four move to Christina's room so the girls can work on the list.

After the girls brainstorm for a bit, Connor looks at them. "Maybe bring the list down to dinner; we are all supposed to meet there."

Emily agrees. "Yes, that sounds like a good idea."

Connor glances at Adam. "Maybe we should go back to our rooms and get ready."

Christina says, "Yes, he is right. We need to do the same." Connor gives Emily a hug and a kiss, while Adam does the same thing.

Emily gazes at Connor. "I will miss you."

Connor says, "Yes, so will I you."

Adam looks at Christina. "I love you. See you at dinner."

Christina responds, "Yes, I love you too."

The boys leave. As they walk downstairs, Connor turns to Adam. "I need to talk to you."

Adam asks, "Ok, what's up?"

"I am concerned things are going too fast between Emily and I. She is already thinking about weddings."

Adam laughs. "I did not think I would see you afraid of anything."

Connor is surprised by his comment. "I am not afraid."

"Sure you are, but it's okay. Women can be scary. Do you think you love her?"

"How would I know? I was never close to anyone like this."

"I get it. With Christina, I knew I could not live without her around, and the last time we were together, when I found out she felt the same way, and after being away from her so long, I knew then I could not stand to lose her in my life. That is why I asked her yesterday. If you think you feel the same way, then yes, you are in love. It does not always take weeks or months. It could be days. We can clearly tell she feels that way about you. Didn't you say she has had a crush on you since we were kids?"

"Yes, she did. Ok, I will feel her out tonight."

"Sure, but you need to talk to her, too."

"Ha, ha, hilarious."

Adam wears a big grin on his face. "Yes, I thought so."

WHILE THEY ARE WALKING AND TALKING, CHRISTINA and Emily are chatting in her room. Christina asks, "So, how do you think it is going with Connor?"

Emily says, "Well, I thought it was great until the conversation about marriage came up. I think we may have spooked him, but I have truly fallen for him."

"Yes, I can see that when you are with him. You're right. I saw his reaction. We will try to be more subtle about it and maybe talk with his mom. You know what? Let's dress up to knock his socks off for dinner. That will help move things along. We need to get him to say I love you. Once he does, you got him. That happened between Adam and I." The girls then go through their closets scanning for just the right dress for each of them. After they get ready, they both stand and look at themselves in the mirror. Christina puts her arm around Emily. "If he does not say I love you after seeing you in this, then he is made of stone."

Emily is excited. "Great, let's go down there."

"No, we need to make them wait so they can see us walk in."

WHILE THE SISTERS STAND BEFORE THE MIRROR, THE guys come down to dinner with their parents right behind them. Esteban, John and Eric are already at the table. As they sit down, Adam glances at Esteban. "Where are the girls?"

"You know women. They are always late." Esteban looks at Sara and winks.

William agrees. "Yes, I can attest to that." Sara lightly punches his arm.

A few minutes later, Christina and Emily come strolling in. As the boys see, they jump up and walk over to them. Connor declares, "Wow, you look amazing," as he stares at Emily. Adam says the same to Christina.

Back at the table, William says, "Yep, my poor son will never know what hit him." The rest of the table hears him and laugh.

Then John and Eric agree. "Nope, he has no idea." The boys escort the girls to the table, helping them sit down.

Esteban states, "I am not sure why I always find myself talking first at these dinners, but I am happy we are together again. I'm not sure how many more times we can do this, as it will get really busy here with everything to prepare, but I want us to enjoy the time we have."

John says, "Thank you for hosting. We are happy to be here together as well." Sara looks at her sons, who can't seem to stop staring at, touching, and kissing the girls, then spots Christina as she winks at Emily.

Sara nudges William, who says, "My poor son."

Connor asks, "Sorry, Dad, did you say something?"

He just grins at Connor. "No, it was nothing."

Slowly, the boys wake up from their trance and join in conversations at the table. When dinner is served, Emily notices Connor is not eating like normal. "What's wrong? You don't seem too hungry. Are you okay?"

Connor says, "Yes, I'm not that peckish right now."

"Why is that?"

"I am overwhelmed with your beauty and everything that has gone on over the past two days."

"Do you want to go outside?"

"Yes, I think so." As they get up, Adam asks Connor if he is okay. He responds, "I just need some air."

Emily says, "I will go with him." Adam nods.

William stares at Sara. "You might be losing him in your plot here. What you see there is him realizing he has been hit."

Sara huffs, "You be quiet."

Christina hears him. "It's okay. Emily will bring him around."

Adam hears what his dad says. "Hit with what?"

William explains, "With the plot from these women here."

"What plot?"

Sara winks at Christina. "Nothing, there is none."

"Well, plot or no plot, you guys might have to back off. I talked to him before we came here. He is scared about how he feels. He has never been with anyone serious before."

Christina says, "Well then, it is a good thing they go outside and talk. Emily is well grounded and can bring him around."

Sara adds, "If not, I can converse with him later."

Eric leans in. "You need to keep in mind he has been a fighter all his life, not a lover. Adam is reasonable. This is all new to him. That is why he is scared."

John agrees, "Yes, Eric is correct. So tread lightly."

WHILE THE CONVERSATION AT THE TABLE CONTINUES, Connor and Emily hold hands, walking outside. When they get to the garden, Connor pulls Emily to him and strokes her face with his hand. "You're so beautiful." Then he gives her a kiss and a big hug.

She pushes him back a little so she can look him in the eyes. "So, what is going on behind that beautiful face of yours?"

He directs her over to the bench so they can sit down. "When I saw you enter the room tonight and could see just how beautiful you are, it made everything we have been doing the past two days more real. I have been a fighter my whole life. Take me to a battle or put me in the middle of a fight, and I know what to do. I do not have to think twice about it. But being here with you has opened all kinds of feelings I did not think I had. Before today, I never even thought about love or marriage, and everything seems to be going at interstellar speed."

"We can slow things down a little." She strokes his face. "But if we are putting everything out there, like I told you before, I have had a crush on you almost forever, and these past two days have just intensified these feelings. I was told not to say this, but I am falling in love with you."

Connor stands up. "Oh wow."

"I'm sorry, I'm sorry. I knew you may not be ready to hear that, but I needed to be honest with you." She reaches for his hand.

He reaches for her other hand and pulls her back up to him. "No it's okay. I think that has been part of the problem. I have been afraid to say those words to you, but now that we are together, I could not stand to live without you. Whoa, this is harder than I imagined, but I think I love you, too."

She throws her arms around him and almost squeezes the life out of him, then kisses his face all over, giggling. "You do? You love me?"

Connor laughs. "Yes." As he says that, he puts his arms around her, leans her to the side as he gives her a big kiss, then pulls her back up.

"So, how do you feel now?"

"Like it lifted an enormous weight off my shoulders. And hungry. I am very hungry now."

"Good, I need you to be fueled up for later."

"Oh, yeah?"

"Yes, you bet." Hand in hand, they go to the dining room to get Connor some food.

As Emily and Connor walk back in, everyone gazes up at them. Adam says to his brother, "So, how are you doing?"

Connor said, "I am starving. That's how." Everyone laughs.

Emily gives Christina and Sara a thumbs up. They then look at each other. Christina says, "He said it."

Adam asks, "He said what?"

William leans over and looks at Adam. "Son, I did not think you were that slow." After saying that, Esteban, John, and Eric start laughing.

Adam has a puzzled look. "Again, said what?"

Christina kisses his cheek. "It's okay, I still love you."

"What?"

She whispers in his ear. "He said I love you."

"OH."

Eric stares at Adam, still laughing. "It's ok. You don't need to think, just fight."

"Ha, ha, you're hysterical."

Connor and Emily sit down again. Christina reaches across the table for Emily's hand and looks into her eyes as they cry a little.

Connor peers at Emily. "What is all this for?"

"I am just happy." Emily kisses his cheek.

Christina hugs Adam. "I love you," she says to him and kisses his cheek as well. They then wipe away their tears.

Eric leans up to Connor, sitting next to him. "So, are you pleased?"

Connor says, "Yes, I am, very. I wasn't looking for this, just like on Zada 5, but it has happened, and I am delighted about it."

John, hearing both Eric and Connor, says, "Good. Then my brother and I are happy for you."

After Connor and Emily finish eating, Christina gets up and sits next to Emily. They talk for a few minutes, then stand, glancing at the boys. "We will meet you guys in a little while. We have something to take care of." They walk away.

Connor asks, "So, what was that about?"

Adam says, "What do you think? They wanted to discuss what you guys talked about."

"Oh, ok, so this is merely the beginning, isn't it?"

William puts in, "Yep, all you can do is hold on and go with it. How do you think your mother and I lasted as long as we did?" As he says that, Sara elbows him in the side, and the men all chuckle.

Sara says, "Don't listen to him. You are doing fine. So is your brother."

Adam says, "Thanks, Mom."

Esteban glances at Connor, now near the other end of the table. "Connor, how are you down there?"

He looks at Esteban. "I am doing much better, thank you."

"Good, I wanted to say I could not be happier you found each other."

"Thank you, sir, so am I."

Esteban then puts his hand on William's shoulder. "You have some great boys."

William agrees, "Yes, I do, thank you."

John and Eric get up. "Well, we have another busy day tomorrow so we are returning to our rooms to retire for the night,"

"Yes, that sounds like a good idea. We will be behind you." At that point, they all leave the room.

Connor and Adam head out to the back garden. While they do, the girls, up in Emily's room and start talking. Christina asks, "So, how did you get him to confess?"

Emily explains, "Actually, I said it first."

"You did? I thought we agreed he needed to start, or it may not happen for a while."

"You had to be there and hear how fearful he was about our relationship. I knew if I initiated, that would open the door for him to relax a little. Did you know he has never had an actual girlfriend before? All Connor has ever done is trained and fought in wars or the competition he won on Zada 5. Tonight, he was afraid to show his true feelings for me. He has never done that before with anyone but his parents when he was a kid."

"I think Adam is a little like that. We have not really discussed his feelings other than how much he loves me."

"Well, they are brothers and grew up together until Adam was shipped off to train with Eric."

"Yes, very true. He has a reputation as a real warrior who has killed several men."

"Does that bother you?"

"No, he is very sweet and tender around me, so he must be ok with it and does not bring it here with him. Next subject. I got access to the boys' rooms. I suspect the boys will be dragging their feet waiting for us, and we can get inside before they do to greet them with just our smiles."

"Oh, I like that idea. Let's hurry." The girls grab a few things and sprint down to the guy's rooms. First, they knock on Connor's door. No answer, so Emily enters. Then Christina does the same with Adam's room. He is not there either. She leans out the door, giving Emily a thumbs up. "Wait, what time should we get up and leave?"

"How about four? The staff does not start until five, so it gives us time to say goodbye and hide in our rooms."

"Yes, I like it." They shut the doors.

A short time later, the boys make their way back to their lodgings. Connor says, "Thanks for the talk earlier. I will see you in the morning." He gives his brother a hug, then unlocks his door to go in. As Connor gets in, he sees Emily lying on the bed wearing nothing but her smile. A big grin comes across Connor's face. "This is a nice surprise."

Emily says, "It would be a nicer one if you were not wearing so many clothes."

Quickly, he undresses and lies next to her. "I am not sure why I was so afraid. This is nice, lying next to such a beautiful woman like you."

She strokes his face. "I really love you."

"And I love you too."

She reaches down between his legs. "So are you going to use this?" He slides into her, making her scream again and again. Connor said, "Remember, my parents are down the hall."

"Yes, but they know what we are doing now."

"But it is still a little embarrassing."

She giggles. "That makes it more fun for me."

"Oh, you are bad."

"Yes, you bet I am." After a while lying there cuddling, they fall asleep for the night.

CHAPTER XIII

THEN IT WAS TWO

A FEW DAYS LATER, ERIC ENCOUNTERS THE GIRLS. "AH, I found you. Do you want to come with me?"

Emily asks, "Sure, what's up?"

"Just follow me."

Christina says, "Can the guys come too?"

"Sure." They all follow Eric up to the third-floor storage room. As he opens the door, he reveals a fully staged lab with the suit lying on the table. They all hurry in.

"This is great, much better than we were envisioning. Thank you."

"You're very welcome. I just hope you two can find a way to help us." Eric then looks at the guys. "Now that the girls will be busy, do you guys want to head to Korbin and sift through Roger's old lab to see if anything still there may help us as well?"

Adam says, "Sure. I will have Dave join us too."

"Perfect, just be back here by the end of the day tomorrow. John said you can use the same place as last time. We have a little over a week before the celebration, and our reinforcements will arrive the day after tomorrow. You guys will oversee them."

Connor says, "Ok, you got it. Fun. I have never been to Korbin before."

Emily says, "Wait, you guys will be gone overnight?" As she puts her arm in Connor's and squeezes. The guys laugh.

Adam assures her, "It's okay. Absence makes the heart grow fonder."

"But I don't know how I can be any fonder of him."

Connor turns to her. "It's okay. We will only be gone one evening. You knew we would have to do this sometime."

"Yes, but I did not think it would be so soon."

Eric grins with a slight laugh. "I am sure you will survive."

Christina winks at Adam. "Yes, we both will. Sis, it's okay. We will be busy in the lab anyway, and tomorrow will be here before you know it."

Emily sighs. "Yes, you are right. Then let's get started." They give the guys a hug and multiple kisses; then the men follow Eric out.

The three go down to John's office, where he is already waiting. When they walk in, John looks at Eric. "Good, you found them." He then eyes the boys. "Did Eric tell you about Korbin?"

"No, I just said we wanted them to take a trip there."

Adam asks, "What's going on?"

John explains, "Since the explosion, after Roger and Andy were taken away, we had the lab locked down, except for our own security. One of our guys dug around, and some of the equipment may have survived. We want you guys to see what can be salvaged and brought back for the girls. They may help us uncover something more to either track or fight Lorenzo and the rebels. But with everything that will be going on here, you have to return by tomorrow night."

Connor says, "Yes, that is what Eric told us. We will be."

"With the girls still here, I bet you will."

Adam snickers. "Yes, what's your point?"

Eric has a big grin on his face. "You kids have been glued together since they graduated."

Connor grins back. "Are you jealous?"

"No, just giving you guys a hard time. We are both happy for you two."

Adam says, "Thank you. Okay, let me reach out to Dave and have him meet us at our ship."

After saying goodbye to the girls one more time, Adam and Connor head to the landing field where Dave is already waiting. He asks, "Why are we returning to Korbin? I didn't think there was anything left for us." Adam tells him about the conversation they had with John as they walk onto the ship and take off for Korbin.

When they arrive, John's security team is waiting for them. The team lead tells Adam about what they found as they walk to the remains of Roger's lab. After several hours of uncovering most of the platform and parts of the power supplies, Adam says, "It's getting late. Let's get something to eat and start fresh in the morning. We have already uncovered quite a bit; the security team has been moving what they had already found to a locked storage room and agreed to meet us back at the lab in the morning." The three walk over the same bungalow they stayed at last time.

The next morning, back at the lab, they search for more pieces. Near the end of the day, as the security team loads everything on Adam's ship, Connor lifts a cabinet in the back and finds a box with some papers in it. A few speak about the suits. Connor shows Adam. "I think the girls will want to see these. Most are partially burned, but they may decode some of this information."

Adam agrees. "Yes, that is an excellent find." They add the box with the last of the stuff for the ship.

Dave says, "Wow, it is later than I thought. It will be almost morning by the time we get home."

Connor mutters, "Man, the girls are going to be mad."

Dave asks, "Girls, what girls?"

Adam explains, "Well, I am engaged to one of Esteban's daughters, and Connor has been dating his other one."

"Are you kidding me? You guys go from one fire to another, don't you?"

Connor asks, "Fire? What do you mean by that?"

Dave laughs. "I mean, the emperor's daughters must keep you on your toes."

Adam agrees. "Yes, you are right about that, but it is worth it."

"I am sure it is. Well, congratulations."

"There will be a celebration for their graduation and an engagement party for us in about a week. I would like you to attend."

"Thank you. It would be an honor."

Connor says, "Ok, I think we are finished here. Let's get going." They depart for Markus 2. As they land, they see Dave was right. It is early morning, and the sun is just coming up.

As they disembark, Dave says, "I will get all this equipment delivered later today if that is okay with you guys."

"That works for me."

Adam says, "Let's clean up and meet the girls for breakfast."

"Yes, sounds like a plan."

The guys get back to their rooms. As Connor opens the door, Emily is still lying asleep in his bed, waiting for him. He sits on the bed and gently wakes her up;

she pops up, putting her arms around him, then kisses him all over his face.

Emily exclaims, "Oh, I missed you so much. We thought you guys were going to be here already. We waited all night for you."

"I know. Time got away from us, but we were able to bring back quite a bit for you girls to inspect."

Emily peers at the time. "Oh man, it is late. We are going to be in so much trouble with Dad."

"Adam and I will clear the way." Connor goes out to talk with Adam when his mom comes down the hall.

Sara asks, "You boys just returned?"

"Yes, and the girls waited. They will be in trouble if anyone sees them."

"It's okay. Have them come to my room. I will say they were with me waiting for you and drifted off."

"Thanks, Mom."

Emily accompanies Sara to knock on Adam's door. Christina opens it and sees Sara. "You girls come to my room; it will be okay."

Both girls at the same time say, "Great, thanks, Mom." All three quickly head to Sara's room; the boys return to their rooms to clean up. The girls wait a while, then leave Sara's room in time for the staff to see them and get ready for breakfast.

Meanwhile, John greets Connor and Adam. "So, how was the trip? When did you guys get back?"

Adam responds, "We returned this morning."

Eric says, "Then you accomplished what we wanted?"

"Yes, we brought a lot back, including some paper files we will need the girls to review. Dave will deliver everything later."

John asks, "Speaking of the girls, where are they?"

"No idea. We got cleaned up and came here thinking they would be waiting." Just as Connor says that, the girls rush in. Seeing the guys, they run over to the table, hugging and kissing them.

Eric laughs. "Well, I guess that question was answered."

Adam asks, "What question?"

"If they missed you."

John says, "Well, it sounds like you will be busy for a while. The boys brought back items for you two to analyze, and they will be occupied with the additional men that just arrived."

Adam looks at Connor. "It's a good thing we will get plenty of sleep when we are dead because we will not be getting any today."

Connor chuckles. "Yep, you're right. We have a lot to do."

The girls exclaim, "Oh no, you guys need to rest."

Adam assures her, "No, it is okay. This is not the first time we have been up for multiple days."

Christina says, "No, I could not image not sleeping every day."

LATER THAT DAY, DAVE DELIVERS THE SALVAGED equipment in one of the storage rooms below the palace. Eric notifies the girls while the men work with the new security team, getting them used to the protocols in the palace and the security checkpoints.

Everyone meets again for dinner. Esteban glances at Adam and Connor. "How are the new men doing?"

Adam says, "I think they will only need another day or two. They have adapted easily."

"Excellent, well done." While they are talking, dinner is served. The guys can barely keep their eyes open. Christina nods at Emily, and she nods back.

Emily whispers, "You two need to go get some rest. We will not be coming by tonight."

Connor asks, "No, why not?" Both Emily and Christina laugh.

Emily leans into Connor's ear. "Because you will be unconscious before we start."

Adam barely hears her and nods. "Yep, she's right." Christina laughs and hugs him.

Esteban asks, "What is so funny down there?"

Christina says, "Nothing, Dad. We are just laughing because the boys are drifting off."

"What time did they get in last night?"

Adam says, "This morning."

"And you two have been up all day employed with the new men?"

Connor agrees. "Yes, sir, we have."

"No wonder you two are nodding off. Girls, if they are done eating, could you walk them back to their rooms to make sure they make it okay?"

Christina says, "Yes, Dad, we would be happy to."

Adam demurs, "We should be fine."

Esteban says, "No, I insist."

Emily adds, "We want to make sure you arrive safely."

Connor says, "Okay, thank you." The four then head to the boys' rooms.

Sara looks at Esteban. "Thank you."

He laughs. "I know the girls have been sneaking into their rooms every night, but tonight, I know they will only be sleeping." The men all laugh.

"How do you know?"

"How do you think I got to be the emperor? I need to know everything under my roof. I asked the girls to be discreet, and they have been."

Sara giggles. "Do you mean everything?"

"Yes, even when they went to your room because they spent the night in the boys'."

"Then what was all that about not knowing when they arrived?"

"Like I said, I know everything, but I do not want them to have any idea about what I know." Then they all laugh as he winks at Sara.

THE GIRLS TAKE THE BOYS TO THEIR ROOMS, THEN HELP them into bed. They lie with them until they fell asleep. After they're outside, Emily glances at Christina. "Should we come back later?"

Christina shakes her head. "No, let them sleep. They need it."

"Yes, you're right. But I miss sleeping with him."

"I do too, but we will have plenty of chances after we are married."

"True, but we are not there yet."

"You will be. It is just a matter of time."

"I hope so after these past few days. It has been almost unbearable not seeing or being with him."

"Yes, I know how you feel. It has been the same for me with Adam."

LATER THAT NIGHT, CONNOR WAKES FROM A DEEP SLEEP with his head pounding like the first time he met Andorra. However, now he can hear her for the first time since he left. His headache slowly goes away as he establishes better communication with her. The discussion is brief, but he assures her he will be back soon. Afterwards, he notices how drained it made him as he drifts off. When he wakes, he feels excited he had talked with Andorra, but tries again, to no avail.

OVER THE NEXT FEW DAYS, AS THE GUYS TRAIN THE NEW men, the girls study the suit and equipment salvaged from Roger's lab. The girls make their way through the recovered notes and build a crude power supply. While it powers the suit, it only does so partially. However, as they test different minerals, they discover Verbraso can incompletely penetrate the shield properties of the suit.

WHILE ALL OF THIS IS GOING ON, THE PALACE RECEIVES multiple deliveries for the celebration, including a very large one with multiple large crates. Since they are so big, the guards direct the delivery to the back. The caterers arrive with the delivery and suggest to the security detail that the crates need to be stored for later, as they will not be used until the day of the celebration, and show the guards a map of the palace with the location of where the crates should go. Since the guards are new and don't know better, they let the caterers deliver the boxes to a lower-level room in the palace. A little while later, they come back, climb into their vehicle, and leave.

OVER THE NEXT FEW DAYS, MORE DELIVERIES ARRIVE, as well as multiple caterers and other people to help set up. The four young adults enjoy each other's company day and night with the girls sneaking back to their rooms, unaware of how much their father knows about what they are doing.

The day before the celebration, Connor visits his mother. Sara asks, "What's going on, son?" She puts her arm around him.

Connor admits, "I need your assistance."

"Sure, why?"

"Would you help me pick out a ring for Emily?"

Sara's eyes light up, and a big grin comes across her face. "I have been waiting for this."

William walks into the room just then. "For what?"

"Connor wants me to help him look for a ring for Emily."

William laughs, then winks at Connor. "Can't hold out any longer, huh?"

Sara smacks William on the arm. "Quit it."

Connor stares at William. "In two days, I leave for Zada 5 and will be gone for three months. I do not think it is fair to just leave like that. This way, she knows how much I really care for her, and she will have something to remind her of how much I love her."

This time, William puts his hand on Connor's shoulder. "I get it. That it is how I felt about your mom before I wed her and every day since." He beams at Sara.

Sara glances at William. "Do you want to get the ring?" William ducks into their bedroom and comes back with a small box and hands it to her. "I sent for this the day you told Emily you loved her. I knew you would propose eventually, so I wanted to be ready." She opens the box to reveal a beautiful ring sitting inside.

Connor asks, "Where did this come from?"

"It belonged to your grandmother, your dad's mom."

Connor picks it up. "Wow, this is beautiful. Are you sure?"

William hugs Sara with one arm. "Yes, we are. Adam has one, and now you have the other. We have been holding both for you two if you each found the right woman, and you definitely have. Emily is a great person who can make you happy and help you build a great life."

As he says this, Sara tears up, then gives Connor a big hug. "I am thrilled for you. When are you going to ask?"

Connor says, "Tomorrow morning in front of everyone."

"I love that idea. Have you talked to Esteban yet?"

"No, I needed to speak with you guys first."

William says, "He will be in John's office shortly, so you will find him there."

"Great, thanks, Dad. I love you both and appreciate your support. Let me meet with Esteban."

Connor heads down to John's office. As he walks in, he sees both John and Esteban sitting there. John looks at Connor. "Hey, what's going on?"

"I came here for Esteban."

He turns to Connor. "You're looking for me? What can I do for you?"

"Can we talk privately for a few minutes?"

"Sure, I can always make time for you both." Esteban gets up, and they walk out to the empty hallway down from John's door.

Connor is not sure how to say it. "Sir, I am sure you already know exactly how much I love and care for Emily."

As Connor talks, Esteban chuckles. "Sorry, I do not mean to laugh, but I have known for a few days what you were going to ask me now."

Connor smiles. "You do?"

"Yes."

"So, you realized I was going to ask to marry Emily?"

"I did, and I would be proud to have you wed her. Like Eric and John, I have always thought of you and Adam as my sons. Now, with both of you marring my daughters, it will be official."

"Wow, I didn't think about that, but thank you."

Esteban shakes his hand. "So, when were you thinking about proposing?"

"Tomorrow morning, so everyone can be there."

"That sounds great. If you do not mind, I will have the caterers update everything to add you and Emily as part of the engagement announcement tomorrow evening."

"Yes, that would be great."

THAT NIGHT, WHEN EMILY AND CONNOR ARE ALONE IN his room, Connor is very quiet, trying hard not to say anything until the morning, causing Emily to be a little concerned. When she asks Connor about it, he plays it off as being tired. They make love several times and sleep like normal. Emily gets up early and leaves Connor's room, so they do not get caught. Shortly after, Connor goes down to meet the staff to have one of them deliver the ring to the table in front of Emily at breakfast.

While Connor meets with the staff, Emily sneaks into Christina's room. "I need to talk with you."

Christina asks, "Sure, what's up?"

"I think something is going on with Connor. Has Adam said anything to you about him?"

"No, not at all. Why?"

"He was very quiet the entire night. We made love, and it was great, like always, but he did not talk much."

"I am sure everything is fine. He may be worried, as they are leaving early tomorrow."

"Yes, fair enough."

"I am sure he will tell you when he is ready. Let's go down early and I will see if I can get anything out of Adam."

"Great, thank you." Emily reaches over, giving her a hug; then they walk down to breakfast. When they arrive, everyone is already waiting.

Christina comments, "Wow, everybody was up early this morning."

John says, "Yes, you bet. There is still a ton of stuff to do before the big party tonight."

Emily says, "Oh, yes, that's true." She sits down next to Connor, then kisses him on the cheek, seeing a big smile on his face. "You look very happy this morning."

"Yes, I am." As Connor reaches for her hand, he nods at one of the staff members, who comes over, placing a silver service with a cover over it in front of her.

Emily peers up at the staff member. "What is this?"

The woman smiles and says, "I think you are supposed to open it," as she walks away. Emily lifts the cover off, and there in the middle of the plate is a small box.

Emily looks at Connor. "What is this?"

"Open it." As she obeys, she sees a ring, then screams as Connor moves away from the table. He takes the ring out of the box and gets down on one knee. Christina, seeing all of this, screams as well. Before Connor can ask Emily, she yells yes and grabs Connor to hug and kiss him. He then puts the ring on her finger. Sara and Christina both start crying.

Esteban signals to the staff, and they bring out champagne. "I know it is still early, but one glass will not hurt. I would like to toast to Connor and Emily. I wish you both a blissful life."

Emily asks, "Is this why you were so quiet last night?"

He smiles at her. "Yes, I was doing my best not to blow it. I love you, and I needed to make sure you knew just how much."

Esteban says, "I have already let the caterers know that there will be two engagements to celebrate tonight." As he says that, both Adam and Christina come around the table and hug Connor and Emily. Then everyone settles down again.

Eric pats Connor on the back. "Nicely done, my boy."

Connor says, "Thank you, but I think I would rather go back to Zada 5 and fight than have to propose again." Everyone laughs; Adam nods his head in agreement.

Emily can't stop gazing at the ring. "This is so beautiful, thank you. I love you so much." She turns, putting her arms around him, and kisses him.

"I love you too, and I wanted you to have something to prove that while I was gone. That ring belonged to my grandmother."

"Wait, I thought Christina had your grandmother's ring?"

"Yes, she does, but that was on my mom's side. This is from my dad's mom."

"I love that." She then leans in so no one else can hear her whisper to Connor, "Don't plan on sleeping tonight after the party, Mister."

He gives her a big smile. "Oh, yeah?"

"Yes, you bet. I am going to wear your ass out before you leave." Laughing, he kisses her on the cheek.

LATER THAT DAY, THE GIRLS STRIDE INTO JOHN'S OFFICE, where the four men, John, Eric, Adam, and Connor are reviewing their plans for their arrival on Zada 5. Eric asks, "Hey, girls, what's up?"

Christina explains, "We have been working on the equipment, but we cannot get any of it to work yet. We created a makeshift power supply for the suit after reviewing the notes, but we will need more time to find any vulnerabilities. Right now, the only thing we can think of is to stomp on the right wrist. It might turn the suit off." The boys stand and hug the girls.

Connor says, "Thank you for trying. We will bring the platform in the cavern on Zada 5 when we return. If Craven shows up, we will get another suit and sword, as well."

Adam adds, "Yes, maybe his head too." The guys all laugh.

Christina says, "That is a scary thought." Adam and Connor just grin at her.

Emily looks at Connor. "It worries me sometimes to think about what you guys deal with."

Connor holds her hand. "Don't worry. My brother and I can handle ourselves."

"Well, I know YOU can." Emily has a big smile.

Eric says, "I think we have everything under control. You kids should go get ready. It is going to be a busy night."

JUST BEFORE THE PARTY STARTS, THE GIRLS MEET THE guy in the main hall. This time, the girls look even better than the day when Connor said I love you. Adam gapes at Connor as the girls come in. "Can you believe how lucky we are to be engaged to women that beautiful?"

Connor says, "No, I cannot." The guys tell the girls how much they love them and how stunning they look.

Christina leans into Adam. "I am not wearing any panties."

Adam sighs. "You are killing me."

"Good. I wanted you to be thinking about it during the party. You guys are leaving at 4 in the morning?"

"Yes, we are. Why?"

"Because you will not get rest tonight. I have plans for you afterward."

"You do?"

"Oh, yeah."

Emily hugs Connor. "I am so happy and cannot believe we are getting married; I am going to make you a great wife."

Connor agrees. "I know you will."

A short time later, all the guests arrive. Dave comes in, and Adam introduces him to the girls. Then they ask how he knows the boys. Dave looks at Adam. "Is it okay?"

Adam nods. "Yes, they know what is going on."

"Ok, good." Then he explains to the girls about what they went through, which was a lot more than the boys revealed. The girls' jaws drop as they start to truly realize what kind of men they are with, true warriors. Then Dave pulls Adam to the side. "Holy crap, they are magnificent. You are right. You and your brother are very lucky."

Adam agrees. "You are correct. We are. By the way, did you ever check the panel back at the lab complex?"

"Not after the explosion, but that is a good point. I will examine it before we leave in the morning."

"Perfect, thank you."

The kids enjoy the party, and the girls introduce the guys to their friends. One girl pulls Christina and Emily aside. "Those boys are they the sons of the duke?"

Emily nods. "Yes, they are."

"We have heard they are both fierce warriors and world conquerors. They are so young. All those rumors can't be true."

Both girls grin; then Christina says, "Well, the gossip does not tell the total story. They are also incredible lovers. We are so happy to be marrying them."

"You girls are so fortunate; they are handsome as well."

Emily agrees. "Yes, we are. These weeks since graduation have been amazing." The three girls look over at the guys with big smiles.

Connor asks, "What are you ladies smiling at?"

Emily walks over and grabs his hand. "Just how lucky we are."

The four laugh, dance, and enjoy multiple conversations with the girl's friends. Dave hits it off with the girl, Carmen, asking about the guys and loves the rest of the night talking and dancing with her. At the end, they plan to meet on his return from Zada 5.

During the party, Esteban dances with each of the girls, then once with all three of them together and reminds them how much he loves them. As the celebration nears the end, Esteban comes over to the guys to tell them how happy he is that they will be his sons soon and he could not be prouder of them. He hugs each of them and walks off.

The girls walk over to the guys. Emily says, "I think we need some alone time now with you guys. It's late, and you are departing soon." The girls take them by the hand, ushering them to their rooms. Emily, once alone with Connor, starts to cry.

Connor asks, "Why are there tears?"

"I am both happy and sad." Emily hugs him.

"I know, but let's make the most of what time we have left." He takes off her dress, and they climb into bed, then make love the rest of the time.

At three, the boys get ready. Each in their rooms, they say goodbye to the girls, leaving them sleeping from a long night as they were not used to being up that long. Adam and Connor hurry to the ship where the security detail is waiting. As they are on the move, Dave comes running up. "That was a good call. Emma left something in the loose panel before everything went to hell."

Adam says, "Great, we can review it on the ship."

As they walk in, Connor glances at the ship's captain. "Has everything been loaded?"

The captain agrees. "Yes, sir, late last night."

Connor says, "Great, we can leave then. We need to hurry before the window closes."

AFTER SEVERAL HOURS, THEY ARRIVE AT ZADA 5. THE guys have been snoozing the entire time since the girls kept them up. The captain has them woken up. Connor walks into the cockpit. "What's going on?"

The captain points to the asteroids around the window. "We are too late. The window is already starting to shut."

"We will be fine. The window closes from the outside in. We just need to hurry."

"I can't risk it." Just as he says that, Adam walks in.

Connor glances at Adam and then says to the captain, "Get out of that chair. I will do it."

The captain says, "No, I can't allow that."

"You better listen to my brother." Adam then pulls the captain out of the chair.

Connor jumps in. "This will be fun." As he speeds up and heads the ship in, he tells Adam, "You better have everyone strap in. This is going to be a bumpy ride." They fly in through the window. Small asteroids pelt the ship. Then they glimpse the window slowly closing in front of them. Connor goes even faster. Having to dodge larger asteroids, getting close to the planet, a larger boulder damages part of the ship. Connor barks, "I am losing steering."

Adam assures him, "Just try to keep it straight." Then they get hit again from the other side, breaking more of the ship. Finally getting out of the window, they are now headed to the planet, out of control.

Connor says, "Hang on, this landing will not be a soft one." As they approach the planet, their speed increases. He puts the flaps up, partially slowing the ship down, but it is still going way too fast.

Adam says, "Can you pull the nose up?"

"I am trying." Connor can only get it to rise a little bit, barely before they hit the ground. The ship bounces several times, pieces coming off along the way, then finally slides to a stop, knocking out both Adam and Connor. Dave, in the back behind the cockpit, still conscious, checks what's left of the ship's cockpit and wakes up the guys to get them out. Once they get out, not seeing anyone else.

Connor looks at Dave. "Do you know how bad it is?"

Dave says, "No, not yet." The three return to see who is hurt, but as they come around and look back, the back half of the ship is gone, with dead bodies and debris scattered behind them. Looking at what's left, they see only two men and Eric are alive. The two men are hurt badly. They wake up Eric, who is not injured badly, but the equipment is damaged or gone. The four check on the scattered bodies to see if anyone is still left alive. Realizing some of them are men they had worked with in the past, they try to keep it together as they examine each man, to no avail. They then gather the dead and bring them close to the ship's wreckage.

After they deal with the dead, Adam looks at Connor and Eric. "So, do either of you have any idea where we are?" They peer around.

Connor says, "Based on the mountain range, we should not be too far from the shipping port. I can hear Andorra; she will come here and get me. Then I can fetch a transport vehicle to collect the rest of you."

Dave says, "Really?"

"Yep." A short time later, a larger image in the sky swoops at them. Connor points up. "There she is."

"A real dragon? Holy crap." She lands, and Connor climbs aboard.

"Ok, you guys, hang on; I will be back as soon as I can."

A FEW HOURS LATER, CONNOR RETURNS WITH MONDO and Renaldo who had been waiting for them to land. They bring transport and a doctor to deal with the hurt men. Connor introduces them to Adam and Dave.

Then Renaldo says, "There are two of you? That is a very scary thought. Sure glad we are all friends." Connor glances at Adam, and they both snort.

Mondo says, "Ok, let's get you back to the colony."

Connor demurs, "No, they should be fine at my home."

Dave asks, "What, you have a home here already?"

"Yes, I do. They have accepted me as a Zandorrian."

Renaldo says, "We wanted him to live here with us because he is the One."

Dave looks confused. "The one what?"

"The chosen one, the one who will tame the dragon, lead our people to freedom, and be the ruler of the universe."

Dave laughs. "Really, the ruler of the universe?"

Mondo and Renaldo chuckle as well. "I know it sounds crazy, but he has already tamed the dragon and is officially a clan leader after winning the competition."

"Sure, I will give you that. I would not have believed it if I did not see it for myself."

Connor says, "Okay, we are here, but we failed to bring any real assistance. We only have a handful of men and no equipment."

Mondo says, "You brought your brother, and if he is like you, we are already doing better."

Eric asks, "Did Craven show up?"

"No, he did not."

"I wonder why. We intentionally shorted the shipment to force him here."

"If he isn't here, then where is he?"

CHAPTER XIV

ONLY ONE WAY OUT

On the day of the celebration at the palace, three men dressed as caterers arrive to take care of the crates delivered a few days earlier. They open them, pulling out the equipment, and placing it around the room. By the time they finish, the party has ended. They send a message to confirm they are prepared for testing, but something is wrong.

After making some changes, they send another message to try again. A pad on the floor glows, and a window opens. A few minutes later, Lorenzo and Craven step through, followed by Ramone. Lorenzo looks at the three men.

"Great job. I will take it from here. You men should get ready."

As the men prepare in the lower level, Emily goes to her bedroom upstairs. Being in Connor's reminds her he will not be returning any time soon, which makes her miss him that much more.

LORENZO GOES OVER TO THE CONSOLE IN THE ROOM on the lower level. After a few minutes, the window gets bigger, and rebels from Ria 6 dressed in the suits and with swords powered up begin to step through. After ten men enter, two of the three caterers, now wearing suits and have swords, slowly open the door. Doing so, they rush out and kill two approaching guards before they have a chance to warn anyone. The rebels slowly move more men into the hallway as others come through the portal. One of them hears a call from a dead guard's communicator asking them to check in. The rebel captain tells the others to be ready. Rebels start going up the stairs. As they do, the emperor's guard come down, but their weapons are useless. The rebels reach the main level with Craven and Ramone right behind them.

AT THE SAME TIME, ESTEBAN AND JOHN HEAR REPORTS from the guards. They are fighting with men in the palace. John goes to Esteban's room, already up and arming himself. Seeing John come in, he shouts, "Go find the girls! Try the boys' rooms first."

John says with a puzzled look, "Really?"

"Yes, they only departed a little while ago, and I bet the girls are still in there."

"Ok, William and Sara are close by so I can get them as well."

Esteban opens a secret panel. "Here, take the back way to them so no one sees you."

CHRISTINA, HEARING THE NOISES FROM THE GUARDS fighting with the rebels, gets up, then slowly opens the door and peers out. As the noises get closer, she knocks on Connor's door for Emily, but there's no answer. She runs down the hall to Sara and William's room and knocks on their door and discovers them up and armed. Sara quickly pulls Christina in, then closes the door. Both Sara and William hold their weapons. Just then, a panel opens near the back of the room, and John walks out.

William says, "Good call," looking at John. "Come, ladies, let's go."

Christina asks, "There are secret passages?"

John explains, "Yes, they were added in the earlier years when there were wars on this planet."

"You mean like now."

"Is Emily still in Connor's room?"

"I don't think so. I knocked on his door before coming here, and there was no answer, so I think she went back to her own."

"Ok. I will go get her after we drop you off in your dad's room." They rush down the passageway back to Esteban's. Slowly, John opens the door. "He is not here. He may have gone to see if he could help. Let's get to the main room. Back this way is a two-way mirror we can look through." They sneak down the back passage to the main room. When they arrive, guards are fighting the rebels and dying. Then Esteban runs in as the rebels capture and bind him.

Christina yells, "DAD!"

John puts his hand up. "Shh, they might hear you; we need to get to Emily. We can go this way to get to the main stairs." They come out from the back of the stairs.

One man at the top says, "We still need to capture Christina and the duke."

Emily hears the men talking and comes out to see what is going on. As Craven and Ramone start up the stairs, she sees Christina below and yells, "EMILY, RUN!"

Craven states, "That must be Christina." He runs up as she starts to flee but gets close enough to shove his sword into Emily's back. She screams as he kills her.

Ramone yells, "No, she is just a young girl." Emily falls to the ground.

Hearing Emily scream, John and Christina duck back into the hidden passage.

William says, "We need to go back out through Esteban's room."

Christina sobs. "She yelled her name. Why?"

John explains, "You heard them. They were hunting for you. She must have heard them and was trying to protect you."

When they reach Esteban's room, they again slowly open the panel. They do not see anyone and come out. Just after they do, several rebels rush in. William yells at John, "Get her out of here. We'll hold them off." John takes Christina back through the hidden pass and blocks the door so no one can follow. The rebels capture William and Sara since they cannot fight against the rebels' swords or suits. They are bound and taken away.

John looks at Christina, who is crying. "You are going to have to toughen up to get through this."

Christina agrees. "You're right."

"There is another hidden exit, but there is only one way out. It is in the garden, so we must get through the main entrance."

As they head for the stairs, Craven meets William and Sara. "Craven, why are you doing this?"

Craven barks, "We will get to that, but first, take them back to their room and hold them for me."

By that time, John and Christina reach the main entrance and head out to the main garden, only to encounter more rebels. Some guards run up to protect them. First, the rebels kill the guards, then go after John and Christina. As they flee, Ramone runs up to them.

John exclaims, "Ramone, is that you?"

"Yes, it is." Ramone then turns to fight the rebels. He gets mortally wounded but is still able to slaughter all those who remain in the garden. As he dies, he hands his sword to Christina. "This will help you." He then grabs John's hand. "Tell Mondo I held up the code," and exhales for the last time. John pulls his hand off and takes Christina out through the other secret exit behind a large trellis.

Christina gapes at John as they go through the long, dark tunnel. "What did he mean? He held up the code?"

John explains, "He was from Zada 5 and was the head of a clan. Part of their code is to harm no women or children, so since you were with me, he had to make sure they did not hurt you, and if I am correct, that is one of the clan swords, rumored to be a dragon killer, but it glowed as he wielded it and could slay his men in those suits. We will need to inspect it further."

"So now how do we get my dad, the duke, and Sara out of there?"

"We cannot worry about that right now. I need to get you safe first."

"NO, we need to get them out."

"What if they are already dead? If we go back in there, then Ramone saving you would have been a waste of life. Also, if your father is dead, you are the heir to the throne. The other issue is Lorenzo is behind all of this, and we need to figure out his endgame. We must get back to my home world for more troops and help. I have a safe house on the other side of town."

"So, how long is this tunnel?"

"It goes almost all the way to town."

"Three miles?"

"Yes, that sounds about right."

While John and Christina walk to town through the tunnel, the rebels hold Esteban back in his room on his knees with his hands tied behind him. After a while, Lorenzo finally walks into the room with Craven. Esteban shouts, "*LORENZO,* what the hell is going on here? Release me right now."

Lorenzo declares, "What is going on is I am in control now, not you."

"What do you think you are doing?"

"I am the new emperor and taking your power away."

Esteban laughs. "Do you really think you are going to stage a coup?"

"Yes, I am."

"No, you will never be the emperor. That will never happen."

"You shouldn't have been coronated. When our mother was alive, she told me I was smarter and would make a much better emperor. She also said you had been adopted. She was going to have Father choose me when he passed. But our father did not listen to her. Then he died and let you rule. He must have felt guilty by giving me control over labs and manufacturing."

"No, I suggested our father do that. You are also wrong. Our father did not adopt me, but your mother was not mine. I was about two, maybe three, when our dad married your mom, but I felt like she was mine, and she treated me like one of her kids. So, I had every right to be the emperor, as I was still part of the family line. But back to my point—I have taken measures to make sure you never take the throne."

"Well, they just killed Christina, and Emily is next once they find her."

"*YOU MONSTER!* She never hurt anybody. If I have my way, you will die a horrible death, but that still will not make you emperor. I have ensured that."

"Once you and your kids are dead, it will fall to me."

"No, it will fall to William's sons."

"You cannot do that."

"It is already finished. A secret group has all the documentation on the line of leadership. I removed you from the list when I suspected you were up to something and weren't honest with me. Now I know why."

Lorenzo, now furious, screams, "Kill him!" With that, Craven swings his sword and slices Esteban's throat, nearly taking off his head.

Lorenzo loses it, throwing stuff around the room. "We need to find the dukes' kids. They were not here, and Eric wasn't either. They nearly caught John and Emily and are still searching the grounds for them, but I am not too concerned about Emily. She was adopted, so she cannot stop me from taking the throne, but may look for revenge, especially if John is with her. If they escape, they will flee to Hmar 4 for more help, so we must stop them. Where are the duke and his wife?"

Craven replies, "I had them taken down to their room at the other end of the palace." They hurry there and go into their room where both the duke and Sara wait. They have been tied up in the living room on their knees, facing each other.

As they enter, the duke shouts at them, "You guys have lost you mind. Why are you doing this?"

Lorenzo walks over and hits William. "Where are your boys?"

"Why should I tell you?"

Craven stands behind Sara. "If you don't, I will kill your wife."

"We were fighting on the same side. Why are you helping him?"

Lorenzo shouts, "Answer the question! Tell us where your sons are!"

Sara says, "They are eager to die. Go ahead and tell them."

William starts laughing. "Ok, I just wish we were there to see them take the life from your body. They are on Zada 5, waiting for you."

Lorenzo says, "Why would they be there for me?"

"Not you. Craven."

"What, why would they be looking for me?" replies Craven.

William grins. "Because they know you have been terrorizing the miners to mine more crystals."

"How did they find out?"

"They didn't. They were searching for Lorenzo's platform."

Lorenzo demands, "How could they have known?"

"Because you screwed up. Remember the first lab explosion? The window opened when John and your brother went to inspect the damaged building, just long enough to see the other side. So, you caused us to go there and discover what you were up to, and now they are working with the Zandorrians to repel your forces, which means they are ready and waiting for you."

Lorenzo looks at Craven. "It doesn't matter. They cannot fight against our weapons. Go there and murder them all. We can bring miners in to get the crystals we need. They stopped being warriors years ago and are just old men, so they cannot help with any fighting."

Craven says, "We will have to wait till the next window. It just closed this morning."

"No matter. I will report them dead and take over."

William responds, "Nope, it does not work that way. The owners of control will have to see the bodies or validated reports, and you cannot fake those."

Lorenzo, now irate over the news, loses control again, throwing things around the room in a fit of rage. "I do not care what it takes. Get there as soon as you can and kill them."

Just before Lorenzo leaves the room, he says, "They are all yours," looking at Craven.

William stares at Craven. "Why are you allied with Lorenzo? We were working on the same side before you disappeared."

Craven says, "Yes, let's talk about that. After we saved Sara's father, you guys left me behind."

"No, we didn't. When we left the building, we noticed you were not behind us. I took her father back to the camp while Eric and John waited to see if you would appear. When you did not, they went back in for you, but they could not find you anywhere."

"I was captured by the rebels and taken to another building behind the one we were in, so I had to escape. Because you did not rescue me, they killed my family while I was on the ship, trapped in space with a broken cryopod. If you had saved me, then I would have been back home and could have saved them. Now Lorenzo is helping me get revenge for my family."

"Killing me will not bring them back."

"You're right, but it will relieve my pain of loss."

"I have been watching you, and you cannot stop twitching. Being on that ship has made you insane. Revenge will solve nothing."

"Oh yes it will, when I see the look on your face as I kill your wife." He shoves his sword through Sara, killing her.

William screams, "My sons are going to kill you!"

Craven yells, "I am not insane." He then swings his sword, cutting off William's head. He turns, looking at his men. "I am done. Let's go." They all walk out with William and Sara lying dead on the floor.

LATER THAT MORNING, JOHN AND CHRISTINA REACH the safe house on the other end of town. Once inside, Christina notices everything had recently been restocked, along with a large supply of weapons in one of the back rooms. "So, when was the last time someone was here?"

John explains, "About three months ago, after Lorenzo disappeared."

"How did you know this would happen?"

"I didn't, but I have been doing security my whole life and always have a backup plan. That said, we don't have a way to fight Lorenzo's weapons yet. If we do not figure something out soon, we will be in big trouble.

In the meantime, I need to look for a way to my home planet."

"I thought you already had a ship?"

"Yes, but the guys took it to Zada 5 and when it is gone, I use your father's. Given what has happened, I do not think we should trust it until we know their fate."

"John, I did not say it, but thank you for saving me and helping me keep it together."

"It's my job. I have always thought of you as one of my kids, so I would have given my life for you. I am sorry we could not save your sister."

Christina starts to cry again. "I am sorry, but this is all too much. Yesterday, I was unbelievably happy. Now my entire world has been destroyed."

"Get it out now so you can focus later. I don't want to leave you like this, but I need to find us a way off this rock."

"No, it is fine. I will pull myself together by the time you get back."

"Okay, if you get hungry, there is plenty of food. The pantry is completely stocked."

A FEW HOURS LATER, JOHN COMES BACK. "I AM SORRY, but I have more bad news. I contacted some of the old staff from the palace. Not only your sister, but your father, the duke, and Sara were all killed, and there will be a price on our heads by the end of the day. But the good news is they believe you are Emily, and they killed Christina."

Christina is steaming mad. "How is everyone thinking I am Emily good news?"

"Lorenzo is not worried about you fighting to reclaim the throne, but we are going to have trouble leaving."

"But if everyone thinks I am Emily, how do I prove who I am?"

"Well, your father never got to give you all the empire updates. He was waiting until we had more information about Lorenzo. There is a secret planet that retains and has control of all family records, including all your information."

"But if the planet is secret, how do I find it and claim my birthright?"

"You do not have to do anything. Your father put a provision in the records. If you die, the empire will go to either Adam or Connor. Once it is discovered you are who you say, it will revert to you if they agree to release it. So, your father already foiled Lorenzo's plan to be the emperor. However, Lorenzo is going to rule until you or the boys show up."

"That is great. It really would not bother me if it went to Adam. We could take the throne together."

"Well, we first need to find a way off this planet. They have locked everything down as they continue hunting for us. We may have to wait a few days for things to cool down and hope they think we already left."

Back on Zada 5, after Lorenzo and Craven killed everyone at the palace, Connor looks at Adam. "While I was fighting to land the ship, I was hit with a massive wave of grief."

Adam sees the sadness on his face. "What are you talking about?"

"I know where Lorenzo and Craven are. They are at the palace. They killed my love, Emily, Esteban, and our parents."

"No, how can you say that?"

"I felt and saw it all. The pain is killing me. But I need to focus. We will be here for three months, and there is nothing we can do to change that. Trust me, once we find out what happened, I will make whoever was involved pay for it."

Adam gives his brother a hug. "I am so sorry. I know how much you cared for her."

With that, Connor breaks down, then stops himself. "No, I can't do this now."

Dave, hearing this, puts his arm around him. "If this is true, I will be there to help you guys make whoever pay."

"Thanks, Dave."

Adam asks, "Wait, what about Christina?"

"I do not have any feelings of pain or saw anything related to her or John, so they could still be okay." When they reach Connor's home, they help Connor and Adam grieve over Emily and their parents.

BACK ON MARKUS 2, THE NEXT DAY, LORENZO puts out a statement to stop the rumors about what happened, stating the duke tried a power coup, but was killed after taking the lives of Esteban and Christina. Emily is said to have helped because she was in love with the duke's son, so Emily, the duke's sons, John and Eric, are all wanted with prices on their heads as accomplices. And to make sure there is no further attack, he brings in outside forces to help him keep control as the new emperor. Lorenzo also sends word to the force on Hmar 4. If they stand down, he will not send his armed forces to take control, as they cannot fight against his army with their new weapons. He also restricts them from leaving their home planet.

Meeting with Craven, Lorenzo presses about John and Emily. "I have our men looking everywhere for them, but no sign. We search the ships before they leave."

Lorenzo orders, "I want them found. Double your efforts."

"Yes, sir, will do."

"What happened to Ramone?"

"We found his body yesterday out in the garden with several of our men and the palace guards who were dead."

"How is that possible? And how did our men get killed?"

"Ramone did it. I think he helped Emily and John escape."

"What? Why?"

"When I killed Christina, he yelled that she was a young girl. He had the same issue when I eliminated the girl at the lab and blew it up. I do not think he could take it."

"That is too bad. He could have helped you control the people on Zada 5. Where is his sword?"

"I don't know. We searched the entire garden, but there was no sign of it."

"That's not good. John may have it and be able to fight against our men. Most of them cannot handle him, so when you find him, you will need to be careful." Craven acknowledges him, then leaves the room.

LATER THAT DAY, LORENZO CALLS CRAVEN BACK. "WHAT are your plans for going back to Zada 5? I need the duke's son's taken care of right away."

Craven explains, "Well, I have been working on this, but we cannot use the portal. If they know it is there and where it is, we can't send people through. We risk them being captured or killed because it takes about a minute for the suits to activate. The next window is not for three months, so no matter how soon you want us to travel, we will have to wait."

"I guess you are right, but you need to make sure you are prepared to take care of them when you get there."

"Yes, we will be."

At their safe house, John works with Christina and the new sword. As he does, they notice it glowing red. The more proficient she gets with it, the brighter it glows. John says, "I am glad to see you kept up your drills when you were at school. It shows. Based on what we will have to do, I am glad you trained with Adam and Connor when you were a kid. Those skills will help us defeat your uncle."

Christina orders him, "Do not call him that. He killed almost everybody I loved; he is now an evil slug sitting on my throne."

"Excellent, I like it. We can start referring to him as the slug."

"Do you have a plan yet for our escape?"

"Yes, but we will need to wait for an old friend of mine to come back for his normal shipment, which is around the twenty-fifth of the month. That is not for a few days."

"With all that has gone on, do you think he will still help you?"

"I will not give him a choice. He will have to."

"Great. I can't wait to leave and planning to get the guys back, then my Empire back from the slug, and kill him for what he has done to our families."

OVER THE COURSE OF THE NEXT FEW DAYS, JOHN LEAVES every day in a hood to check the shipping port for his friend Evan. Finally, on the sixth day, Evan lands. John waits for him to leave his ship. John follows Evan to the back of a building where he gets some of the product he smuggles to other planets. John walks up to Evan and pulls down his face cover. Evan turns and looks at him. "Why are you here? Do you realize how much heat there is on you? Your name is all over the empire."

John explains, "I need you to take us to my home planet."

"You mean Hmar 4?"

"Yes."

"And who is us?"

"Esteban's surviving daughter and me."

Evan says, "There is no way. You are both too hot. If I get caught, it will be over for me as well."

"You would not be breathing right now if it were not for me."

"I knew you would bring that up."

"I saved your life and never asked you for anything, have I?"

"No, nothing. Well, I guess it is fair that I risk my life helping you, but if I do this, we are even."

"Yes, your debt is paid in full."

"This is still going to cost me a lot."

"I can give you two thousand sovereign credits now and twenty thousand more when we land on Hmar 4."

"That will work. Be back here tomorrow morning at eight, but you need to make sure nobody recognizes you when you get here."

John puts his face cover back on. "That will not be a problem. You better not double-cross me, or I will hunt you down and kill you when I get out of here."

"I would not do that to you. I need to clear the books between us."

"Thank you. See you in the morning." John leaves and makes his way back to the safe house.

THAT AFTERNOON CRAVEN REPORTS TO LORENZO A strange person has been seen around the shipping platforms, and he has doubled the security around that area. Lorenzo asks, "Do you think it could be John?"

Craven snarls, "I hope so. I owe him."

"I do not want him killed before we find out where Emily is."

"Yes, sir, you got it."

THE NEXT MORNING, CHRISTINA AND JOHN DISGUISE themselves and make their way to the shipping platform near Evan's ship. When they arrive, John points out Evan's ship, an old Magnus 10 modified with interstellar engines. "We need to wait here a minute. There have been more patrols in this area." Evan comes out of the ship and signals to John, letting him know to hurry. They look around, not seeing anyone. Quickly making their way across the pad to his ship, they draw the attention of two rebels, who yell at them, "Hey, who are you, and why are you all covered up?" They face them; the rebels first yank the hood off John, then yank the hood off Christina.

One rebel yells, "It's both of them." They quickly draw their swords. Christina and John do the same. Evan runs back in the ship and fires it up. John wields his sword first, but as he does, it is deflected and cut in half by one rebel.

Christina, not wasting any time, thrusts her sword into the rebel in front of her. "That is for my sister, you piece of shit." He looks at her in disbelief, thinking he could not be hurt, but she has just dealt him a fatal blow. The second rebel, shocked by it as well, hesitates, allowing her to spin around, slicing his head off, and yells, "That one was for my father." Then they quickly run into the ship, and Evan launches.

"I knew you were going to be trouble when I saw you yesterday. I hope we have a few minutes before those guys are discovered." But as he takes off, a small fighter pulls in behind them, then comes over the communicator, telling them to land. Evan tries to stall them. While he does, he points to a panel behind him, telling John to push the red button when he tells him to. He speeds up, getting ready for interstellar travel. The fighter fires just as they bolt off. Evan yells at John, "Hit it now!" When he does, the ship disappears, and they hit interstellar speed, leaving the fighter looking for them.

John asks, "What was that button?"

"I have an illegal cloaking device. That fighter has no idea where we are now, but if they have figured out your identity, they will know where we are going."

"That's ok. We have a secret base away from everything else, and they do not know it's there."

Christina says, "Well, if you can get us there, I will owe you."

"Owe me? John, you said I was getting paid sovereign credits?"

John assures him, "Do not worry. You will be, but what she is talking about is worth a whole lot more."

"Why? What do you mean?"

"This is not Emily, Esteban's adapted daughter. This is Christina, the true empress with Esteban gone."

"Are you kidding? Lorenzo sent out a message saying she had been killed."

Christina explains, "No, Emily saved me. She made them think she was me, so they killed her, allowing me to escape. Keep in mind you are the only one besides John who knows."

"Your highness, your secret is safe with me. If there is ever anything I can do to help you, all you must do is ask."

"Well, you are going to be sorry you said that."

Evan laughs. "Why? What do you need?"

"A ride to Zada 5 in a little over two months."

Evan says, "Zada 5, why there? It is just a mining planet."

"Yes, it is, but that is where my fiancé, his brother, and Eric are. We will need their help to get my empire back."

"John, what the hell have you got me into here?"

John shrugs. "Hey, you are the one that volunteered."

Evan laughs again. "I guess you are right. So, who is your fiancé?"

Christina explains, "Adam Balcazar."

"Wait, isn't he the duke's son?"

John puts in, "Yes, he was before they killed the duke."

"Then I am sure glad he is on your side. I have heard rumors about him, and they are scary."

Christina agrees. "Now you know why I need to get there."

John adds, "But we really do not require Evan. We have plenty of ships on our planet."

"But do they have illegal cloaking capabilities?"

"No, they do not. That's good. You are already thinking like a warrior."

Evan asks, "Wait, why are they on Zada 5?"

"With the information we had at the time, we thought Lorenzo's soldiers would be there. The guys went there to confront them, but they showed up at the palace, killing everyone. If they had stayed, they may be dead now as well. This will be the last time Lorenzo—oh, sorry, the slug—outguesses us."

"The slug?"

John laughs. "Yes, that is what Christina calls Lorenzo." Evan laughs as well.

Christina asks, "How long can you stay cloaked?"

Evan says, "If my crystals are fully charged, about thirty minutes."

She then looks at John. "Then how long will it take to get through the window on Zada 5?"

John says, "Not that long. Ok, so what's the plan?"

"Well, if we must fly in while Craven and his men do, then the last thing we will want is for them to see us."

"I like the way you are thinking."

CHAPTER XV

WHERE DO WE GO FROM HERE?

AFTER LEAVING THE FIGHTER BEHIND ON MARKUS 2, the group finally gets to Hmar 4 a few hours later, and land at the secret base on the far side of the planet. When they arrive, John's nephew runs out to see who was landing there. When he gets close to the ship, John comes walking out. As he does, John's nephew Abel first gives him a hug and tells him he is glad he is ok, but then he tells him they cannot stay. "We have been warned that if you show up here, we have to turn you over to the new emperor, or there will be retaliation. We are working hard to build up our forces, but right now, we are no match for his army with their new weapons." As they talk, Evan and Christina join them.

Hearing this, Cristina looks at Abel. "You are here to protect the emperor, are you not?"

"Yes, we were, but he is dead."

"But I am not."

"You are not the heir to the throne. Christina was, and she is deceased."

John looks at Abel. "Nope, that is not true. She is Christina. They killed Emily trying to protect her."

"Your Highness, I am sorry, but wait, how do I know for sure you are? Who you say you are? I was told you two looked like twins. If so, you could just claim you are."

"Yes, that is the case, but they were not really twins, merely close in looks. There are two reasons you need to accept what she is saying. I was there from the time she was born. I helped raise both girls when Emily was brought to us by William and Eric."

"And the second reason is?"

"She has a dragon birthmark."

"I thought that was just a myth?"

Christina says, "No, it is real. At least I was told it was, having never seen it myself."

John adds, "I have, and that is all that matters."

Abel says, "I am sorry for doubting you. I am also sorry about your father and sister."

Christina assures him, "No, you have every right to be suspicious. These are dangerous times. The days of being happy and free of fear are gone for now, but we must fight to regain control and bring life back to what it was when my father ruled."

"But we still have the issue with the emperor's new weapons. We have no way to defeat them from what I have been told."

John puts in, "Not true. We have a sword that deflects their swords and penetrates their suits. Christina here killed two of them before we left Markus 2."

Evan adds, "Yes, and I witnessed it for myself."

Abel asks, "So, if that is the case, how do we make more?"

John explains, "Well, that's the problem. This sword is ancient. It comes from Zada 5. We are looking at a clan master sword of the Zandorrians. It is said they were created to kill dragons and were crafted for the heads of each clan."

Christina says, "We need a fully stocked lab, so I can try to analyze it. Once we do, then we can create more."

Abel says, "We have a problem then. The only lab like that is on the main base. Let me see how we can get you access without being caught by Craven's rebels."

John exclaims, "There are rebels here on Hmar 4?"

"Yes, they got here two days ago hunting for you two. We had to agree or risk retaliation. That is why I am here. The rebels are still unaware of this base, and I needed to make sure it stayed that way. But give me some time to plan. In the meantime, let me set up some accommodations for the three of you."

As Abel walks away, Christina looks at John. "I didn't think Eric had a family?"

John explains with a smile on his face, "No, Abel is the son of our sister, but she died in childbirth."

"Oh, like what happened to me."

"Yes, you're right, but when he was old enough, we took him under our wing and had him trained as we did with Adam and Connor."

"Then there is the commander of our army till we can get to Zada 5."

John laughs. "You are not wasting any time planning your takeover."

"I can't. The longer he is in power, the harder it will be to get him out, but with all that has happened, one thing bothers me. If they snuck into the palace, they did not use the hidden passage, so how did they get in?"

"I have been thinking about that. They may have snuck a platform into the palace, because from what I first heard, the guards claimed they came from the lower levels and then up the stairs. Since we had additional guards, new to the palace, they would not have focused on those levels, as there was too much happening on the main floors."

"That makes sense, and maybe we can use that to our advantage."

"What do you mean?"

"Didn't you guys say there is a platform on Zada 5?"

"Yes, there is. Why?"

"Well, if we can make that one work, maybe we can use it when we are ready to get back into the palace."

"I would enjoy using their own weapons against them."

"Just promise me when we get to that point, I'll kill the slug. I want him to see my face, knowing I ended him."

"If and when we reach that point, I promise, but we still have a long way to go."

LATER THAT DAY, ABEL COMES BACK. "I THINK I CAN get you in, but it will only be for a few hours."

Christina says, "I will need days, not hours. So, there is nowhere else on this planet with a fully stocked lab?"

"No, not that I have ever been aware of."

John says, "What about the old base on the edge of the dead zone?"

"Yes, there was, but no one has been to that part of the base in years. I do not know what kind of shape it is in or if there is any power to run it."

"It is worth a shot. I doubt the rebels will go there."

"You are right. They would not unless they think you could hide out there, but if they are looking, I will try to find out when they will leave. Give me a day or so. I do not want to raise any suspicions."

Christina says, "Ok, that sounds good to me."

While waiting for an update from Abel, Christina and John train. As they do, other guards ask to join, all are put to shame by Christina's skill level and how easily she can defeat them. John laughs about their embarrassment as most of them are men, so easily beaten by a girl. After a while, Abel returns, but when he does, he asks what Christina is doing to his guards.

John says, "Nothing, just training and beating them."

Abel responds, "Yes, I heard that. John, how long have you been training her?"

"Not me."

"Then who?"

"Adam and Connor."

"You mean the duke's sons?"

Christina agrees, "Yes, the very ones."

"No wonder. So, then all the rumors are true?"

John and Christina laugh. Then Christina says, "We hear that same thing every time they are mentioned."

"Well, if they trained you, then how about sparring with me?"

"Sure," she says. They each wield their swords, striking back and forth several times, before they lock at the hilt, pushing back on each other to the point they have to shove away. Abel spins around, trying to get behind Christina, but she is as quick as he is, putting her sword behind her to block his before twisting around herself. They try to outmaneuver the other, neither one able to get the best of the other. After a half hour of evenly matched combat, both are putting everything into it and are almost worn out.

John says, "Ok, I think no matter what the two of you do, this is always going to end in a draw." They both glance up at him and nod their heads as they can barely breathe. After letting them rest for a few minutes, John looks at Christina. "You picked well."

Abel asks, "What are you talking about?"

John defers to Christina. "Do you want to tell him?"

"Tell me what?"

Christina says, "I want you to be the commander of my army till we can get to Zada 5."

"What? Why me and why Zada 5?"

"Because you can handle yourself, and that is where Adam, Connor, and Eric are."

"Why are they there and not here in this middle of this mess?" John explains the whole reasons they are there. Then Abel says, "Wait a minute, back up. You want me to be your commander until we can get Adam, Connor, and Eric? When can we reach them?"

John comments, "It sounds like he is in."

"I did not say that."

John laughs. "Yes, you did when you said until WE can get them."

Abel chuckles. "I guess I did. So how soon do we leave for Zada 5?"

Christina explains, "The window does not open back up for a little over two months now, which gives us time to work on this sword. To that point, what is the story about going to the base by the dead zone?"

"We will have to wait. The rebels have brought more troops, and they are checking all the bases, including that one. Should be in a week or two. In the meantime,

I will gather supplies we can take there in case it is not still stocked."

Cristina looks at John. "So why is it called the dead zone?"

John explains, "From what I was told, several hundred years ago, two military factions here held a battle for control that lasted almost a year, with our family winning out. During that war, a new bomb was tested. Something went wrong. The base was missed by miles, but when it exploded, it killed everything around, coming very close to the base we are talking about. Since then, it is still hard to breathe, and nothing grows near the base, so people have stopped going in there. We tried to keep the base running, but a few years ago, it was deemed no longer needed, so it was reduced to minimal staff. But really, it was too close to the zone and is not comfortable working there."

THE NEXT DAY, EVAN PACKS UP TO LEAVE. CHRISTINA sees this. "You're leaving? What about helping us get to Zada 5?"

Evan explains, "Don't worry. I will be back in time, but I still must earn a living. There are people I owe, and if they do not get paid, I will not be around to help you."

"I understand. Thank you for all your help so far."

"I am happy to do it, your highness." Evan then steps onto his ship and heads off.

John walks up. "Where is he going?"

Christina says, "He said he owes people and had to make sure they were taken care of."

"Ah yes, the life of a smuggler."

"He said he would be back in time to transport us. Do you think he really will be?"

"He has never been that reliable, but with him knowing who you are and how it could work to his advantage, my guess he would kill himself to get back in time. So, I would not worry."

"Ok, good."

Two weeks go by. In that time Christina has built a reputation with all the guards at the base as unbeatable. In those prior weeks, guards, one after another, wanted to spar with her, trying to defeat her, but the only one who could end the contest in a draw was Abel.

Later that day, Abel comes by shortly after Christina defeats another guard. Abel, seeing another one of his guards defeated, just shakes his head. "This is getting embarrassing. Every one of my soldiers that loses to you has to go through another two weeks of intensive defense and combat training."

John, hearing this, starts to laugh. "Maybe you should have Christina train them."

"That may not be a bad idea, but maybe when we come back from the base near the dead zone."

Christina's eyes light up. "Really?"

"Yes, the rebels were just there. They have been making multiple trips to each of the bases, but if they come back, we can lock up that end of the base, saying we are getting ready to shut it down completely. Since they have already visited and seen only minimal staff there, they will not question it."

"Great, when do we leave?"

"First thing in the morning. I have transport fully stocked with anything the lab does not have, so you should be able to accomplish your analysis."

"I wish we would have been able to get a suit so I could test that as well."

With a grin on his face, Abel opens his pack and pulls a piece of material out to show it. "You mean one of these?"

John exclaims, "How did you get that?"

"I had one of my guys steal it when the additional rebels came with more supplies, which included more suits. We did not think they would miss this one."

Christina asks, "You didn't happen to get the power supply as well, did you?"

Abel pulls another piece out of the other side of his pack. "This?"

Christina is excited. "You're wonderful."

Abel again has a grin on his face. "It is all in a day's job."

THE NEXT MORNING, THE THREE WALK INTO THE transport vehicle. As they leave, Abel reminds them, "It will take several hours to get there."

Christina asks, "Why didn't we fly?"

John explains, "We did not want to take a chance of being tracked. This is a much safer way."

"What do you tell the rebels you are doing when you are gone?"

Abel shrugs. "I don't tell them anything. I don't report to them, and when they are looking for me, my men have been ordered to claim they do not know where I am since I'm their superior. If there are any issues, they know how to reach me. The rebels have tried a few times to have one of my men reach out to me, and when the rebel asked where I am, I told them it's none of their business. I allow them to be here with no trouble. That is all I agreed to do. It will cause problems down the road, but I do not want to give them the idea I am a pushover and that they can do whatever they want. Once we figure out how to get through their suits, it will be 'no more mister nice guy.' My men are already tired of their crap. It is all I can do to keep them under control at this point."

John agrees. "Yes, they have been trained to be the aggressor, and none of them believed the story Lorenzo sent out. They all know who William was, but they also know they took our men out in a very short time at the palace. That is the only thing holding them back."

A little while later, still headed to the base, Abel looks at Christina. "I have to ask, how old were you when you started training with Adam and Connor?"

Christina says, "I was about seven."

John agrees. "Yes, that sounds right."

Abel exclaims, "Seven! Didn't your father have a problem with it?"

Christina says, "Well, we would use Emily as the lookout in case anyone came, so they would not know what we were really doing."

John laughs.

"What's so funny?"

John explains, "Your father knew the whole time and actually encouraged it. You never wondered why you were hardly interrupted? You would do it at about the same time almost every day when the boys were there. We just made sure no one came around." Both Christina and Abel chuckle.

Christina says, "So poor Emily had to keep watch when she could have been there training with us as well?"

"Yes, I am afraid so. Your father wanted to make sure you were prepared in every way to take over if anything happened to him, but once you and Adam got into trouble on Lucas 2, we knew it was time to expand your training to the sciences."

"Wait, learning the sciences was my choice, not his."

"Ok, if you want to think so."

"It was. There were some other courses, but they were full, so I opted to try the sciences and stayed with them. No, wait, don't tell me he set that up as well."

John smiles at her. "What do you think?"

"Because of that SOB? So, he drove my whole life, and I did not know."

"You don't think he became the emperor without knowing what to do?"

"Well, he always seemed to know everything, and we could never figure out how he did it."

"Your father was better than anyone I knew about reading people and understanding their plans. That is why he sent us off after his brother. Unfortunately, Lorenzo was almost as good. That is why we are here in this situation now."

Christina starts to cry, but then stops herself. "No, I can't do this. I need to focus."

"It's ok. I know this is hard to talk about and it is bringing up a lot of feelings about your father."

"Yes, you're right, but holding the pain inside strengthens me."

Abel comments, "Yes, I get that, and part of the reason you are so hard to beat when sparring is you use that anger."

"Everyone I fight, I think is the slug, and want to kill them."

"The slug?"

John explains, "Yes, that is what she calls Lorenzo."

Abel laughs. "I like it. That will catch on."

Christina, stoic, almost sad, from their discussion, then says, "Also, I have been thinking about it, and it is no longer Christina. It is now Chris."

"Why is that?"

"Christina was young and unaware of how cruel the world could be around her, but Chris is hardened and bent on avenging her family and will do whatever it will take to get the throne back."

John says, "I understand that, but do not make your thoughts of revenge turn you bitter. Once we take back the throne, you will need part of Christina."

"I will try to remember that."

AFTER ANOTHER COUPLE OF HOURS, THEY FINALLY GET near the base. As they do, Abel stops the vehicle and looks with his long-range glasses. "We will have to go in a back way. There are rebels here."

Chris asks, "How do you know?"

Abel hands her the glasses. "Look at the window on the right side of the main building. See that blue flag in the corner?"

"Yes, I do."

"That is the signal to our guys when the rebels are in the building."

"So, what can we do?"

"There is a spot behind the base just inside the dead zone. We will be fine there. I can hike over, then find out their location."

John says, "Ok, that sounds like a plan."

Abel drives into the dead zone to an area with a group of dead trees far enough away they cannot see it at the base.

It takes Abel a while to get into the back of the building. After a few hours of waiting, both John and Christina, concerned, start to head to the base, but about halfway, Abel walks back towards them. They wait for him. "Sorry for taking so long, but I had a run-in with some rebels. They demanded I tell them what I was up to and why I was there. At first, I insisted it was none of their business. They threatened me, but I finally told them there were only a few of them, and I had elite killers on the base. They may kill a few but end up losing their lives. Then it would be on. If they tried to send more troops, we would blow them out of the sky. One of them said the discussion was not over. I told them it was for me." Looking at both John and Christina, Abel tells them they better get the vehicle to the base and unload it before the rebels return, so he can lock down the back.

AFTER UNLOADING, CHRIS STUDIES THE SWORD WHILE Abel secures the back half of the base. She pours herself into her work, testing the sword relentlessly from every angle. After a few days, John comes in. "You have been up for ages working on this and really need to get some rest. You don't want to miss anything." Chris, haggard and exhausted, argues at first. John pushes back and makes the point that she's running the risk of missing something. Finally, she agrees and gets some actual sleep; then she goes right back to it.

Chris determines the sword contains several minerals, including Zando Crystals and Verbraso, but because they are bonded with the base metal from the sword, she cannot figure out the actual formula to create a new sword. It would take months of trial and error to get it right. She starts testing the suit powered up. Same as she did with the sword. After going for almost two more days, John again pushes on the issue of getting some sleep. This time, she doesn't argue.

But as they are having the discussion, Abel tells them they need to be quiet. The rebels are back near the area they are working in. Chris shuts everything down. As the three of them sit quietly, they can hear talking and someone checking the doors. Chris draws her sword. Abel puts his hand up silently, telling her to stand down. After a few minutes, the rebels walk away. They wait for a while to make sure the rebels are gone. Chris starts up again, working on the suit for a few more days while taking time to sleep in between.

When Chris is finally finished, she tells the guys she is ready to report on her findings as she tells them about the sword. Abel asks where they can get these minerals, and John responds they can all be found on Zada 5.

Abel responds, "Why does everything lead back to Zada 5?"

John comments, "Well, it is the largest mineral production planet, but the Verbraso is extremely rare and hard to find, even there."

Chris says, "Then that answers that question. As for the suit, I found a small weakness in the back of it near the power source. You can penetrate it with a regular sword."

Abel says, "Great, so all we have to do is get them to run away. Then we can stab them in the back."

"There is one more option. If you can knock them to the ground and stomp on their right wrist, the suit should shut down."

"None of this is great news, so where do we go from here?"

They all sit for a while not speaking; then John gets up. "Maybe it is time to start the war."

"Are you insane? We can't. They have weapons we cannot fight against."

"True, but we can start by stealing from the four that are here."

"How?"

Chris agrees. "John is right. We have my sword and this suit," she holds it up, "that you can wear. You can draw them out, and I will kill them."

"But when they do not report in, and it's discovered they were killed here, what next?"

John says, "Think about where we are. We put them in their vehicle and drive them deep into the dead zone. Their search will give us time for phase two. We will not draw them out and kill them. We are going to use one of our small sonic bombs on them to see how they respond. It should knock them unconscious. Even if it stuns them, we can take them out. We should still have a few of the bombs near the supply closet in weapons storage."

"How can we win with only four suits and swords?"

"You're right, but that is the start that leads to phase two."

"That will only work if the sonic bomb succeeds. And when it is discovered that the four men are missing?"

"I am sure they will send more men, and we use the bomb on them. This is how we will build up our weapons to fight back."

"Are we really going to start a war?"

Chris points out, "You knew it was going to come to this point. It was just a matter of when."

"I guess you're right, but I thought we could be better prepared. This way, we may lose a lot of men."

John agrees. "Yes, but how much more of this crap are you willing to take from those rebels?"

"Not much more. If we have the right weapons, I would have destroyed them the last time I faced them."

"And how do you think your men feel?"

"The same way. They are almost to the boiling point now."

Chris says, "I am sure they are. At least this way we let your men know we have a plan and a way to fight back if phase one works. So, John, how do we get started?"

John looks at Abel. "Can you sneak out, get to the weapons storage, find one bomb with the remote trigger, and place it under their vehicle? Then we will see what happens when they get close to it."

Abel consents, "Yes, I should be able to do that. Give me about an hour to place it. I will also find a place where we can monitor them, so we know when to detonate the device."

A LITTLE OVER AN HOUR LATER, ABEL SNEAKS BACK IN. "Ok, I found a spot in one of the old security offices that is not being used but is still active." Abel shows them the way. It is close enough to activate the detonator, but still off the path of the rebels. When they get in the office, Abel points out a display revealing the complete front of the building with the rebel's vehicle.

Chris asks, "How far are we from their vehicle?"

"We are about five minutes away from the front door. Why?"

John says, "Oh wait, you're right."

"Right about what?"

"We do not know if it will work, but if it does, how long it will affect them being in those suits?"

Chris adds, "How close can you get to their vehicle without being seen or damaged by the bomb?"

Abel says, "If I am in the building, it will not affect me at all. Our buildings were updated against these bombs. There is an office real close where I can see most of the front, so if you set off the explosive, I can run out right after and get their swords."

John adds, "You will need to get their rings too."

"Their rings?"

"Yes, the ring activates the sword."

"Ok, let me sneak into that office."

Chris hands him the suit. "Here, wear this just in case."

"Good point."

John says, "Once we set off the bomb, we will run out there as fast as we can. If we do not see them drop, we will have to come up with a new plan."

Chris says, "Yes, we just pull them out of the vehicle and kill them." John and Abel laugh. "What's so funny?"

"You seem to have a one-track mind here."

"Can you blame me?"

Abel soothes her. "No, we can't. If they had done to me what they did to you, I would feel the same way."

AFTER ABOUT AN HOUR OF WAITING, THE FOUR REBELS exit the building. When they see this, John detonates the small bomb as they enter their vehicle. They drop to the ground. All three head for the front door. Abel gets out to the rebels first. He takes the swords and then pulls off their rings, but as he does so, they stir. John and Christina run out after Abel, pulling off one of the suits, only to discover the rebels are waking up and fighting back.

With three of the four rebels partially disarmed, Chris yells, "Kill them!" As she says that, she draws her sword, stabbing the first one through the head, killing him instantly. She then swings, cutting the throat of a second one.

John draws his sword, but as he goes to stab the one in front of him with an opening in his suit, the rebel moves, causing John's sword to slide across. Chris runs over just as the rebel jumps up. When he does, Chris runs her sword through the suit and into his chest. He wears a look of shock as he falls to the ground. At the same time, the rebel in front of Abel rises. Abel picks up one of the rebel's swords and runs it through the middle of his opened suit, killing him as well.

With all four now dead, they look at each other and smile. Then John says, "Well, now we know the sonic bomb will work, but just not very long." While he says that, Abel collects the rings, and they finish taking off their suits. They put the dead bodies in the back of the rebel's vehicle. "Go get our vehicle and follow me into the dead zone so we can get rid of them." Abel leaves and comes back a short time later. When he does, John looks at Chris. "Why don't you take the suits and swords to the lab? We will be back as soon as we can."

After several hours of waiting, Chris gets concerned. Not knowing where they are, all she can do is wait. After about another hour, they finally return. "What took you guys so long?" she says with an excited tone.

John explains, "Sorry, but I thought about it on the way. We sent their vehicle over the ravine, but it was further than I remembered. It will take a long time for the bodies and vehicle to be discovered, if ever. So now we need to think about whether we push the issue and start the war or try to be covert."

"As much as I would really like to get things moving, it would be prudent to be more clandestine. Then we can steal more suits and swords."

While they talk, Abel picked up a sword and puts a ring on, activating the sword. "These swords glow blue, but yours glows red, and you do not need a ring for your sword. So, I have two questions. The first one, do you know if this sword will keep turning on as long as you have the ring?"

Chris shrugs. "I have no idea. We will have to test it. But if it deactivates, then we will have to figure out what powers it and how it gets loaded. Ok, your second question?"

"Your sword pierces these suits. Do these?" He holds up the rebel sword.

"That is a great point. We have been assuming they would, but clearly, the two swords are different. I will have to test it." With a smile on her face, she adds, "Hey, you are still wearing one. We can try it now."

"Ha, ha, very funny."

THE NEXT DAY, CHRIS RETURNS TO WORK IN THE LAB, this time testing the suit with the sword. After several hours, she discovers a way to remove the handle from the sword at the hilt. Once she does, she figures out most of the minerals are Zando Crystals with a small amount of Verbraso. Chris determines the sword, with a full amount of minerals, would last about six hours. Next, she attempts to penetrate the suit with the rebel sword, but the best she could do was burn it.

A short time later, as Chris is finishing her examination, the guys came back from patrolling the base. Abel asks, "Were you able to successfully test everything?"

"Yes, I was." Chris tells them what she discovered and points out the sword seems to cut through almost everything except for the suit, but they can fight back with rebels' swords.

John says, "Well, we can reload the swords for a short time. We have plenty of refined Zando Crystals, but we will need more Verbraso, which is on Zada 5."

Abel comments, "Again, everything leads us back there."

"Then we need to obtain as many swords as we can before we go to Zada 5."

"But if we take all the men that have them there, we will leave our bases defenseless against the new emperor's forces—sorry, the slug's forces. We will need to meet with the troop leaders and come up with a better plan, or by the time we can leave Zada 5, no one will be left here, and the war will be over before we can ever get it off the ground."

John and Christina, at the same time, agree.

John says, "Ok, we should get back to the secret base and work on a better strategy. We are running out of time before the next window."

CHAPTER XVI

THE NEW EMPEROR?

On Markus 2, Lorenzo establishes himself as the new emperor. He brings the rebel forces he and Craven had been building up on Ria 6 to take over as the new emperor's army. But since he cannot legally claim the rights thanks to his now-dead brother, Lorenzo eliminates anyone that tries to push back against the rights he claims. Since he is not officially the emperor, he cannot access any of the empire accounts, so in the meantime, Lorenzo uses the diverted finances from the sale of extra minerals to build his army and has to continue. Now that he has proclaimed to be the new emperor, he can force all the mining colonies on every planet to produce more and reduces the amount been shared with all of them prior. After coming up with this plan, he calls Major Johnson and Craven in to meet with him.

Craven and Major Johnson walk into Esteban's old office where Lorenzo sits. They enter, and Lorenzo goes over his plans. Doing this, Craven asks how he is going to force all these colonies to produce so much.

Lorenzo tells him they will need to send troops to each one that resists, and they may need to make examples of a few of them to help force the others to fall in line.

Major Johnson comments, "If we send troops to all these colonies, we will not have enough left to guard you or the area surrounding the palace."

Lorenzo replies, "Then we will have to train and arm more men."

Craven objects, "But we barely have enough weapons for the men we have already trained, and I will need men when I go to Zada 5 to take care of the duke's sons."

Lorenzo is getting irritated with the questions. "I DON'T CARE WHAT IT TAKES! This is what I want to be done, and you two need to make sure it happens."

"Yes, sire, we will. But when will we get more weapons?"

"I have the labs working on them now, but we are running short on Verbraso. That you will have to get when you kill the boys on Zada 5."

"But it will take me three months to return."

"Once you have killed the boys, the threat will be gone. Then you can use the portal."

"But how? The device was only set up to receive, not transmit. I cannot send you any messages from there."

Lorenzo is even more irritated. "Why do I have to come up with all the solutions? I am looking for generals here that can think on their own!"

Major Johnson looks at Craven. "We will turn on the portal once a week at the same day and time. Then we can have the minerals sent each week, and you can come back once you have taken control."

"Yes! See, that is what I am talking about, answers, not negativity and more issues." Lorenzo studies Major Johnson. "I have always called you Major Johnson. What is your first name?"

"It is Thomas, but I go by Tom, sire."

"Well, Tom, you are now General Tom Johnson." He shakes his hand.

Tom, with a big smile on his face, continued to shake Lorenzo's hand excitedly. "Thank you, sire, thank you."

Clearly mad over this, Craven glares at Lorenzo. "Wait, what about me?"

Lorenzo says, "Well, if you really want the title Chief of Security for me, then prove it by killing the duke's sons on Zada 5 and get us more Verbraso so we can create more weapons. There are already plenty of suits, and we are having the swords built, but we will need rings and the minerals to power them."

"Chief of Security! Yes, sire, it will be done. You can count on me."

"Next on my list, Hmar 4. Are we getting any pushback there with the duke's men?"

"No, they have been silent. They seem to be concerned about our weapons. Our men have been inspecting the bases for Emily and John but have seen no sign of them so far, either. There has been some minor resistance from the guards there, but nothing major."

"Very well. Continue to have our men patrol there. We cannot afford any type of rebellion."

General Tom agrees, "We will, sire. You can count on us. If they start anything, we will stop it as soon as it starts."

A FEW DAYS LATER, TOM GETS A MESSAGE. FOUR OF HIS men are missing on Hmar 4. Knowing Lorenzo and his temper, not wanting Lorenzo to think he cannot control the situation, he keeps it quiet. In the meantime, Tom has additional men sent there to find the missing soldiers. After a few days of tracing the steps of the men who disappeared, the rebels cannot find them anywhere. Since Hmar 4 is mostly covered with dense trees and vegetation; the rebels would have to find them from the ground. So, they assume the men got drunk and crashed somewhere, as most of the rebels have a reputation for drinking heavily and having crashed multiple vehicles back on Ria 6. Finding them from the ground with the limited resources they have on the planet would take forever. This is the report sent back to Tom. He responds to his men that they can no longer drink while on Hmar 4, not being sure what else to do at this point.

Since Tom is now responsible for the entire force supporting Lorenzo, he turns the planets into zones with a commander for each, to control his troops better. Since each planet has its own mining guild, the commanders take charge of these guilds with a few rebels dispatched to each mining planet to control the miners that resist. As there is no way for any to fight back against the rebels, they have to accept Tom's control. At Lorenzo's request, the miners increase their production while the commanders keep more of the profits from the mined minerals.

Despite everything Lorenzo has put in place, he grows angrier about not being the official emperor or having internal restraints, which limits his abilities to overtake certain parts of the empire. What's more, the cost of building his new army, weapons, and new fighters keeps increasing as he expands his rule. He finds this unbearable and demands that Craven come and meet with him.

Craven takes several hours to get back from Korbin. By this time, Lorenzo is completely irate, waiting for Craven to arrive. As soon as he walks in, Lorenzo starts screaming, "What are you doing about killing the duke's sons? They are still in the way."

Craven, not wanting to increase Lorenzo's anger, explains, "The window for Zada 5 opens in a few weeks, and I have been working to face Adam and Connor and finish them off. Once they are taken care of, I will send all the minerals through the portal. Also, the reason it took me so long to get here is I was on Korbin, where I am staging everything to go to Zada 5 since it is closer."

Lorenzo now smiles. "Well, it sounds like you are well on your way to becoming my Chief of Security for the empire. I just hope you understand who you are really up against."

"First, thank you for trusting me. I am doing everything to accomplish this for you, and yes, I am aware how dangerous they are, but with our new weapons, along with my knowledge and experience, we will defeat them. Now, if there is nothing more, I need to get back to Korbin, so we are ready."

"Yes, how will you find them on Zada 5? It is a large planet."

"There are currently only a few mines that provide the crystals. All ships come from the same place, so that is where we will start our search for them."

"Very good. Thank you for coming. I feel better now about what you are doing to help me get ownership of the empire. Please do not let me hold you up anymore. Come see me once it is done."

"Yes, sire, I will." Craven exits the room.

Once Craven leaves for Korbin, the pilot looks at him. "That was a short meeting. You had to fly all the way back here for that? Why could you not have done it over the communicator?"

"The new emperor does not like to use them. He is afraid someone could monitor them and hear everything."

"But they can be made secure."

"You know that, and so do I, but you cannot say so to him. It is much safer for me if I just come here and go back. It kills the day for me and puts me way behind, but I would not tell him that either. The emperor is extremely smart but has no patience and a terrible temper. His new power makes it easy for him to have people disappear, never to be heard from again. So keep that in mind if you ever have to deal with him."

"Yes, I will. Thanks for the heads up."

LATER THAT DAY, CRAVEN GETS A REPORT THAT SOME of Tom's men went missing on Hmar 4 and reaches out to Tom. Craven presses him on what happened to the lost men. Tom responds they got drunk and ran off the road into a deep ravine, not wanting Craven to know they could not find them. Craven, unhappy with that answer, keeps pushing. Tom finally tells Craven to mind his own business and not worry about it. Craven responds, "It is all my business. I own security, and Hmar 4 will continue to be a big issue for us."

Tom responds, "You still need to kill the duke's sons before that job is yours. Until then, I am the general over all the troops, including the ones going with you to Zada 5."

"Are you sure that's the way you want to play it?"

"What do you mean, if that's the way I want to play it?"

"I mean, once I kill the boys, you will work for me, and I will remember this conversation."

"Is that a threat? I am not worried about you or what you think you can do to me. Lorenzo made me the general, and you cannot change that. You seem to forget I have worked with both of you over the past couple of years while you guys planned to overthrow Esteban and his team. The troops have always answered to me, not you, and I know how the both of you think."

Craven gets hot over his comments. "Think what you want, but you do not know everything. I will leave it at that."

"I'm not worried." Then Tom ends the communication.

Right after their discussion stops, Craven screams as loud as he can in frustration. Everything Tom said is true. He cannot control Tom with intimidation once he is made Chief of Security and will need to have Tom either replaced or eliminated, with someone he *can* control once Lorenzo promotes him. Right now, he needs to focus on killing the boys first, then work on his new plan for Tom.

SHORTLY AFTER TOM'S CONVERSATION WITH CRAVEN, Lorenzo calls Tom into his office. Tom is using John's old room, trying to stay as close to Lorenzo as he can. He is in with Lorenzo in a matter of minutes. Walking in, Lorenzo asks if Tom is making any progress with the miners. Tom lays out what he has done with his commanders, the guilds, and zoning the planets. Lorenzo, with a big smile on his face, tells Tom how pleased he is with the plans and his ability to think for himself. Lorenzo then tells him to keep up the good work while giving him regular updates on the progress. Tom, feeling good about the conversation, informs Lorenzo about the missing men on Hmar 4, but he has replaced them with a larger group as they continue to search for John and Emily. Lorenzo tells Tom he is comfortable with how it is being handled, if Tom is. Tom tells him he is and thanks Lorenzo for his support, then leaves the room.

When Tom is out of earshot, he thinks to himself that if he keeps it up, he can replace Craven and have him eliminated with Lorenzo's support.

Once Tom returns to his desk, he sends a message to the captain selecting the troops that will go with Craven to Zada 5. The captain needs to replace most of the men with newly trained soldiers, telling him they will be more effective, but in reality, they do not have the experience needed to deal with both Adam and Connor. This will make it harder for Craven to be successful. Tom also tells the captain not to concern Craven with the changes. He will notify Craven. The captain agrees and replaces the men with the alternatives. Since Craven does not know most of the rebel troops, he is unaware of the swap. This change only leaves four experienced pilots going with Craven. Tom hopes making this change puts Craven's life at risk in the battle against Adam and Connor.

BACK ON HMAR 4, CHRIS, JOHN, AND ABEL plot to take down four more rebels that have come to the base by the dead zone before they could leave and also dump them in the ravine, just like the last ones. This time, instead of using a sonic bomb, they face the rebels as soon as they get out of their vehicle, with two additional men using their own weapons against them. They force the rebels to attack Chris one at a time, but once she kills the first one with her sword, the other three men surrender right away. Abel comments, "Well, we did not plan for this. Where are we going to hold them?"

John says, "The lower level can be locked up. We can hold several men down there."

"Ok, we will have to get more men to help guard them."

While working out how to hold and guard the rebels, the group takes the dead rebel and their vehicle to the ravine in the dead zone and dump them. This time, Chris goes with them, and on the way there, she looks at John. "What kind of crap do you think this will stir?"

"Well, I do not think they will accept that they got drunk and drove off a cliff somewhere this time. We need to get the other six or force them to come to us before they send more men. Once we have captured the rest of the men, we will prepare for war. We have no choice now."

Headed back to the base now with Abel in the vehicle, he glances at both John and Chris. "Well, we have done it, so how do we go after the other six?"

Both John and Chris laugh. Then Chris says, "We discussed that very thing on the way there."

"I guess war has started whether or not we want it to."

John agrees. "You're right."

THAT NIGHT, THEY FIND OUT WHERE THE REST OF THE rebels are going to be and plan to meet them, along with more of Abel's men. This time, when the rebels see nine warriors facing them with the same swords, all surrender right away. Knowing it will not matter if they were seen, they use the rebel's vehicle to take them back to the base, along with the other captured men. Now they have fifteen suits and fourteen swords. John and Abel pick fourteen of their best men and arm them, but warn them to only power the suits when absolutely needed. They demonstrate how to reload their weapons while pointing out that currently, there is only a limited amount of minerals.

Back on Markus 2, the next day, Tom gets a report: ten more men are missing. He becomes concerned if he sends more men, they will also disappear. With that in mind, he builds a blockade around Hmar 4 and warns all on the planet they will need to file a flight plan and must get official approval to leave the planet, or they will be destroyed, and the same goes for anyone trying to land. He does all this one week before the window opens for Zada 5.

On Hmar 4, Chris, hearing this, looks at John. "Do we have any idea where Evan is? We need him more than ever now."

John assures her, "No, but if he said he will be here, we have to trust that, but we will start sending out communications to find him."

Again, on Markus 2, Lorenzo, hearing the announcement about Hmar 4, demands Tom meet with him. Tom quickly comes down to Lorenzo's office, telling him he was sorry for not asking before doing it, but he could not lose any time. Lorenzo is totally irate about the loss of the ten men, wanting to start a war with Hmar 4. "Everyone on that planet was trained by the duke, John, and Eric."

Tom agrees. "You are correct. They also instructed most of the emperor's army, with many still loyal to them. That is why I put up the blockade. We cannot start a war with them right now. We are spread too thin and would have to focus all our troops on Hmar 4. Since they are the elite military, skirmishes could take a long time, and we could lose too many men. Once you are the official emperor, they will have no choice but to accept you."

Lorenzo calms down. "Yes, you are right. You are truly proving to be someone I can depend on. Keep it up."

"Thank you, sire. I will."

On Korbin, while Craven is almost done loading everything he needs, he plans how he and his men will approach and attack Zada 5. While this is going on, Craven hears about the missing men and the blockade on Hmar 4. He gets ready to communicate with Tom but then stops and thinks to himself to stay out of it. John and Eric's men on Hmar 4 will not sit still for this very long. Even with the new weapons, Tom cannot handle a full attack from them, not with the limited amount of training Craven could provide the rebels. They are no match for the men and women trained on Hmar 4. Even if they were outnumbered four to one, which would take every rebel they have now.

With only three days left before the new window, Craven just sits back with a big smile on his face, thinking to himself, this will be the end of Tom.

ON HMAR 4, TWO DAYS BEFORE THE WINDOW OPENS, John tells Chris they finally heard back from Evan. "He has been on the outer edges of the empire and had some problem to deal with, but will be back on Hmar 4 early tomorrow, the day before the new window. This will give us just enough time to load and leave for Zada 5."

Clearly, Chris is upset Evan is cutting it close but acknowledges they can do nothing but wait for him to show up. "Please make sure we have everything ready waiting to be loaded as soon as Evan lands."

John looks at her and laughs. "You think this is my first time?"

"No, you are right. I am sorry. I am just nervous about the guys, and we need to make sure they are safe."

"I understand. Don't worry. We will get there as soon as we can."

THE NEXT DAY, TRUE TO HIS WORD, GETTING CLOSE TO Hmar 4, aware of the blockade, Evan turns his cloaking on. He is also starting to get low on fuel. Just as he passes the blockade, his cloaking automatically turns off when the low fuel notification turns on. The rebels in the blockade see Evan's ship suddenly appear, headed for Hmar 4. They tell him to turn around and go back, not to land. At that point, Evan realizes the cloaking deactivated on its own. At first, he does not acknowledge. They tell him again, this time saying they are going to fire on him. He then claims he is having trouble with his ship and needs to land. They tell him they do not care; he needs to stop, and they will take him to the nearest spaceport, but he cannot arrive on the planet below.

As they send fighters after him, he speeds up, trying to outrun their ships. They fire on him. He tries dodging their fire but gets hit several times, causing major damage. John and Abel get word Evan is in trouble. Abel tells his ground team to attack the fighters with their large pulse cannons. One fighter gets hit and explodes, causing the others to break off and head back to their main ship.

Evan, barely able to keep his ship flying, bounces on the landing field as he tries to bring his ship down. John, Abel, and Chris run to Evan's ship just as he comes out. As he walks off, Evan shakes his head. "Well, I made it. My ship took some hits, but I am here."

Chris looks at John and Abel. "Can we fix this pile of junk before the window tomorrow?"

"It is not a pile of junk." As Evan slaps the side of his ship, part of the wing falls off behind him.

"It's not?"

"Well, yes, it has some damage, but nothing that cannot be fixed by a good mechanic." Part of the landing gear breaks, and the ship partially falls to its belly. Evan throws up his hands. "I need a drink. Where's the bar?" He strides away.

John and Abel turn to Chris. "We will have our guys work on this all day and night, but there is a lot of damage here."

Chris asks, "What other options do we have if we cannot get this ship ready by tomorrow?"

John explains, "We really do not have any. You saw what they did to Evan just trying to land. They have pulse cannons on their ships and will blow apart any vessel that tries to leave. We would have to send too many ships to get one through."

Chris tears up for a minute. "No, I have to stop this," she mutters, talking to herself. She glares at John. "We have to get there. You know they are going to throw everything they have at our guys. They will need our help!"

"They have been in worse, especially Adam and Eric. It is also clear Connor knows how to take care of himself."

"You're right, but they do not understand about the vulnerability of the suits that could help them fight back."

"True, but knowing my boys, I am sure they have already come up with preparations of their own."

"I hope you are right."

CHAPTER XVII

FIGHT FOR THE RIGHT

On Zada 5, everyone discusses Connor's vision of what may have happened on Markus 2. Eric laments, "It was all as Esteban feared. Lorenzo's ultimate goal was to take the throne, and if Lorenzo and Craven are back on Markus 2 killing everyone, as Connor said, then we have to assume Lorenzo will have to come here next to take care of us. We will need to plan for that because we will threaten Lorenzo's grip on power. Especially seeing as Esteban also took steps to make sure Lorenzo could never take the throne."

Adam asks, "What's this now?"

"If Esteban died, then it would go to Chris, not Lorenzo, and if he could kill Chris, then it would go to you two, first Adam, and, if anything happened to you, then your brother."

Connor says, "So even more reason for them to come here to kill us, as I am sure that Esteban would have taken solace in telling Lorenzo about his plan before being killed, knowing he could tell his brother how he screwed him. I know that's what I would have done if I were him."

Eric agrees. "I am sure you are right."

Adam says, "So if that is really the case, then we will be first on his list when he comes here. Maybe we can figure out a way to use that to our advantage."

Mondo and Renaldo hear all of this. "Ok, then we have three months to prepare."

Adam looks at Dave. "Hey did you read the report from Emma? I spent the whole time sleeping and never got to it."

Dave says, "No, I didn't either. I put it in the lockbox on the ship and forgot all about it."

"Do you think it could have made it through the wreck?"

"Well, it was stored on part of the ship that is still there."

Connor glances at Renaldo. "Can you take Dave back to the crash site and see if you can find that report? If so, it may have something in it that could help us fight against Lorenzo's new weapons."

Renaldo asks, "New weapons? What new weapons?" Adam explains about the suits and swords, along with what transpired while Eric and Connor were still on Zada 5. Renaldo and Mondo are taken back a little by this news.

Mondo says, "Then let's see if the report is still on the ship and it has some good news."

Renaldo adds, "Speaking about new weapons, the blacksmith has Connor's swords ready. We can go get them after we visit the ship." He looks at Dave. "Want to see some of our country? The trip is long. If we leave now, we can be back late tomorrow."

Dave agrees. "Sure, I would like to check things out." A short time later, Renaldo and Dave head for the wrecked vessel.

Right after Renaldo and Dave leave, Connor goes out alone to talk with Andorra. Adam looks at Mondo. "What is he doing?"

Mondo explains, "He did this a lot when he was last here. He seems to talk to her. There is a bond between them no one can explain."

"I struggle to believe that dragons are real and that my brother can talk with it. My parents did not believe it either."

"Yes, your father, I am very sorry for your loss, if Connor is right. He and I started out as enemies, then became good friends. I will miss him."

"He was a great role model for me, someone I really looked up to. It is hard for me to accept he may be gone, but like my brother, we are here for three months, and I cannot dwell on the possibility. Let's change the subject. Connor told us he is part of one of your prophecies."

"That is true. So far, he has tamed the dragon and won the battle for head of the clans. The only thing left is Emperor of the Universe. Now, based on what Eric said, he is actually in line for that title if anything were to happen to you. Not that we ever want that to happen."

Adam laughs. "Right, neither do I."

"That is why all the clans got together to give this house to your brother and made him an official Zandorrian."

"So, he wasn't kidding about any of it."

Mondo chuckles. "No, he wasn't. We wanted to encourage him to stay with us and show him how much we cared about him."

Adam smiles. "Well, I am glad he has so many people who do."

"You are his brother. That affection falls to you as well."

"Thank you. I truly appreciate it. But if my father is really gone, then I would have to go back to Hmar 4 to take over what my family built."

"I can understand, but you will always be welcome here."

Eric, hearing Adam and Mondo talking, looks at Adam. "I understand how you feel, but once we leave here, we will have to fight and defeat Lorenzo. If he is sitting on the throne now, he can do a lot of damage before we can leave."

Mondo agrees. "Eric is right. If we can do anything to help, consider it done."

Adam turns to Eric. "Do we still have a secret base on our home planet?"

Eric says, "Yes, we do. Why?"

"Once we defeat Craven and can leave, we will have to be stealthy so Lorenzo does not know where we are. Then we can manage our plans for overthrowing him."

"I like it. You are already thinking like your father would have."

As Adam speaks with Mondo, Connor stands alongside Andorra. She tells him how sorry she is for the loss of his mate. Connor takes in her sympathy. She tells him she has seen her end coming soon. As she speaks, visions of a fierce battle overwhelm Connor. Men fall in droves, and the bloodshed is overwhelming.

"Do you have the same visions?" he asks.

Andorra reassures him, "I do, but I don't worry. I've seen you will not die."

"Andorra, I am going to miss you."

"Do not mourn me. I've been able to communicate with a human after years of being hunted. It is a fitting end to my life."

"Even after you go, you'll always be a part of me." Connor and Andorra stand there in front of her barn with the sun still rising behind them.

Connor enters his home and says, "I just had another vision while talking with Andorra, with a lot of blood and death all around us."

Adam responds, "I am not sure what we can do with what you are telling us, other than try to limit our exposure to whomever we will be fighting."

"I understand, but I wanted you to know."

Eric comments, "Maybe part of it is what we are doing to them during our battle."

Mondo nods at Eric. "I like the way you are thinking. You could be right, especially if they are not expecting us to stand up to them, thinking we are no longer warriors like we were many years ago."

Connor agrees. "Yes, you're right. But to that point, we need to gather all the men we had trained back here so we can keep it up. There is a lot they can learn from my brother as well."

Adam adds, "Yes, I would like to see how well they can handle themselves."

Eric looks at Adam. "I think you will be surprised how well they fight after learning from your brother and I."

Mondo says, "I will get the word out that you are back, and we can continue their guidance with you guys. They have been doing a lot on their own, so I think you will be surprised how much better they are. About another twenty clansmen want to fight with you." Mondo puts his hand on Connor's shoulder.

Adam exclaims, "Twenty? How many men do we have then?"

"Well, we are at about forty now."

Adam wears a big grin on his face. "Wow, that is much more than I thought. I'm with Eric—the blood and death will mostly be Craven's men."

As Adam and Connor talk, Renaldo and Dave reach the remnants of the crash ship. Dave finds the box broken open and the report partially burned on the outside, but when he pulls it out of the cover, it is mostly intact. Renaldo sees the report. "Well, it looks still readable."

Dave concurs, "Yes, it is, and there may be some good news about fighting the rebels. Emma found a gap we can expose."

"Great, then let's go get us some new weapons we can use as well. I recalculated the time; it will take us about a day and half there, then the same back."

"Let's get moving."

Early in the morning, a day and half later, they arrive at the home of the blacksmith. As they get to the door, the son opens it. "You must be Renaldo. I was told to expect you. I have what you came for in here." The son leads them to the back of the blacksmith's home and out to his workshop. He walks over, picks up a long box on the table, and hands it to Renaldo, "My father made this for Connor, the One."

Renaldo takes it with a puzzled look on his face, "Where is your father?"

"He died the morning after he told you the sword was ready."

"What happened, and where are the other swords? He was going to build five for us."

"My father had been sick for a long time, but he wanted to do this for the One. The night before he died, I think he knew it because he handed me this." He puts his hand on top of the box Renaldo holds. "Then told me it was the best work he had ever done. This was his crowning achievement and was proud to give it to the One. If Connor were truly the One, it would protect him against anyone." The son then lifts the lid on the box. "If you look near the hilt, that is not just a design. It is Connor's name in Zandorrian script on one side and 'The One' on the other."

"This is a beautiful sword. I am sure that Connor will love it, but where are the other four?"

The son points over to the forge. "There, but they are not finished yet. I found the instructions to complete them lying next to my father when I found him the next morning. This is how I know he knew he was going to die that night. I really think he felt this was what he was meant to do and could finally let go. With the instructions, I will finish them, but I will need another month or two."

"I am very sorry for your loss. Looking at this sword, his craft will be a significant loss to us all, and we appreciate your willingness to pick up where he left off. Do you think you can bring them to us when you are finished? That will be close to the new window, and we cannot come back here until much later."

"Yes, I would be happy to if I can meet the One."

"Absolutely. I am sure he would like to thank you personally."

"Great, consider it done. I think you will be happy with my finished product. I learned a lot from my father."

Dave puts in, "Well, if they look even close to what your father created, I am sure they will be amazing, too."

"You will not be disappointed."

Renaldo agrees. "I am sure we won't. Thank you very much for everything, but we must be going. There is a lot to do, and we need to get back."

"Of course." The son then walks them out, and they head back to Connor's with his new sword.

THE NEXT DAY, AS RENALDO AND DAVE MAKE THEIR WAY back, Connor and Adam meet the men as they show up. A few days before, Mondo sent out the word that Connor was back looking to train with them again. As they come down, Connor sees several familiar faces. Some he fought against and some who tried killing him, along with his bodyguards, who are all friends now. While greeting the men, he introduces them to his older, fiercer brother. They all laugh. Adam asks, "What so funny?"

One of them comments, "We all know how strong the one is. We struggle to believe anyone else could be worse."

Connor looks at Adam, raises his eyebrows, and grins.

Adam laughs. "Ok, I get it. You have already proved yourself, and they do not know me yet, but they will as we train. That will come later. First, let's review the plan." Adam and Connor have the men gather around as they lay out their plots with all the work that will need to be done over the next couple of months.

SEVERAL HOURS LATER, THEY START TO PREPARE FOR THE coming fight. Near the end of the day, Renaldo and Dave show up, Dave with Emma's report and Renaldo carrying the box with Connor's sword. Renaldo strides over to Connor, handing him the box.

Connor looks at him. "What's this?"

Renaldo smiles. "Open it and see." Adam walks over as Connor obeys.

"Wow, this is beautiful. Whose is it?" As he says that, Mondo comes over, leaning in between Adam and Connor to look.

Mondo comments, "That's a Clan ruler sword. I have only ever seen images. The tale is the last one was destroyed during the clan wars."

Connor stares back at Renaldo. "Again, whose sword is this?"

Renaldo puts a big smile on his face. "He made this sword for you. The blacksmith put your name on it."

Mondo walks around, picking up the sword, but this time, everyone else comes over to see. As Mondo holds it, he says, "On this side is your name, and on the other side it says, 'The One.' This is written in our old language, Zandorrian script." Mondo kneels in front of Connor. As he does, so does everyone else. "I believe the official words were," Mondo holds the sword up to hand it to Connor, "My lord, this is yours to help lead us out of the darkness." He then hands the sword to Connor.

As he takes it, first, the writing starts to glow, and then the entire sword burns bright red. Everyone gasps in surprise. Connor then points it to the sky for everyone to see.

Mondo states, "You and the sword are now one."

Renaldo says, "Clearly, that is your sword, or it would not have glowed like that. The old man died shortly after making it, but the son told us it would protect you if you were truly the One."

Everyone but Eric, Dave, and Adam still kneel. Connor tells them all to please get up.

Adam looks at Dave and Eric. "Wow, I have seen nothing like that in my life."

Dave and Eric agree, "No, me either."

Dave comments, "I guess there is no question. Connor was meant to be here."

Adam put his hand on Connor's shoulder. "Yes, I think that is clear."

Connor still gazes at the sword with a big smile on his face. "So, where are the other weapons?"

Renaldo explains, "Well, the old man died after completing yours."

"So, no one else can make more?"

"No, his son said he will finish the other four, but he needs two more months."

Adam puts in, "That will be cutting it close, but we still do not know if they will hold up against the rebels' armaments."

Dave says, "Oh, yeah, I forgot with all this going on. Here is the report from Emma. I read through it a few times. In there she talks about both the rebel sword and the suits. She heard a rumor the swords were built by Lorenzo and came from a clan design. She does not say what clan, but Zada 5 has been the only place I have heard the word used."

"But the rebels' swords glow blue."

Eric remarks, "True, but maybe they are missing something which would make these swords better."

Mondo says, "Let's hope you are both right."

Dave adds, "There is better news. Well, maybe better news. According to her report, there is a weakness in the suits near the power pack in the back on the right side."

Adam says, "Great, we just need to get them to turn their backs, then try to stab them. How is that good news?"

Dave shrugs. "At least there is a weakness. We just need to figure out how we can expose it."

Connor says, "Dave is right. Maybe we can practice making them turn to one of us while the other strikes them from behind."

Renaldo remarks, "That is not very honorable."

Adam agrees. "No, you are right, but we really are not being given much of a choice."

Mondo adds, "Adam is right. This war is not of our making."

Connor ends the chitchat. "We can discuss this later. We have a lot to do. Let's get back to work."

For the next month, they all busy themselves near the freighter landing area, digging trenches, a killing zone with hidden traps, setting up ways to get behind the rebels to exploit the gap in the suits. After those inventions, they train and practice using what they just built, where they should hide and stand, while working on their offensive moves. Since they believe the fight will happen right after the window opens in the morning, they utilize the overarching shadow from the mountains behind them to help with their defense. During this time, the men also discover how truly fierce Adam can be with all his years of experience doing battle on several other planets. He teaches them a few more defense moves Connor could not.

Meanwhile, Dave brings up the concern about their lack of fighter craft. Mondo had to explain After the Zandorrians became miners, there did not seem to be the need for anything like that till now. Then Dave suggests they salvage one of the pulse cannons from their craft. Adam tells him it's a great idea, so he has Renaldo take them back to the damaged ship, trying to piece together a workable cannon. After several hours, they come back with everything they could retrieve from the wrecked ship.

Over a week later, Dave and Adam piece together one pulse cannon, but the power supply limits the ability to fire before overheating. Knowing they will only have a limited time, they will have to make every shot count before allowing it to cool down. Dave maps out how and when to fire it. He then trains a few of the men in its use just in case they get hurt or if he cannot access the cannon. Dave then had the men place it behind the front line.

A few days later, Andorra asks Connor what they are all doing at the place where the flying ships go. "Getting ready for the men that will come soon?"

Connor asks, "What do you know about the men coming?"

"They want to kill you and your brother. This is where your visions of blood and death start. I also saw that they gave you a sword like what killed all my family when I was young. Why do you have it?"

"You're right. We believe there are men coming to kill us. That is why we are working so hard to be ready for them. The visions are getting worse. As for the sword, I did not realize that is what they were built for, but they crafted this one for me to help us fight the men. They have weapons we do not know how to combat. We are hoping this sword can help us. Please do not think it was meant for you."

"I was scared at first seeing, but I knew you would not hurt me, so my fear slowly passed."

Connor says, "You are right. I would do nothing to hurt you or put you in harm's way. When these men come, I want you to hide in the cavern where we found you until I come to get you."

"No, I will not do that. You could get hurt. I can't let that happen, either."

Connor responds, "People get hurt all around me, but I will be fine. That is what I am seeing in my visions. But they have weapons that could hurt you. Please promise me you will go to the caverns."

Andorra says, "I promise."

"Thank you."

Very early, before the window opens, Adam, Connor, and all the men set up for anything that may come through. They store weapons in the hideaways, then power up the cannon. Connor orders Andorra to go to the cavern. A few minutes later, he sees her fly that way, but instead of going in, she sits on the top of the mountain where she can see everything down below, since Connor will be focused on what's in front of him and not looking for her.

On Hmar 4, later that same morning, before the window opens on Zada 5, the team repairs Evan's ship, but it will take several more days before the vessel will be ready to fly again. Abel goes to Chris to wake her up, then tells her, but when he gets there, she is already up. Seeing his expression, Chris sighs. "You don't have to tell me. I can see the ship is not ready to leave the planet, is it?"

Abel agrees. "No, you are right. It will take a few more days. I'm so sorry. We had everyone working as hard as they could, but there was way more damage than we thought once we got started."

"It is not your fault. I am sure everyone did their best, but now we have to hope Adam and the guys can hold out until the next window. We can't get a message to them, even with an open window?"

John walks in just in time to hear her. "No, we have tried before, but there's too much interference no matter what we do or how much power we crank up."

"Well then, all we can do is hope they can hold the rebels back somehow."

"Knowing the boys and my brother, I am sure if there is a way, they have found it."

BACK AT ZADA 5, CRAVEN WAITS NEAR WHERE THE window opens in the outer atmosphere with forty of his men on their transport ship, along with four fighters next to them. He sees the freighters sitting as well to pick up the next shipments of Zando Crystals. Craven tells the captains not to come in until he has someone check it out and tell them it is safe. They wait for a short time; then the window slowly opens. Craven tells the captains again, "Remember, do not come in until you are told to." Both captains acknowledge him.

As Craven says this, his ships enter. He tells the fighter to make sure the landing field is clear to land their transport ship. The fighters fly in, not seeing anything other than empty trenches near the field with some equipment scattered around. One of the fighter captains tells Craven it is all clear. There does not seem to be anyone around, and it is safe.

After a few minutes, while the fighters circle around, Craven's ship lands with his men. They run out, lining up in front of the ship facing out towards the warehouse. Still not seeing anyone, he tells two of the fighters to also land. As the two fighters arrive, Adam and Connor stride out of the warehouse. Craven, shocked to see just those two alone, first looks around. Then Adam says, "I hear you are looking for us?"

Craven barks, "Do you know who I am?"

"Yes, you're Craven. You used to fight with my grandfather, then turned traitor. I saw you kill Roger on Korbin, so that is how I recognize your face, but John and Eric told me."

"Ok, but how did you know I came here for you two?"

Connor says, "I told him."

"But you were here. How could you have known?"

"I know more than you think. You killed our parents."

"Again, that's not possible. You were here, not there."

Adam exclaims, "So it's true!"

"Yes, I did, and now I am here to kill you both."

Craven then yells at his soldiers to mobilize. Adam shouts, "Now!"

As he does, they fire the pulse cannon, blowing one of the fighters out of the sky. When that happens, the men come out of hiding from the trenches and start yelling, causing Craven and his men to pull back. At first, they can't believe they are faced by that many. Quickly, the enemies realize the Zandorrians do not have suits or powered swords, then go running toward them. While they fight, Adam and Connor run back through the warehouse to join their men. Craven tells his two fighters on the ground to take off and destroy the ships on the landing field so no one can get away, then take out the pulse cannon. They miss the cannon, but, despite this, it locks up. The Zandorrian fighters come at the rebels from the side, trying to turn them and expose their weakness, killing several of them. But at the same time, several Zandorrians get slaughtered, not being able to stand up against the rebel swords. As more rebels fall, the Zandorrians pick up the rebel blades and kill them with their own weapons.

Andorra, at the same time, seeing Connor's men dying, joins the fight. She flies in, grabbing one fighter and destroying it. As she does, the pilot tries to eject; she drops what is left of the ship, then seizes the pilot, ripping him in half. She takes off after one of the other ships. After chasing it for a bit, she tears it apart. The last fighter aims a rocket at the guys; she flies into its path, blocking it. The rocket strikes her and explodes where she had been wounded in the cavern, severely hurting her and causing her to crash to the ground.

At that same time, Dave fires the pulse cannon again, taking out the last fighter. Connor runs over to Andorra, giving Craven an opportunity to catch him off guard. Adam, seeing this, tries to block Craven, but cannot fight against his powered sword. Connor turns to help Adam just as Craven cuts through Adam's sword and into his chest, mortally wounding him.

As he falls back, Connor grabs Adam to stop him from hitting the ground. Andorra roars extremely loud, scaring Craven and the remaining rebels away from Connor, still holding Adam. Mondo, Renaldo, and Eric run over. Mondo swings his sword at one rebel, almost cutting him in half. They realize the clan swords can penetrate the rebels' suits.

Running from Andorra, Craven looks back just in time to see Mondo cut through one of the rebels. He then tells what is left of his men to get back to the ship and instructs the still-waiting freighter captains they need to turn around and go back, hoping to stop Connor and Eric from leaving Zada 5 before he can return with more troops.

As Craven flees, Connor tries to save his brother. He tears rags from his shirt and drapes them over the wounds across his brother's chest, but no matter how much he helps, he cannot stop the bleeding. Mondo kneels down, trying to assist. Adam, barely able to talk, squeezes Connor's hand. "Connor, stop. I know I'm dying. Please tell Christina if she is still alive how much I loved her. Promise me you will help her take down Lorenzo, avenge our family, and keep her safe."

Connor screams, "NO, Adam, I can't lose you too."

"Promise me."

"I promise." As Connor says that, the life leaves his brother's body.

Mondo, seeing Adam is dead, tries moving him off Connor and tells him to release his grip on Adam. "I am sorry your brother's gone."

Renaldo, standing next to Andorra and watching Connor deal with Adam, can hear Andorra is having a hard time breathing. He reaches down, putting his hand on Connor's shoulder. "I am sorry, but your dragon may be dying as well."

Connor quickly turns and yells, "Andorra!" Mondo moves Adam off him.

She can barely respond. "I told you I would pass away soon."

Connor still weeps from the loss of Adam. "NO, I did not want you to get hurt. You promised me you would go to the caverns."

"Yes, I agreed and went there, but knew I was going to die here by saving you. Like I told you, I have had a long life, and meeting you made the end of my years worth it. I promise you will never be alone, but this is the end for me. Just remember how much I cared for you." Right after she says that, she gasps her last breath, and her body drops as the life leaves it too.

Mondo, Eric, and Renaldo, seeing all of this, have tears rolling down their faces, then come over to hug Connor, but he pushes them back. "No, no, this can't be happening." He just stands there staring at both his dead brother and dragon, wiping his eyes, trying to stop himself from crying. "I need to hold on to this and turn it to hate."

Mondo hears him. "No, that will not help you. Let it all go. The hate will make you bitter. That is not who you are."

"I know, but they have taken everything from me now, and they need to pay."

Eric agrees. "You're right. We will help you."

Diego comes over. "Connor, sir, I am sorry, but I need to tell you we also lost Juan and Ramon. They fought bravely, sacrificing themselves, allowing others to get behind to pierce the rebel suits, killing more of them."

Connor sobs, "This is all too much. They all need to pay."

As the guys console Connor, a tiny ship lands near them on the edge of the landing field, and a woman comes strolling out towards them. All four of them have shocked looks on their face seeing this person land and just walk over with all the dead bodies still around them. As she marches up to Connor, the rest of the men run over to make sure she is not there to harm him. All stop when they get close, seeing she is not carrying any weapons. She is wearing a nice suit and holding a book. She points over to Andorra. "Is that really a dragon?"

Connor says, "Yes, that was Andorra."

She then reaches out her hand to shake Connor's. "I am sorry. I see you are grieving, and it looks like I just missed a horrible battle. My name is Mandora. I'm from the hidden planet of Terra-Drez. I was sent here looking for either Adam or Connor. Is one of them you?"

Connor still wears a puzzled expression on his face. "I am Connor. Why are you looking for me?"

"We were instructed to give this to your brother Adam or you if something happened to him. Then you should be the emperor, should Esteban and his daughter be killed."

"Well, that was my brother." He points to Adam's lifeless body still collapsed on the ground near them.

"Oh my, I am so sorry. I did not mean to sound insensitive, but I was told I would find both of you here, and there is only a short time for the window." She hands him the book.

"Ok, but what is this?"

"This is your proof you are now the emperor, not his brother Lorenzo, who is currently trying to tell everybody the throne is his."

Mondo yells, "The prophecy is true. He is the One." They all kneel around him.

"I am sorry—he is the one what?"

"Our prophecy states the man that tames the dragon, becomes the leader of all clans, and leads us out of the darkness against our enemies will become emperor of the known universe. The only gap is Connor was not born of this world."

Mandora peers at Connor. "Can I see that book for a minute?" Connor hands it back to her, and she opens it to the beginning, then thumbs through a few pages. "Ah, here it is. Actually, your prophecy states a man not of this world will tame the dragon, defeat the head of all clans, then lead their people out of the darkness and become the emperor of the known universe."

Eric exclaims, "Oh wow, so Connor is really the One then."

Mondo asks, "Can I see that book?"

"Sure, it is right here." Mandora points as she hands him the book.

Renaldo demands, "So who are you that would know this?"

"On our planet we record everything, including all history from every planet and their prophecies. This book has a list of emperors from the beginning, along with prophecies from each of the planets if they point to the emperor, as this one does." Mondo hands the book back to Mandora, which she then returns to Connor. "All I need from you is to sign it here." She indicates a page. "Then I need to sign it acknowledging I saw you do it." She points to Mondo. "If you would also sign it as a witness, this will be your proof that I have given it to you, and you are now the ruling emperor."

As all three sign the book, Connor looks at her. "What if Christina is not dead?"

"But Lorenzo says he killed her, so how could she still be alive? Her sister Emily is still alive, not Christina."

Connor smiles for a minute, thinking that could be possible, but then loses his smile. "No, he is wrong. I felt the pain of her death, but I did not feel Christina's."

"You felt it? Oh, right, you have the gift of second sight."

"How do you know that? There are only a few people aware, and most of them are here."

"As I told you, we record everything. It has been known to us since you were small, but if you are right, and she is still alive, we will need proof that she is who she says she is."

"How can she do that?"

"She has a special birthmark."

Eric nods. "Ah, the dragon, you mean."

"Yes, that is it. But how did you learn of it?"

"Esteban told my brother and me in case something happened to her."

Connor asks, "She has a birthmark of a dragon? How is that possible?"

Mandora explains, "Well, within the Colon family, it has happened two other times and only with the women, but back to your original question, you would have to agree to release the empire back to her if she can prove who she is. Do you have any more questions? I want to make sure I leave before the window closes."

Eric inquires, "Would you be able to take us back with you to our planet of Hmar 4? They have destroyed our ships here, and we cannot reach any others before the window closes."

"I would if I could, but my ship only supports one person."

"It was worth a shot."

Connor asks, "Wait, would you be able to get a message to Eric's brother John?"

Mandora asks, "Sure, I can do that. Where is he?"

Eric says, "If he could get out of the palace, he would go back to Hmar 4, but if John is not there, give the message to my nephew Abel." Eric puts a message together.

"Well, if there is nothing else, I wish you good luck, sire, and I hope you are successful in removing Lorenzo from the throne."

Connor asks, "You won't help us?"

"By giving this message to John or Abel, I am more involved than I should be. As I said, we are a hidden planet and record history. We do not change it. Think of us like secretaries, not warriors." She gets into her ship and leaves.

Mondo looks at Connor. "Why don't you go back to the house? We will take care of your brother and dragon."

Connor disagrees. "No, I need to do it. They would if things were reversed."

Renaldo adds, "Our men need a warrior funeral, too."

Eric says, "Yes, they all do, but we need to get the rings off the dead rebels."

Mondo asks, "Why?"

Connor explains, "The rings power their swords. Did you guys wonder why the swords did not activate when you picked them up?"

Renaldo says, "Yes, they were almost ineffective as we were wielding them."

"Yes, that is why." Eric hands Renaldo a ring. "Here, put this on, then try one." Renaldo obeys and grabs one of the rebel's swords. As he does, it lights up blue.

He then swings it at a nearby tree stump, nearly cutting it in half as if it were hot butter. "Oh, wow, no wonder we lost so many men."

Mondo puts in, "Our clan sword does almost the same thing when it lights up, but ours does not need a ring." At that point, Connor and Eric explain their discovery about the rebel swords.

Renaldo comments, "Well, we have ten of their swords and rings for the next time they return, and we will have four more clan swords when the blacksmith's son is finished with them."

Eric states, "With those and the two Connor and Mondo each have, that's sixteen. And if I know Craven as I do, he will bring a lot more men in the next window. We have lost the element of surprise. We will have to find a new place to attack."

Mondo notices Connor staring at his brother and Andorra still lying there. "This is all well and good, but we can plan tomorrow. Today, we should take care of our dead."

Eric also looks over at Connor. "Yes, you're right. They deserve our attention now."

The few men left collect wood for an enormous bonfire to place the dead warriors on. While they do, Mondo, Eric, and Dave help Connor build two separate ones for Andorra and Adam. Dave says, "I understand we need to do something for the dragon, but I thought they were fireproof."

Mondo explains, "Yes, you are right, but only when they are alive. The rumor was the armor in their skin softens when they die."

Once they have built the bed for Andorra, all the men help Connor move her onto the bed of logs for her burial fire. Adam is already on his bed. By this time, it is getting dark. Connor lights a torch standing between Andorra and Adam. He lights Adam's bed first, then Andorra's. They both rapidly burst into flames, causing Connor to back away quickly. As he does, the flames grow larger, allowing them to be seen from far away. Connor stands there silently, saying goodbye to both. Mondo and the others set the fires for the other dead warriors, then do the same for the dead rebels to honor them as well.

Tears rolling down his face, Connor, unwilling to leave, watches Andorra and Adam while the fires burn until early the next morning, slowly turning to ash just as the sun rises, with only wisps of smoke rising.

Connor wipes his face. Everyone stands there behind him, not wanting to leave him. He then turns. "Ok, what's our plan? How do we kill Craven and Lorenzo so we can take back the empire?" They all walk up to him.

Eric put his arm around Connor. "Let's go back to the house, clean up, and then get some sleep so we can scheme with a clear head."

Mondo agrees. "Yes, that sounds like a good idea." Renaldo tells the remaining men to go home and do the same, then meet them back in a few days once they have a plan.

CHAPTER XVIII

YOU FAILED!

CRAVEN, ON HIS WAY BACK TO MARKUS 2, THINKS TO himself how to tell Lorenzo he failed to kill both brothers, playing the battle over repeatedly in his head. As he does, he realizes while he and his men fought, the rebels died when struck from behind. Seeing those images repeatedly, he calls one of the men to come over, stand up, and power on his suit. He then tells him to turn around as he takes his ring off and draws his sword from over his back. Clearly seeing the sword is not powered up, he then lunges towards the rebel's back on the right side near the power pack. He punctures the rebel's back, causing him to bleed. The rebel yells, "What are you doing?" as he wheels around to face Craven, grabbing his back. Craven orders him to have the medic check him out.

The man looks at him. "You're insane."

With anger in his eyes, Craven shoves his sword at the rebel's throat. "Never say that to me, or I will kill you." The rebel, knowing he cannot be hurt with his suit still powered up, just puts his hands up and steps away. Craven scowls at the rebel walking to the back of the ship as he tries to calm down. For another minute, Craven continues glaring at the rebel, then finally sits down and decides what he is going to tell Lorenzo.

LANDING ON MARKUS 2, AFTER A FEW HOURS, CRAVEN heads to the palace to face Lorenzo and report his failure. Tom sees Craven quickly walk by, realizing he is already back from Zada 5, which means he had to leave before the window ever closed. It must be bad news, or he would still be there to mine the Verbraso and send it through the platform when they activated it.

Craven walks into Lorenzo's office. Sitting behind the desk, Lorenzo looks up, surprised to see Craven. "Why aren't you still on Zada 5? Did you kill the duke's sons like I told you to?"

Craven explains, "Well, I killed one of them, but they were way more prepared than we ever thought. They knew we were coming and that we killed everyone here."

Lorenzo abruptly stands up out of his chair, then starts screaming, "You failed. You only killed only one! I needed them both dead, and how did they know?"

"The young one seems to be able to see things."

Lorenzo, still angry, speaks loudly. "Then the rumors are true. Connor has the ability of second sight, but you still had the four fighters, suits, and swords. You should have defeated them."

"They had a pulse cannon that took out one of the fighter, and the dragon took out two of the last three, before we killed it with one of the rockets." While all of this is being said, Tom walks in behind Craven and has heard everything so far.

Tom then asks, "What about the suits and the swords?"

Craven, a little startled, turns to see Tom. "The suits are flawed."

Lorenzo snaps, "What do you mean, flawed? They are perfect!"

"No, there is a gap in the back. They knew and were exposing it, killing several men. Then once I eliminated the older brother, we realized the dragon was not dead and had to leave with what men we had left."

Tom demands, "How could they have known about that gap in the suits?"

"Remember the suit and sword I took back before blowing up Emma's lab here? She was working with Adam, remember? She must have figured it out and let them know before I killed her." Craven glares directly at Tom. "But she would not have been able to if your men had been doing their jobs properly on Ria 6."

"So, this is my fault?"

"I was not the one that allowed them to get the suit and sword." He turns to face Lorenzo. "You said the Zandorrians were no longer warriors but old men now. Those men we fought were well trained by the duke's sons and made our rebels seem like trainees." Tom looks down, knowing that is basically what he had sent with Craven, who then continues. "I killed the older son, Adam, when the dragon crashed to the ground. I was going to take out Connor, but Adam jumped in front of him, and I sliced through his chest with my sword before the dragon rose after us. We destroyed their ships so they could not leave. They will be there when I go back with a lot more men."

Tom thinks this is his chance to get Craven removed, then looks at Lorenzo. "No, he had his chance. I will take them all out."

Lorenzo agrees. "Tom is right." He glares at Craven. "You blew your chance. I want Tom to finish the job you couldn't."

Craven shouts, "NO! I will take care of it. Just give me more men."

"Nope, you had your chance. I want Tom to kill Connor, then get Eric too." Craven finally agrees, knowing Lorenzo will not back down. Maybe there is a way he can cause Tom to fail as well somehow.

ON HMAR 4, AS SHE PROMISED THE NEXT DAY, MANDORA arrives. When she reaches the blockade, she is told she cannot pass; she responds she has come on official empire business. When the rebels check the digital marker from her ship, it is listed as part of the empire fleet with emperor priority. The rebels, thinking Lorenzo sent the ship, agree and let her fly through. When she lands at the main base, the commander comes out. As he does, Mandora exits her ship.

The commander looks at her. "Can I help you?"

Mandora replies, "Yes, I was asked to deliver a message to either John Aristo or his nephew Abel."

"And who are you?"

"Oh, sorry, I am Mandora. Eric and Connor asked me to come here."

"You talked to them, and they are still alive?"

"I did yesterday, and they are still both alive, but the battle they were in looked brutal."

"What about Adam?"

"I think this message will explain everything."

"Fair enough. Can you give it to me, or do you need to deliver it in person? I know where Abel is, but it will take him some time to get here."

"I think I can trust you if you promise to give it to him."

"Yes, I promise. If they have questions, can they reach out to you?"

"No, they cannot. I am already more involved than I should be by delivering this message, but I think it will tell them everything they need to know."

"I understand. Thank you for bringing this to us."

"You're welcome and good luck with your war. I am rooting for you guys."

"War? What war?"

"Oh, I am sorry. Maybe I misspoke; I think I have said more than enough. Goodbye." She then gets back into her ship and flies away.

The commander sends a message to Chris, John, and Abel that the guys on Zada 5 have contacted them and to get here quick. Since the rebels are not sending any more men down to the planet, John and Chris take a chance to go with Abel to the main base. Evan wants to accompany them since they are still working on his ship; he has nothing to do, and there is no bar at that base.

They take a few hours to get to the main base. When they land, the commander greets them, then hands the message to John. He tells them about the women that delivered it and that she specifically asked for John, or Abel if John was not there. John asks, "How did she know to look for me here?"

The commander explains, "She would not answer questions." Since the message was loaded on a digital chip, John asks them for a terminal they can use. The commander leads them to an office just inside the main building, John plugs in the chip, putting in the encryption key, knowing what Eric would have used, and it unlocks the message, informing them about the loss of Adam and Connor's dragon. As Chris hears Adam is dead, she completely loses it and weeps uncontrollably for several minutes, then stops.

"I cannot do this. I need to hold all this anger." Chris then tells them to continue reading.

John, Abel, and Evan tell Chris how sorry they are for her loss. Chris tries to compose herself. "It is not any of your faults, and we could have landed right in the middle of everything and possibly died. That is why we will need to think about the next window, so we have time to join the guys without ending up in the middle of it. Then decide how we get them back here."

Evan says, "Well, if it is just Connor and Eric, I should have enough room on my ship if I remove the storage."

His comment takes Christina back to losing Adam, and she starts to cry again, then says, "No, no, I need to stop this."

John looks at her. "It is okay. You should let it out. That may help you deal with it better."

"No, I need the hate for killing that slug on the throne."

Abel says, "But the message says Connor is the new emperor."

"Yes, but only because everyone thinks I am dead. We can work that out after I slaughter that slug."

Evan replies, "I think we are all forgetting they could fight off the first wave and still be alive. Isn't this good news?"

John says, "Evan is right. It is horrible we lost Adam, but we still have Connor and Eric."

Chris agrees. "You are correct. There is a reason to at least try to be happy. At this point, we need every piece of good news we can get."

Abel says, "I am going to share this news with our troops, so they know we are fighting the good fight."

A FEW DAYS LATER, AT BREAKFAST, CHRIS LOOKS AT JOHN. "Did you guys ever figure out where Lorenzo was hiding before they got into the palace?"

John replies, "No, we never did, but they are using the Ria 6 rebels. I recognized their uniforms in the palace, and we all thought he could have been hiding there."

"Ok, and if we still think they snuck one of his platforms into the palace, then they had to have one on Ria 6."

"Sure, what's your point?"

"They should have a platform there."

"Ok, again, what's your point?"

"And there is a platform on Zada 5 as well."

"Yes, there is. So, are you thinking of using them somehow?"

"Well, I need to see how the one on Ria 6 works. Then I may be able to modify the one on Zada 5 to reach the palace."

"That sounds like a great idea except for all the guards just waiting for anyone to try something."

"You may be right, but wouldn't it be worth a shot?"

Abel puts in, "I think she is correct. They would not be expecting that. Isn't that what they did to you guys?"

Chris agrees. "It is, and you are right. They would have no idea."

John says, "We are getting way ahead of ourselves here. We do not know if it is even possible or if there is one actually on Ria 6. If you want to go there, we should wait for things to calm down a little. Knowing Lorenzo, he is going nuts right now and will have everyone spun up because he is not the official emperor, he could not find us, and Craven failed on Zada 5. So, we will need to wait a week or two."

"Since you are the expert, I will let you make the call."

John and Abel laugh. "Oh, ok, good. I am glad I have your approval."

A little embarrassed, Chris reaches out and pushes his shoulder. "I am sorry. You knew what I meant."

John winks. "It's ok. I was just giving you a hard time."

Back on Markus 2, Lorenzo's bad mood continues. Craven, back on Korbin, works with the people in the labs, trying to solve the suit vulnerability issue. But every test or modification fails. Craven drives everyone crazy because Lorenzo takes it out on him when he reports another failure. Tom remains in the palace near Lorenzo, intently watching him berate Craven. Every time Craven calls, Tom comes down to Lorenzo's office to add fuel to the already roaring fire in Lorenzo's head, slowly convincing him Craven is not who Lorenzo thought he was.

Lorenzo, still angry, shouts at Tom in a loud voice, "What are you doing about finding John and Emily? It has been several months now with no report of them anywhere. They didn't just vanish!"

Tom explains, "We believe they got to Hmar 4 somehow, but every time we send men down to the planet, they disappear."

"Then we just need to order a bunch of men there and kill anyone who gets in our way."

"I am not trying to push back, but I thought we already talked about this. They are the elite guards, and we could lose over half our men trying to do so. Those that were trained by the duke's sons slaughtered half the men, even though they had none of our weapons. They have trained the men on Hmar 4 the same way. I was not going to tell you this, but a month ago, a ship appeared just in front of our blockade. We tried to get it to turn around, but it kept going and when we sent a fighter to stop it, it fired a pulse cannon, blowing up our ship. So now, if we try to land, we run the risk of losing half our troops."

Losing it, Lorenzo throws stuff around in his office. "What do you mean, they shot one of our ships? This is war now."

"Yes, it is, but you are still not officially the emperor, and we do not have enough men to tackle everyone. We need to continue to control what we can. I have taken the rest of my men from Ria 6 to train on Korbin, where I am staging for my siege on Zada 5." Lorenzo calms down while Tom continues. "Once I have killed Connor and Eric on Zada 5, then you can formally take the throne, at which point everyone will have to accept it. We can build up our troops so we can really fight back. Right now, no one knows how many we have, so we appear to have more than we do. A war with Hmar 4 would kill that illusion."

"Ok, I get it. Thank you for talking me down here. I realize why I made you a general. Once you have taken Connor and Eric out, we can discuss your future with me and our empire."

"YES, SIR! I look forward to that conversation when I return from Zada 5."

On Ria 6, Tom collects more men for his trip to Zada 5, leaving only a skeleton crew of his elite guards to protect the base and Lorenzo's lab. He thinks he won't have to worry because no one would want to deal with his men. After all, they are trained to kill anyone who attempts anything on sight, no questions asked, creating fear among all the locals.

Back on Hmar 4, Abel has his men monitor messages throughout the universe for anything that could help them. After a few days, one man hears a message that most of the rebels are being moved to Korbin from Ria 6 to prepare for a big objective.

Abel goes to the lab on the main base, where Chris studies the suits and the swords to see what else she can do with them. As Abel walks in, both Chris and John look over at him. "I got a message I am sure you guys will want to know about. They have moved most of the men off Ria 6 to Korbin."

Chris, grinning, looks at John. "Can we go now?"

John says, "I guess now would be as good a time as any, but keep in mind there will still be guards, so we will have to be careful. We will sneak onto the base, then find that device, if it is even there."

Chris sits down and starts sketching. After a little bit, John walks over to her. "What are you drawing there?"

Chris explains, "Well, based on the parts you brought us at the palace," she then holds up the image she drew, "this is what I think the platform and equipment will look like, so we will all know what we are searching for. If we split up, we can find it faster."

Abel walks over to study what she is holding up. "Ok, good, as I would not have known even if I were standing in front of it."

John comments, "Actually, that looks close to what was on Korbin before they blew it up." John then pulls out the images from the lab on Korbin.

Abel looks at Chris. "Wow, how did you know? This is almost identical."

Chris replies, "I had been studying this stuff when we were in school, albeit not quite this advanced."

Abel replies, "Well, it is too bad that your uncle went so wrong. I am sure you guys would have made a great team and really advanced our technology."

"Not my uncle, the slug, but yes, that was our hope after we graduated. Emily's and mine, that is."

John says, "If we are going to Ria 6, we should probably head out when it is dark so we have a few hours to get ready. We will need Evan's ship. The work has been completed, and we need to test it anyway. Docs anyone know where Evan is?"

Abel says, "Yes, he is at the bar. It has just opened, so he has not been drinking for very long. I'll fetch him."

"Ok, Chris and I will load the ship."

A short time later, Abel helps Evan stumble back toward the ship. John glares at Evan. "Great, you're drunk already."

Evan, barely able to talk, slurs his words. "I am not; I am fine. I can still fly my ship."

John then looks at Abel. "Just put him onboard and let him sleep it off. We can use him to monitor the radar from the ship once we land. You can fly this ship, right?"

Abel answers, "Yes, it's older than me, but I can. Also, we have two men who want to help. They are some of our best and will help make the search quicker."

Chris says, "Great, it will be a little crowded, but we should all fit."

"Did you guys load extra fuel? We will need it. The cloaking burns up the fuel fast."

"Yes, of course we did." She looks at John and winks. "This is not my first rodeo."

Both John and Abel laugh, then John comments, "Well, yes, it is."

"I know. I was just trying to be funny."

The other two men help John and Chris finish loading, then walk inside. Evan sleeps in the back with Abel in the front, doing his final checks. As Abel fires up the ship, he asks, "Is everything onboard? Are we ready to take off?"

John answers, "Yes, let's get going."

Abel reaches around behind him and turns on the cloaking devices, which respond with a slight hum. After a minute, the ship disappears, and they proceed into space, flying right past the blockade ships without being noticed. Once they get clear of the blockade, Abel then turns off the device as they continue to Ria 6.

John walks up. "Are you doing okay? It looks like you have everything under control."

Abel replies, "Yes, this ship is easy to fly, but we will be there a little early, based on the navigation report. It will not be dark yet."

"Then we can locate a spot that is not too far away from the base. The quicker we get in and out, the better I will feel about this. I just hope we find something. I do not want to think we are risking our lives for nothing."

"I agree. We need every break we can get at this point."

When they reach Ria 6, it is still light. As they get close, Abel again reaches around and pushes the switch, turning the cloaking back on. They near the main rebel base and look for a place to land. John, seeing an area close by, points to it. "Look over there. That's a good spot."

"Yes, I like it." Then Abel lands.

As they do, Evan finally wakes up and comes to the front. "Hey, where are we?"

John turns around. "Finally decided to join us, did you?"

"Yes, I guess so, but again, where are we?"

Abel explains, "The planet Ria 6. I guess you don't remember our conversation in the bar?"

"No, I suppose not. So why here?" John tells him the whole story, to which Evan excitedly responds, "So we are near the rebels' base, the same ones that tried to kill me on Hmar 4?"

Abel looks at John. "I guess he's awake now."

Evan remains a little excited. "Why am I here?"

John explains, "We need you to monitor the radar while we try to find the portal."

Evan says, "So you are really going into the lion's den?"

Abel responds, "We have to if we are going to find it."

Evan is now almost panicked. "But what if you don't?"

John shrugs. "Then this will have been a waste of time, but we needed to try something, and we think the odds are about 80-20 that it is present based on what we have put together."

By this time, it is nearly dark. Chris comes up to them. "Well, are we ready to go? It should be night by the time we get to the base."

John peers at Chris. "How do you want to do this?"

She responds, "You're the expert. I leave it to you."

"Okay, well, I will go on my own. Abel, you leave with Chris and you two." He points to the two men that came with them.

"Wait, is everyone wearing a suit?"

Abel answers, "Yes, under our dark clothes."

John, being six foot three and weighing about 280 pounds, admits, "I'm not. It was too tight, and it didn't feel right when I move, but I have one of the swords."

"We all do."

Chris says, "Great, then we are ready. I was thinking about it. The platform will be in the slug's lab and should have its own building. That way, the slug can control who goes in there."

John says, "Okay, so we are searching all the single buildings first."

Abel consents, "That works for me."

Evan says, "Then I guess I am just staying here by myself."

John agrees. "Yes, and keep an eye on that radar and let us know if anyone comes our way."

All of them head for the base. They come to the end of the trees about twenty feet from the fence surrounding the base and all the buildings. Looking through, they see just a few guards and no one else. Only a few buildings have the lights on.

Abel comments, "They were right. This base is almost deserted."

All of them watch, timing the guards' patterns. They take about thirty minutes to go out and come back. They wait for the guards to reach the far end of the base. Then John puts one of the rings on and pulls the sword from his back over his shoulder, activating it to cut through the fence. As he does, he looks back at them. "This is slick, but we will have to be careful with the glow. The guards will see it."

Abel replies, "But from far away, they will think we are rebels too."

"Yes, but let's try not to assume."

Chris says, "Okay, let's get going. We are wasting time."

Abel agrees. "She's right. Let's go."

They all sneak through the fence and onto the base. "I will go this way." John points to his right. "You two," he adds, signaling to Abel and Chris, "go that way," pointing to the left. "And you two go that way." He indicates for the two guards to go straight. They split up and search through the single buildings, only to discover all of them are locked. They peer through the windows while trying to stay out of sight of the rebel guards.

After about thirty minutes, Abel and Christina reach one of the larger buildings, standing alone on the other end of the base. They cannot peek in, as it has no windows. Chris states, "This is it."

Abel asks, "How do you know?"

"This is the building I would use if I did not want anybody to see what I was doing."

"But the door is locked."

"Then use the key."

"What key? I don't have one to this door."

Chris quietly laughs. "Yes, you do. It's on your back."

Then Abel laughs. "Oh, yeah, the sword will cut through it. Keep a lookout for the rebels." He slices between the door and the doorjamb, cutting the latch. They push the door open and walk in, closing the door behind them, but it will not stay closed, so Abel moves a box in front of it. Chris turns the lights on. There, in the center of the room, is a platform.

Chris says, "I knew it. This is it."

Chris inspects the device and everything feeding it. She turns to Abel. "I need about an hour to figure this all out, but we need to take those with us." She points to the tubes partially loaded with refined Zando Crystals. A short time later, John and the other two men come to the building, and Abel lets them in. Chris, deep in thought, goes through everything.

Abel looks at John, pointing at the glass tubes. "She said it will take her about an hour here, but we can bring these back to the ship."

John agrees. "Ok, we will do it. You stay here with her in case the rebels try something. We will have to make two trips, and that will be almost an hour." The three transport the first three tubs back to the ship. As they bring them in, John walks up to Evan, barely awake, and smacks him on the back, causing him to jump up. John says, "We need you to stay conscious. We are almost done and will be back shortly with the next set of tubes."

They leave and come back about twenty-five minutes later with the last three tubes. John orders the two men to stay there.

When John gets back to Abel and Chris, he looks at her. "Are you about ready?"

She responds, "Yes, just a few more minutes, and we also need to take these." She points to the two metal boxes inside one of the open cabinets.

Abel pulls them out; then John grabs them. "I will handle these. Let's get going."

"One more minute. We will be right behind you."

John steps out and scans the area, but doesn't see anyone and heads towards the ship. Just then, one rebel emerges from behind the next building. John quickly turns to see him, but as he pulls his sword, the rebel runs his into John's side, severely wounding him. John hits him as he is pulling his sword, causing the rebel to fall back, yanking his sword out of John's side.

Chris, emerging from the building, yells as she sees John stabbed. As John pushes the rebel back, Chris pulls her sword and drives it through the middle of the rebel, killing him instantly. Abel runs over to John and props him up to get him to the ship, but two other rebel guards rush towards the three of them. Chris tells Abel, "Get him out of here. I got this."

Nodding, Abel drags John to the fence. The guards dash up to Chris. She wields her sword at them. As they fight, she pushes them back to the point they are merely trying to prevent themselves from being killed. They continue to get pushed back and one of them falls. While he does, the other one drops his guard just enough for Chris to run her sword through him. He wears a look of shock as he dies, thinking himself invincible from the suit. The other guard tries to rise just as Christina draws her sword back out of the first rebel.

Then she swings, slicing his throat. He grabs it, gurgles from the blood gushing out, and collapses. Chris then turns, running for the fence. As she gets through, two more guards run up to the two rebels, now both dead. Not believing they were killed wearing their suits, they gape at each other.

"Shouldn't we go after whoever that was?"

"Do you want to die? Because I don't. They have weapons we have never seen. Even our sword can't cut through our suits."

While the rebels discuss whether or not to chase them, the three reach the ship. John is still bleeding badly. Abel yells at Evan, "Get us out of here!"

Evan asks, "Do I need cloaking?"

Abel demands, "No, just take off right now!" Evan does as he is told, and they get into space, hitting interstellar speed almost immediately. Abel and Chris try to stop the bleeding, but the medical kit was damaged in the crash, breaking the laser needed to close John's wounds.

John grabs Chris's hand and looks into her eyes. "Please do not think this was your fault. We needed to come here if we were going to win. The wounds are too bad. I already cannot feel my legs."

Chris, crying, shouts, "NO, I NEED YOU."

"It is over for me. Abel will help you save my brother and Connor. They will help you win the fight."

Chris still sobs. "No, you helped my father, and I need you to help me."

With his eyes slowly closing as life starts to slip away from his body, with all that is left of his strength, he reaches for Abel's hand and puts Chris's hand in it.

"Here is your help." He then gasps his last breath and goes limp.

Chris screams, "NO, I can't lose you too!"

At the loss of his uncle, tears roll down Abel's face. "I am sorry he's gone." They all sit with their heads down. Chris cannot stop crying this time.

After a little while, Abel adds, "He would not want you to mourn him. John had a significant life and achieved more than most men dream. I was proud to know John and to have him as my uncle."

Evan comes over. "If it was not for him, I would be dead now. I owe him my life; that is why I am here assisting you."

Chris wipes her eyes. "You are both right. He was a great man; we will remember him always. We must make his loss count by taking out the slug sitting on my throne."

At this, one of the two men who accompanied them responds, "Ma'am, I think I can speak for every one of us on Hmar 4. We will follow you no matter where you go until the throne is yours or we all die trying."

Chris says, "Well, get ready. We are going to war."

CHAPTER XIX

WHAT'S THE PLAN?

BACK AT HMAR 4, THE CREW BRINGS JOHN'S BODY OFF the ship and places him on the small logs set up as a bed, but they wait for that evening to start his fire. While waiting, more and more people gather to pay their respects and say goodbye. Chris stands by, steadfast. Finally, darkness falls. The commander brings a lit torch to Abel, who takes it over to Chris. "Here, you should light it." Tears run down her cheeks, thinking about everything she has lost. She takes the torch and lights the base. It quickly takes off, lighting up the skies. Everyone gathers around the fire and sings their national songs, saying goodbye to John, a legend to all of them.

ON KORBIN, THE DAY AFTER THEY BROKE INTO LORENZO'S lab and killed the two guards on Ria 6, Tom gets the word from his captain Irate about the news. He grills his captain over how it could have happened and questions him about whether there are any identifying images. The captain responds that the assailants entered in a dead zone between the cameras, so they have nothing. Tom orders his captain not to say anything to anyone else and continues to focus on working with his men, getting ready to go kill Connor and Eric. But while Tom plans how to protect himself going after Connor, his men hear rumors that a sword exists that can cut through their suits from the front, not just from the exposed gap in the back the labs are currently working to correct. Tom, learning these rumors from his men, proceeds to tell them it is merely that, a rumor, even though he knows that is not true. But no matter how much Tom tries to stop the whispers, they keep going, rising to fear in the men slated to go to Zada 5.

ON HMAR 4, CHRIS AND ABEL MAKE PLANS OF THEIR own. Since they can only bring a few men with them, they look at what weapons they can bring, knowing they will also need to carry extra fuel to support cloaking both going there and on return to Hmar 4. Abel also works with Evan, mounting a small cannon on the front of his ship. Once they open the doors and the cannon drops to fire, it appears outside of the ship's cloaking, making part of the ship visible and gives anyone a target to fire back at. So, they spend some time dropping the cannon, firing, and then pulling it back in and quickly changing direction to throw off anyone shooting back at them. Evan comments,

"You know I have never flown any kind of fighter, nor have I ever been a warrior."

Abel laughs. "Well, I guess this will be a crash course for you."

"Please don't use that word."

Abel is still laughing. "What word? Crash, yes, maybe that was a poor choice of, but I am going to be busy firing the cannon, and you will have to fly the ship."

Evan says, "Why am I getting a bad feeling about how wrong this can go?"

"Don't worry. If we keep practicing for a while, you will be fine."

"Well, ok, if you say so."

AT THE SAME TIME ABEL AND EVAN ARE WORKING ON his ship, Chris is back at the lab studying her notes from Ria 6 after visiting Lorenzo's lab, going over everything from his platform. She then analyzes the large tubes, the fuel cells for the platform, to determine the combination of Zando Crystals and other minerals used to make it work. The crystals were refined at a much higher rate along with the Verbraso she found as part of the combination of minerals. Fortunately, they have a small refinery near the main base. She works with others at the refinery to set up a process to match those rates, but since they only have a small amount of Verbraso, it is barely enough to fill the six tubes, not leaving any left to power up the captured suits. Chris warns Abel that the suited men must only power them up if it is a critical need in a battle against any of the rebels, since they have no more fuel once they have used up what they possess.

Abel responds, "This will not be a problem as we have their swords, which is all we really need." Chris also points out the swords will have the same problem once they use up their power source. "Then, I guess we better make sure we bring back more of the Verbraso if we are going to really start a war with them." Abel then asks about her sword and how it has the same abilities as the rebels' but does not seem to require anything to work. She points out that they would have to cut apart her sword to build a duplicate. But if she could not completely replicate the process, they would have no new swords, and her sword would be gone. Maybe if her sword really came from Zada 5, then they will know how to make more or may even have some there. "Good point. Then I think we can wait until we visit and see what questions we can get answered if we can help them."

Chris says, "Knowing Connor as I do, he is driven right now the same as I am, looking for any way to get revenge for his family against the slug and for any opportunities to take care of Craven upon his return. So, I am sure we will be able to help. It will just be how."

"With the cannon we mounted on Evan's ship, we should be able to vaporize a few of the fighters, if we can get close enough and keep up the cloaking while hiding it after we fire. But since Evan has never fought and is not a warrior, only five of us can attack on the ground once we land. Hopefully, Connor and Eric can recruit more men to assist as well. Also, we have two small sonic bombs left that we will bring in case we have an opportunity to use them. My men reloaded the suits and swords so they will be good for several hours. We will bring the additional swords. They will not cut like the ones powered up, but they will hold up to fight with."

On Zada 5, Connor and Eric have also been preparing with Mondo and Renaldo for Craven's return. A few days after the burial fires, Diego and Dutch arrive with the only remaining clansmen who fought Connor, but they have ten more. Connor emerges from the house, seeing all these men, and walks over to Diego, Dutch, and the new arrivals. "Diego, who are all these recruits?"

Diego explains, "They came to me after hearing how we still pulled off a victory, despite how many men we lost. They all want to help. Most of them have never really fought in any type of battle, but they are willing to learn how from you."

Connor takes in all of them. "Well, I appreciate it. I'm not sure what happened was a victory. Yes, we chased the rebels away, but we are sure they will be back with more fighters and men. All of you need to be aware of what we are up against."

Renaldo, Eric, and Mondo come up as Connor tells them this.

Renaldo asks, "Why would you warn them?"

Connor replies, "We suffered severe losses with less than what we will see this next time. I did not want anyone to be surprised. Don't get me wrong. I am very glad to see them here and would be happy to train them."

Diego turns to Renaldo. "Don't worry. I already warned them they could all die, and they are still here. All of them want to say that they could learn, train, and fight with the One. They come from warrior families and will not let you down."

Connor says, "You all have my appreciation already. I am sure you will work hard, and I will show you everything I know."

Mondo looks at Dave. "My technicians will help you work on the pulse cannon, so we do not have the same issues as last time, especially if Connor is correct. If they bring more fighters, we do not have Connor's dragon to help take them down this time—sorry, Connor."

"No, you are right. We need to do whatever we can with what we have. There is no time to really mourn our losses now. We will have to honor them by taking the empire back. But first, we need to win here and then go after Lorenzo for the throne."

Renaldo puts in, "Not to change the subject, but I heard back from the blacksmith's son, and he will have the other four swords here next week."

Mondo exclaims, "Great! Then you, Eric, Dave, and Diego will each have a clan sword and we will have rebels' swords for the others so we can maintain a solid front against whoever comes, at least for as long as the blades stay powered up."

Eric comments, "Since they will not need to be powered to train, we can save what power they have left for the battle with Craven."

Connor remarks, "Speaking of Craven, he's mine. He really needs to pay for everything he has done to my family."

Mondo agrees. "We all understand, and he is coming to kill you."

Eric says, "I am sure he will be headed towards you anyway, but if not, we can drive him your way."

Connor says, "Thank you."

A FEW WEEKS AFTER, THE BLACKSMITH'S SON DELIVERS the new swords to Renaldo on Zada 5, but as they practice with them, they barely glow, not like Mondo's, and Connor's is even brighter than Mondo's. When Renaldo reaches back out to the blacksmith's son, he tells them the blacksmith himself forged them, but the son had to finish them and followed his instructions as written. He does not know why they won't light up the same way, but he assures Renaldo they should still be as powerful as Connor's. Renaldo thanks him again for his help and work providing the swords.

Later, as Connor and the men are training, he looks at Eric and Mondo, standing next to each other. "As we plan for where we will make our stand, we need a spot for Christina and Abel to land their ship." Both Eric and Mondo wear puzzled looks.

Eric speaks. "What are you talking about?"

"I have seen it. They are preparing to come here, but it is a small ship with only a few men."

"Ok, but why isn't John with them?"

Connor walks over and puts his arm around Eric. "I am sorry. He died on a raid at Ria 6."

Eric pushes Connor back. "What? No, he can't be dead too! You're wrong. How could you know that?"

"I saw it. Not sure how to explain it, but my visions have gotten clearer now that Andorra is gone. I don't know if it is from the pain of her loss or if I just gained it from her as she passed. It also only seems to be when people close to me think about me or are close to me get hurt. I'm not able to see what is going to happen with the next battle, like the last one, seeing all the fierce fighting and blood. I will keep trying to improve on it. But again, I am so sorry about John."

Still not willing to accept it, Eric sits down, starting to feel the loss.

Mondo hunkers down next to Eric. "I am sorry too. If Connor is correct, this is a significant loss for everyone. Your brother was a great warrior and will be remembered always." As Mondo says this, tears slowly run down Eric's face. Mondo reaches over and pats Eric's back. "It's ok to grieve for losing your brother."

Eric jumps up, looking at Connor. "No! You have to be wrong. He cannot be gone. I won't accept it. I will need to hear it from Abel if they truly come. You can't say your visions have been totally clear, so you could be wrong, true?"

Connor admits, "You're right. They have not been crystal clear, but I was not wrong about my parents or the emperor, was I?"

"No, you weren't, but we still do not know for sure whether Emily or Christina was killed, either."

"I know. And you will too when they come. But to your point, I really do hope I am wrong about John. We can stop talking about it until we know for sure."

"Thank you."

Renaldo says, "Eric is correct. Maybe we should get back to training and planning to take our minds off it." Eric gives Connor a hug, and they return to work.

THE NEXT DAY, DAVE COMES UP TO CONNOR AND ERIC. "The pulse cannon is 100 percent now, and I was thinking if we use the entrance to the mine as a backing for us, we can hide the cannon in the trees right next to it. If they come to the loading area for the crystals, you can almost see the landing area for the freighters from there, giving us the element of surprise. We may neutralize a couple of fighters before they head our way."

Connor smiles at both Eric and Dave. "I like the way you are thinking. Let's go out there to see how we can defend it. Tell Mondo and Renaldo to come with us while Diego continues to train the other guys."

At the mine, the five of them look around near the front of the entrance. Connor points to each side. "If we cut trenches going towards the landing area and hide them like last time, we can drive the rebels towards us, leaving their backs exposed using the weakness of the suits. We should be able to kill them off. Once they realize we have multiple swords, they will go running like last time."

Mondo says, "Yes, but didn't you claim they will bring more men than they did last time?"

"With the ten extra men that have come over the past few weeks, that gives us twenty-five, counting the five of us."

"You're right, but we do not have swords for the new recruits."

Eric puts in, "I see where he is going. They will steal their swords from the ones we kill. We just need to drive it into their heads to grab the rings when they pick up the blades."

Renaldo agrees. "Yes, then the twenty-five of us can handle fifty of them."

Dave asks, "Wait, now we are saying fifty of them, which is a lot to face at one time."

Connor put his hand on Dave's shoulder with a smile on his face. "Are you saying you cannot handle two at a time?"

"No, two at a time is not that hard for me."

"Nor me either. If we each take two, there are the fifty."

Renaldo says, "I do not want to be the pessimist here, but most of the men we are training have never fought before, and they will face weapons they have never seen, either."

"Yes, you are right, but they are fighting to protect their home, and the rebels will not understand why they are here. That will give us the edge we need."

Eric agrees. "Connor is correct. I have seen this before on other worlds. It is much harder to fight against someone who has a reason and knows what he must protect. We just need to remind our guys why they are here."

Mondo adds, "One more thing that concerns me is this is the same mine we were trapped in battling your father way back when."

Connor says, "Yes, I remember that conversation, but we still have the opening created for Andorra. It will be a bit of a climb, but we can get out."

"Oh right, good point. I forgot. With that, I am good here."

A FEW DAYS LATER, MONDO COMES UP TO CONNOR AND Eric with someone they have never seen before. Mondo says, "This is Simon, one of our lead scientists, who has spent his life tracking the alignment of the moons. He has some information you should hear."

Connor shakes Simon's hand. "Hi there. I am Connor. Pleased to meet you."

Simon says, "Yes, sir, I know who you are. The pleasure is all mine. Thank you for seeing me."

"You're welcome. What can I do for you?"

"No, it is what I can do for you. There are changes happening with the moons' alignment. Normally, there is an opening for about a day and a half, but that window has been getting shorter. I heard that when you came this last time, the window was closing on you, which is what damaged your ship and forced you to crash."

"Yes, you're right. We thought we had more time to get through and had to force our way in getting here."

"Well, you were correct. You should have. Right now, that time has shortened to just over one day, and the next time in a few weeks will be about half a day. Based on my calculations, there will eventually not be an opening long enough to get through at all. Right now, we do not know why it has been speeding up, but we also have no idea how long this opening has been happening either, as we were not even aware of it until we started spaceflight. Before we recorded our history, we believed that at one time there were four moons, two big ones and two small ones. For one reason or another, a big one exploded, causing all the debris that surrounds our outer atmosphere, but this has made the most sense."

"Ok, thank you for the history lesson, but how much time do we have before we can no longer leave or come back here?"

"Well, it could be as soon as six months or as much as a year, but no more than a year."

"Thank you, Simon, for the news. If anything changes, please come see us as soon as you know."

"Yes, sir, I will. Thank you for meeting with me."

"Well, I cannot say I am happy you came and talked with me, but we really appreciate the information."

"You're welcome, sir." Simon then turns and leaves.

Eric exclaims, "So, on top of everything else, we now have to worry about being able to leave."

Renaldo says, "Yes, it sounds that way, but there are at least two more windows, and if you cannot get out on this one coming up, you can depart on the next one."

Connor laments, "But I am torn here. If we leave, I can never return."

Mondo says, "Wait, what about that platform thing in the back of the cavern?"

Eric agrees. "Mondo is right. Maybe we can get back that way."

Connor says, "But that is only if someone can still activate it from a sender and if we knew where one of those were. The only ones we were aware of have both been blown up."

Renaldo puts in, "The other issue is we only have one ship left capable of leaving our planet unless the freighters come back."

"Can we park that ship behind my home?"

"I think it is small enough it should not be a problem, but if they are bringing fighters, they will see the ship, as your home is a little out of the way, but still between where the freighters land, the mine, and our attack area."

Eric agrees. "You're right, but we will need to risk it if we are going to fly out after fighting the rebels, since the window is open for only a day." He glances at Connor now. "I thought you said Abel and Christina are coming with their own ship?"

Connor says, "Yes, but what if it is not big enough to carry all of us?"

Dave muses, "That is a good point. As nice as this planet is, I really do not want to live here. I have a life elsewhere, and once we are done fighting, I would like to go home."

Renaldo responds, "That's fair. I'm sure I would feel the same way if I were not fighting on my home world."

Several days later, after setting up the pulse cannon and digging the trenches to get ready for the rebels, the men practice how they will attack. They also spend time on the rear exit in the second cavern, building better ways to climb out just in case they are forced to retreat for some reason, then climbing out so they know what it will take and how long.

Mondo says, "We should set charges near the cavern entrance just in case they try to follow us if we need to use this to exit."

Connor agrees. "Yes, good point. They will have no idea where we will come out and will not know of the path out through the top, but I am not sure we should have this option. My feeling is we need to win or die trying."

Eric comments, "I understand how you feel, but if you are truly the emperor, you need to survive to rule at all costs."

"You're right, well, at least until I can give it back to Christina."

Mondo points out, "That also means you will need to be the first one in and the second one out."

Connor asks, "Second one out?"

"Yes, someone will need to make sure the path out is clear before you."

"This being the emperor is getting complicated. The sooner I can give it back to Christina the better."

Eric says, "That will change nothing because even if you will not be the emperor, you're already the duke with you father and brother gone."

"You're right. I forgot about that."

BACK ON HMAR 4, CHRISTINA COMES TO ABEL AND Evan. "Well, what's our plan?"

Evan says, "Don't look at me. I am barely holding on at this point."

Abel laughs at Evan's comment. "I have been thinking this through. If we stay cloaked waiting for the window to open, we can see anyone else trying to get in. Then we'll know what we are dealing with and can follow them in, maybe take out a few of the fighters when we get close. The only problem is, we do not know where Connor will be. We have to hope Craven does, as they already fought once before. But if they want to get the element of surprise, they will change their location. That's what I would do, so we will have to wait until we know their location for sure before we can fire on the fighters, or we could be in big trouble."

Chris says, "Then, Evan, the question is, how long can we stay cloaked?"

Evan explains, "Well, the longest I have used it has been about thirty minutes, but I guess technically, as long as we do not run low on fuel or overheat, we can continue to stay cloaked."

Abel exclaims, "Overheat? You have said nothing about overheating."

"No, I am not saying we will, but like I said, I have never used it longer than thirty minutes, so I do not know how it will react."

"Ok, fair enough. Then we will just need to keep an eye on the systems once we get to that point."

On Korbin, Tom has spent a lot of time keeping the rebels that went with Craven to Zada 5 from seeing or talking with the men he has been working with. He wants nothing to distract them, or for them to hear any rumors about the last time. But a few days before the next alignment, some men sneak out to a tavern in town, running into some rebels that went with Craven. Tom's soldiers start to ask questions about what happened and why they came back so soon after getting there. Craven's men explain about the dragon, the cannon, and how fierce the men were that they encountered.

The next morning, those men that had snuck out inform the rest of the troop about their conversation. At that point, the rumors begin to fly about the dragon still being alive and what fierce fighters the Zandorrians are. Tom, hearing the men talking, gets mad and tells them they are letting the rumor scare them. The dragon is dead, and Craven lost his nerve; that is why they left so soon. The men ask if anyone actually saw the dragon die. Tom lies to them, trying to stop the rumors, telling them that Craven did witness the death. Then he insists with all the training his men have been through, they are even better than the Zandorrians.

The night before the men leave, most cannot sleep, worried about what they will head into. Tom sleeps like a baby, thinking that with his thirty men and six fighters, they will finish Connor, Eric, and what is left of his men off quickly, and he will finally force Craven out.

On Hmar 4, that same night, Chris stands out by Evan's ship, just looking up at the stars, thinking about all they have lost and how everything is now riding on rescuing Eric and Connor and bringing them back. After a little while, Abel walks over to Chris. "Why are you out here still?"

Chris sighs. "We have a lot, depending on what happens tomorrow. I just couldn't sleep."

"I know, me either." Just as he says that, Evan steps out of his ship. Both Chris and Abel are surprised to see him. "What are you doing in there?"

Evan admits, "I am not afraid to say it. I am terrified about what is going to happen. I'm not a warrior and will be running into battle in the morning."

Chris walks over to him. "We just need you to fly. We will do the rest. Once we land, find a safe place to hide."

Evan says, "No, I cannot do that. You guys will fight while I hide. Abel gave me one of the good swords and has been teaching me."

Abel agrees. "Yes, I have. You're not as bad as you think you are." Evan has his back to Abel, who's looking at Chris and mouthing, yes, he is bad, as he shakes his head.

Chris, with a slight laugh, still looking at Evan, puts her hand on his shoulder. "Don't worry about it. Just stay behind us, cover our backs, and you'll be fine."

Abel says, "Well, it is late, and none of us will be any good if we don't get some sleep."

BACK ON ZADA 5, THAT SAME NIGHT, ALL THE MEN ARE sleeping in the minc, close to where they will fight in the morning, not knowing how soon anyone will show up. Connor wakes and walks out to the skirmish area in between the two trenches. He stands there gazing up at the flicker of stars through the haze of the asteroids encircling the planet. A tear runs down his cheek, thinking of all he has lost and how they need to avenge them. After being out there for a while, Mondo joins him. Connor turns to him. "You can't sleep either?"

"No, I can't. But I am more concerned about you." He walks up, putting his hand on Connor's shoulder. "You are carrying the weight of the world on your shoulders, and it has been this way since your brother died."

"You are smarter than you look. We cannot lose tomorrow. We have lost too much and need to make sure they did not die in vain."

"If you do your best, the rest will take care of itself. Every man here has your back and will gladly give up their life for you. Do you think our enemy feels the same way?"

Connor smiles. "No, you're right. They don't. Thank you."

"You're very welcome. Now come on, let's get some sleep. We will all need it."

CHAPTER XX

WHERE S CRAVEN?

Very early the following morning, Tom leaves with his men in a freighter and the six fighters from Korbin headed for Zada 5. About the same time on Hmar 4, Christina, with Abel, Evan and three men that volunteered to go with them, also leave. Since Korbin is closer, Tom and his men arrive at Zada 5 first, waiting near the alignment window. The two freighters that tried to land last time are back. Tom, not knowing the procedures, asks the freighters why they are there. They inform him about their normal trips to the planet. Tom, not wanting anyone to leave the planet without his approval, tells them they have an hour to pick up their freight and leave, but they cannot take on any passengers. Both captains agree, not wanting to argue with him and his six fighters.

A short time after, just before getting to the planet, Evan activates his ship's cloaking. A few minutes later, as they get close to the window entrance, they see the two normal freighters and a third one sitting next to six fighters. Evan calls Chris and Abel up front. As they join him, he points out the ships. He looks at Abel. "Well, now what do we do? We can't fight all of those."

"No, those are not all the rebels, those two ships." Abel points to the normal freighters. "They must be the normal transport for the mined crystals."

"Ok, I feel a little better, but the other can still have a lot of men on it, and I have never seen fighters like those before."

Chris agrees. "Yes, those must be the ones that Adam saw, but we do not know what they are capable of, so we need to destroy as many as we can."

As they finish talking, the path opens while the three of them watch. Evan exclaims, "Holy crap, would you look at this? That is amazing. I was always told it was worth seeing. And now that I've seen it, I can say they were right."

Abel barks, "Ok, if you are done sightseeing, can we proceed?"

"Oh yes, sorry, here we go." As they enter, they are right behind Tom's freighter. "What if we fire on their freighter and force them to crash? We can kill a bunch of them, and all we have to deal with is the fighters."

Chris says, "As much as I love that idea, if we kill Craven before Connor has a chance to face him, we will rob him of a way to avenge his family."

Abel agrees. "Yes, she is right, but we can still damage it and force them to crash, so they cannot use it to leave."

"I like that plan better. Just before they land, fire on the engines."

They follow behind the freighter. Once it approaches, landing near the others, Abel drops the cannon and fires on the back of the ship. As they do, the back of the ship explodes and drops to the ground and slides into one of the regular freighters, destroying it as well. At the same time Abel fires, the pulse cannon on the ground shoots at one fighter, but its shield protects the ship since it was too far away. Two of the fighters split off, hunting for the pulse cannon on the ground, while the other three look for Evan's ship. Abel quickly draws their cannon back up, as Evan pulls up in the other direction, almost hitting one fighter.

Abel says, "Evan, head up high above them. I notice something when they turned back around at us."

Chris asks, "What did you see?"

Abel points at one of them as they turn sideway to bank.

"I see it. They disappeared. You cannot spot them from the ground. They have no way of knowing where they are down below, only when they turn away." As they look, the rebels running out of the freighter, away from the two ships. Abel, with Evan, searches for an opportunity to dismantle another fighter. Just then, one of the two ships off in the distance is hit by the pulse cannon on the ground as it makes its turn back. It crashes to the ground and explodes.

Chris says, "I saw the flash. I know where they are."

Abel responds, "Ok, good. Let's see if we can take out these fighters." Abel points at one of them. "Evan, see that one there? He splits off from the others. As he does it again, get behind him, and I will shoot him down." Evan drops down off to the side of the fighter's path and waits for him to turn. As he comes back around, Abel drops the cannon and fires, blowing up the fighter. But when he tries to pull the cannon back up, alarms start going off all over the ship.

Evan says, "We just lost our cloaking. Everyone can see us now. The ship is overheating. We have to get out of here."

"We need to land over there." Chris points to where she thinks Connor is.

"I will try, but this is not a fighter, and the controls are not working very well." He heads for the spot Chris pointed at. Two fighters bank towards them and start firing. One shot hits, causing the ship to bounce. "I'm not sure we are going to make it that far." At that same time, the other fighter, seeing Evan's ship, appears headed for it as well. Abel fires at it, but they are too far away, and it bounces off the ship's shield, forcing it off course and out of their way.

There are still two ships behind them. Just as Evan drops trying to land, they fire the pulse cannon below, destroying the closest ship behind them. With Evan's ship damaged, not able to land easily, it hits the ground, causing more damage to his ship, but not hurting anyone on board. Meanwhile, the pulse cannon takes out one more ship.

As the five of them quickly disembark, Connor, Eric, Mondo, and Renaldo run over. Connor says, "Christina, it is you. Everyone kept telling me they killed you, and Emily survived, but I knew it was not true."

She runs over and hugs Connor. "I am so sorry. She saved my life."

"I know, and I am sorry about Adam. He saved me too."

Abel steps over to Eric and grabs his hand. "I am sorry to tell you this, but John is also dead."

Eric laments, "Connor told me. I did not want to believe him, but I knew he was right."

"Wait, how could he have known?" He looks at Connor. "So, it's true. Then you really have the gift."

Connor agrees. "Yes, I do. But we can talk about that later. Welcome to the party."

Evan says, "So, who is manning the cannon? I want to shake his hand; he saved our asses."

Renaldo says, "Let's get back there. The rebels are headed our way."

"And we definitely have different definitions of what a party is." They dash back to the front of the mine.

Connor explains, "Gentlemen, this is the true empress of the universe, Christian Colon."

She then says, "It's no longer Christina. It is now Chris."

"Well, ok." They all introduce themselves to her.

Mondo notices her sword, as she has it drawn, ready to use. "Where did you get that sword?" he asks.

Chris says, "You're Mondo? This was given to me by a man I never met before, but John knew him and told me his name was Ramone. Just before he died protecting me, he told John to tell you he followed the clan code."

"We will need to talk about this further when we are done here."

By this time, Tom and his men come close to where Connor and the others are, with the rest of their men still hiding in the trenches off to the sides, out of sight. Tom sends one of his men out to talk. Connor steps out close enough to hear him. The man standing there asks, "I was told to ask for Connor and Eric. Would you be one of them?"

Connor says, "Yes, I am. What do you want?"

"Our general would like to talk with you two."

"Ok, I will listen to what he has to say." He then signals for Eric to come over at the same time the man walks back, waving at Tom. Eric walks up next to Connor while Tom approaches. "Who the hell are you and where is Craven?"

Tom laughs a little. "I am General Tom Johnson. I control the armies for the emperor. As for Craven, he failed the emperor and sent me in his place. Why would you concern yourself with someone like Craven? He has been betraying you all from the beginning. When I was a recruit, Craven worked with our leaders, getting them the newest weapons through a secret supplier, and he gave up Connor's grandfather since he wanted to take over."

Eric demands, "If that was the case, then why did he help us get Bernard back?"

"My guess is he had no choice when the emperor got involved."

Connor asks, "This is all well and good, but why are we talking to you?"

Tom explains, "You fought brilliantly till now, but I still have two fighters flying overhead, and we only lost two of our thirty men. I only see ten of you, so why don't you give up so I can turn you over to the emperor? You can't fight our weapons."

Connor now draws his sword. "Why don't I just kill you and stop this boring conversation?"

Tom thinks he cannot be hurt with his suit on while having a powered sword. "You're kidding, right? We have you outnumbered, like I said, with superior weapons. You have no chance."

"You think so?" He then yells at Dave, "Now!" As Connor says that, Dave blasts another fighter out of the sky. Tom starts to run back to his men. While doing that, the hidden Zandorrian warriors emerge.

Connor yells, "Your weapons are crap! Let's get to it." The one fighter left fires on the men. As it does, Dave tries to shoot again, but the cannon just shuts down. Tom yells at the fighter to take out any ships in the area they can use to get out. As he says that, the pilot tells

Tom he only sees one sitting behind a building off in the distance. Tom orders him to destroy it.

As he is doing that, the warriors run at the rebels along with Connor, Chris, and the others. Connor yells at Chris, now next to him, "That arrogant SOB is mine!" He points his sword at Tom.

When they get close, Tom turns, still thinking he cannot be hurt and will take out Connor. He swings his sword at Connor, who blocks it. Doing this, Tom sees Connor's sword glowing bright red, which catches him off guard. Still believing his suit will protect him, he goes back at Connor. When he does, they hear and see an explosion off in the distance,

Renaldo, fighting on the other side of Connor, says, "I think they destroyed our last ship." This just makes Connor madder, so he swings even harder at Tom, cutting his sword in half. Tom, stunned, pauses just long enough for Connor to drive his sword into Tom's chest.

With a surprised look on his face, he says, "This is not possible," before falling to the ground dead. When this happens, several rebels near the back of the group, seeing Tom die, turn and run to the last freighter. They get into the ship, then force the captain to take off, leaving a few of their men behind.

Dave, able to get the cannon to fire again, shoots down the last fighter, causing it to crash. As the freighter ship takes off, Dave asks, "Should I shoot it down?"

Connor says, "No, let them go." At that same time, all the warriors cheer. Chris then hugs Connor just as Dave comes walking up. Connor looks at Evan. "This is our cannon operator." He pats Dave on his shoulder.

Evan beams at Dave. "Let me shake your hand." He clasps Dave's hand. "How were you able to see those fighters? You really saved us."

Dave comments, "It was easy once we realized what they were doing. I used an old pair of infrared glasses that showed me the heat blooms from their afterburners and just led them when I shot."

Eric walks over to Connor and pulls him aside. "I saw what you did there. How do you feel?"

Connor asks, "What do you mean?"

"Wasn't that your first kill?"

"Yes, I guess it was. As for how I feel, I thought I would have some remorse, but after everyone we have lost, I have nothing but relief for killing that arrogant piece of slime."

"Well then, you have really grown up in a very short period. If you had made that same kill on Castia trying to save Adam, I am sure you would have been very remorseful and it would have affected you differently."

"Yes, I think you are right. I am not that same person."

As Connor and Eric rejoin the group, Abel says, "Well, that was fun, but now what can we do? Our ship has been damaged, and we do not know if it is even repairable at this point."

Eric explains, "The window timing is shrinking. Now it closes again tonight."

Chris says, "Wait, we thought it was open for about a day and a half. Is this not the case?"

Mondo explains, "It used to be, but not now. The scientist has no idea why, and soon there may be no more."

Evan shouts, "WHAT? I can't be stuck here. We have to get off this planet."

Connor says, "Well, the ship we stashed behind my house may have been blown up, but we still have to check."

As they discuss this, Diego marches up with some of the other warriors and the rebels that survived, but did not make it on the freighter. He addresses Connor. "What should we do with these men?"

Connor looks at Renaldo and Mondo. "What do you guys normally do with prisoners?"

Mondo says, "That's a good question. We have not had to deal with them in a really long time."

Connor frowns at the rebels. "If we let you go, will we have to worry about retaliation?"

One rebel steps up. "I think I can speak for all of us. We really did not want to come here in the first place, and we hold no ill will. We would be willing to help you with anything you need, but I have a question, if I may ask?"

"Sure, what is it?"

"Are you really the new emperor, as the rumors have been saying, and the reason we were sent here to kill you?"

"Yes, the man sitting on the throne now is lying to everyone."

The rebel says, "Then I am glad we are here, and we offer our services to you, sire."

Diego says, "I will find somewhere for them to live and sleep for now."

Connor responds, "Thank you, Diego."

Abel starts to ask a question, and Connor holds up his hand, telling him to wait. After the rebels are far enough away, where they cannot hear any of their conversations, Connor looks at Abel. "Ok."

Abel asks, "Why did you not tell them Chris is the empress?"

"Because we were just fighting them. I did not want to open up anything until we know we can really trust them. That is also why I wanted you to wait to speak."

"You're right."

Eric says, "Well done. You are really thinking like a leader."

Chris agrees. "Yes, well done. Thank you."

Connor says, "We need to get to my house now and see what happened there."

Renaldo comes back after walking away for a bit. "We only lost three of our men, but over ten of the rebels died. I asked the men to set up for burial fires while we check if the ship survived."

Abel puts in, "I will have our men help as well."

While the men take care of the dead, Connor, Chris, and the rest head to Connor's home. As they get close, they see Connor's house and the ship completely leveled and still burning. Connor says, "Well, this is just icing on the cake. After everything else, I have now lost my home."

Chris puts her arm around Connor. "I am so sorry."

Mondo says, "Don't worry. We have lots of help, and we can rebuild it even better and bigger if you want."

Connor agrees. "You're right. I just need to be happy we are all still alive."

"Yes, we need to celebrate. But first, let's go back and mourn our dead."

Eric says, "Good point."

Abel asks, "So, we have no way back home at this point?"

Connor says, "Not unless we can repair Evan's ship before the next alignment."

Abel glances at Chris. "Wait, isn't there a platform here, and isn't that why we went Ria 6?"

"Yes, you guys went back there. Why did you do that?"

Chris fills him in on what they speculated about the palace invasion and where Lorenzo was hiding and the platform there on Ria 6.

Connor asks, "So, you think you can make the platform here work?"

Mondo jumps in. "But this one is a receiver. I thought we would need a sender."

Chris admits, "Well, yes, and yes to both of you. I think I can make the receiver here work as a sender if we can get the right equipment. We were taking what I thought we would need, but when John got stabbed, he dropped the two boxes. But after seeing their contents, I think I can build it. We already have the units to power up the system for transmission, but it will take me some time to craft everything else."

Mondo says, "That is great. The technician that looked at it the first time can help you if you want."

Chris says, "That would be wonderful. The more help, the quicker we can get it working."

Renaldo puts in, "When you're ready, if you get me a list of everything you think you will require, I can source it for you."

Abel states, "In the meantime, we can repair Evan's ship to see if we can get it to fly again."

Dave says, "I can give you guys a hand with that."

Mondo adds, "And we can take parts from the damaged freighters if they will work."

Evan explains, "My ship has been rebuilt so many times with anything available. I am not sure there are any original parts left on it, so anything will help, thank you."

Back on Ria 6, much later that day, the remaining rebels that hijacked the freighter arrive on their home world. The base captain comes up to the ship right as it lands, trying to find out what is going on since no ships like this have landed there after the palace was overtaken. When he gets to the ship, the rebels rush out. The captain yells at them to stop and tell him what's going on and why they are there. One man says, "Sir, they killed him. They killed General Johnson. We were on Zada 5, and they killed him."

The captain demands, "Who killed him?"

"That person they sent us to kill, Connor. He did, sir. He put his sword through the General's suit like it was nothing."

"Then why did you come back here? Why didn't you go to Markus 2 and tell the emperor? He needs to know this. If not him, then Craven on Korbin."

The rebel says, "No, sir, we cannot go back there. We are not going back to Zada 5 ever. It was a slaughter. They had some of our swords from the last time our men were there, and the leaders had swords that cut right through our suits. These suits are useless against their weapons. They were all well trained and made us look like amateurs."

"What about the new stealth fighters? You must have taken some of them with you?"

"Yes, sir, we took six, but they seemed to see those as well. Their pulse cannon blew them out of the sky with no problem at all. They destroyed part of our ship as we landed, so we had to hijack this ship." He indicates back at the freighter. "The men that were left got out of there as fast as we could."

"You must come with me. We need to see the emperor and let him know what happened there."

"No, sir, I am never leaving this planet again."

"Get it together, soldier. I require someone who was there to explain this to the emperor. Now clean yourself up and let's go."

The rebel does as he's told. He comes back several minutes later to meet the captain at one of their smaller ships, and they fly off, headed for Markus 2.

It is almost dark by the time they land on Markus 2. As they get off the ship, the captain can see the rebel is clearly terrified at the thought of facing the emperor. The captain assures him, "It will be all right, son. Just be clear and to the point as to what happened there, and you will be fine." As he puts his hand on the rebel's back, he notices the rebel is no longer wearing his protective suit. "You took your suit off?"

The rebel says, "Yes, sir, it is clearly useless against our enemies now with their new weapons."

"Maybe you're right." They go to the front of the palace, with several rebel guards out front.

One guard says, "I am sorry, sir, but no one is allowed in unless you have a special pass."

The captain barks, "Do you know who I am?"

"Yes sir, I do."

"Then let us in. This man just came back from Zada 5, and we need to see the emperor right away."

The guard says, "Alright, follow me." The three of them go into the palace and down the hall to the emperor's office. When they arrive, Lorenzo looks up as he hears the guard walk through the door.

The emperor glares at the guard. "Yes, what do you want?"

"Um, sir, sorry to interrupt you, but there are men here with news from Zada 5, and they are asking to talk with you." He looks at the time, thinking they are here late, so it must be good news.

He smiles. "Great, send them in."

The guard waves them in. The captain and the rebel enter. Now Lorenzo's expression changes from happy to surprised. "Who are you and where is Tom?"

The captain looks at the rebel. "Go ahead. Tell him what happened." He pushes the rebel closer to the emperor's desk.

The rebel, clearly shaking at this point, tries to calm himself to talk. "Um, well, um, they killed the general." He then blurts out, "IT WAS A SLAUGHTER. THEY WERE KILLING EVERYONE!"

Lorenzo snaps, "Calm down and tell me what happened. You were all wearing your suits and had your new swords, right?"

"Yes, sir." The rebel then tells the emperor what happened, like he did to the captain about the suits, the crash, and the fighters.

Lorenzo begins to shout, "So the rest of you ran away like cowards, leaving Connor and Eric still alive to threaten me!"

The rebel cries, "They would have killed us too. We had to leave!"

Lorenzo jumps up from his desk, quickly grabbing his sword, then yells, "You coward! Connor is still alive." and drives his sword into the rebel's chest. Both the guard and captain stand shocked.

The captain yells, "SIR," as the rebel falls to the floor.

Lorenzo, completely pissed off at this point, looks at the captain. "What? Do you have something to say?" He tosses the sword back on the desk, dripping blood all over it.

The captain looks down. "No, sir, I do not."

Lorenzo, still clearly angry, looks at the guard. "I need you to get hold of Craven. He should still be on Korbin. I must have him here NOW!"

"Yes sir, right away, sir." The guard then runs out the door.

Lorenzo then looks at the captain. "It took a lot of guts for you to bring that sniveling coward to me. What's your name?"

The captain says, "Yes sir, thank you, sir. It did. My name is Jeff, sir."

"Well, Colonel, thank you for doing that."

"Sir, I am a captain."

"No, not anymore. You are now a colonel."

"Yes, sir. Thank you, sir."

"With Tom gone, I need someone to take his place. His office is down the hall. It is now your office. You now will work here in the palace with me."

"Yes, sir, thank you, sir."

"I also want you involved when I talk with Craven later tonight to hear our discussion."

"Yes, sir, I will be."

As it gets late, Jeff continues to look for Craven, since it has already been a very long day for him. A short time later, Craven arrives, clearly pissed off, stomping down the hall. Jeff waits a minute, then follows in behind Craven to Lorenzo's office. He stands up, looking at Craven. "Finally, you're here!"

"Yes, why?" Still mad, Craven glares back at him.

Lorenzo states, "The man behind you, Jeff, brought one man that came back from Zada 5 to tell me we had another failure. And Tom is now dead. So, what are you going to do about it? Connor is still alive, and I'm losing my patience."

Craven now has a grin on his face. "The window there should still be open until tomorrow midmorning, and they will not be expecting it. So, we will have the element of surprise this time, but we will have to act quickly. There are three fighters left with men personally trained by me on Korbin. I should be able to get back to Korbin, collect what we need, and then reach to Zada 5 by early morning tomorrow."

Jeff asks, "Should I go with you?"

Both Craven and Lorenzo at the same time yell, "No!"

Craven says, "You have not been training with my men and would be in the way."

Lorenzo states, "Jeff, I will need a plan from you if Craven fails again."

Craven glares at Jeff. "I will not fail this time, so don't worry about it." He then looks back at Lorenzo. "I am leaving now unless there is anything else. I have a lot to do, and no time left to do it."

Lorenzo watches Craven walk out. "No, nothing else. Just bring me back a win."

As he says that, Craven looks at Jeff and tells him to walk out with him. "I remember you. Aren't you the captain of the guards back on Ria 6?"

Jeff explains, "Yes, I was until tonight. The emperor made me a colonel and told me I am taking the general's place now that he is gone."

"Oh, he did? Ok, aren't you responsible for the break-in on the base several weeks back?"

"Um, well, my men were. I was not there at the time, but I made the general aware of it, and he told me not to tell anyone. The guards that were on duty are now dead. But how did you find out?"

"I still have my contacts that inform me of everything. I don't want you to say anything about the break-in either. That will stay between us."

"Ok, yes, sir."

Craven now thinks he has something over Jeff, in case he tries to do the same thing Tom did. "You need to keep in mind you are still just a colonel, so no matter what the emperor says, you really work for me."

Jeff, still new to all of this and not wanting to stir things up, agrees. "Yes, sir, whatever you say."

"Good, keep all of this in mind and we will get along fine."

"Yes, sir, anything you need, I will be there." Craven then walks away to get back to Korbin.

When Craven arrives, he rushes out of his ship to where his troops are sleeping, then wakes them up, telling his men they have an hour to load and be ready to leave. By this time, it is already very early the next morning. All the men jump to and rush around, but they take almost an hour and a half to get ready and everything loaded. Craven hurries everyone onto the ship, then tells them to take off. As the ship departs, the men question what is going on. Craven tells them about what happened the morning before with Tom, his men, and how they are going to finish what Tom started on Zada 5. The men voice concerns among themselves about all the rumors. Craven, hearing the rumblings of his men, gets mad. "We have the element of surprise and will be successful this time, so I want all the noise to stop." They do as he says, but quietly try to think about how they will survive this time.

A few hours later, clearly early morning where they should be landing, as they near the planet, they see the window is closed. The pilot calls for Craven to come up front. As Craven walks in, he can see the issue. Craven looks at the pilot. "Are you sure you're at the right location?"

The pilot points to his panel. "Yes, there is the location right there. The window is closed already."

"No, that can't be. We have a day and a half. We should still have several hours before it closes."

"Yes, you are right. That is the same thing my charts say. It opened yesterday is what they tell me."

"This is not good." Craven then mumbles to himself, "This will not be a fun conversation."

"I am sorry. What did you say, sir?"

"Nothing, never mind. I guess we have no choice. Take us back to Korbin."

"Yes, sir, you got it."

When they get back, Craven tells the men to unload. They are done for the day. He then goes over to his ship and heads to Markus 2 to let the emperor know what happened, not really wanting to deal with his anger. After Craven lands and gets to the palace, he reaches Lorenzo's office. He sees Jeff sitting in his office and waves at him. Jeff, surprised to see Craven so soon, jumps up and quickly follows him. As Craven walks in, Lorenzo jumps up from his chair, angry to see Craven back already. "Why are you here? You should have been killing Connor by now. What lame excuse could you possibly have for this?"

Craven glares at him. "Lame excuse, really? I don't have to take this crap from you. The window for Zada 5 is already closed. We had no way to land on the planet to get to Connor."

Lorenzo shoves everything off his desk and shouts, "Failures! I am dealing with nothing but failures! Connor needs to be dead. I cannot wait another three months to officially be made the emperor. We must use the platform to get there."

"And what happens if they are guarding it? They will kill us as we walk through, as our suits and swords will not work for at least a minute."

"Then we need another solution."

"There is none. There is no way to get through the asteroid field surrounding the planet, so I do not know how else we could get there. Do you?"

Lorenzo gets even more irritated. "If I could do that, why would I need you? That is what you are here for. You need to figure this out. I need better control of the universe, the mining colonies, which means more men for the army, which means more money. The empire has a ton of wealth coming in, but I cannot access it until I am officially the emperor, and you are stopping me from getting there." Still looking at Craven, he continues to get madder. "Just leave. You have two days to come back to me with a plan to solve this for me."

Craven, wanting to tell him that if he had sent him instead of Tom, he would have brought back the win, just says, "Sure, okay."

As Craven leaves, Lorenzo looks at Jeff. "Do you have any suggestions?"

Jeff says, "I am sorry, sir. I have never been to Zada 5, so I know little about it, but I will see what information I can get on it to find any other options."

"See, that is what I am talking about, someone who will take initiative. If you can discover a new way in, that will lead to another promotion for you."

"Wow, thank you, sir. I will do my best to not let you down and will get started right away." Jeff then leaves his office as well.

CHAPTER XXI

HOW DO WE GET THERE?

On Zada 5, the next morning, Connor and Chris sit in the back corner of the dining hall, the same place Connor and Eric first met Mondo. They spend the morning catching up with each other. Chris shares about how the palace was invaded by Lorenzo and Craven, and Emily's sacrifice to save her. Connor talks about how they crashed, what they did to get ready for the first attack with Craven, and how Adam and Andorra were killed protecting him. Connor then asks Christina why she now wants to be called Chris. She tells him Christina was the name of a young unjaded girl with a lot of ideas and no thoughts of how cruel the world can really be, but Chris is mature, battle-hardened, and well aware how harsh life truly is.

Connor says, "Sure, I get it and feel the same way. But do not completely lose that young girl with lots of ideas. That is who my brother fell in love with. I know she is still in there." He points to her heart.

With that, a tear rolls down her cheek. "Thank you for that. We had little time together, but I loved him so much that it's hard to think about because it hurts." As she says that, more tears roll down her cheeks.

"I know you did, and how much it hurts. I feel the same way about Emily. I find myself starting to think about her, then having to stop because the pain is too great. I'm sorry, but when Mandora showed up saying you were dead, and Emily was alive, I dared to hope for a minute, but I knew it was not true."

"No, don't be. I would have felt the same way. I could see for myself how much you loved her; she truly loved you too. Wow, is this really my future life? This aches so much." She wipes the tears away with her sleeve.

While doing that, Abel and Eric see it as they come walking up. Abel looks at Chris. "Are you okay?"

"Yes, I am fine. We have just been updating each other about what has gone on with each of us, and some of it has been painful to talk about." She then puts her hand on Connor's shoulder. "But it helps to talk with someone who knows exactly how I feel, because he feels the same way."

Eric asks, "Should we leave you two alone to talk more?"

Connor studies Chris. "No, I think we are ready to change the subject here."

Chris smiles at Connor. "Yes, I agree."

Connor and Chris stand up and all walk over to sit down to eat. As they do, Mondo, Dave, and Renaldo join them. Abel asks, "Has anyone seen Evan?"

Mondo and Dave start to laugh. Then Dave says, "Well, I don't think we are going to for a while. Yesterday was an eye opener for him. I take it that was the first actual fight he had ever fought in, and his nerves were shot. Not sure I have ever seen anyone drink that much before."

Abel laughs. "No, he can really drink, but normally, he is up and ready to go the next morning."

Mondo comments, "I would be dead if I drank as much as he did last night. We had to get him to his room. I am sure he was out before he hit the bed." A few minutes later, Evan slowly comes walking in with his eyes barely open and sits down next to Dave.

They all chuckle, and Dave says, "So you did survive last night."

Evan declares, "Yes, and I am never drinking again. I think last night was a new record. My head is killing me."

Mondo remarks, "I am surprised you are upright."

"Me too. But when I woke up, I figured I'd better get up or I never would."

Abel says, "Good call. After breakfast, you can help Dave and I work on your ship. Then you can sweat the hooch out of you in the hot sun."

Evan holds his head up with his arms on the table. "Oh man, not sure how much help I will be today, but I will go back out there with you to see how bad my ship is."

Abel looks at Dave. "We will find him sleeping on the ship is my bet."

Dave agrees, "Oh, I'm sure."

Evan says, "You understand I can hear you."

Abel replies, "Are we wrong?"

"No, I just wanted you to know." Both Dave and Abel laugh.

"Okay, next subject." Renaldo looks at Chris. "The two technicians will meet you at the platform in the cavern later this morning."

Chris says, "Great. I am eager to get started working on it and make the modifications. Abel, before you start working on the ship, can you have someone bring me the power modules?"

Abel agrees. "Yes, no problem."

Connor says, "I will have some of our men do that so you guys can focus on the ship."

"Thank you, sire." Eric, Mondo, and Renaldo start to chuckle. Abel stares at them. "What's so funny?"

Eric explains, "Nothing, really. It is just Connor has a hard time being called sir or sire and spent a lot of time telling the men here they did not have to call him that, like you just did."

Abel gawks at Eric. "Well, right now he is truly the emperor, isn't he?"

Connor agrees. "Yes, you are correct. But at this table, we are all the same where I am concerned. What's more, once we get off this planet, Chris will be declared the rightful heir."

Renaldo puts in, "How about we put the rebels to work? They really have nothing to do now anyway, and we can see where their heads are at the same time."

"Great idea. Diego can monitor them."

"Perfect. I will have Diego bring them out to the ship."

"Ok, thank you. While you do that, we will take Chris back to the mine so she can see the platform." Everyone but Evan gets up.

Abel looks at Dave. "Can you wake him?"

Dave pushes on Evan's shoulder, and he jumps up. "What did I miss?"

"We are leaving now."

"Oh, ok, I'm ready." They all laugh and start to exit. Evan, still dazed, wanders off in the wrong direction. Abel walks over to him, grabs his shirt, and pulls him in the same direction everyone else is headed.

As they come out of the building, Renaldo heads off to talk with Diego and the stranded rebels. Abel and Dave leave with Evan in tow to work on Evan's ship, assess the damages, and determine if it is even salvageable, while Connor, Chris, Eric, and Mondo head to the mine to check out the platform in the cavern.

A LITTLE WHILE LATER, DIEGO COMES UP TO THE damaged ship while Dave and Abel repair it with the rebels behind him. "Hi, I am Diego. We did not get the chance to meet yesterday."

"Hi, I'm Abel. Glad to know you." He shakes Diego's hand. "You are amazing warriors."

"Yes, we are thanks to Adam and Connor. We thought we were good until the training we got from the One and his brother."

"The One?"

Diego smiles. "Yes, Connor, he is a great man. I actually tried to kill him before he took me down and disarmed me. Then I understood who he really was."

"Wow, and now you fight beside him."

"Yes. I would gladly give my life for him."

"Your men clearly fight like it. I am glad we are on the same side."

Diego has a big smile on his face. "Yes sir, we are."

At that moment, a rebel comes walking over. "Do you need help on this ship? If so, that was my main job when I was still at Ria 6."

Dave hears him. "Sure, this is a wreck, and we need all the help we can get if it is ever going to fly again." He comes over, peering at the rebel. "So, what's your name?"

"It's Rodney."

"Well, Rodney, if you can help us get this ship flying, you will have cleared your name with us."

"Thank you. That is all I am looking for. We never wanted to come here in the first place."

Diego, listening to Dave and Rodney talk, looks at them. "Okay, then I will have the others help me take the stuff Connor was asking for to the cavern, if you can show me what it is."

"Yes, follow me on to the ship. I can show you." Abel and Diego go into the craft, where Evan sleeps in the corner. Abel points out what they need to take. Diego looks at Evan, then back at Abel, who glances at Diego and laughs. "Don't ask." Diego smiles and nods; he then goes to the door and waves for the others to come in to help him. Once they finish, they load up everything and head to the mine not very far from the damaged ship. Diego and the other three men take the stuff inside through the cavern to the back, where Chris, Connor, and the others are inspecting the platform. As the men set the equipment down nearby, one of them looks at Chris and Connor.

"I helped Lorenzo with one of these on Ria 6." Everyone focused on the platform looks up at the rebel.

Chris asks, "So, how did you assist?"

"I put some of it together and made changes."

Connor peers at him. "But you are just a private, right?"

"Yes, sir, I am, but I was a scientist before being forced to fight with the rebels. They pressed a lot of us back home to join or else."

Chris asks, "Then you know how all this works?"

"Well, most of it. But Lorenzo would not let me see everything, and I was not there when he started testing, but I understand the basics."

"What's your name?"

"My name is Manuel."

"Manuel, welcome to the team."

Diego, standing there hearing this, laughs. "Well, I guess it is down to the three of us," looking at the last two rebels.

As he says that, Renaldo strolls in and smacks Diego on the shoulder. "That's okay. I could use your assistance with Connor's home."

Both Connor and Mondo respond, "We can help too. We are not needed here, and are really in the way."

Chris looks at Connor with a smile on her face, then winks at him. "Yes, you are."

Connor winks back. "I thought so. This is all way above my head."

Laughing, Chris pats his face. "That's okay. You're cute and good with a sword. That is everything you need."

Connor, grinning, looks at Renaldo. "Let's get out of here before I earn any more insults." As he says that, everyone laughs. Then they follow Renaldo out to what is left of Connor's home.

As they leave, Chris turns to Manuel. "So, how much do you really know about this device?"

Manuel says, "Okay, first thing. You cannot go anywhere with this unit. It can only receive based on all I see here."

One of the two technicians, that had looked it over when Eric and Connor arrived, interjects, "I was right. That is what we figured."

Chris shows them the diagrams she has put together. "Ok, good. Then we are all on the same page. If you look at these, this is what I designed based on studying the one on Ria 6."

Manuel comments, "Wow, this is much better than what I helped Lorenzo build. If I am reading this correctly, this device, after we have made the changes, will work both ways. Is that right?"

"Yes, that is what I was thinking. We do not have everything here needed to make all the changes. We will need to alter what we can, then list the rest and hope we will be able to either find or build what we need to complete these modifications."

One of the two technicians says, "We are very good at building complex devices if we know what we need it for. If you can design it, we can build it."

"Great, let's get started." Over the next week, they spend long hours making all the changes they can with what's there and compiling a list of equipment needed to build the rest.

At the end of the week, while at breakfast with everyone else, Chris gives the document to Renaldo.

Renaldo looks it over. "This is an extensive list, and some of what you are asking for is very hard to find, so I will need some time to source all of this."

Connor, Eric, and Mondo are sitting there and hear what he says.

Connor gazes at him with a big smile. "Keep in mind your success or failure in acquiring all of this only means the fate of the universe."

Renaldo laughs at Connor. "Oh, okay, so no pressure here. But seriously, what if I cannot find everything?"

"Well then, we have to wait for them to come and try killing us again and hope we can grab their ship."

Dave and Abel are still having trouble repairing Evan's bucket of bolts. They walk in just as he says that.

Dave says, "Correction, just bolts. There is no bucket yet."

Evan objects, "Hey, that is my ship you are talking about."

"Saying it's a ship would imply that it can fly. So, can it?"

"Well, no, but I have faith you, Abel, and Rodney can breathe life back into it."

Connor, amused, looks at Renaldo. "After hearing this, do I need to say any more?"

Renaldo says, "No, I get it. I will have Diego help me. Give me a week and I will update you on the progress."

Chris says, "Thank you, Renaldo. We appreciate it. Also, keep in mind, if you can't locate everything, your technicians may be able to build some it if they can get the pieces."

"Ok, that helps. Let me get started." Renaldo then departs.

Days after Renaldo left to source parts for the platform, Abel, Dave, Rodney, and Evan continue rebuilding Evan's ship. In order to do so, they have to modify parts taken from the damaged freighters, as no other sources available will work with Evan's vintage ship. But they have trouble making the parts function correctly, so their progress is slower than they hoped. They ask Chris to assist Evan with the cloaking device as it was also damaged, and no one really knows how it works since someone other than Evan added it to the ship as payment for a shipment he delivered. She takes most of the device apart, trying to understand how it functions. After a few days, Chris completely redesigns the unit and ties it directly into the ship's main engines, making any part of the ship invisible when the cloaking is turned on. When Chris is finished, she tells Evan and Abel what she could do, then tells them she can duplicate this on the rest of their ships if they make it back to Hmar 4.

Rodney hears this. "So, you guys could destroy the blockade, and they would not understand what hit them."

Abel agrees. "Yes, that is my thought."

"What if I show you how to disable their ships so you don't have to kill all of them? Some of the men and women on those ships are friends of mine, and I would not like to see them dead."

Chris says, "I get it, but all your friends have been trying to kill us."

"Yes, that's true, but only because we have been ordered to. Our superiors would slaughter us for not following orders. Most of my friends, just like me, have been forced into rebelling. If you give them the option to surrender and attack with you for their freedom, they will jump at the chance."

"If you are right, I am willing to try it."

Abel says, "Not so sure I am. What stops them from trying to murder us in our sleep?"

Rodney asks, "Have I tried that here with you guys?"

Dave, who is also there, comments, "No, but you really have nowhere to go if you did, so that is not much of an argument."

"You're right. I am not sure what assurance I could give you, other than my word, from one warrior to another."

Chris says, "Maybe we could house them separately until they can prove themselves."

"That sounds fair, but I have a question. Right now, the emperor wants to kill Connor. But everyone calls you Chris and treats you the same as Connor. Isn't Chris short for Christina? If so, are you the true ruler? I thought everyone said you were dead."

Abel turns to Chris. "Don't answer that."

"It's ok. You don't have to, but based on your response, you already have."

Dave says, "Why don't we all get back to repairing the ship?"

"You're right. We still have a lot to do."

AT THE SAME TIME THE GUYS ARE WORKING ON EVAN'S ship, Connor, Mondo, Diego, and the engineer Donovan have finished tearing apart the remains of Connor's home and started to restore it bigger and better. While they are building, Donovan asks if they saw the rich veins of Verbraso when they constructed the escape path through the top of the cavern.

Connor says, "I did, but I did not realize that was what we were looking at. But if that is truly Verbraso, then we could build enough swords for any army."

Donovan replies, "Sure, I guess you could if you wanted to."

"I remember when you were creating the opening. You talked about rich veins, but we were focused on other things at the time. I will let Renaldo know when he returns. Thank you for reminding us."

"My pleasure. I am always happy to help the One."

Connor smile at him as he puts his hand on Donovan's shoulder. "It's Connor to you."

"Thank you, Connor, sir."

AT THE END OF THE WEEK, RONALDO MAKES GOOD ON his word and returns with a lot of items. He meets Connor and Chris that morning and shows Chris the list and what he could get, along with several parts to craft the other pieces she was looking for.

Chris exclaims, "You are amazing. When we take out the slug and I officially take over, would you like to come to work for me? We could do some great work together with your skills."

Renaldo says, "Thank you, your highness, that would be a great honor."

Connor pats him on the shoulder. "Nice. I like to see good things happen to great people like you. One other thing, I am not sure you remember, but I was talking to Donovan the other day, and he reminded me about the minerals in the top exit to the cavern."

"Yes, I remember."

"But what he did not say and what we did not realize is that mineral is Verbraso, and there is a lot."

Chris gasps, "Verbraso, are you sure that is what it is?"

"Yes, that is what he told me. We can build a lot of swords with it."

Chris pulls out her weapon. "You mean like mine and yours? You guys know how to create these the correct way?"

Renaldo explains, "Well, no, not us. But the son of the blacksmith that made Connor's does."

"That's great, but we will also need a lot of Verbraso for the platform. That is part of the fuel."

Walking up, Mondo hears their conversation. "I will reach out to the miners to pull out all they can from the cavern. Then we can see how much we have to determine how much we need for each."

"Thank you, Mondo. That will be a great help."

Renaldo says, "Diego and I will deliver the parts back at the cavern for you to work on. I also have some leads on the rest and will be back in a few days."

Connor says, "Thanks, buddy. That will be a big help."

Chris adds, "We will be out there shortly to start work again. Thank you."

Dave and Abel stride in with Evan right behind them. Connor looks at them. "So, how are we doing with Evan's ship?"

Dave turns to Abel. "Well, do you want to tell them, or do you want me to?"

"Great, now what?"

Dave has a big grin on his face. "We're kidding. We will test it later today. There are just a few things we need to take care of."

"Really?"

Abel smiles too. "Yes, Dave is correct. Evan's bucket of bolts should be able to leave the ground sometime this afternoon."

Evan adds, "To that point, once my ship is flying again, how soon can we actually leave this planet?"

Connor says, "The window should open again in about two months."

"Then we have to wait two more months to get out of here?"

"Not so quick. We do not know if they are planning to return again, but based on the past effort, we need to plan as if they are, so we cannot leave until we have finished any fighting. If Chris is successful with the platform before the window opens, we can surprise them."

Chris puts in, "I will know by the end of next week if I can make it function or not. Then we can come up with a plan from there."

At the end of the day, Abel and Dave, with the help of Rodney, finally fly Evan's ship. There are still some issues, but it is leaving the ground. Evan comes out of the vessel with a big grin on his face, kind of bouncing around. Abel looks at Evan. "Why are so you happy?"

Evan says, "After this last crash, I did not think it was ever going to fly again. Thank you, thank you all for doing this for me."

Dave replies, "You're welcome, but this was not just for you. We all want to get out of here, but if we have to wait until the new window and the next battle, we will need to find somewhere to hide this ship, so they do not blow it up like all the others."

"Blow it up! No, we just got it to fly again. I need this ship to survive."

Abel reassures him, "Relax, we will figure it out."

"No, you're right. I am just really concerned about getting out of here."

Dave looks at Evan. "I am right there with you. Being here all this time has been intense, but I feel like we are almost at the end of it."

"I hope you are correct."

Abel asks, "Have I got you this far with only a few scratches?"

"Yes, you have, and I appreciate it, but all this fighting has been way too much for me."

Dave agrees. "I get it. This could be a lot for someone who is not in this kind of life, but we will keep you safe until we can all leave."

"Thanks, guys. Let's get something to drink." The guys call it quits for the day and head back to where they are staying.

On Markus 2, Lorenzo calls Jeff into his office. "So, do you have a plan yet?"

Jeff states, "I have been working on a few options, but all the scientists are telling me none of them will work. I am sorry for failing you, but I keep getting told the only way in is with the moon alignment." Saying this, he expects Lorenzo to lose it, but how relatively calm he seems to be with his news surprises him.

Lorenzo says, "That's okay. I knew that was the answer, but I wanted to see if you could find any other options. I am still pushing Craven to be ready so we can finish this once and for all with the next alignment. I have asked him to come back here before then so we can all review his plans looking for any gaps. He does not like that idea, but I cannot have a third failure."

"I understand, sire, but we have all heard he does not like to be second-guessed."

"That is not my concern. He works for me and needs to control it. Once he has succeeded and I can officially proclaim myself as the emperor, I can resolve his continued plotting and plans. He thinks I do not know what he has been up to, but I know he told you that you work for him, not me."

"But, sire, how could you have heard? We spoke in private."

"Just because I am not officially the emperor, I still have the power to see and hear all. Craven is wrong. You work for me, not him, so keep that in mind."

Jeff puts on a big smile. "Yes, sire, I will."

Back on Zada 5, a few days later, Renaldo returns with the rest of the parts Chris and the technicians need to finish rebuilding the platform. A couple of days later, Chris announces that if everything continues as planned, they can start testing.

Connor cautions her, "That is great, but we will need to be careful. You do not know what could be waiting for us on the other side if you can successfully open up a window."

Chris agrees. "Yes, you're correct. That is why I want all of us there when testing so we can handle anything that either comes through, or that we have to deal with when all of us step through."

Eric says, "Ok, good, just let us know when you are ready, and we will be there."

ON KORBIN, CRAVEN WORKS WITH THE LABS, DRIVING the engineers crazy, pressing on them to resolve the gap issue in their protective suits. No matter what they try, the changes do not resolve their problem. A few days later, one scientist invents a new way to power up the suit from the bottom, attaching it to the boot. It leaves the right one vulnerable, but now makes it a non-life-threatening injury. But the tradeoff is, with the smaller unit, the suit can only be active for a few hours before the power unit needs reloading. Craven accepts the downside, realizing his men will be more comfortable knowing where the gap is for their modified suits.

Later that day, Craven tells his men about the changes and shuts down the rumors about a sword that can still cut through their suits. On Zada 5, they used the gap in the suit to kill their men, and the dragon is dead, so they will be victorious this time. Craven's message calms most of the men, but a few do not believe him as he trains them for their next battle.

CHAPTER XXII

CAN WE GET THERE
FROM HERE?

Back on Zada 5, early in the morning, Connor and Chris are in the back corner again, talking a few days before Chris is ready to test. Connor asks, "I have been thinking. Do you really believe we can get back into the palace?"

Chris says, "Yes, if everything works the way I think it should."

"If that is the case, I do not think we will have to worry about any guards near the portal. Your uncle has been arrogant about all of this and will have no idea we could modify his invention to use against him. If we go in a few weeks before the alignment, all their plans will center around them coming here."

"First off, he is not my uncle. He is a slimy slug."

Connor laughs. "Sorry, you're right."

"But to your point, I think you're right. He has no reason to have anyone guarding the portal there, and if it is in the lower level where I think it is, we can sneak in a bunch and get to the slug before his guards can rush us."

"Okay, to that point, the slug is yours, but Craven is mine."

"We are in complete agreement."

"I was not sure I should ask, but did you see them kill everyone?"

Chris looks down. "No, I heard them go after Emily when they called my name. I wanted to go back for them, but John told me if they were dead, I would have been too. The next day, the slug announced your parents were trying to take over, executing my father and me. Why are you asking? Do you think they could still be alive?"

"No, they are dead. I know that. My concern was about what you had to see. I did not want you to have to live with those images in your head. I am glad you don't have to. It was bad enough to see John die. It was the same when I watched my brother and Andorra die in front of me. I am hoping killing Craven will give me some peace."

"You're right. I remember John being murdered all the time when I close my eyes. I guess that is why I do not sleep very much."

Connor smiles.

"Why are you smiling?"

"In the not-too-distant past, I recall a girl telling me she could not imagine not sleeping all night."

Chris smiles too. "Yes, that feels like an entire lifetime ago now."

Mondo comes walking up. "What was a lifetime ago?" he asks.

"Being able to sleep without seeing the dead."

"Ah, yes, trust me, it never goes away. But you learn how to live with it. You need to remember neither of you created this life, but once we take care of your uncle and Craven, that should give you some peace."

Connor agrees. "That is what we said. Chris will handle the slug, and I will get Craven."

Mondo laughs. "The slug, that is what you call your uncle?"

Chris says, "Yes, he is not family. He is nothing to me, just slime that I need to scrape off my shoe."

"I can understand that. I am sure I would feel the same way if he had done this to me. But this was not the reason I walked over here. I wanted to tell you the miners could get all the Verbraso out of that vein. There is more than we thought there was."

"Great. Do you have a way to refine the minerals here?"

"No, we never have. That happens after we ship the crystals."

"Then that is going to be a problem for creating more fuel for the platform."

At the same time, Renaldo joins them. "What's a problem?" he asks.

"Refining the Verbraso and Zando Crystals."

"There is an old location we were going to use to do that, but it would be easier to just send it off world."

"Do you think the equipment could still be functional?"

"It has been sitting there for a long time, but some of our people can try to get it working."

"That would be great. If it runs, I can show them the process to make the fuel."

"Okay, give us a day or two and I will see if we can get it off the ground. But if I can ask, I thought the fuel cells you brought with you were full already?"

"Yes, but I do not yet know how long they will last. Once I get the platform working correctly, we will need to turn it on a few times so we can return. If there is one at the palace like we think, I do not know if it can send or if it only receives."

Mondo says, "But if we are there, someone will have to stay behind, and if they do, how will they know when to turn it back on?"

"We will need to come up with a plan, but we still have some time to work that out."

As the four of them finish talking, Evan and Dave walk in, with Abel and Eric following behind.

Abel inquires, "What is the plan for today?"

Connor says, "Well, we need to prepare for the next wave from Craven just in case Chris cannot get the platform working in time."

Chris laughs. "Really? You don't think I can?"

Connor smiles at her. "I was not saying that, but we want to have a backup just in case."

"No, I get it. You're right. We need to have a plan for everything like we were talking about for the platform, so we never get caught off guard again."

Eric looks at Chris. "We have already suffered too much loss. We cannot afford any more."

Shortly after their discussion, Connor and the rest of them leave to prepare for the return of Craven and the rebels. Dave works on the cannon with two of the guards that came with Abel. They also talk to Evan about hiding his ship up above the cavern in the opening created for Andorra, made bigger by the miners when they excavated the Verbraso.

When Evan tries to land inside, the walls are still too close, so they plan to turn on cloaking and fly the ship just inside the hole, waiting until the combat is over, as the previous battles only lasted an hour. They discussed using the cannon on his ship, but if the cloaking failed like last time, they could risk damage and not be able to use it to leave. They all agreed not to take that chance.

While the guys finesse the battle plans, Chris is in the cavern at the platform with the technicians and Manuel. One technician says, "If we keep up this pace, we should be able to test in a day or two."

Manuel agrees. "Yes, that was my thought as well."

Chris says, "Ok, I will let the guys know so they can get ready."

"I am sorry to ask this, but do I need to step across with everybody else? As much as I would like to get home, I really would prefer not to have to fight guards. Some could be friends of mine."

"We would not do that to you. Plus, we will need someone to stay behind to help whoever else we leave here to turn this platform back on."

Manuel has a smile on his face. "Yes, I would be happy to do that, and once the fighting is done, I can come over and change the one on the other side if it is needed."

"That would be a big help, and this could be an actual job for you once I take back the throne. That goes for you two as well, if you want."

"Yes, your highness, thank you."

After a couple of days, as Chris plans with Connor for her testing, Renaldo comes up to tell Chris, "I think we can adjust the equipment to refine the crystals. If you want to come with me and show us, our team there will see if this equipment can support what you need done."

Chris goes off with Renaldo. When they arrive, a woman there shows Chris some samples they produced.

Chris inspects them and then looks at the woman as she pulls one of her samples out of the bag she has been carrying. "These look good," she shows the women her version, "but we need to reduce them to this finer level. Do you think you can make the adjustments?"

The woman studies her sample and then says, "Yes, I think we can, but we may need a day or so. Can you leave your sample with us to measure against?"

"If you think you can handle the changes, that would be very helpful. I would be happy to leave it with you."

"Thank you very much, your highness."

Surprised, Chris glances at Renaldo. "Your highness?"

Renaldo shrugs. "Don't look at me. I said nothing to them about you."

The woman is startled at Chris's reaction. "I am very sorry. Did I misspeak?"

Chris assures her, "Oh no, I was just surprised you know who I am. I did not think anyone outside of our group realized."

"Well, we did not think it's confidential. Everyone in the colony is aware who you are, and that Connor is the one for now, but he is going to give the throne back to you."

Chris and Renaldo laugh. "I'm glad we are among friends, as there seem to be no secrets around here."

Renaldo has a smile on his face. "When electronic communication does not work, word of mouth does very well here."

"I guess so." Chris winks at the woman.

STILL PREPARING FOR CRAVEN'S RETURN, RENALDO AND Chris meet the guys near the front of the mine. Chris tells them they will need a few more days before they can experiment, as she needs to be sure they can make more fuel.

Connor says, "That's fine. We still have a little time before they can come. In the meantime, why don't you practice with us? We want to cut off Craven from the rest so I can take him out. Once the rebels see you can also strike through their suits, it will scare them off, leaving Craven on his own to face me."

Chris asks, "How many Zandorrian swords do you have?"

"Seven counting yours."

"Wow, that many. Great. I think that will be enough to scare off any brave soul on their side."

"We also have mines placed throughout if we need to use them, but Abel was telling us they may only slow them down, as the sonic mines only seemed to stun them for a short time."

"Yes, he's right, but if they are dazed, it could buy us some time to deal with them after."

Eric agrees, "That is what we were thinking because my guess is they will come with about fifty or more this next time."

Connor says, "Yes, but if I can attack Craven right away, that will stop the rest of them."

"That makes sense to me after what we saw this last time."

Dave puts in, "Right, they all went running scared when Connor killed their general."

A few days later in the afternoon, Chris and Renaldo go back to the refinery. The woman comes up to them as they walk in and shows Chris her sample, then what they could refine. When they compare the two, they look almost the same. Chris exclaims, "This is great. They are not identical, but close enough that I think the platform should work the same. It may burn this fuel a little faster than what we have there now, but that is fine if we can make more."

Renaldo says, "Based on what we have, we should be able to fill twelve fuel cells like currently in the mine. That will still leave enough for the blacksmith to construct five more swords."

"That is great news. How long will it take to refine the rest of the crystals, then?"

The woman says, "I will need three days."

"Okay, that will work. We still have about three weeks before the next alignment, if my math is right."

Renaldo tells her, "Yes, you are correct."

"Great, then we can start experimenting at the end of the week." She then turns to the woman. "I am sorry.

I have been rude. I'm just focused on what I need and never asked your name."

The woman says, "You all have a lot going on. No need to be sorry for that. My name is Rema."

Chris reaches out and shakes her hand. "Rema, thanks for all your help. I really appreciate it."

"You are very welcome, your highness."

Chris still holds her hand. "No, it is Chris to you."

Rema wears a big smile. "Oh wow, thank you, Chris. It is my pleasure to know you."

Chris and Renaldo meet the guys back at the complex in the main room upstairs. Evan asks what everyone is going to do after they successfully overthrow Lorenzo.

Chris, hearing him, objects. "I am not sure that anyone is really ready to talk about any of that yet. Sure, I have told a few people I would like them to work for me when we get to that point, but our own lives are hard to think about, at least for me, and I am sure Connor feels the same way."

Connor agrees. "Yes, Chris is right. The life we both had been looking at before all of this was completely different. We have asked the question several times now. *Is this really my future life?* For me, every time I have asked, things have changed drastically. So instead, I think about our plan to survive the next task and don't look too far into the future."

Chris has a tear rolling down her cheek. "When I try to imagine what the future can be, it brings me right back to what I thought it would be with the people I loved the most and have lost." She wipes the tear from her cheek. "I am sorry. You are excited about going home, and I just brought everyone down."

Connor comes over and puts his arm around her. "It's okay. We understand."

Smiling, Chris kisses his cheek. "Thank you for that. Now let's change the subject. We should have everything we need to power up the platform a few more times and start testing at the end of the week. We have all been working really hard, and maybe we can rest for the next day or two."

"That sounds great, but I still need to at least train for a few hours to keep my edge."

Renaldo starts to laugh.

"What's so funny?"

Renaldo comments, "Well, not everything has changed from your past. This is how you have been since you first arrived here."

Connor grins. "Wow, you're right. I have been able to hold on to something. I guess that's a start."

EARLY THE MORNING OF TESTING, CONNOR AND CHRIS sit and chat at the same spot in the main room, since neither one could sleep the night before. Connor says, "I have been thinking about this all night. When you have the platform active, and you think we are in the palace, I will go in first."

Chris asks, "Why?"

"You need to stay here in case something happens with the platform so you can get me back. You know it better than anyone at this point."

"Oh, ok, I was thinking you were going to say because I was a woman."

Connor laughs. "Well, that too."

Chris socks Connor on his shoulder. "I am just as good as any man here."

Connor is still laughing. "Almost any man."

"Oh, so you don't think I could take you?" Chris pokes at him.

Connor smirks at her. "No, I am sure of it."

Every time they talk, Connor continues to look away and not at her all the time. "I need to ask you something."

"Sure, anything," he responds.

"Why is it when we're alone, you have a hard time looking at me? Have I done something?"

"No, not at all. When I look at you, I see Emily, and every time I find myself thinking you are her, I have to remind myself you're not. Then I have to turn away."

Chris reaches for his hand. "I am so sorry. I did not realize that was going on between us, but being near you has helped me feel like your brother is still with me. Maybe in a way we both have been doing the same thing."

"I have felt better sitting here talking with you, just the two of us, but it is difficult for me at times when I see her in your face."

Chris pulls Connor to her and hugs him, then kisses him on the cheek and whispers, "It will be okay. We can get through this together." As they each pull back, tears run down his face. Chris reaches up and wipes them off. Connor then takes her hand and leans in like he is going to kiss her, but just as he gets close enough to do so, he jumps up and turns away.

It surprises Chris. "What's wrong?"

"I almost kissed you!"

"I know. It's okay."

"But you were going to marry my brother, and I was going to marry your sister."

Chris stands up next to him and puts her hand on his arm. "Yes, you are right. But they are gone now, and we are standing here."

"Yes, I know that, but I was thinking you were Emily, not yourself."

"I understand. But we can make each feel better," she says.

"Thank you, Chris. But if we get involved, I would like it to be because I care about you, not your dead sister."

She puts her arm around him. "I understand how you feel. It makes sense. I just want to get closer to you."

"Don't get me wrong. You are beautiful, and touching you feels great, but I still feel disloyal to Emily and Adam."

Chris steps in front of Connor and gets close. "Would you not want them to be happy if we were gone and they were standing here?"

"Yes, I guess you're right. I would."

Chris leans up to kiss Connor, not realizing some guys are walking into the room. Connor grabs her arms and whispers, "We will have to do this another time," as he steps back.

Just then, Eric joins them. "Sorry, did I interrupt something?"

Chris quickly turns around. "No, um, we were just talking."

Smiling, Eric looks at them both. "Oh, talking, is that what they call it?" He then winks.

"Yes, talking."

Eric is still smiling. "It's okay. I am glad you two are talking." He reaches out and hugs them. "It has been hard for both of you, and you need something to be happy about."

Chris says, "Thank you, Eric. I was telling Connor the same thing."

While Connor, Chris, and Eric chat, the rest of the team walks over to them.

"Okay, what's the plan for today?" Abel looks at Chris and Connor.

Chris declares, "Well, we are all going to the cavern, and you guys are going to watch. If I can get the platform activated, then we can enter the palace on Markus 2. We are going to really stir things up."

Evan asks, "Great, but do I have to go too?" They all laugh at his remarks.

Chris strolls over, putting her arm around Evan. "No, we need someone to stay behind and help get us back."

Evan first smiles, but then his face changes to puzzled. "Great, but how can I do that?"

"Don't worry. I will show you everything you will need. Plus, Manuel will be with you. He knows how everything works as well."

"Ok, good, but when do I turn it back on?"

Connor puts in, "Yes, that's a good point."

Chris says, "I was thinking once we all get across, we turn it off to save fuel."

Abel agrees. "Yes, that's a good point. What about the fuel?"

Renaldo replies, "I will bring more over as you all go to the cavern and Chris tests the platform."

Chris says, "Thanks, Renaldo. If you guys agree, I was thinking we turn it back on after two hours as a checkpoint."

Evan asks, "But what if they are there waiting for you?"

Connor responds, "And how would that happen? Even if we could trust none of the rebels here, they have no way of warning anyone."

"You're right, but they could have a ton of guards in the palace."

Chris agrees. "Yes, that is possible, but Connor and I grew up there, and no one knows that place better. I know where the hidden passage is, so we can sneak around any of the guards. Plus, we will have seven swords, and we can take out a whole lot of men before they know what happened."

Connor agrees. "She's right. Once we get there, it is all or nothing for me."

Eric demurs, "Let's be smart about this. We cannot just rush in, guns blazing." He addresses Connor and Chris. "I understand you both have revenge on your minds, but you are also our future, whether or not you want to think that far out. So, Diego, Mondo, Renaldo, and I will go through first, and if it is clear to the main floor, then you two can follow with Abel as your backup. This is not up for debate."

Mondo adds, "Eric is correct. We need to be smart here. If you two die, then all is lost."

Chris groans. "We get it. Your plan makes the most sense. We do have revenge on our minds, but that can wait until we take control."

Connor agrees. "I am with you and two hours makes sense. We should have control by then, or we will all be dead."

Evan shouts, "ALL DEAD! If you guys are all dead, then what?"

Chris says, "When you turn the portal back on, if no one is there, I guess wait twenty minutes, then turn it off again. There are still about two weeks before the next alignment, so let's say the day before, at nine in the morning, you turn it on again. We will need to synchronize so we are all looking at the same timing."

Renaldo agrees. "Good point. Okay, let's go get started now that we have a plan."

"I am eager to see if we can get the platform to work."

Evan points out, "But you never answered the question about what to do if you are all dead."

Chris says, "Well, if the two times you turn it on, none of us are there, when the alignment starts, get out as soon as you can, then make it back to Hmar 4. You will be on your own from there unless you hear different when you arrive."

"That is a joyful thought."

Connor puts his hand on Evan's shoulder. "Don't worry. We are not going to die."

"I really hope you are right."

LATER, AS THEY ARE IN THE CAVERN WAITING FOR THE platform to respond, Connor decides to go back to the other cavern where he met Andorra for the first time. The last time he was there, everyone was focused on creating an exit out the top. This time, he is going to find some of her eggs, but just as he heads that way, Chris calls him back. She is ready to turn everything on. Just as he joins them, Chris gets the platform running, with everyone standing there in anticipation. Connor asks, "Should we be seeing something yet?"

Chris responds, "I would have thought so, but right now, it is still looking for a destination to link with. I'm looking through the system controls to see if anything shows up, but maybe it is having some trouble with the asteroid field."

Eric says, "If that's the case, then why was it able to link up from Markus 2 before your uncle destroyed the lab there?"

"That's a good point. Let me increase the power. That will take a few minutes." She works with some controls. After a bit, the system locates other platform signals. "Okay, I can see a link to the one on Ria 6, and it is still searching for others."

Abel asks, "How is it able to see the one on Ria 6? I thought you took all the stuff out of it."

"Not everything. The main controls are still there, and we could not visit as we took the main power supplies out. That is also a good point. We will need to bring more fuel with us just in case, as we do not know how much is left there."

Renaldo says, "Okay, let me fetch another storage container. It will take a little while to go there and get back."

"I will just see if I can open a window to the palace, then shut right back down."

Connor asks, "Do you really think that is a good idea? All we need is a guard down there for some reason as the window appears and goes away."

"Yes, that makes sense. Okay, Renaldo, we will wait for you to come back before we try, as I can see in the system a platform that we can activate. It is just labeled P0R3."

"Were you hoping it was going to say palace or something like that?"

Chris laughs. "Well, maybe you're right. Why would it be that simple? While we are waiting for Renaldo to return, Evan, why don't you see what I do to first shut it down, then turn it back on?"

Manuel looks at Evan. "So, you get to stay behind with me?"

Evan says, "Yes, I am really not a fighter. I have spent some time with Abel learning how to use the sword he gave me, but I would prefer not to step into somewhere with no idea about what we are going to find."

Connor comments, "What do you mean? We know what we are going to find. Possibly lots of guards, the slug, and hopefully Craven."

Evan looks at Manuel. "Now you see why I was concerned."

Manuel says, "I get it."

So, while they wait, Chris walks Evan through, shutting the platform down, bringing it back up, and how to find their location. She then shows him where the fuel cells are, and reloading them. She does this a few times to make sure Evan understands everything, then tells him to try it since Renaldo is still not back. After a few attempts, with a little help from Manuel, he can activate the system and shut it down.

After several hours of waiting, Chris turns to Connor. "Should we just go? It is getting late."

Connor says, "I am getting concerned. Renaldo should have been back a long time ago."

Diego asks, "Should I go look for him?"

"Yes, if you would. Maybe we should return to the complex and wait there since it is closer."

Chris sighs. "Yes, I guess you're right. Plus, we need him and his sword."

Diego leaves to find Renaldo while the rest head back to the complex. After they wait, Diego and Renaldo finally come walking in. Connor gawks at Renaldo. "What happened to you?"

Renaldo explains, "I have bad news. Rema is in the hospital. The two men that she was working with are dead, and some of the refinery equipment was damaged."

Chris says, "Oh no, is she going to be okay?"

"Yes, they seem to think so. They hit her on the back of the head with a pipe or something like that. I found her lying on the ground with the others not too far from her, so we got her some help. Everything is okay now, but we do not know who did it. We don't have any monitoring equipment in there, since we did not think we would need it. I also posted a guard out front just in case whoever tried to destroy the equipment strikes again. But I still need a storage container for the extra fuel. I will have that later tonight if that's okay?"

"Of course it is. In the meantime, can you take me to see Rema? I would like to see how she is."

"Yes, I would be happy to. I think she would really like that."

Chris and Renaldo leave to visit Rema. When they get there, she is very pleased to see Chris. Chris tells her not to worry and to get better. Chris also asks her if she can remember anything, and Rema tells her she saw nothing. She was focused on her work until she felt the pain of being hit, then woke up there. She did not even hear the front door open, so they must have come in from the back. As they leave, Chris tells her she hopes she feels better soon.

When Chris and Renaldo reach the complex, two of the Zandorrian warriors stand guard out front. Once they head upstairs to the main room, Renaldo looks at Mondo. "What's with the guards out front?"

Eric says, "That was my call. I just thought, with the fact we will be leaving in the morning, and with no idea who was responsible for the killing at the refinery, I wanted us all to be safe tonight and not have to concern ourselves with everything else going on."

Chris agrees. "Eric, yes, thank you. That makes sense. It is going to be hard enough for me to sleep tonight." Chris then walks over to Connor and quietly says, "Do you want to continue our conversation from this morning?"

Smiling, Connor hugs her. "Are you sure you want to add to everything else we have to deal with right now?"

"Maybe not, but I still need to do this." As he is much taller than her, she pulls him down to her and gives him a kiss on the lips.

Connor comes away with a big grin. "I'm sorry. I did not hear you. Maybe you need to tell me again."

Beaming, Chris kisses him even longer this time, not realizing everyone is watching. They both turn at the same time, seeing everyone looking at them and smiling.

Mondo remarks, "It's about time." Both of them turn red from embarrassment.

Eric says, "It's okay. We are all happy for you two. We have been taking bets on how long it would take for the two of you to figure it out."

Connor replies, "We really have figured nothing out yet. We are still working through it."

Renaldo says, "At least you have started the conversation, so to speak."

Connor doesn't know what to say. "Well, ah, we have a busy day tomorrow, and I need to get some sleep." He hugs Chris, then looks at her this time without looking away. "If you can't sleep, you know where to find me."

Chris grins. "Yes, I do, right over there." She points to the spot in the back of the room where they have been talking.

CHAPTER XXIII

THROUGH THE WINDOW

Just like he said, very early the next morning, Chris enters the main room, and there on the couch, asleep facing the window, is Connor. Chris walks over, sits down on the edge, and strokes his face. As she does, still partially asleep, he says, "Emily, you're back." Waking, he then realizes it is Chris. He jumps up. "I'm sorry."

Chris responds, "Don't be. You were sleeping, and I woke you up."

"No, I meant for calling you Emily."

Chris reaches for his hand. "Please sit down." He obeys. "I know what you meant, and it's okay. You were in the place where you wanted to believe she was still alive. I am there almost every night, so I understand." She squeezes his hand. "You're right. Maybe I am pushing too hard."

Connor puts his arm around her. "No, it is me. I have strong feelings toward you, and I would like to move things forward between us."

"But?"

"If today goes the way we hope it will, things will change drastically for both of us, and we will both have to make hard choices after. I keep playing things over in my head. I was really happy before I went to sleep last night, thinking of the possibilities between us. Then everything else started creeping in. You are going to be the ruler of the entire universe, and I do not want to be in the way."

"Wait, right now, you're the official emperor, not me. You are putting way too much into this." She stands up and pulls him up to her. "Come with me." Still holding his hand, she takes him down to her room.

"No, I am not—" Before Connor can say anything else, she puts her finger across his lips.

"Shh, don't talk, just go in." She then tells him to lie down. "It's way too early, and we both need sleep." She then climbs into bed behind him, putting her arm over him. "Just relax, close your eyes, and let everything else go." Connor closes his eyes.

When he wakes up, it is several hours later. He rolls over, seeing Chris lying there, still asleep. He strokes her face, and as he does, she slowly opens her eyes and smiles at him.

Connor says, "Thank you. I really needed that."

Chris agrees. "We both did." She then kisses him softly and puts her arm over him again. "You were right. We have a lot to do today. Since we both have powerful feelings for each other, we will have time to figure it out. We don't need to rush into anything here.

Knowing you care about me, and I do you, is enough for now. Do you agree?"

Smiling, Connor kisses her back. "Yes, I do."

"Great, let's go get our empire back." She then smacks him on the shoulder and pushes him to get up. They both stand, and Chris hugs him, then says, "Stop worrying so much. We have time." Still hugging, Connor lifts her up, squeezes her, then sets her back down. "Wow, thank you for that. Let's go. Everyone will be waiting."

As they both walk out the door, they almost knock into Renaldo and Abel, passing by her door.

Abel smacks Renaldo on the shoulder. "I told you. I win."

Connor laughs. "No, we just slept."

Abel replies, "Yeah, right. Is that what they call it?"

Chris frowns at Abel. "Nothing else happened."

Abel smirks at them. "Yes, your highness, whatever you say."

Connor says, "Never mind. They won't believe anything but what they want to, no matter what happened."

The four walk into the main room. Everyone else sits there at the main table. As they settle down, the joking about Connor and Chris goes on for a few more minutes. Then Chris asks Renaldo about the extra fuel. Renaldo says, "Yes, the case was delivered late last night. We still do not have any idea who killed the men yesterday, but we still have some of our guys looking into it."

Connor remarks, "Then maybe we should just focus on breaking into the palace and let the guards investigate what happened for now."

Several hours later, they all go to the platform in the cavern. Chris takes a bit to fire everything back up. After a minute or two, a window opens, revealing on the other side what seems to be a room in the lower level of the palace. Nervous energy fills in the room. Mondo looks at everyone. "Are we ready?"

Chris glances at Evan. "Do you have this?"

Evan assures her, "Yes, I do. Please don't die, any of you."

Abel slaps him on the back. "It's not us you need to worry about. We have this."

As he gets ready to step through, Diego draws his sword. "Is this safe?"

Chris, not having any idea, crosses her fingers. "Sure, it is just like going through a door."

Connor says, "Wait, Eric, you need to go through first, then Diego. You know the palace."

"Yes, you're right." As Eric steps through, he comments, "Wish me luck."

There is a few second delay before appearing on the other side, followed by Diego, Renaldo, Dave, then

Mondo. As they get over there, Eric tells them, "Yes, we are in the palace. This is one of the main storage rooms we cleared quite a while ago." He slowly opens the door, peers around, and comes back. "Okay, we are good. The stairs are right there, and they are all clear."

Mondo returns to the window and tells Connor, so he then steps through, followed by Chris. She reminds Evan to only keep the window active for thirty minutes, then to reopen it two hours after. He nods, and Chris steps through, followed by Abel. Once Connor steps through, he walks over to the door where Eric is standing.

Eric looks at Connor. "What are you doing? We talked about this."

Connor agrees. "Yes, but we are through the window now. I am bigger and stronger. Let me lead. If you back me up, I will be fine."

"Well, I am not sure I like that idea, but go ahead."

Seeing what Connor is trying to do, Chris comes up to him. "Why are you going first?"

Connor assures her, "It's okay. I have this. You guys are here to guard me. I will just need you to show me where the passage is by the main stairs when we get there."

Eric explains, "Ok, when you open the door, there is a hallway, and the stairs to the left lead to the main entrance."

"I know. You forget, we used to play all over this palace as kids."

"Yes, you're right."

Dave demands, "Are we going to sit here talking or go for it?"

Connor gives a slight laugh. "Sorry, we're leaving now." Connor slowly opens the door and looks out. As he does, a guard marches the other way right by the stairs. Connor rushes out and runs up to the guard. Putting his hand in front of his mouth, he shoves his sword up through his back and partially out of his chest, killing him instantly. As Connor draws his sword out, the rebel drops to the floor. Eric helps him drag the body behind the stairs. Then they head up the stairs with everyone behind them. Connor points. "There's one."

Dave nods. "Ok, we're counting."

Abel adds, "It's on."

Chris tries to be quiet. "What's on?"

Renaldo explains, "The body count. When we are done, who got the most."

"You guys are twisted, but I'm in." They all nervously laugh. At the top of the stairs, Connor turns to peek at them, and puts his finger to his lips. He then opens the door, just as the three men that accompanied Abel and Chris come running up.

"Did you really think you were going to do this without us?"

Abel turns to face them. "Right, what was I thinking? Welcome to the party."

Connor still stands behind the door, waiting for everyone to be quiet. After the noise stops, he slowly opens the door, revealing another hallway at the end of the palace, leading them to the main floor near the front door. He sees two guards and steps back, then holds up two fingers.

Diego steps forward. "Let me." Grinning, Connor nods his head. Diego peeks out, seeing the two walking away. He rushes out and kills them before they know what happened. As he does, Connor and Eric trail right behind him. Diego smirks, holding up two fingers.

Renaldo and Abel then come out. At the other end of the hallway, two more guards enter through the secure door with their swords drawn. Renaldo deflects one rebel's sword as he swings, shoving him into the other rebel. Abel tries to impale the one rebel as he falls, but cannot get through his suit. Seeing this, Renaldo shoves his sword through the one rebel while Abel drops and kicks the other, knocking him to the ground. As he does, Chris and some others rush through the door now. Chris stabs the rebel on the ground, killing him. She then holds up one finger.

Abel whines, "This is not fair. My only chance of scoring is if I can get them in the back." They check for an open door off the hallway to hide the bodies, dragging the bodies in there. Connor, Eric, and Diego continue down the hall, with the others following behind. Chris tells Renaldo and Mondo to pull up the rear as their Zandorrian swords can penetrate the rebels' suits.

Connor nears the end of the hall. There, six more rebels stand at the main entrance, but he cannot see the front doors to know if there are more outside. Connor has to assume there are. He holds up six fingers and points at Diego with two fingers, then at Eric with two fingers. They both nod, then rush the rebels, each taking on a pair. As Connor swings at his two, he forces one off balance, spinning him around. Abel runs up to stab the rebel from behind while Connor cuts the other rebel. Diego and Eric quickly take care of their two.

Connor looks at Abel. "Feel better now?"

"Yes, I do. Thank you." But as Abel says that, three more rebels come running in.

They yell, "We are being invaded!" The three men with Abel run up, but can't kill the rebels. Chris, Renaldo, and Mondo kill them, but as they do, more dart their way.

Chris yells, "Follow me," as she runs to the back of the stairs and opens a door to the secret entrance.

Diego responds, "You go. We got this." Chris, Connor, Eric, and Mondo duck in the door, leaving Diego, Renaldo, Dave, and Abel with the three others to cover their exit.

Once in the secret passageway, Chris says, "This way to my dad's room. I bet that is where the slug is." They sneak down the passageway to Esteban's old room. As they get to the panel, they have to take off John's block, then rush in.

Several rebels flank Lorenzo, who is surprised to see them enter from that back panel. The rebels turn, rushing at Chris and Connor, who kill them quickly. Renaldo and Mondo also run into the room, leaving

Lorenzo standing there, holding his sword up, pointed at them. Lorenzo demands, "How did you get in here with all our guards out front?"

Chris barks, "I am in control here. First off, tell your men to stand down."

"Why would I do that? You are completely outnumbered."

Connor replies, "If you don't, we will show them your head after I cut it off your shoulders. You just saw what we did to your guards here, SO TELL THEM NOW." He points his sword at Lorenzo's neck.

Lorenzo drops his sword and communicates to the guards. "So, are you going to tell me how you entered?"

Chris sneers, "We modified your platform from Zada 5."

"No, that is not possible. No one but me knows how to make the changes to a receiving unit." As they talk, Jeff runs in, sword drawn. When he does, Eric knocks the blade out of his hand and puts his weapon at Jeff's throat.

Connor looks at Lorenzo. "Who's this?"

Lorenzo states, "That's Jeff. He is nobody to you."

Mondo interjects, "He must think he's somebody coming in here trying to save you."

Jeff says, "He's right. I am no threat to you now. Clearly, you are in control here."

Mondo stares at Jeff. "Go over there and give me your ring." He grabs his sword as Jeff sits in the corner.

Chris scowls at Lorenzo. "Now, back to you. We took a trip to Ria 6. I went through your platform there and saw what you did before we stole the fuel cells, power supplies—oh, yeah, and killed three of your guards."

Jeff demands, "That was you?"

Lorenzo glares at Jeff. "Why did I not know about this?"

"Um, ah, Craven told me not to tell you."

Pacing, Lorenzo loses it. "If I had known that, they could never have done this, and we would still be in control."

As she points her sword at him, Chris yells at Lorenzo, "SIT DOWN!" He is clearly upset, but obeys.

Lorenzo gapes at Chris and Connor. "Then are you Connor? And you must be Emily, right?"

Chris states, "No, I am Christina. Well, Chris now, thanks to you and yes, this is Connor."

Lorenzo's expression changes to surprise. "Craven killed Christina. You're Emily."

"They killed my sister. You have been screwing up all over the place. Your team failed twice to execute Connor. Then you thought you slew me when you had my sister, and Craven hid my trip to Ria 6."

Connor demands, "That brings up a good point. Where's Craven?"

Lorenzo glares at Connor. "He is still on Korbin, getting ready to kill you."

"Oh, something else you have failed at, as we are here with you, so do yourself a favor and get Craven to join us."

"Sure, why not? This is all his fault anyway." He gets up, looking at Chris.

She says, "Go ahead. Just know we are watching you and can hear what you tell him."

Lorenzo walks over to his desk and picks up his communicator, calling Craven. "I need you here right away. We have a 602 failure, and I need your attention."

Craven answers, "Yes, sire, I will be there immediately."

Connor states, "Just so you know, it does not matter what you told him. We are going to be holding you out front when he shows up with however many troops."

Lorenzo responds, "I do not know what you are talking about."

"Do you think we are stupid? We developed most of the procedures used at this palace. You think we don't know you just warned him you are being held hostage? When he arrives, you are going to tell the troops to stand down, or they are going to see you die by Chris's hand right in front of them."

A SHORT TIME LATER, THEY TAKE LORENZO OUT FRONT, where the rest of the guys wait. At least twenty rebels lay dead. Lorenzo stands in shock. "How is this possible? They're all wearing my new protective suits."

Chris pushes her sword into him just hard enough to cut the skin. "It does not protect them from our Zandorrian swords like mine. By the way, this is Ramone's. He gave me it before he died. All because Craven killed my sister."

"But I thought he had the last sword?"

Mondo answers, "No, actually, there were two, the one Chris now has and mine." Mondo points at him with it.

"Then how did you get more?"

Renaldo comments, "We have the correct formula to make more like mine."

Connor gazes at everyone that is left. "We need to get ready. More rebels are coming to kill us."

As he says that, Eric drags Jeff out, "I just told him to send word that we have captured Lorenzo, and the true emperor is here."

When he says that, an entire battalion of the emperor's original army dashes up in front of the palace, and the major moves in. "Connor, is that you, sir?"

Connor says, "It is. Hey, wait, didn't my brother and I work with you in a training exercise?"

"Yes, sir, we did. The word is out. You are here trying to overthrow the tyrant, so we came to see if we could help."

"Major, your timing is perfect. Have your men disarm the remaining rebels."

"Yes, sir, that will not be hard. Once they heard you captured the dictator, they all went running. We are getting the word out everywhere. The real emperor is in power now."

"Well, we have more rebels coming from Korbin."

"Then we will be ready. Whatever you need, sire."

Connor looks at Chris. "Maybe we surprise Craven and have these men overtake them after they come up."

Eric agrees. "Yes, I like that idea. There can't be that many rebels left. Even if they bring fighters, we have many more, and with the pulse cannon on the roof, we can blow them out of the sky."

Dave asks, "Did you say pulse cannon?" They all laugh.

Connor says, "Yes, Dave, it is all yours."

"Sorry, I just love to blow things up in the sky, then watch gravity take over."

Renaldo asks, "Do you think you can demonstrate how to work it? I would like to blow something up."

The major grins at them. He goes to the door and waves for a few of his men to come in. As they come in, he looks at them. "Show them where the cannon is and give them a hand."

One of them responds, "Yes, sir, and, sire, we are glad you are finally here. We heard rumors you could still be on Zada 5, but did not know what we could do to bring you back."

"I am happy to be back here with you all again." Then they tell Dave and Renaldo to follow them up to the roof. As the Major leaves, Connor says, "Major, one more thing."

The major asks, "Yes, sire?"

"I am not the emperor."

"Sorry sir, we all heard that they had made you the emperor."

"That was only if they killed Christina."

"Yes, sire, and we were told they killed her, and she is Emily." He points to Chris. "Sorry, ma'am, I did not mean to point."

Chris laughs. "That's okay, Major, I am Christina. They thought they killed me, but they murdered my sister, Emily."

He kneels in front of her. "Sorry, your Highness, we did not know."

Chris pulls him up. "It's okay. It was safer that way until I could bring Connor back to help me fight the war for the throne."

"Yes, your Highness, Christina."

She responds, "It is just Chris."

"Yes ma'am. May I go now to get everyone staged?"

"Yes, thank you."

Eric says, "Major, wait. Can you take this guy and lock him up with the other rebels?" He pushes Jeff towards the major.

"Yes, sir, will do." Then the major grabs Jeff and forces him through the door to some of his men standing outside.

Back on Zada 5, just as Evan and Manuel shut the platform down after everyone went through, Rodney sneaks up behind them. They do not notice him in the darkness of the cavern. Rodney hits Manuel over the head with the large pipe he is holding. Then he swings at Evan but only partially makes contact, knocking him to the ground. Evan rolls and grabs his sword, holding it up to stop Rodney from hitting him again. He kicks Rodney, knocking him away, giving him a chance to get up. As Rodney comes at Evan again, he swings his sword, hitting the pipe and deeply slicing Rodney's chest. Rodney drops the pipe and grabs his chest. Evan, now holding his sword, ready to hit him again, looks at Rodney. "Why are you doing this? I thought we were friends."

Rodney gasps, "I'm sorry. It has nothing to do with you. I can't go back to prison."

"What are you talking about?"

"Before becoming a rebel, I was in prison for killing two men in a fight. The rebels broke me out, along with many others, to help them. Now, with Connor taking over, he will eliminate the rebels on Ria 6, and they will send me back."

"Okay, but why are you trying to kill us?"

"It's not you, just whoever controlled that device. I needed to stop anyone from coming back until after the alignment so I could leave in your ship. That is also why I had to stop them from refining any more fuel, just in case."

"So, you killed the men there, too?"

"Yes, I had to."

"You were going to steal my ship?"

"Yes, I could have gone where no one would know who I was."

"But you helped us. All you had to do was tell Chris your problem. I am sure she would have helped you."

"Yes, but I could not take the chance she wouldn't." While he is talking, he bends down towards the pipe.

"Don't do it."

"Sorry, Evan, I have to." He stands up, grabbing the pipe again, and swings it at Evan. Evan slashes his sword into Rodney, slicing him deeper this time. Blood gushes out, and he drops to the ground.

"Why? You just forced me to kill you."

"Yes, I know. You gave me no choice." He then lies down and dies.

After killing Rodney, Evan rushes over to Manuel, lying on the ground next to the platform, bleeding badly from his head. Evan checks to see if he is still alive. He is barely breathing. Evan runs out to the front of the mine for the guards. Seeing they are present, he tells them to go get help quickly, as he does not know how much time Manuel has left. One guard calls for medical aid and is able to reach help. Evan runs back to help Manuel, but when he gets there, Manuel is no longer breathing. Evan tries everything to revive him, but nothing works, no matter what he does.

A short time later, two men run in and over to Evan, who is still trying to revive Manuel. The two men pull Evan away so they can attend to Manuel. As soon as they inspect him, they can see Manuel has been dead for some time now. "We're sorry. He's gone."

Evan is looking down at the ground. "Yes, I know, but I couldn't stop trying."

The two men cover Manuel with the blanket they brought, then look at Evan. "We will have someone come and take both bodies away."

"No, just that one there." He points at Rodney, then Manuel. "I will handle him. But help me move him over there." He gestures off to the side of the platform.

"Sir, is there anything else we can do for you?"

"No. Thank you for coming to help."

The men leave, taking Rodney away. Evan is now all alone with Manuel's dead body as he stands by the platform, waiting for the time to turn it back on.

BACK ON MARKUS 2, AFTER JEFF WAS PUSHED OUT THE door, Chris asks, "Wait, what time is it?"

Mondo says, "We have thirty minutes before Evan opens the window again, if that is what you mean."

Connor says, "Ok, good, we have about an hour before Craven arrives."

Chris glances at Connor. "Then what's the plan?"

"We are going to tie up the piece of crap." He pokes Lorenzo with his sword. "We'll set him right outside the door, then wait for Craven to show up."

Eric cautions, "You know he is going to come loaded to slaughter everyone with men and fighters focused on whoever has that dirtbag."

Lorenzo thinks he can still get out of his situation. "That's right, and they will kill you all. Your men cannot fight mine with our superior weapons."

Connor replies, "That is what they will think until I show them how well our swords perform."

Chris says, "And how are we going to do that?"

"Simple, we take one of these dead rebels and prop them up like they are still alive and show them how well our swords work against their suits, then tell them we have armed our men with these. They will have no choice at that point. We will set that up while you and Mondo return to the platform and tell Evan what's going on."

Chris and Mondo go back down the hall to the stairs to the room with the platform. It is almost time for Evan to open the window again; they wait about ten minutes. Finally, they see him stand in front of it. Evan asks, "Can you hear me?"

Chris peers at his face. "What's wrong?" Evan explains what happened to Rodney and Manuel. Chris steps back through the window. As she does, she sees Manuel's covered body off to the side.

Chris hugs Evan, and he starts crying. "I am so sorry."

Chris assures him, "This is not your fault. You didn't know Rodney was going to do this. I am sorry, but we only have a little time." She yells for Mondo to come back through and help Evan bring Manuel across.

When Mondo comes over, he asks, "Why are we taking Manuel over there?"

"I want to give him the same funeral as the rest of our guys. He deserves that much."

"Sure, that makes sense." While Evan and Mondo move Manuel, Chris checks the platform system and the fuel cells, now less than half full. She looks at Evan, who has come back to the Zada 5 side. "Okay, the platform can run for about an hour and a half at full power, so if you fill the fuel cells before you turn it on again, there should be no issue coming back."

Evan says, "Then I will see you all in about two weeks. I am very glad you guys did not die."

Chris hugs him again. "Thank you. So am I; you take care." Chris then steps through the window. Evan waves and shuts the system down.

Once the window closes, Chris turns to Mondo. "We have to hurry. Craven will be here any time now." As they reach the main entrance, all the dead bodies have been cleared away, and Connor waits out front with Diego, Abel, and Eric. Chris and Mondo rush out the door.

Connor looks at Chris and Mondo. "Glad you could join us. I just got a report. Craven with four fighters has entered our airspace and will be here shortly. I told the major to take down the shield for the palace."

Lorenzo, hearing Connor, adds, "Yes, and when they get here, you will all die."

Chris sticks her sword into his back, cutting him a second time. "The first one to die will be you if you open your mouth again." As she says this, she pushes her sword against him with each word. Realizing he has lost control, Lorenzo just nods his head.

A few minutes later, Craven lands his ship right in front of the palace. Twenty men come running out with Craven as four fighters hover above and behind them. Craven walks through the middle of his men, approaching the palace entrance. He is shocked to see Connor on one side, and who he thinks is Emily standing on the other side of Lorenzo, on his knees with his hands tied behind his back.

Craven asks, "How could you be here now and with Emily? That is not possible. The window for Zada 5 will not open for two more weeks. You had no way off that planet as they destroyed all your ships. At least, that is what we were told."

Connor says, "For one, she is not Emily. This is Chris. You blew it and killed the wrong girl. Second, we used your own equipment to get here."

"No, that's not possible. You had no way of knowing how the platform worked on Zada 5, and it was only a receiving unit."

Hearing this, Lorenzo gets mad all over again and then yells, "This is all your fault! They raided my lab on Ria 6, you idiot. You gave them everything they needed to do this!"

"That was your fault. You put that braindead jerk, Tom, in charge. His men allowed them in."

"*Enough.*" Connor glares at Lorenzo as he puts his sword in his side. "Tell them to drop their weapons now or else."

Craven hears this. "Or else what? We are in control here. You only have a few men. You are outnumbered, and we cannot be hurt." He points to the suits.

"What, you think four to one is a problem for us? I think not." He shoves his sword through the dead rebel propped up on Connor's side. The rebels and Craven all gasp as Connor pushes his sword through the rebel's suit like he's wearing nothing. The rebels drop their swords. Craven yells at his men to pick them up, but they all step away.

"It doesn't matter. I still have our fighters here that can blow you away."

Connor then says with his communicator, "Dave, do it now." They fire the cannon at one fighter, blowing it to bits, with pieces on fire falling to the ground. "Okay, send the rest." Eight more fighters come in behind the three left for Craven, and the major's men surround Craven and his men.

Craven says, "Okay," as he drops his sword.

Connor marches forward towards Craven while staring at him. He points his sword at Craven's on the ground. "Pick it up. Let's finish this."

Thinking he has the upper hand, Craven smiles.

Craven bends down not taking his eyes off Connor, grabs his sword, and rushes up the three steps to the main landing at the front of the palace where Connor stands. He swings his sword at Connor, who knocks it away. With all his might, Craven slashes at Connor again, who bats it away again, though this time he slices Craven's chest. "That was for Adam."

Craven, shocked, not willing to believe Connor just cut through his suit, holds his sword up as if he is going to swing at Connor again. Connor smacks it away and slices Craven's right cheek. "That was for my mother."

Craven brings his sword back up, and Connor smacks it away again, slicing his left cheek. "That was for my father."

Using the last of his strength, Craven swings at Connor, and Connor again deflects it away like nothing. He plunges his sword into Craven's chest and yells, "That was for Emily. You killed my family, and I just killed you!" Craven grabs Connor's sword with a shocked look on his face as he falls to the ground and dies.

While Connor and Craven battle, the rebel fighters land, and the pilots surrender along with the men on the ground. The Major has his men take the rebels away and approaches Connor. "Sir, we will leave a few men here to guard the palace with your permission."

Connor shakes his hand. "Thank you for all your help."

"Yes, sir, happy to. We are glad that you and Her Highness are back."

Connor looks at Chris. "Okay, it is your turn."

She glares at Lorenzo. *This slime has been responsible for killing everyone I loved.* She then swings her sword, cutting Lorenzo's bonds. "It's your call. Do you want to die with a sword in your hand or like the slime you are on your knees?"

He stands up, then turns, smiling at her. "It will not be as easy for you as it was for Connor. Can someone get the sword from my room?"

"You mean my father's?"

"No, we killed your father, so it's mine now."

Chris swings her sword at Lorenzo. As she does, Connor yells, "NO, wait till he's armed." She stops, almost cutting his throat, stepping away, fuming. "Calm down. He's baiting you."

Chris paces, swinging her sword back and forth. "You're right. I just want him to die so bad."

"I know, but we have to be better than they were."

Eric returns with Lorenzo's sword. He looks at Chris. "Are you ready?"

Chris agrees. "Yes, I am."

Eric then throws Lorenzo's sword on the ground in front of him. Lorenzo demands, "You will not hand it to me?"

Eric snaps, "You're lucky she is allowing you to die with it at all. I would have cut off your head and been done with it."

Just like Craven, Lorenzo bends down while looking at Chris. He grabs his sword, then spins around to hit Chris, but she blocks. As she does, she slices his leg on her return swing. He then strikes from overhead, which she deflects as well, holding his sword in front of him.

"Connor, I learned how to use my sword when I was young. Your grandfather taught me."

Connor lunges at him. "That's a lie. Why would he?"

Eric stops him. "That is possible. Your grandfather trained many people, so he could have."

Connor looks at Chris. "It doesn't matter. You are much better."

Lorenzo, thinking he has caught Chris off guard, strikes again, but Chris slices his arm as she deflects his swing. They volley back and forth, and as they do, he continues to talk, trying to get into her head. "How can you kill me? I am your uncle."

"You're no uncle of mine. If you were, how could you have killed your own brother?" As she says that, he swings, slicing her arm.

Connor barks, "You are letting him get in your head. Stop it." They volley a few more times.

Chris snaps, "Ok, I am done with this." As she says that, she slices his stomach, his eyes open wide. He tries to hit her again, but she blocks it and strikes him across the chest. Now he sees he is not fighting a young girl who knows nothing. He tries to hit her again, but she swings down, cutting him from his chest to his stomach, and connecting the two other cuts.

Realizing he is going to lose, he drops his sword and falls to the ground on his knees with his head down. "No, no, please don't kill me."

Chris puts her sword under his chin and forces him to lift his head. "Did you give my father a chance before you murdered him?"

"No, it wasn't me. Craven killed him."

"Whether or not you actually did it yourself, they would not have killed him without your say-so."

Lorenzo, with his hands clasped in front of him, begs for his life. "Not true. I told them to save his life."

Chris screams, "You're a liar! This is for my father and sister." With all her might, she shoves her sword down into his neck and out his back. A look of shock appears on his face, just like Craven. He gurgles when Chris pulls her sword out of him, then falls to his side and dies.

Connor hugs her. "How do you feel now?"

"Anger as I did it, then relief, and now, I feel bad as he was my uncle. I should have been better than him."

"I know it is a hollow victory, but they did not think twice about hurting us, and they would have if they had the chance."

"Yes, you're right."

After giving them a few minutes, all the guys come over in a big group hug. Eric excitedly says, "We did it. We got the empire back, thanks to you two."

"We did. We really need to celebrate, but first, where is Renaldo?"

"I am right here," he responds.

"We know who killed the men at the refinery. It was Rodney."

"Why?" Chris explains what Evan told them and that Manuel's body is downstairs. They will deal with him the same way as their other men.

While they talk, one of the lead staff members, Dunsmore, joins them. He reaches out and touches Chris's arm. Everyone is shocked; they all quickly turned to look at him. As they do, he steps back. "Sorry, I did not mean to scare anyone."

Chris says, "It's ok. He is part of the staff."

Dunsmore agrees. "Yes, ma'am, I need to speak with you."

"Sure, you can speak freely here. What can I do for you?"

"No, ma'am, it is what we have for you."

"For me?"

"Yes, ma'am, if you can follow me, I will show you. They can all come too if you want." Everyone follows him down the hall. The other way from where they entered, he opens a door leading to a set of stairs down to the lower level. At the bottom of the stairs is the main kitchen.

Chris asks, "Where are you taking us?"

Dunsmore says, "We are almost there, ma'am." He leads them to the far back part of the kitchen and a large steel door. "This is a storage freezer. We use this when we have big parties." As he opens the door, four covered bodies lie there in the back corner, each on a table.

"NO, who is that?" She starts to cry. "Is that my father and sister?"

Connor says, "Oh, wow, and my mother and father?"

Dunsmore says, "Yes, ma'am, yes, sir, we recovered them hoping that one of you would return." Chris turns and hugs him as he continues. "They were great people and deserved to have a proper funeral with people that loved them as we did. We heard rumors that you two, well, Emily and Connor, were still alive fighting to get back here."

Chris sobs. "Thank you, thank you." Connor comes over and shakes his hand excitedly; then Chris and Connor hug, and Connor starts to cry.

Eric pats Dunsmore on his shoulder as a tear runs down his cheek. "Nicely done."

Dunsmore says, "I know you are still in the middle of taking over. They can stay here until you two are ready for them. But we all wanted you to know they were safe."

Connor pulls the sheet down from Emily's head, exposing her face. As he does, Chris comes over, putting her arm in his. Connor, with tears rolling down his face, strokes Emily's cheek. "I am so sorry we were not here to protect you." He covers her again, then turns and hugs Chris. "Now we can say goodbye the right way."

She squeezes him. "Yes, we can."

Chris then looks back at Dunsmore, still standing there. "I do not know what else to say, but thank you so much. This is the perfect way to allow us to celebrate."

Dunsmore says, "Ma'am, we are just so glad to see you and sir back here."

Chris walks back and kisses him on the cheek. "Not ma'am. I am Chris to you. We owe you so much for this."

"Well, ma'am—sorry, Chris, it was not just me. It was our entire staff." They walk out of the freezer. The staff is all there, and as they exit, the staff claps and cheers.

Chris and Connor both say, "No, it is us that should clap for you. We owe you all more than we can say." As they walk out, they hug and shake everyone's hands, personally thanking each of them.

Diego interjects, "This may not be the right time, but this day has been very intense, and I am starving."

They all laugh. Dunsmore grins at Diego. "Yes sir, absolutely. We would be happy to help you with that. If you go back up to the main dining hall, we can have food up there shortly."

Diego shakes his hand. "Thank you."

They all laugh again and go up to the main dining room. On the way there, Mondo smacks Diego on the back. "Have you been taking lessons from Connor?"

Diego can be very literal. "You know I have."

Connor chuckles. "No, Diego, he is talking about me being hungry all the time."

"Oh, ok, I get it now." They all laugh again. By this time, they reach the main dining hall, and everyone but Connor enters.

Seeing this, Chris goes back to Connor, looking at him. "What's wrong?"

Connor, standing there seeing the room, feels the pain of loss. "This is hard. The last time we were in here, everyone else was too."

Chris puts her arm in his. "I know, but this is our house now, and I will help you through it." They then go into the room together, sit down to eat, and celebrate what they all were just able to accomplish. Chris and Connor both watch as everyone enjoys themselves, laughing and eating, while trying not to remember how most of the people they loved are gone.

CHAPTER XXIV

WHAT DO WE DO NOW?

WITH EVERYONE EXHAUSTED FROM THE MONTHS OF hard work preparing, fighting, and all their effort to enter the palace, it takes a few days for them to recover. Chris and Connor finally learn to sleep, each still in their own beds. Chris comes down to Connor's room a few days later in the morning and knocks on his door. Connor yells, "Come in. It's not locked."

She walks in and looks around. "Wow, your room looks just like Adam's did."

"Yes, I know. I could not change it."

"Well, maybe if you are not ready yet to stay in my room, you should move into your parents' old room."

"I am not sure I can do that either, not yet. Have you moved into your father's old room?"

"No, but that's not the same."

"And why not?"

"Because the slug was staying in there, and I need to have everything burned, then start over."

"Then why don't you?

"You know."

Connor grins. "I do, for the same reason I can't move into my parent's old room, too many memories. Plus, it has only been a few days. We both need time to adjust."

"Yes, you're right."

"So, should we talk about the funerals for our families?"

"Yes, I think so. We have many other plans we need to talk through as well. Why don't we meet the others?"

"Great, I am starving."

Chris laughs. "I knew you would be." She puts her arm in his, and they walk down to the main room.

Everyone else is already there eating. Abel comments, "Well, it's about time. I bet you're starving."

Connor smiles. "Yes, I am, as a matter of fact."

Renaldo asks, "Did the two of you have a good night?"

Chris answers, "Yes, we did. Thank you."

"I bet you did. That is why Connor is starving." As Dave says that, they all laugh.

Connor objects. "No, again, nothing happened. She slept in her room, and I was in mine."

Abel comments, "Is that why the two of you came in together?"

Chris looks at Connor. "Never mind. Let it go. They will not believe you, but we know." She kisses him on the cheek, and they sit down.

Mondo begins, "Eric and I were talking. We need to take care of our dead warriors today."

Chris agrees. "Yes, we are on the same page. Connor and I were just discussing a funeral for our family too."

As she says that, Dunsmore walks up. "Ma'am, if you like, I can take care of all the arrangements. I had to do this for others in the past."

"If you could, that would be wonderful."

"Yes, ma'am, my pleasure. Give me a few days."

Renaldo adds, "In the meantime, we can have a warrior funeral for our fallen men."

Connor says, "The Major can get some men to help us."

Dave agrees. "I will reach out to him."

"Thanks, Dave."

Eric says, "Ok, on to the next topic. With the rebels on the run, maybe we should finally clear out what is left on Ria 6?"

Connor concurs. "That's a good point. I am sure our men on Hmar 4 are ready to turn the tables on them."

Abel agrees. "Yes, that's an excellent point. I will take charge of that one."

Connor says, "Great, thanks, Abel. Hey, I never asked who fired the cannon the other night."

Dave brags, "I let Renaldo take over, and he did a great job."

Connor smirks at Renaldo. "Was it fun?"

Renaldo wears a big grin. "Yes, it was an excellent feeling to fire that weapon."

"Well, maybe that can be your new job."

Chris objects. "Hold on, I already gave him a new job as head of all procurement."

Connor bumps her with his shoulder and smiles. "You're not the official empress yet, and you're already hiring people?"

"Yes, you bet. I need to make a start before you get a big head and try to keep the throne."

Mondo winks at Chris and Connor sitting across the table from him. "Oh no, I am not doing this again. Taking it back once was enough for me."

Just as he says that, a guard walks in. "Ma'am and sir, someone out here is asking to speak with sir." He looks at Connor. "Is it ok if I send them in?"

Connor says, "Sure. Who is it?"

"Sir, she said her name is Mandora."

"Mandora, really? Talk about timing. Yes, send her in."

The guard leaves, and a few minutes later, Mandora strolls in. As she gets close to them, Connor stands up to shake her hand. "Everyone has heard about what you did here. We are all so happy."

Chris says, "Wait, is this the person who left the message for us on Hmar 4?"

"Yes, I am the one. Are you Christina?"

"Yes, but it is Chris now."

"It is a great pleasure to meet you. I am here to make it official."

"I am sorry. Make what official?"

Connor laughs. "She's here to crown you the empress and relieve me of the power, just what we were talking about."

Mandora agrees. "Connor is correct. Just one formality. I need to see your birthmark."

Chris asks, "Birthmark?"

"Yes, the dragon at the base of your hairline on your neck."

"Oh, yes. I completely forgot about that, as I have never really seen it." As Chris is sitting down, Mandora comes over, and Chris leans her head down. Mandora looks at her neck. She continues to search for a while. "Are you not able to find it?"

Mandora says, "No, it does not seem to be there."

The guys all look at each other. Connor turns to Eric. "Any ideas what could be going on here?"

Eric first shrugs his shoulders. "Oh wait, Mandora, do you have a multicolor light?"

Mandora asks, "Are you thinking it only shows up in a colored light?"

"Yes, I think it needs to be in the blue spectrum."

"I may have one back on my ship. Let me go check."

Chris says, "I don't remember that."

"Yes, it was very prominent when you were born, but faded when you turned about three. I think that is how we found it back then," Eric says.

While they chat, Mandora goes back to her ship. A short time later, she comes walking back in. "I found one." She holds it up and walks back over to Chris, who bends her head down again. After a few minutes of changing the light color, Mandora exclaims, "Ahh, there it is."

Eric says, "Ok good. The next thought would have been to look at Emily's body downstairs."

Mandora, hearing Eric, says, "Wait, you still have her body?"

Connor explains, "Yes, we have all four of them. The staff saved them for us."

"Not to be indelicate, but they are all dead, right?"

Chris is a little annoyed at the question. "Yes, they are. *Why?*"

"I'm sorry if I offended you, but it makes everything easier to document if I can see their bodies. Until now, it has just been the word of your uncle."

"He was no uncle of mine!"

"Again, I am sorry. I am just here to document."

"I understand."

"So, can I see the bodies?"

Eric steps in. "It's ok. Let me take her down."

Chris says, "Thank you, Eric. It will be hard enough at the funeral."

A short time later, Eric and Mandora come back, looking at Chris. "Thank you for that. Now, Connor, do you agree to return the empire back to Christina?"

Connor smiles. "Hum, I'm not sure. It has been nice being the emperor."

Chris socks him in his shoulder. "You're funny. Tell her it's ok."

"Well, what's in it for me?"

Chris strokes his face and kisses it. "If you let me, I can show you my gratitude tonight."

Dave excitedly says, "I knew it!"

Connor blushes. "Calm down. Like I said, nothing has happened." He then looks at Mandora. "Well, she talked me into it. Yes, I agree."

Mandora asks, "Is this something else I should know about?"

Chris says, "No, not yet."

"Ok, sure, I get it." She then walks Chris through the same process with a newly updated book as she did with Connor, only this time, she has Connor sign, agreeing to turn the empire over to Chris, and again has Mondo witness it. "I am so glad that everything has worked out the way it has, and I look forward to all the updates."

She then asks if they have any questions, to which they reply, "No, we are all good. Thank you."

Mandora leaves them with a copy of the official book and walks out.

Eric comments, "Well, now that you are officially the empress, I think we need to have a coronation to show the universe you're in power, and everyone throughout can breathe a sigh of relief, knowing things will go back to normal."

Chris replies, "Not exactly. We now have the technology to deploy portals throughout, but the problem is obtaining enough Verbraso."

Renaldo puts in, "Then I guess that will be my first task, I'm assuming."

"See, that is why you are perfect for the job. You know what we need without me having to say anything."

Diego asks, "Not that all of this has not been fun, but when do we go home?"

Connor points out, "Actually, some of us are home."

Diego replies, "Wait, are you saying you're going to live here? You're the One. We rebuilt your house, and you became an official Zandorrian."

"No, I am not saying that. Zada 5 will always be home to me now, but I have responsibilities here and on Hmar 4 as well. If Chris successfully deploys the portals, that will make it easier for all of us to work and live wherever we want."

"Sure, I get it. Zada 5 will always be my home, but I will be there for you, wherever you need me, just as long as I can return."

"I promise you can always, but to your question on when, Evan should open the portal in a little over a week from now."

Mondo adds, "To Chris's point, how do we start building and deploying portals?"

Chris says, "We will have to get the labs building all the parts needed. How would you like to help with that?"

"Are you now offering me a job, too?"

Chris smiles at him. "What do you think? Could you do it? You seem to know how to talk to people and get them to work together. That's half the battle."

"But I have no technical knowledge."

"You will have people to handle that."

"I am willing to try."

Chris replies, "Great. The way they split everything up, with my father not able to know what his brother was up to, that is not happening with me."

Eric puts in, "Chris, I think a better spot for Mondo would be security. With my brother gone, you really need someone in charge of that."

"But I thought Connor would."

Connor remarks, "Wait, so now I am working for you?"

"No, I did not mean it like that."

"How did you mean it?"

"Sorry, just, who better than you to protect me? That way you are always with me, but if that doesn't work for you, tell us what you want to do."

"No, sorry. I am watching you settling into your life already, and I have no clue what I should do yet."

Eric comments, "You're forgetting you are still the duke. All security efforts run through you and all the men under you on Hmar 4, just like you told Diego."

"I understand, but what is that?"

"You are overthinking it. We need to spend some time back on Hmar 4. Then I can show you everything your father was responsible for."

Chris hugs Connor. "Yes, Eric is right. Everything will happen in its own time. We have the whole universe to do what we want."

Connor says, "You're right. I was getting a little jealous seeing you working out everything already, when I have no clue yet, now that you are the empress."

"You don't have to be. It's ours, not mine, to run."

THE REST OF THE DAY, CHRIS INSPECTS HER FATHER'S old office, finding several things she had given him over the years, reminding her of their life together. At the same time, Eric and Connor set Mondo up in John's old office while showing him how to access everything, along with the tricks Eric used with John when they sent encrypted documents to each other.

That night, Connor meets Chris in the garden. As he walks out, Chris is sitting on the bench with tears running down her cheeks. Connor settles next to her and wipes her tears away. "What's wrong? Why are you crying?"

She quickly turns and hugs him. "You're right. This is hard. I just spent the day going through all my dad's stuff. There were way too many memories in there. Then I come out here." She sighs. "The last time I was, it was with Adam."

Connor kisses her cheek. "Yes, I get it. And I was thinking about it. This cannot be our home if we are going to make it work between us. This has to be just the place we do business."

"So, what do you suggest?"

"I have a real home on Zada 5 that was just rebuilt, and with your platform already there, we can visit whenever we want."

Chris kisses his face all over. "I love that idea." She stands, reaching for his hand, and pulls him up. "Follow me."

"Where are we going?"

"Shh, don't ask, just obey."

Connor says, "Oh, ok." As they walk back into the palace, Dave and Abel stand off to the side by the stairs. They wave.

Dave asks, "Where are you to off to?" Connor shrugs.

Chris turns and heads down the hall to Connor's room.

Abel remarks, "Oh, I know."

"Me too. It's about time."

As Chris reaches Connor's room, she pushes him against the door. With his back to it, she puts her finger across his lips. "When I open the door, do not say a word. I think we have waited long enough."

Connor says, "Ok."

"No talking." Chris opens the door, then pushes him in, closes the door, and moves him to the bed. They hurriedly pull off each other's clothes while kissing and trying to crawl into each other's skin. Because of all the pent-up rage and loneliness from loss, they make fierce, passionate love for several hours before falling into a deep sleep till late the next morning.

THAT MORNING, CONNOR IS THE FIRST TO WAKE UP with Chris behind him. He rolls over, seeing Chris still sleeping. He strokes her face while watching her. She slowly opens her eyes. Connor says, "Hi there."

Chris responds, "Hi yourself." She then kisses him softly and strokes his face. "You were quite the animal last night."

"Me? So were you. I think that was the stress relief we both needed."

"Yes, that was a real workout, and I don't know about you, but I am hungry."

Connor laughs. "Hey, that's my line." They quickly get dressed and go to the main dining hall, where everyone has already been waiting for a little while. As Chris and Connor walk in, hand in hand, they all start clapping and cheering. Both are clearly embarrassed. "What's all this?"

Dave says, "You can't tell me nothing happened last night. The whole palace heard you two."

Chris puts her hand in front of her face. "Oh no, were we that loud?"

Renaldo agrees. "I think they could have heard you back on Zada 5."

"Ok, yes, we did finally do it, and it was amazing." Connor puts his arm around Chris. "And she is amazing."

Eric stands up. "Well, we are all happy for you two. You both deserve it."

"Thank you, Eric."

Then they both sit down, and as they do, Dunsmore stands there. "Ma'am, I have made all the arrangements, and the funeral will be the day after tomorrow. There will be several heads of state from all over the universe here as well. It is going to be a grand event."

Chris gets up to hug him. "Thank you so much for all your help."

THE FUNERAL HAPPENS AS PLANNED, WITH THOUSANDS of people from all over the universe attending, paying their respects to the dead and the new empress. Chris and Connor have the chance they needed to say goodbye properly to their loved ones, with their friends surrounding and supporting them through it.

As the days go on, Chris and Connor make love and sleep in her room, as there are no memory ghosts from past relationships floating around there.

THE DAY AFTER THE FUNERAL, ABEL FLIES TO RIA 6 WITH his men from Hmar 4 and disarms the few rebels left while dismantling what remains of their armory and bases, then turns the buildings over to the locals. As they do all of this, the leader of the mining coalition for the planet comes to Abel. One guard tells Abel someone would like to meet with him. Abel assents, "Sure, send them in."

A gruff older man enters. "Sir, first, thank you and all your men for what you are doing. We have been under the thumb of those rebels for far too long. I am here because some time ago we discovered several mines with rich veins of Verbraso, but we have kept it a secret from the rebels, as we knew they were searching for it to supply their war machine. We already have large stores of this mineral mined and are ready to ship wherever you need it." Abel provides this news to Chris and Renaldo.

This allows Chris to expand the platforms across the universe. It also changes for the better the lives of the people of Ria 6, oppressed for so many years.

SHORTLY AFTER ABEL LEAVES FOR RIA 6 AND THE DAY before Evan will open the window for all to return to Zada 5, Connor tells Chris he needs to finish their new home while bringing some things back. Chris laments, "But I can't go with you."

Connor says, "I understand. You are the empress; your duties are here."

"But we have not been apart since we crashed on Zada 5."

Connor smiles at her. "Are you saying you will miss me?"

"What do you think?"

"Well then, give me a reason to miss you."

Chris grabs him between his legs, making him jump. "The challenge is on." That night, Chris is good at her word. She blows Connor's mind, making love with him, wanting to make sure she is giving him a reason to come back.

THE NEXT MORNING, DOWN IN FRONT OF THE PLATFORM, Renaldo, Diego, and Mondo are already standing there when Chris and Connor come down. Connor teases, "What, are you guys in a hurry to go home?"

Diego answers, "Yes, you bet we are." A few minutes later, a window opens over the platform. As it does, they see Evan standing there. They all step through.

Evan says, "It's about time. I am ready to go home." Everyone laughs.

"Why do think we are here?"

"No, I am talking about leaving this planet."

Chris looks over the equipment, then at how much fuel is left in the cells. "Ok, we are good to go." She hugs and kisses Connor.

Evan asks, "Hey what did I miss?"

Renaldo says, "Actually quite a bit. We can talk later."

Chris puts her arms around Connor. "I know we have not said it yet, and I am ok being the first."

Connor puts his finger across her lips. "Are you sure? Once you say it, you can't take it back?"

Chris pulls his hand down. "Yes, I am sure." Putting her arms back around him again, she gazes into his eyes. "I love you, Connor."

He puts his arms around her too. "I love you too, Chris. And I will miss you." They kiss again.

Chris holds his hand as she goes back through the window. "I will see you tomorrow." From the other side, she looks at Evan. "You make sure you get him back to me safely."

Evan states, "I will." He then turns off the platform, and all but Connor leave.

Mondo eyes Connor, who is looking off at the path to the other cavern. "Connor, are you coming?"

Connor replies, "I need to do something first and will see you guys soon." He then walks off to the second cavern, walking back to where he first met Andorra. Not sure why, but feels a powerful presence pulling him there. As he continues to a far corner, he hears a strange cracking noise. When he gets to the sound, rubble falls, exposing several large dark gray eggs. One egg is shaking and cracks open. Connor smiles. "Now I know what she meant. I would never be alone. *This is my future life.*"

THE END?

SNEAK PEEK

Want a FREE sneak peek of the next book? Continue the adventure with Adam and Connor in book 2, *Zada 5: Slipping Dimensions.*

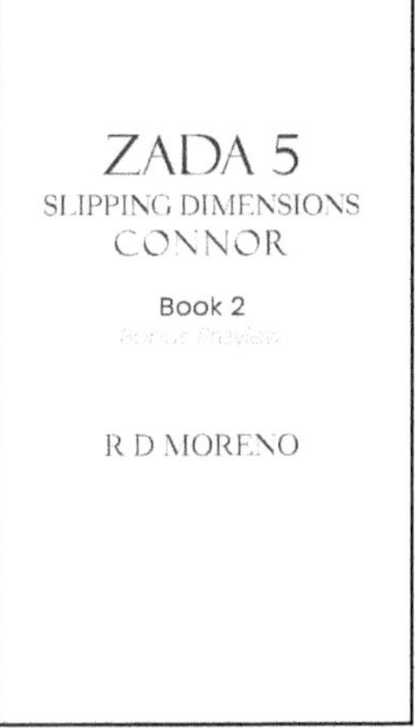

www.rdmorenoauthor.com/
slippingdimensionspreview